THE STONES OF ANGKOR

(BOOK 3 IN THE BABYLON SERIES)

SAM SISAVATH

The Stones of Angkor
Copyright © 2014 by Sam Sisavath

All rights reserved.

Disclaimer: This is a work of fiction. Names, characters, businesses, places,
events and incidents are either the products of the author's imagination or
used in a fictitious manner. Any resemblance to actual persons, living or
dead, or actual events is purely coincidental.

Published by Road to Babylon Media LLC
www.roadtobabylon.com

Edited by Jennifer Jensen, Samantha Gordon & Wendy Chan

ISBN-13: 978-0615965659
ISBN-10: 0615965652

Books in the *Purge of Babylon* Series
(in order)

The Purge of Babylon: A Novel of Survival
The Gates of Byzantium
The Stones of Angkor
The Walls of Lemuria
The Fields of Lemuria
The Fires of Atlantis
The Ashes of Pompeii
The Isles of Elysium

Also by Sam Sisavath

Hunter/Prey
The Shadow Operators

To all the brave souls who took a chance on a nobody and picked up The Purge of Babylon, then did it again with The Gates of Byzantium. This is all your fault. Thank you.

The war for survival continues.

The fight for Song Island is over. Despite suffering losses, Will and his group have claimed the island as their own and achieved the safe haven they've longed for since The Purge.

Months later, Will makes contact with another group of survivors, and travels to their base in hopes of striking an alliance and gathering much-needed medical supplies. Instead, he finds himself in the middle of another bloody battle.

With Will gone, Lara must take up a leadership position on the island, and is immediately confronted with a difficult choice. It's a lot of pressure for a third-year medical student, especially when her decisions may cost lives.

Meanwhile, the ghouls have launched yet another startling new phase of their master plan, forcing Will to venture deep behind enemy lines to collect valuable intelligence. What he discovers will change everything.

Where The Purge begins, and the Gates hold, the Stones will crumble...

BOOK ONE

ARRIVALS AND DEPARTURES

CHAPTER 1

WILL

IT WAS DARK and dank in the tunnel, and his face was sticky with dirt and sweat, so of course Danny was making with the jokes.

"It's been ages since Old Man Tom's gotten laid. His wife isn't interested in sex anymore, so one day Old Man Tom goes to the barn and starts looking around. He spots a very nice-looking gelding with white spots and a great coat of brown fur—"

"What's a gelding?" Will asked.

"What?"

"What's a gelding? Do I need to know what that is in order to get this joke?"

"It's a horse."

"Then why didn't you just say 'horse'?"

"'Cause it's a gelding. Now, you want me to finish this joke or not?"

"Wait, are you saying I have that option? Why didn't you tell me this before?"

Danny said something, but Will couldn't hear it over the shotgun blast, the ear-splitting noise magnified in the tight confines of the tunnel. For the briefest of seconds, bright red and yellow fire lit up the darkness, revealing the skeletal forms of three ghouls, black-prune skin rippling as they lunged at him—just before the silver buckshot vaporized flesh from bone.

Will racked the shotgun and fired again as three more poured out of the blackness, only to disappear in a shower of buckshot. He racked and waited…but nothing else moved, except for the clumps of flesh splattered against the curved walls.

Smart. They're attacking three at a time now.

"Sorry about that," Will said. "You were saying?"

"What happened?" Danny asked.

"A little housecleaning."

"Still? What the hell are they doing down there?"

"I'll be sure to ask the next one I run across."

Will stepped over the bodies sprawled on the wet concrete floor. His boots crunched bone, and thick, oozing liquid clung to the soles. He breathed through his mouth to avoid taking in the acrid stench.

The tunnel was huge, running underneath Beaufont Lake and emerging out of the Power Station on Song Island. At its lowest point, the construction reached thirty meters to the bottom of the lake. The partially round structure was twenty meters in diameter, with a flat bottom big enough for two simultaneous lanes of traffic. Condensation dripped from the high ceiling, and drops of water dangled from broken lights evenly spaced out for maximum coverage. The *drip-drip-drip* had been a constant ever since they'd stepped inside. Steel pipes and conduits snaked along the sides.

The tunnel extended just over one full kilometer underneath the lake, and it wasn't until they were three-fourths of the way through that it split up into two paths—one continuing forward and the other diverging left. Except the one that went left ended at a solid concrete wall after about ten meters. They were close enough to the island that Will guessed the unfinished portion—probably designed for the customers—led to the resort hotel, while the workers continued on to the end of the line and the Power Station directly above it.

Blaine moved loudly behind him—which was to say, Blaine moved the way only he knew how. The big man was armed with the same Remington 870 tactical shotgun, the shells loaded with silver buckshot. Silver was the only thing that could kill the ghouls. The only *other* thing, anyway. The sun was more lethal, but it was hard to walk around with the sun in your holster. The rifles over their backs were backups, because Will never liked to venture far without the M4A1. Lara insisted it was superstition. He called it habit.

"How many does that make?" Blaine asked, his voice echoing slightly in Will's right ear.

Will wore an earbud that was connected to a comm gear, with a throat mic and a radio Velcroed to his stripped-down assault vest. "Twenty?"

"I thought it was more. Where are we now? Feels like we've been down here for a couple of days."

"We should be underneath the island by now."

"Like rats scurrying through the darkness," Danny said in Will's ear. "Foul-smelling, hairy, no-shower taking rats. I can smell you guys from up here."

"Really?" Will said.

"No, not really."

They had been moving steadily through the pitch-black tunnel for the last two hours, navigating by night-vision goggles. It was slow going because there were more ghouls inside than Will had anticipated. Too many, in fact. He wondered what they were still doing down here. Waiting for the door on the island to reopen? That wasn't going to happen. He and Danny had sealed the entrance with multiple thick layers of concrete months ago. Nothing was getting through that.

And yet here they were, having dug their way through the rubble, only to wait…for what?

Will and Blaine had left a ragged line of dead ghouls in their wake, all the way from the tunnel entrance. Or what was left of it after Danny's C4 had collapsed it three months earlier. The creatures, undeterred, had begun digging their way back in the very first night after the demolition, moving the makeshift wall of concrete piece by piece until they could slip back inside the dark and damp structure God knew how long ago. A month? Two months ago?

What the hell are they doing down here?

"You hear anything?" Will asked.

"Nothing," Blaine said. "Maybe that's all of them."

Danny chuckled through their earbuds. "Captain Optimism, this guy."

"Maddie, give me a sitrep," Will said.

"Hot, sweaty, and oh yeah, hot," Maddie said in his right ear. "How's it going down there?"

"Slow."

"Take your time. I love the heat. No, really."

"I don't think she likes the heat," Danny said. "I could be

wrong, but I think that was sarcasm."

"You think?" Blaine said.

"I'm pretty sure, yeah."

They moved in the dark for another thirty minutes, anticipating more ghouls to jump out at them with every carefully plotted step. The ground was soft and muddy despite the concrete floor, a product of heavy condensation and dirt that the ghouls had tracked in while they were using the tunnel as their point of entry into the island.

Eventually, the tunnel started to angle upward noticeably.

"We're close," Will said.

"You're right; I can hear you guys from up here," Danny said.

"Really?"

"No, not really. Man, you're gullible. What's that, the third time now?"

"Nice," Blaine chuckled.

"We're definitely going up, though," Will said.

"See you when I see you," Danny said.

It didn't take long before the tunnel leveled out again. They continued along a flat surface for another five minutes before reaching a wide, circular room.

Tap.

Will froze.

"What?" Blaine whispered from behind him.

Tap, tap.

Will watched it moving toward him. It was small and painfully thin, even more so than the ones he had been killing on his way here. He wondered how long it had been down here, waiting for something that never came. Flesh hung loosely from deformed bones, and it seemed to be sniffing him. Maybe it knew there was silver in the shotgun, or maybe it was just too smart to make a frontal attack.

For a second, just a second, Will stared back at it through the night-vision goggles, wondering what was going through its mind, what it was seeing, and what *(who)* else was looking back at him through those dead, black eyes.

"Shit," Blaine said, stepping forward and shooting the ghoul from a meter away. The creature's head was severed from its narrow shoulder blades, and it flopped to the floor as if it were a sack of meat.

Blaine racked his shotgun. "What the hell was it doing back here all by itself?"

Good question.

Will continued into the room, stepping over the decapitated ghoul.

The room looked about forty meters in diameter, with concrete floors covered in old, cracking, mud-caked footprints. The place had the feel of a staging area, like a supply warehouse without the supplies. That stark emptiness gave it a cavernous vibe, and Will couldn't help but wonder how many had been down here that first night they spent on the island.

Hundreds. Maybe thousands…

On the far wall was the empty car of a freight elevator, and from its position, he guessed it led straight up to the generator building on the surface. And next to it, the first of many steps leading up.

Will clicked the Push-to-Talk switch on his radio. "We're underneath the Power Station. Looks like they never got around to finishing the elevators."

There were bodies in the room, though not as many as he had expected. Old, wrinkled skin draped over bones that looked bleach-white against the neon green glow of his night vision. He counted a dozen skeletons, give or take, in a jagged line toward the stairs. They had been here for a while.

Blaine moved closer to get a better look. The hulking, six-two Blaine had a good three inches on Will, and looked like some kind of alien insect with the protruding lens of the night-vision goggles.

Blaine craned his head to look up the stairs. "I see a door."

"That'll be the shack."

There was a steel door at the top of the stairs, slathered with dry skin and thick clumps of coagulated liquid. Will went up the steps first, skirting around still-gooey layers of flesh in his path. The stairs were wide, designed to accommodate more than one person at a time, but it got noticeably narrower the higher it went. A door gleamed against his night vision, even underneath the cake of dried blood.

When he finally reached the top, he banged on the door as hard as he could. There were barely any echoes, just the dull thuds of flesh against unyielding steel.

"Can you hear that?" he asked.

"Barely," Danny said in his ear. "Do it again."

Will banged his fists against the door a second time.

"Okay," Danny said. "Now do *Camptown Races*."

THEY CLIMBED OUT of the makeshift hole—a one-by-two meter-long jagged opening near the top—and slipped and slid their way down the loose pile of rubble. The tunnel entrance, or what remained of it, squatted along the eastern shore of Beaufont Lake and was little more than a wall of destroyed concrete. It would have looked like just another unfinished construction site—gray and uninteresting—if you didn't know what was on the other side.

He had been seeing the world through the night-vision goggles for so long that the sudden afternoon glare gave him an excruciating headache. The scorching late-September heat didn't help, a reminder that there wasn't much of a difference between Texas and Louisiana when it came to climate.

Maddie was waiting for them with a baseball cap to keep the brightness out of her eyes. She seemed even smaller than usual against the expansive, barren landscape behind her. "What were they doing down there?"

"Good question," Will said.

"It looked like they were waiting," Blaine said.

"Waiting for what?" Maddie asked.

"I don't know," Will said, "they weren't in a conversational mood. Come on, let's get this thing sealed back up."

"I was hoping you wouldn't say that," Maddie sighed.

It took them two hours laboring in the heat until they could replace all the concrete slabs that the ghouls had removed from the rubble to regain entrance into the tunnel. It was heavy work, and they created an assembly line, passing pieces big and small between them, with Blaine tossing them up into the pile until they couldn't see the opening anymore.

"Will that hold?" Maddie asked later.

"Not in this lifetime," Will said. "But it'll slow them down. When they get it open again, we'll close it back up. Next time, we'll just seal the fuckers in."

"The fun never ends," Blaine said.

"Sorry I couldn't lend a hand," Danny said in their ears, "but you know, island duty…and stuff."

"Yeah, yeah," Maddie grunted. "Rub it in, surfer boy."

"It doesn't look like much, does it?" Blaine said, looking the tunnel over.

He wasn't wrong. The entrance, before Danny blew it up, was a large, wide open half-circle surrounded by a concrete bunker. There were no doors and it was big enough for a truck to drive through, and when they had first located it three months ago, they saw old tracks and faded footprints leading in and out. The land around it was flat and sun-bleached, with a few shacks scattered among the dead, brown grass. There were signs that a construction crew had once been here, including an abandoned Port-A-Potty lying on its side and a trailer with deflated tires. But there were no vehicles now, as if everyone had simply packed up and went home one day.

Will glanced at his watch: 2:15 P.M.

He clicked the PTT. "Gaby, we're on our way back. Anything?"

Will looked west, across the lake and at the easily identifiable long structure jutting out of Song Island. The Tower. A combination lighthouse and radio tower, with windows along the second and third floors that offered a perfect view of the island and the surrounding shorelines to the east, north, and south. There was nothing in the west except water.

"Lots of big, fat nothings," Gaby said. "Well, except for you guys."

He couldn't see Gaby, but knew she was on the third floor of the Tower right now, providing overwatch with her M4, probably peering through the ACOG—the Advanced Optical Combat Gunsight—riflescope at him at this very moment. The ACOG gave them long-distance shooting capability, something at which Gaby had proven surprisingly efficient.

From shoo-in high school prom queen to military-trained sniper. I wonder where you put that on the college admissions form.

"All quiet?" he asked.

"Good to go," Gaby said.

Will looked back at Blaine and Maddie, both still catching their breath, all three of them standing in shirts and pants drenched in sweat.

"We'll keep an eye on it from the Tower," Will said. "Until we can get it permanently sealed, this'll have to do for now."

They headed back to the Jeep parked nearby. The land around them was flat but impossibly bumpy, with the nearest paved road, Route 27, a good five kilometers away. The Jeep made the trip bearable, if just barely.

They were halfway to the vehicle when Will stopped suddenly.

Blaine almost crashed into him. "What?"

"Listen," Will said.

It was like the flutter of feathers in the air—a soft, teasing *whup-whup-whup*. Will knew what it was, because he had heard it often enough in Afghanistan. And he remembered that night on the island while waiting for the collaborators to attack the beach. It had come and gone, never to be seen again...until now.

It was tiny, but that was only because it was still far away. The only reason he could even hear it at all was due to the stillness of the world around him. Sound traveled these days, especially the very odd, foreign noise of helicopter rotor blades whipping across the air.

"Holy shit," Blaine said. "Is that what I think it is?"

"It is," Will said.

"Is it the same one from last time?" Maddie asked.

"Maybe," Will said. "Gaby, what do you see?"

"Helicopter," Gaby said.

"But what do you *see*?"

"Looking." Then a few seconds later, "White." He could hear frustration in her voice. "That's all I got, Will, sorry. It's still too far away."

"Okay. Keep your finger on the trigger."

"Will do."

Will slung the Remington and pulled the M4A1 free. Blaine did the same thing with his M4.

There were no doubts about it; the helicopter was moving in their direction. If it was armed and had hostile intentions, they were pretty much out of luck, even if they could make the Jeep.

The helicopter began to slow down as it neared them, its tail turning slightly as the pilot eased up on the controls. It was close enough now that Will could see it was a civilian chopper. Best of all, there were no signs of a shooter leaning out of the open side door.

"What should we do?" Maddie asked.

"Don't shoot unless it shoots first," Will said.

He walked past the Jeep and watched the helicopter hovering for a moment, as if the pilot was trying to gauge the reaction to its presence. Eventually, it started lowering itself to the ground forty meters from him.

"That's a good sign, right?" Blaine shouted after him.

Hope for the best...

Will covered his eyes at the swirling storm of dust and dirt biting into his exposed face and neck. "Stay here!" he shouted back at Maddie and Blaine.

They took up positions behind the Jeep, shielding their eyes from the debris.

Will waited for the helicopter to fully touch down, its landing pads rocking slightly as they settled on the uneven earth.

A *click* in Will's right ear, then Danny's voice: "Nice ride. You gonna bring it over so we can all go for a spin, too?"

"Looks pretty friendly."

"I can't see anything but a white bird. A big-ass white bird."

"It's civilian, and no armaments as far as I can see."

"That's a good sign."

"But just in case, stay frosty."

"I'm so frosty, Gaby's catching a cold over here."

"Oh my God," Gaby said. "I don't know what Carly sees in you."

"I go places where other guys don't dare, or can."

"I think I just threw up in my mouth," Gaby said.

Will tuned them out and walked toward the helicopter. He saw only one person inside the cockpit, a ponytail whipping behind her as she pulled off her helmet and climbed out of her seat.

The helicopter had blue stripes and sported a big, round number 3 inside a red circle, along with the letters KTBC. The Bell 407, a popular helicopter brand with news channels, looked weathered from time and the elements.

The woman climbed out wearing khaki cargo pants and a sweat-stained white T-shirt. She moved across the flat land toward him, careful to keep her hands at her sides, just far enough away from a holstered sidearm—and the black pistol inside it—but still close enough to go for it if everything went to shit.

"Don't shoot," she called. "I come in peace."

Now that she was closer, he guessed she was in her early thirties, with an athletic five-eight frame. He slung his rifle and saw her let out a noticeable sigh of relief.

Will met her halfway and stuck out his hand.

"Jen," she said, shaking his hand.

"Will." He pointed back at the Jeep. "Blaine and Maddie."

"They're not gonna shoot, are they?"

"Hopefully not. You took a risk coming down like this, alone."

"Yeah, well, end of the world and everything, what's a little risk, right? Besides, you folks are the first moving things on two feet I've seen in days."

"Can you use that thing?" he asked, nodding at her holstered sidearm.

"Haven't had any reasons to use it yet."

"You've been lucky, then."

"Really lucky, yeah." She looked past Will, across the lake, and at the Tower. "You folks from the island?"

"We are. Why didn't you go straight there?"

"I didn't see any safe landing zones when I made my passes three months ago. Overgrown grass, lampposts, and palm trees everywhere. There was a beach, but that's always risky. Plus, I saw a lot of people with guns outside a house farther down the shoreline. What happened to that house, anyway?"

"I burned it down."

"Ah." She waited for him to continue, and when he didn't, "Got a reason, right?"

"Yes."

He got something back that looked halfway between an amused smirk and a grin.

"A man of few words; I can dig it," she said. "By the way, where did you people get palm trees in Louisiana?"

"I have no idea. We found the place like that."

A *click* and he heard Lara's excited voice: "Danny said the helicopter came back?"

Will let Jen know he was keying his radio. She nodded and waited, as he said, "I'm speaking to the pilot now."

"What does he want?"

"She. And I haven't asked her what she wants yet."

"Maybe we can do some kind of a trade," Jen said. "I don't have much inside the helicopter, but if you need medicine, or medical equipment, I have a hospital."

"How much of the hospital?" he asked.

She grinned. "How'd you know?"

"Hospitals are big places. You'd need an army to hold all of it. Do you have an army?"

"No army, and we only have the top floor."

"Maybe we can work something out. We happen to be running a little low on medical supplies these days."

"Should I ask why?"

"It's a long story."

"Does it have anything to do with that house you burned down?"

Will smiled. "Maybe."

CHAPTER 2

LARA

LARA WATCHED THE helicopter swoop over the island, with Maddie peering out from the cockpit passenger seat, before angling toward a makeshift landing zone Will, Danny, and Blaine had carved out of the hotel grounds. It had taken about an hour to chop down three trees and saw two lampposts within the 100x100 feet square box in front of the two pear-shaped swimming pools.

The kids—Elise, Vera, and Jenny—stood next to Carly and Lara on the raised, open patio outside the front doors of the Kilbrew Hotel and Resorts. She couldn't blame them for being excited. It wasn't every day you saw a helicopter at the end of the world. As the helicopter landed, its rotor blades threw around a healthy chunk of grass and dirt, some landing on the roof of the unfinished hotel behind them.

Jen, the pilot, climbed out with Maddie.

"Oh, great," Carly said. "She's blonde, hotter, and taller than us, too."

"Hey, I'm blonde, too," Lara said.

"But she's taller."

"Don't worry, you're safe. Danny likes 'em young."

"Well, I'm good for a few more years, then."

Danny had gone back to pull overwatch in the Tower, on the eastern side of the island behind the hotel. That left Will and Blaine to greet Jen and walk her over to the patio.

"Time to put on the hostess hat," Carly said. She adjusted her bright red hair a bit, then jogged over to meet the group.

The girls ran after Carly, passing her by to get a better look at the helicopter. Carly led Jen over, stopping every few seconds to point out something around the island. Jen looked impressed.

Will climbed up the patio and leaned against the railing next to her. "What do you think?"

Lara reached over and flicked at flecks of dirt, grass, and what looked like dried mud and flakes of concrete clinging to his brown hair. "You need a haircut."

"About Jen."

She looked back at the pilot. "Given how fast we've been going through our medical supplies, it'd be nice to re-stock. That, or we could just stop getting shot and blown up."

"Now what would be the fun of that?"

"I forgot who I'm talking to. If you could stop getting into trouble, you wouldn't be, well, you."

"I'm not sure that was a compliment."

"It wasn't."

"Ah."

"But I love you anyway. Even if you do smell like rotten cabbage."

He sniffed himself. "Yeah. It was pretty rank down there."

She looked toward the shoreline, where she imagined the tunnel entrance was—not that she could see even a little bit of it from here. "Have you figured out why they spent all these months digging their way back in there? Could they have eventually gotten through the shack and onto the island?"

"I don't think so. The shack's solid steel with reinforced brick walls. Nothing's getting through that."

"So what were they doing down there?"

Will shook his head. "I haven't a clue. Waiting, maybe."

"For what?"

"Orders would be my guess. They're foot soldiers. Have you ever heard the phrase, 'Hurry up and wait'?"

"Is that a joke?"

He smiled. "Just something soldiers say."

"You think she's still out there, don't you? Kate."

"I *know* she's out there."

"So why hasn't she attacked? It's been three months."

He looked toward the shore, and she could tell he had been turning the question over in his mind for some time now, too.

Why haven't they attacked yet?

She remembered those anxious first few days on the island after the fight. Waiting—and fully expecting—every single day for an attack that never came. Everyone was hurt. Danny, Gaby, Maddie, even Will. She was hurt, too. *Everyone.*

And they waited, and waited…but it never happened. Instead of relief, each passing day without an attack was suffocating, as if they couldn't breathe because of their own overwhelming anxiety. Or at least, it felt that way to her. Will had kept them afloat, never resting, always moving, doing everything until Danny was back on his feet. Gaby had been instrumental in those first few days and weeks, and Lara couldn't recall a day where the teenager wasn't stuck to Will's hip like a devoted little sister.

"I don't know," Will said finally. "This island, us… What are we, in the larger scheme of things? Insignificant would be my guess. What's a handful of stubborn humans compared to what's going on out there, in the rest of the country? The world?"

"What is going on out there?"

"I don't know. That's what bothers me."

Lara reached over and took his hand, then leaned against his shoulder.

"I thought I smelled like rotten cabbage?" he smiled.

"You do. But I'm used to it by now."

"Okay, now I *know* that wasn't a compliment."

She laughed.

LARA WATCHED JEN tear apart a thirteen-inch white bass, gobbling up the meat and sighing with so much pleasure that Lara felt almost guilty about not appreciating the never-ending dishes of fresh fish more than she did.

They were inside the hotel lobby watching Jen indulge her amazing appetite. A flurry of dirt blew across the marble flooring, pushed through the wide-open spaces by a sudden breeze from the open windows. The lobby was aired out against the heat, and she couldn't imagine how much hotter it would have been without the black marble that covered the mostly finished portions of the hotel. Thank God it would be cold soon, with November and December on the horizon. But then they would have to worry about heating…

"These are insane," Jen said.

"You have Sarah to thank for that," Lara said. "If it was just the rest of us, you'd be eating canned fruit, SPAM, or MREs."

"We have boxes of those disgusting MREs at the hospital. The guys 'rescued' them from a nearby surplus shop a few months back. Before then, we were surviving on vending machine chips, sodas, and whatever else the cafeteria had in stock before we lost it."

"Sounds like us in the beginning," Carly said.

"How many of you are there?" Will asked.

Jen licked her lips and reached for another fish. "Twenty-six in the beginning, but over time we added two dozen more, so forty in all."

"That's a lot of people."

"It's a big hospital."

"But you only have the top floor."

"Correct. The hospital itself has ten floors."

"And you're just doing recon out here?" Will asked. "Like you were three months ago?"

Jen nodded. "We've been scavenging the areas around the hospital for food, but it's becoming scarce." She paused. "This may sound crazy, but some of us have a theory. We think the creatures have been purposefully sabotaging food near us so we can't use it." She looked at them over fish bones to gauge their reaction. "Sounds nuts, right?"

"No," Will said. He glanced over at Lara, then Carly.

Jen picked up on the look. "What? Wanna share with the new girl in class?"

"What do you know about how they did all this?" Will asked.

"I know as much as anyone, I guess, which isn't much. Why, you guys know more?"

Will told her about what they had managed to piece together. How the ghouls took over the big cities first during The Purge, using the population to grow their army exponentially. How they then moved into the countryside on the second night, conquering the smaller cities. When he got around to the blood farms, Jen listened intently and stopped eating. He told her about the collaborators, about the blue-eyed ghoul. Lara thought Jen might gag back up everything she had eaten in the last ten minutes.

"Jesus," Jen said when Will was finished. "We've been hunkered down in the hospital for all these months, just trying to keep them at bay. If what you're saying is true, we're truly fucked, aren't we? Are we just delaying the inevitable?"

"Not necessarily," Lara said. "This island, for instance, is safe. There's something in the water—the mercury content, maybe—that the ghouls don't like. So there are three certain ways we know of to fight them. The sun, bodies of water, and silver."

"What about silver?"

"Silver kills them," Will said.

He drew his knife, the one that used to be a cross but that Will had sanded down into a double-edged bladed weapon. He handed it handle-first to Jen, and she took it carefully.

"What is this, some kind of cross?" she asked.

"It used to be," Will said. "The silver on the outer edges is what's important. Have you tried shooting them?"

"Of course."

"What happens?"

"Nothing. They just shrug it off."

"Not with this. They can be killed. You just need to use the right ammunition."

"Silver," Jen said.

He nodded. "Silver."

Will drew his Glock. He pulled out the magazine and thumbed a bullet free.

Jen took it and turned it over between two fingers. "Silver bullets?"

"Hi ho, silver," Carly said. "It sounds ridiculous, we know, but it works."

"Ridiculous?" Jen said. "There are undead things crawling around in the darkness of that hospital, and every single night they try to break through to the tenth floor to get at us. Compared to that, silver bullets make perfect sense."

Lara smiled. That was as good an answer as she had heard. "One question," she said.

"Shoot," Jen said, handling the bullet back to Will.

"What took you so long to come back? It's been three months."

"I had a list of sites to check out first and not a lot of fuel. And to be honest, after I saw all those guns back at the house, this place didn't seem all that safe. I know it's crazy, but I sort of have an unnatural fear of getting shot out of the air."

"When are you due back at the hospital?" Will asked.

Jen glanced at her watch. "Tonight, actually, but now that I'm already down here, and you folks seem friendly enough—i.e., no one has shot at me yet—I guess I could stay the night. It'd be nice to sleep on a real bed again. You guys have any spare rooms?"

"Um, maybe one or two," Carly said.

AFTER LUNCH, JEN was back inside her helicopter's cockpit, talking on the radio with her hospital. Lara watched her from the lobby window, wondering what it felt like to be able to climb into something that could fly you away whenever you wanted. She could go anywhere, at any time, and not have to worry about the creatures that lurked in the darkness.

I need to learn how to fly one of those things.

She felt a pair of strong arms slip around her waist. Will slid his body against hers and kissed her neck. He had poured water over his face and changed clothes, but he still smelled of sweat and dust. They all did, these days.

She leaned her head to one side to give him better access.

"What are you thinking?" he asked.

"Isn't that my line?" she smiled.

He chuckled.

I wish I could fly, she thought, but said, "That we could really use supplies from that hospital. We're running dangerously low on everything."

"I agree. That's why I'm going back with her, to work out a deal with this Mike guy that runs the place."

"I should go, too."

"One of us has to stay here."

"So you stay."

"Right, that's going to happen."

"You don't know what we need."

"You can make me a list."

"It's not the same thing."

"I'll go back with her first, see if it's safe over there. Maybe I can help them get some of the other floors back. Jen's telling Mike about silver right now."

"You sound as if you're planning on being gone for a while."

"We've been out here by ourselves for too long. We need allies, babe. That kind of relationship takes time. And that helicopter will come in handy one of these days."

"Starch?"

"Yeah. We left a lot back there. That helicopter would make the trip easier, faster, and safer."

She watched his face closely. Will always had a look about him when he was thinking ahead. *"Hope for the best, prepare for the worst"* was a motto he and Danny had lived—and survived—by since The Purge. It had gotten them this far, and this island.

"So how are we going to convince Mike we're his new best friends?" she asked.

"You know what every soldier likes during wartime?"

"Sex?"

"Besides that."

"More sex?"

"Bullets. The only thing soldiers like more than bullets? Even more bullets."

"I'll pretend that actually makes sense."

"Think about it."

"I'd rather not. Anyway, so who else is going with you and Danny, if not me?"

"Danny's not going. I need him here. So it's either Gaby or Blaine."

"Gaby's just a kid, Will."

"She's eighteen going on thirty. In a few years, she could be in charge of the island's security."

"You can't be serious. Take Blaine."

"Why Blaine?"

"He's bigger."

"Is he supposed to be my bodyguard?"

"Something like that."

"I'd feel better if Blaine was here with you. Danny's very good at what he does, but he's only one man. That leaves Gaby."

"What about Maddie?"

"Gaby's better."

"Better than both Blaine and Maddie?" she said doubtfully.

"Yes," he said matter-of-factly.

"How is that possible? You've been training both Blaine and Maddie, too."

"Gaby's a natural," Will said. "Some people were just born to be shooters."

AFTER SHE GOT Jen settled into one of the many available rooms in the hotel, Lara showered, spending her full five minutes. That was their daily limit: five minutes in the morning and another five at night if they needed it. She always needed it. After all those months on the road, every shower counted.

Afterward, she stood nude in front of the sink and dried her hair, while Will leaned against the open bathroom door and watched her. She didn't acknowledge him for a while, and he seemed content to just stare at her with that smile on his face that all men got when a woman took her clothes off in front of them.

Finally, she said, "My hips are fuller, have you noticed? Must be the steady diet of seafood."

"Your hips? I haven't really noticed your hips."

She rolled her eyes at him. "You're such a charmer, Will."

"Is that why you love me?"

"Uh huh. Your ability to shoot things in the face was a close second."

"Good to know, good to know."

He walked over and picked her up. She yelped and turned around in his arms, wrapping her legs around his waist and kissing him.

Will carried her to the bed and laid her down, then sat back and watched her for a moment.

She stretched her arms and legs lazily in front of him. "Like what you see?"

"Very much."

"So do something about it."

"I should let you know. I expect my good-bye sex to be spectacular."

"You've had a lot of experience, have you?"

He shrugged. "Ladies like a man in uniform."

"You're not wearing a uniform."

"I could put one on."

"You have it with you?"

"For the purpose of this conversation? Yes. Yes, I do."

"Lame-o," she said, and pulled him down to her.

◄━━━   ━━━►

AFTERWARD, SHE LAY in his arms, their bodies sticky and tangled, glistening from either the heat or the sex, she wasn't entirely sure. It should have been uncomfortable, but it wasn't. Maybe she was just used to it. She had learned to get used to a lot of things these days, but this was one of the more pleasant ones.

She stared at the darkening patio window across the room, secured in the knowledge that they were safe here—in this hotel, on this island. It hadn't been easy after that first night, when they uncovered the island's true purpose. But day after day, week after week, it got easier, until she stopped looking at every coming nightfall with mounting dread. It still happened every now and then when she least expected it, but they were rare these days.

"You're awake," he said softly.

"Uh huh."

"You okay?"

"I'm fine. Better than fine."

"Good."

"When was the last time we were apart for longer than a day?"

"Before Starch."

"Not since?"

"I don't think so. Why? Are you tired of me already?"

"Yes, but that's not the point."

"What is the point?"

"I was just wondering…"

"The good kind of wondering, or the 'I think we should see other people' type of wondering?"

"Really? And what other people would I be seeing at the end of the world? Blaine? Danny? Maddie?"

"Maddie?"

"What, you think I should limit myself to just the boys?"

"Then why not include Carly?"

"Gross. She's like my little sister."

"I'm just saying, if we're already going there…"

"That's disgusting, Will. Don't ever talk about me and Carly like that again."

"A guy can dream, can't he?"

"Only if he's Danny."

"Gotcha."

"Anyway, I was *wondering*…about this thing we have. You and me."

"What about it?"

"It's been good. This thing."

She saw a ghost of a smile creasing his lips in the semidarkness. "You're not trying to get me to buy you a ring and make this official, are you?" he asked.

"Perish the thought. Besides, where would we find a minister?"

"Whew, escaped the noose by the skin of my nose."

"Oh, that's funny."

She punched him as hard as she could in the chest. He laughed it off, grabbed her by the shoulders, and reversed their positions until she was lying on the bed underneath him. He kissed her, then pulled back a bit to trace the length of her breasts with his fingers as if they had all the time in the world.

She loved these moments. The quiet and solitude of the island, especially in the evenings, was a gift she was determined not to waste. To have someone to share it with, someone who had been through everything she had, made it all the more special.

Please, God, don't take this away from us.

Lara watched his face, letting herself become lost in his soft-brown eyes. They didn't speak for a while. It used to drive her crazy, the way he could be silent for so long. Will could do that. He was so unlike Danny in that respect. Unless someone was shooting at them—and even then—Danny always felt a need to fill the void.

Will, on the other hand, could look at her in the darkness for hours without saying a word.

"By the way," she said, "you still owe me one."

"I do?"

"Oh, right, you forgot. Give me a break. You didn't forget when you reminded me it was your turn last time."

He laughed. "I'm going to take your word for it."

"Trust me, you definitely owe me one."

"I was hoping you'd let me get away with it. After all, I am leaving the island for who knows how long."

"Nice try. Now get down there."

"Yes, ma'am."

He kissed her on the lips, then moved down to her breasts. By the time he was at her belly, the last remaining light in the room had begun to fade and she was only aware of Will, existing in this space with her, at this moment.

His touch against her skin, the warmth of his breath against her belly...

As he continued moving southbound, she sighed into the darkness, closed her eyes tightly, and found his shoulders somewhere around her waist. She held on and tried to make the night last as long as possible.

CHAPTER 3

GABY

SHE WAS HAPPY. The last time she was this happy was when she finally hit something with the M4. After that first hit, it was all uphill. It was like sex that way—once you got it over with the first time, the second—and third, and fourth, and fifth—times came naturally.

Training on the M4 and the Glock with Will and Danny were some of the best times of her life. For the first month, it was almost exclusively Will, with Danny still recuperating from his wounds. Will didn't so much as teach her to become a soldier as he taught her how to become *more*. More than she had ever thought she was capable of, or realized she had the potential to become.

"Muscle memory," he had told her. "When you can do it without thinking about it, that's when you can stop."

By the end of the second month, Will had enough faith in her abilities to give her overwatch duty when either he or Danny were occupied elsewhere. She became, essentially, the third most valuable shooter on the island, and Gaby didn't take the job lightly. Their trust in her put her on a high that she still hadn't come down from yet.

So when Will came to her room last night and asked how she would feel about coming with him to the hospital with Jen, it was all she could do not to blurt out, *"Hell yeah."*

She was packing for the trip the next morning when Danny showed up. He had a palm full of blueberries, one of the island's more abundant fruits, and his mouth and hands were already stained with blue and purple juices. From a distance, Danny could have passed for an old teenager and not a thirty-year-old ex-Army Ranger.

"Ready to go?" he asked.

"Almost." She stuffed only the bare essentials into the field pack she was bringing with her—a pair of shirts, pants, underwear, and socks—before filling the rest of the space with spare magazines for the Glock and M4 that she couldn't fit into the pouches around her waist.

"Your first field work."

"Got any advice?"

"Stay close to Will and do what he says."

"That's it?"

"What were you expecting? Something more Mr. Miyagi-like?"

"Who?"

"Mr. Miyagi."

"I don't know who that is."

He grunted. "Never mind."

"What else?"

"Always use a condom."

"My mother could have told me that."

"Don't go into the barn."

"The barn?"

"It's tough getting hay out of ass cracks."

"Good to know."

"And finally, always follow the Army Ranger creed: It's not your job to die for your country, it's your job to make the other guy die for his."

"That's the Army Ranger creed?"

"Of course. Would I lie to you?"

"Yes."

"I'm hurt." Danny touched his chest, then went the extra mile and slid down the wall and let his hands flop away, the berries spilling onto the floor.

"Finally, he shuts up," Gaby said. She slung her pack, grabbed her M4 off the bed, and stepped over Danny on her way out into the hall. "You're cleaning up my carpet before you go."

"Yes, ma'am," he said after her.

SHE FOUND LARA on the patio outside the hotel, watching Will, Blaine, and Maddie loading three heavy green ammo cans into Jen's helicopter.

Lara smiled at her. "Excited, afraid, a little bit of both?"

"A little bit of both, but mostly excited."

"You'll do great."

"Thanks."

Of all the people on the island, it was easiest for her to bond with Lara. The fact that they could have passed for sisters didn't hurt. Gaby was a few inches taller, but they had almost the exact same blonde hair, except Gaby kept hers tied in a ponytail so it wouldn't interfere with her aim.

"Do me a favor?" Lara said. "Blonde to blonde?"

Gaby smiled. "Sure."

"I really love him. If you could bring him back in one piece, I would really appreciate it."

"Okay, but if he accidentally puts his hand on my thigh, can I accidentally shove my tongue down his throat?"

"Only if he puts his hand on your right thigh."

"Not the left?"

"No. The left means he's only mildly interested. The right is the serious thigh."

"Deal."

Lara turned around and hugged her, and Gaby felt a sudden flood of emotions she wasn't prepared for. It almost got the best of her, but she managed to push it down so she wouldn't start crying like a girl.

Girls cry. Soldiers don't. You're not a girl anymore.

"Take care of yourself, Gaby," Lara whispered. "And him too, if you have the time."

"I will. He and Danny are like the brothers I always hated."

Lara laughed. "You've been spending too much time with Danny."

"You think?"

"Just a tad."

"That would explain the strange desire to punch myself in the face for absolutely no reason."

They heard the helicopter's rotor blades starting up behind them, the *whup-whup-whup* getting faster and faster, pushing the wind all the way over to the patio.

She looked over, saw Will waving at them.

"That's my signal," Gaby said.

"See you soon," Lara said.

Gaby hurried off, jogging down the steps and running across the lawn, afraid that if she hesitated for even a second, she might change her mind and convince herself that she wasn't ready for this.

She passed Blaine and Maddie, bracing against the onslaught of swirling wind. The whine of the helicopter's turbine engine was already deafening even before she got close. Will opened the back door for her and she slipped inside. He slammed the door shut, then climbed into the cockpit's passenger seat.

Will held up an aqua and black headset and motioned for her to put hers on. She grabbed a pair off the seat next to her. Will's voice came through loud and clear. "We good?"

She nodded back. "We're good."

Will turned to Jen. "How far to Lafayette by air?"

"Eighty miles, so call it an hour, give or take," Jen said. "I like to take the scenic route whenever I can, in case I run across survivors below."

"How many survivors have you found over the last year?"

"Exactly thirteen."

"Lucky thirteen."

"Lucky for them, I showed up."

The helicopter lifted into the air, gaining speed and altitude with each passing second. Gaby looked out her window, saw Carly outside the front patio with Lara and the kids leaning against the railing around them. It wasn't until she saw the girls waving good-bye that the realization she was leaving the island for the first time since arriving here with Josh and the others three months ago finally struck her.

"How are you for fuel?" Will was asking Jen up front.

"There's enough to get us to Lafayette and back, if necessary. Don't sweat it."

"Sweating things is what I do."

"Is that how you landed the hot doctor?"

"That, and my charming personality."

"Is that what she told you?"

Will chuckled.

Gaby became slowly aware of an insistent *clicking* noise. It took a few seconds to track it down to the ammo cans on the floor next to her, shaking from the vibrations that coursed through every inch of the helicopter. The rectangular boxes were dull green with handles on top, and the bullets inside were trembling against the sides, the metallic *click-click-click* sounding disconcertingly like a bomb's timer.

Jen pointed the helicopter northeast, and Gaby watched Song Island slowly fade behind them.

SOMEWHERE BETWEEN BEAUFONT Lake and Lafayette, Gaby drifted off to sleep. When she opened her eyes, the first thing that flickered across her mind was—

Josh.

How long had it been since she thought of him?

Too long…

Josh is dead. Move on, girl.

She pushed him out of her mind and sat up in the backseat. In front of her, Will and Jen were talking, their voices coming through the headset that had slipped down to her neck while she slept. She pulled it back up over her ears.

"The city's almost completely empty," Jen was saying. "I flew this chopper over every inch of it before I started expanding out into the countryside. I was sure there would be survivors at Lake Charles. If anyone can survive the end of the world, it's got to be gamblers, right?"

"Where do you land this thing in the city?" Will asked.

"I've been landing and taking off from the hospital rooftop. Every time I leave it up there overnight, I'm always dead certain the next morning I'll find it in a hundred pieces, that they—the ghouls—would sabotage it. But they never did. I don't know why."

"It's a good question."

"You don't have any theories?"

"Not really. They used a car against us once. They lifted it up and crashed it into a brick wall."

"Ouch."

"Yeah."

Gaby had heard that story before. Will and Lara had lost a couple of people they were traveling with that night.

We've all lost people.

She thought about everyone she had lost over the last year. Her parents, her friends, her neighbors…

Josh…

"What was he in the Army?" Will was asking in the cockpit.

"Mike was a lieutenant," Jen said. "You?"

"Corporal."

She grinned over at him. "So what was it, a general lack of ambition? You don't strike me as the kind of guy who'd be happy pulling down a corporal paycheck for the rest of his life."

"I didn't see the point. I left the Army after my enlistment was up, joined the Harris County Sheriff's Office. Danny and I were working SWAT when all of this happened."

"Damn, Will, I didn't know I was flying a badass soldier-slash-ex-SWAT commando around. I'm practically trembling with excitement."

Will smiled. "You want an autograph?"

"Will you sign my breasts?"

"Are they big enough?"

"Wouldn't you like to find out."

◄━━▌ ▐━━►

LAFAYETTE, LOUISIANA, ACCORDING to Jen, was a city of 112,000 people. Dull, gray concrete highways had replaced open prairie below the swiftly moving helicopter, and she glimpsed large buildings and skyscrapers in the distance. Marble and glass curtain walls, something she hadn't seen in a while, glinted underneath the sun's glare.

Jen reached forward and hit some switches along her helicopter's dashboard—they all looked the same to Gaby—before speaking into her headset. "Mercy Hospital, this is Jen, I'm on approach. Anyone manning the radio over there? Over."

There was static through Gaby's headset for a few seconds, before a male voice answered: "We hear you loud and clear, Jen. Welcome back. We thought you'd abandoned us for good this time. Over."

"No such luck, Mercy Hospital. I'm ten minutes out. Over."

"Roger that. ETA ten minutes. Over."

"Inform Mike I'm rolling in with two new people. They're armed but not dangerous, so no one get ants in their pants. Over."

"Will do," the man said. "Mercy Hospital over and out."

"You guys have problems with other survivors before?" Will asked.

"Here and there, but nothing we couldn't handle," Jen said. "We've never had to fight off a whole army of collaborators, though. Mike's done a hell of a job keeping us going, but…" She paused.

"But?"

"I don't know. We're not soldiers, you know? There are a couple of soldiers at the hospital. Mike and a couple of his guys, but the rest of us are just civilians. If there was a fight like the kind you guys had to deal with…" She shook her head. "I don't know."

"Sounds like you've been lucky so far."

"So far, yeah," Jen nodded.

AS THEY NEARED their destination, Jen veered the helicopter away from the I-10 Highway and angled south, until they came up on a large group of buildings—a baseball field, a football stadium, and the roof of a large, domed structure. A dozen parking lots, with only sprinkles of cars, filled the rest of the open space. It looked as if they were flying over a college town.

On the other side of the sports facilities was Mercy Hospital, a ten-story brown and black building that looked as if it were molded from clay. Gaby wasn't sure if the architect purposefully designed it to represent a cross when viewed from the air, but that was what Mercy Hospital looked like to her as they glided toward its rooftop. Four separate towers joined at the center, forming a squatting cross. It also looked a bit like a giant Tetris piece, waiting to be inserted into a larger puzzle.

"Welcome to Mercy Hospital," Jen said. "People check in, but they don't check out. Unless they have a helicopter. Which, happily, I do."

Two figures appeared out of a building along one of the towers and jogged over to the center of the rooftop. Jen hovered above them for a moment before starting the helicopter's descent.

"How many times have you landed on this roof?" Will asked.

"Too many times to count," Jen said. "Easy as pie."

"Are all rooftop landings easy as pie?"

"Just like driving a tank. You wanna learn? I bet a smart soldier like you could probably pick it up in no time."

"Maybe on the next trip."

There was a slight bump and rocking motion as the helicopter touched down.

Jen flicked at switches along the dashboard. "You're welcome to keep your weapons. Just do us all a favor and try not to point them at anyone, okay?"

"As long as no one points their weapons at us first," Will said.

"Fair enough. Oh, and one more thing."

"What's that?"

Jen looked back at Gaby. "There are a lot of guys down there. Teenagers, early twenties, mostly. Don't be offended if they stare. They're only human."

"Thanks for the warning," Gaby said.

"Don't sweat it. Girl power, and all that."

Gaby grinned back at her, then unbuckled her seatbelt and climbed out. She was wearing combat boots, and loose but hard gravel crunched under the soles. The helicopter was winding down behind her, its engine the only sound for miles.

Jen waved the two guys over. They were both young, and their eyes went from Will to Gaby, where they stayed for much longer than necessary. She guessed they were in their early twenties, though neither one had shaved in a while, so it was hard to know for sure. One had a shotgun, while the other was cradling an AR-15 that looked brand new.

Jen snapped her fingers in front of them to get their attention. "Hey, boys, stop staring at our guest and grab the boxes from the helicopter." Jen motioned to Will and Gaby. "Come on, I'll take you to see Mike."

They followed Jen to the access building on the north tower rooftop. The steel door was fortified on the other side with a second sheet of repurposed metal, possibly a tabletop with its legs sawed off.

"How often do they attack the door?" Will asked.

"They used to do it more often in the beginning," Jen said, "but not so much these days."

"But they're still around. They know you're here."

"Oh, they know," Jen said, and something about the way she said it made Gaby slightly nervous.

They stepped into the stairwell, their path illuminated by a single LED portable lamp hanging from a makeshift hook. Gaby leaned over the railing to get a look at the nine floors below them, but only saw a big slab of concrete instead.

"There's only one rooftop access on the north tower," Jen said. "And that's only accessible from the tenth floor. The nine floors below that share a common stairwell, but you need to use a separate door to get up to the rooftop."

"So you didn't have to barricade the entire stairwell in order to keep using the rooftop," Will said.

"Uh huh."

Jen pushed open a second door, this one with no extra fortification. Two people standing guard on the other side glanced over as they emerged out of the stairwell. There was another door directly to their right, reinforced with thick slabs of wood.

"Guys, this is Will and Gaby," Jen said. She indicated the redhead. "That's Claire—" and pointed at the man, who was staring at Gaby "—and this slack-jawed idiot is Miles."

Miles look offended, but Claire chuckled and said, "Welcome to Mercy Hospital."

"Benny and Tom are bringing some heavy stuff down," Jen said. "You might want to leave the door open for them. And Miles, make yourself useful and give them a hand when they get down here."

Claire nodded, while Miles looked sheepishly away.

Jen continued on, leading them through the hospital's tenth floor.

Gaby noticed the smell right away. She recognized it from all those days and months living inside other people's basements before she joined Will's group. It was the suffocating smell of forty people living, sleeping, and surviving on a single barricaded floor with very little (if any) ventilation. After three months on the island breathing in the fresh air, the sudden attack of enclosed space came as a major shock to her system.

The dirty floor under her squeaked, and portable LED lamps strategically placed along the ceilings lit their path. There was barely any natural light, with the windows along the hallways boarded up with doors and furniture, which explained why some of the empty rooms they walked past no longer had doors.

Jen seemed to know where she was going, though Gaby thought they were just walking from one hallway to another. There was a mazelike quality to all the turns, but maybe that was just her mind trying to orient itself to the layout after having the wide open spaces of the island as her backyard for so long.

Every now and then, people came out of their rooms to watch them. Most didn't bother to wave or say hi. They all had long and pale faces, weary eyes, and gaunt cheeks. They didn't look sickly or malnourished, but she imagined the lack of light and physical activity had something to do with their unhealthy appearances.

She glimpsed more doors plastered over windows inside the rooms, and stray spills of sunlight here and there. Some of the windows had what looked like steel rebars soldered over them, like some kind of prison.

Must have run out of doors...

"How many rooms?" Will was asking Jen.

"Over 200," Jen said.

"That's a lot of access points."

"We removed every door from the rooms that weren't being used so we could cover the windows, and we even raided a construction site next door for supplies."

"The rebars."

"Yeah."

"That must have taken a while."

"It took forever. Luckily, we have people who had done construction before. They taught the rest, and we got them up eventually."

"So the floor is safe."

"We haven't had an incident in months."

"Don't jinx it," a voice said behind them.

They stopped and looked back at an attractive Asian woman in her late twenties coming out of a room behind them. Like everyone they had met so far, she wore cargo pants and a sweat-stained T-shirt.

"Welcome back," the woman said to Jen. "I thought you were gone for good this time."

"You wish," Jen said. "Will and Gaby, this is Amy Park, our resident doctor. Amy, this is Will. He used to be a corporal."

"I guess that means I outrank you," Amy said, walking over and shaking Will's hand. "I was a lieutenant."

"Only if the United States government is still in operation," Will said. "Do you know something I don't?"

"About the U.S. government? Not a thing. Lucky for you, or I'd insist you call me 'sir.'"

"I was taking them to Mike," Jen said. "You know where he's keeping himself?"

"He's in the central hub," Amy said, before giving Will an unconvinced look. "So, what's this I hear about silver?"

GABY WASN'T SURE what she had expected when they finally saw Mike, a twenty-something who, like most of the guys she had met so far, hadn't shaved in quite some time. He was reasonably handsome underneath sleep-deprived eyes, but a tired face didn't do him any favors.

"Welcome to Mercy Hospital," Mike said, walking over and shaking their hands. "It's not much, but it's kept us alive and you can't ask for more than that."

"Been busy, I see," Will said.

"Almost done. We've been using what you've told us about the silver. Unfortunately, there wasn't nearly as much of the stuff on the floor as we thought, but some of us brought personal items, like crosses. I had no idea so many people were holding on to those."

There were a dozen or so men and women gathered inside what Amy called the "central hub," a large, circular lounge that connected the hospital's four towers. A wide, dark cherry desk sat in the center, the glass tabletop featuring a map of the building. At the moment, Mike's people were using it to hold makeshift weapons. Silver gleamed underneath the LED lights and what little sunlight managed to pierce through the barricaded windows around them.

The weapons had once been crosses and everyday items such as candle holders, but had since been sharpened, sanded down, and forged into bladed weapons. There had to be a good fifty, maybe sixty, dangerous-looking items piled on the tabletop. More than enough for all forty people in Mike's group.

Will pulled out his cross-knife and showed it to Mike. "Brilliant minds think alike."

Mike turned the cross-knife over. "And it works?"

"I've probably killed over a hundred with just that thing. More with silver buckshot and bullets. It works."

"You don't know how glad I am to hear that. I'm tired of shooting these things with a whole magazine just to watch them keep coming. It'll be nice to see them stay down for a change. Speaking of which, Jen says you brought some goodwill gifts."

"The boys are bringing them over now," Jen said.

"And you need medicine?" Mike asked.

"If you can spare it," Will nodded.

"We can. But I was hoping we could expand our relationship beyond that."

"I'm listening."

He gestured around him. "I have forty people here who would rather be someplace else. Jen tells me you have an island. And the creatures can't get to it. Is that right?"

"We've been there for three months, and they haven't tried to cross the water once."

"And they know you're there?" Amy asked.

"We see them on the shores every night," Gaby said.

She spent most of her time in the Tower's third floor keeping overwatch and switching shifts with Danny, Blaine, and Maddie. During her night shifts, she could see the ghouls on land, moving around like little black ink dots through her night-vision binoculars. The sight of them used to disturb her, but she had learned to tune them out.

"I was there last night," Jen said. "Not a single creature. It's safe, Mike."

"Is it the water they don't like?" Mike asked.

"We think it might have something to do with the mercury content," Will said. "Probably."

"But you don't know for sure?"

"I don't know anything for sure. Just that some things worked, and others, not so much."

"What about ultraviolet? Jen says you've killed a few with those, too."

"More than a few. The facility we stayed at before the island had industrial ultraviolet lamps they were using to grow plants. Those things killed the creatures on the spot, but we haven't been able to duplicate that kind of success on our own."

"Some flashlights and portable lamps have ultraviolet. The LED ones."

"So do the solar-powered lamps on the island. But the creatures just run through them without any effect."

"Wrong wavelength, maybe?"

"Or maybe just not enough of the right kind of UV. The guy who built the facility wasn't exactly a stickler for building codes. Those lamps could have been more than just ultraviolet despite what they told us." Will shrugged. "I'm just a grunt, Mike. I'll leave the science fair experiments to the officers."

Mike handed the cross-knife back to Will. "Still, it might be worth going back to that facility to find out for sure. That kind of weapon would be invaluable."

"I wouldn't mind heading back there myself. We left a lot of supplies behind." He looked over at Jen. "How about you? Texas is pretty nice to look at this time of the year."

Jen snorted. "Oh, I see. You were after my Bell all along, weren't you? And here I thought it was my winning personality."

"That, too."

There were loud shuffling movements and grunting behind them as Tom, Benny, and Miles each lugged a heavy ammo can over. Sheets of sweat covered their contorted faces. Gaby guessed they hadn't seen this much physical activity in a while, probably not since the barricades went up.

"Where do you want these?" Benny asked between grunts.

"Over there," Mike pointed.

The men *(boys)* brought the green cans, each eleven-by-five-by-eleven inches over, but only Tom managed to stare at her long enough to get caught at it.

People gathered around them, peering curiously over each other's shoulders at the ammo cans.

Mike opened one of the green, rectangular boxes and took out a 9mm silver bullet. He held it up to the light. "How many?"

"A thousand 5.56x45mm rounds and another thousand 9mm," Will said. "Add another 500 shotgun shells to that."

"A .50 cal can should be able to carry over 1,200 rounds."

"Who's counting?"

Mike grinned back at him. "You guys actually pounded out over a thousand silver bullets on that island of yours? That's a hell of a feat."

"We had a lot of time on our hands."

"And a lot of ammo, I see."

"We drove through Texas. There was no shortage of ammo along the way. And we found some more on the island."

"God bless Texas," Mike said. "Hell, I guess it can't be any worse than what we've tried." The former lieutenant stood up and turned to his people. "Everyone start swapping out your regular ammo with silver. If you're not using 9mm or 5.56mm, it's time to change now."

"Free bullet buffet, kids, all-you-can-eat," Jen said, flicking open the other two ammo cans.

Mike turned back to Will. "Now. Let's talk about what it'll take to get my people over to that island of yours…"

CHAPTER 4

LARA

THE ISLAND ALWAYS looked so different when viewed from the Tower's windows. The structure stood almost 150 feet high, and gave them a complete view of the island and the surrounding shorelines. In the back of her mind, she always remembered how Karen's people had sneaked onto the island three months ago. It had almost cost them their lives.

She climbed the spiral cast iron staircase, pushing up on the thick wooden door to access the third floor, and stuck her head up. Because of the Tower's conical shape, the third floor was smaller than the second, which was smaller than the first.

Danny was over on the east window looking through binoculars. "What's up, doc?"

"Is that still funny?"

He grinned. "Only if it annoys you."

"Then I guess it's never going to stop being funny."

"Ha!"

She glanced up at the ceiling for a moment. There used to be a big gaping hole up there, the result of a grenade launcher finding its mark. The new roof had a skylight that looked out into a cloudless sky, with the middle of the floor bathed in bright, rectangular pools of warm sunlight. It was easy to tell which part of the third floor was rebuilt after the attack. The top half of the walls were noticeably brighter—almost white—against the dark and weathered gray of the old construction.

"How's everyone adjusting to life without Will and Gaby?" Lara asked.

"Maddie'll take over Gaby's spot and we'll cycle through the nightshift so everyone gets daylight duty every other day."

"Why, Danny, are you actually being responsible for once?"

"Yes, but don't tell anyone."

"And the arm?"

Danny moved his right arm around in a circular motion, like a baseball pitcher winding up for a pitch. "It only hurts when I do this."

"So don't do that."

He grunted. "Set you up pretty good for that one, huh?"

She smiled. "And I appreciate it."

"Did I ever tell you the joke about the priest and the clown?"

"I don't wanna hear it."

"Ah, come on, without Willie here, you're the next best thing."

"There's Blaine."

"Too scary."

"Maddie."

"Too short."

"Sarah?"

"Too always-cooking-something."

"I guess you're out of luck, then."

Lara grabbed one of the binoculars hanging along the wall. She peered south and saw Blaine and Maddie working on the boat shack on the beach in front of the piers. Elise and Vera were building castles, while Jenny struggled with a fishing pole, screaming excitedly at the other girls.

"Jenny caught another fish," Lara said.

"Fishing pole?"

"What else would she use?"

"I threw a rock into the lake this morning. Two fish floated to the top."

Danny was exaggerating, but not by much. Beaufont Lake was teeming with fish. Without fishermen to thin the herd, there was enough sea life in the water to feed them for a long time. Lara found that both reassuring and oddly a little depressing.

Still better than cans of SPAM, I guess.

"Anything from Will?" she asked.

Danny glanced at his watch. "He's only been gone for two hours, Lara. Relax. It usually takes Big Willie at least three hours to pick up a girl from the bar. The forever love that knows no bounds you two crazy kids share is still safe for at least another hour."

"I knew I could count on you to cheer me up, Danny."

He chuckled. "That's what I'm here for. But just in case you'd like to remind him you have something better to offer back home, I wrote down the hospital radio's frequency, along with the one for Jen's helicopter."

Lara hung the binoculars and walked over to a table on the other side of the room. There was a ham radio on the tabletop and a sheet of paper duct taped next to it. An antenna extended outside the Tower gave the radio excellent range, not that they had made use of it in the last few months. Surviving, waiting constantly for Kate to attack, had taken precedence over broadcasting out into the world. Besides, without the computer that once ran Karen's automated FEMA signal, the idea of manually calling out seemed like too much of a crapshoot—and too much work.

"Give it half a year," Will had said. "If we're still around then, we'll see if anyone's still out there. Right now, we need to help ourselves first."

The radio was one of the things they had found in the Tower's basement, one of the few places on the island she dreaded visiting. Every time she did wander down there—and usually only when she absolutely had to—she couldn't help but feel a great sense of loss and tragedy. The equipment, the supplies, and the clothes stacked in piles were reminders of the poor souls that had come here seeking hope, only to find tragedy. It never failed to depress her.

She sat down in a swivel chair and turned the ham radio on, then manipulated the frequency dial for a moment until she found the correct one.

She pressed the transmit lever and spoke into the microphone. "Hello, this is Song Island to Mercy Hospital. Can you hear me?"

"Say 'over,'" Danny said behind her.

"What?"

"You have to say 'over' when you're done talking. It's a radio thing."

"I used to talk on the radio all the time when I was a kid, and I never said 'over.'"

"Well, you're all grown up now. Different rules."

She turned back to the mic. "This is Song Island to Mercy Hospital. Are you receiving this? Um, over."

She waited, listening to static on the other end.

"Say it with more conviction," Danny said.

She pressed the lever again: "This is Song Island to Mercy Hospital. Can anyone hear me over there? Over."

She waited again, but there was still no reply.

"Are you sure this is the right frequency?" she asked Danny.

A male voice answered through the radio before Danny could respond: "This is Mercy Hospital. We read you loud and clear, Song Island. Over."

"Told ya," Danny said.

"Shut up," she said. Then into the radio: "Roger that, Mercy Hospital. I'm looking for one of ours. He should have arrived by now. His name is Will. Over."

"He's here, Song Island. I'll go fetch him for you. Over."

"Thanks. Uh, over."

"Ask him if there are any hot girls over there," Danny said.

"What do you care? You already have a hot girl here."

"Hey, I like to keep my options open."

"I'll tell Carly you said that."

"Go ahead. She's keeping her options open, too."

Before Lara could reply, a familiar voice spoke through the radio: "Hey there, beautiful, you were looking for me?"

She smiled at the sound of Will's voice.

"What's he talking about?" Danny said behind her. "I wasn't looking for him."

Lara ignored him, and said into the microphone, "How was the ride?"

"Slightly bumpy," Will said, "and the flight movie kinda sucked. How are things over there?"

"It's only been two hours, but we've managed to get by without you. Although it's been tough. You are, after all, indispensable."

"That's what I've been trying to tell you."

"How's the situation over there?"

"What Jen said. They've sealed the entire floor off from the ghouls, but that still leaves nine infested floors below them."

Lara felt the hairs along her arms and neck prickle at the

thought. "Great. Fresh nightmares for tonight. Thanks, Will."

He laughed. "Sorry."

"Sounds like they've gotten by so far."

"So far, yeah. Anyways, I was talking to Mike, and he wants to make other arrangements."

"What kind of 'arrangements'?"

"He wants to bring his people over to the island."

"You think that's a good idea?"

"I'll tell you tomorrow. Right now, it's just an idea. But we have to be open to it, or something like it." He paused, then continued, "So, tell me how much you've missed me already…"

SHE FELT REFRESHED after talking with Will, and walked down to the beach along the cobblestone pathway that serpentined around the island like the many heads of a hydra. The short walk through the woods between the beach and the hotel grounds always allowed her to pretend there was nothing wrong with the world. It was quiet and cool, the trees supplying plenty of shade against the September sun.

When she stepped onto the beach, Lara stayed on the path and watched the girls darting in and out of the lake, splashing each other with water. The fish that Jenny had caught was nowhere to be found, and she guessed they had released it. With so many fish already in the freezer back at the hotel kitchen, it was overkill to do more than just catch and release these days.

Another luxury we didn't have three months ago. Please, God, let us never run out of luxuries.

She smiled to herself. What would her mother say if she knew her little girl had begun praying to an unseen, unknown, and un-named God? Her father would probably have chuckled in amusement, but her mother…

Sorry, Mom, try not to be too disappointed.

Maddie was on top of the boat shack, a long, rectangular brick building that squatted in front of the piers. She sat in a lawn chair with her M4 rifle across her lap, binoculars hanging from her neck, and a bottle of sunscreen nearby. She looked like a teenager sitting in cutoff jean shorts and a T-shirt.

"I hope you remembered to put that sunscreen on," Lara called up to her.

Maddie, in dark shades, sat up a little and smiled down. "Always, doc."

"See anything up there?"

"Does the sun count?"

"Just make sure it doesn't try anything funny."

"That's what the rifle's for," Maddie said, and went back to reclining.

Will wanted to build a guard tower on top of the boat shack, to give the beach the same kind of coverage that the Tower provided. It was another item on a to-do list that was getting longer every week. Not that she minded. If you didn't work or enjoy running around the beach every day, there wasn't much else to do on the island.

"Where's Blaine?" Lara asked.

"He went to the hotel for a bite," Maddie said. "He'll be back to relieve me in a few hours."

"Keep an eye on the girls for me."

"You got it, doc."

Lara headed back up the path. She liked Maddie. The country girl had come to them with Blaine and a young man named Bobby. Bobby was gone, killed during the attack on the island. It had been a bad night for all of them, but to look at the island now, she couldn't even see signs that there had been a bloodbath on the beach just three months ago. The bodies were buried in the field behind the marina, and the blood had been washed away by the tide.

◄━━▌ ▌━━►

SHE HEARD LAUGHTER from the kitchen, and inside she found Blaine leaning against one of the counters, picking at a plate of baked fish wrapped in aluminum foil, while Sarah ate from her own plate with a fork. Sarah's cheeks look flustered, her long blonde hair—the longest on the island by far—in a ponytail that went all the way down to her waist.

Blaine was licking his fingers when she came into the kitchen. "Hey, want some fish?"

"Smells good," Lara said.

"It would be nice if we had some vegetables to go with it," Sarah said. "Cilantro or basil would be wonderful."

"Zucchini or green olives, too?"

"See, I knew there was a cook in there somewhere."

"She must be very well hidden, then."

There was suddenly awkward silence, and Lara got the sense she had interrupted something.

She quickly turned to go. "I'm going to go do something…that isn't here. Carry on."

She caught Sarah blushing a bit as she left, but Blaine was already out of her peripheral vision so she couldn't tell his reaction.

Blaine and Sarah? Was it possible?

She reminded herself what Blaine had lost just to get to the island. For the first few days after the fight, they weren't even sure he was going to stay. At one point, she remembered Will telling her not to be surprised if Blaine disappeared into the western section of the island, into the woods, and never came back. Blaine was looking noticeably less haggard in recent weeks, and whether it was the island weather finally doing its job, or the *(Sarah's)* company, he seemed to have more life in his eyes now than in all the time she had known him.

She was happy for him, for Sarah. Or maybe she was reading too much into what was really just a simple, innocent moment? She hoped it was true. The two of them had been through a lot. They all had. To find a little slice of peace, maybe even happiness, was more than any of them could have asked for when so many people had lost their lives.

She thought of Will again and couldn't help but smile to herself as she walked through the hotel. Sometimes she forgot she was on an island, that just beyond those waters were creatures that shouldn't exist, but did. But here, now, in this place that was designed for rich people but had never been finished, none of the world's problems mattered.

This is our home now. God help those who try to take it from us.

Lara found Carly in the laundry room, near the back of Hallway A—the main hallway that connected the completed sections of the hotel—past the ballroom and squeezed in between some employee lounges and large storage rooms. It wasn't quite the bowels of the hotel, but it was close.

Carly was folding bedsheets and humming some pop song Lara vaguely recalled being popular on the radio. Lara tapped her on the shoulder.

A month ago, Carly would have jumped, but this afternoon she just glanced over and pulled free one iPod earbud. "Hey. How you holding up during this separation from your lover?"

Lara groaned. "Please, dear God, don't ever say 'lover' again."

Carly laughed. "Agreed. I died a little as soon as I said it."

Lara grabbed some dry sheets and clothes out of the industrial-size machines that lined one wall and dumped them onto an island counter. Washers took up space on the other side of the room, with a large pantry stuffed with detergent and drying sheets, along with spare baskets and miscellaneous inventory. Washing what they used was a good way to cut down on unnecessary supply runs for clean clothes, and allowed them to focus on more valuable items like silver, medical supplies, and ammo. There was no such thing as "too much" ammo.

She began folding what looked like the girls' clothes. Elise's or Vera's, or possibly Jenny's. Not that it mattered. Everyone needed clean clothes.

"How's your neck?" she asked.

Carly self-consciously touched the bullet scar along the left side of her neck. It was tiny, but visible if you peeked. "Vera thinks it makes me look like a badass."

"And you don't have any trouble breathing? Or swallowing?"

"Danny hasn't complained."

Lara made a face. "Oh, gross."

"Come on, we're both adults here. A girl's gotta do what a girl's gotta do to keep her man happy, am I right?"

"I don't know if I'd go that far. As Gaby would say, TMI, Carly. Way too much information."

Carly laughed again, and Lara joined her.

When they finally calmed down, Carly said, "Speaking of which, I'm not a big fan of Gaby going with Will. She's just a kid."

"She's just two years younger than you."

"Oh, right, bring facts into this."

Lara smiled. "Anyway, I told him the same thing, but he disagrees. He says…" She paused.

"What?"

"He says she's the best shooter by far after him and Danny."

"That's what Danny says, too."

"Is that...good?"

Carly shrugged. "I don't know. They seem to think it is."

"What do you think?"

"If none of this had happened, Gaby would be getting ready for the prom and college, not learning to shoot and fight. I bet she never thought she'd be doing that a year ago."

"I don't think any of us thought we'd be doing this a year ago."

"Yeah, laundry was never in any of my plans," Carly said.

"Well, you're really good at it."

"Shut up, that's not funny. How long did Will say he'll be gone, anyway?"

"He should know by tonight. Right now, he's talking to Mike— the guy leading the group over there."

"Their version of Will."

"Uh huh. He says—"

She didn't get to finish because the radio clipped to her hip squawked, and they heard Danny's voice: "Heads up, we have vehicles on approach."

Lara unclipped her radio. "How many, Danny?"

"Four. Three trucks and one van." He paused, then added, "They're pulling into the marina."

"I'm on the way."

Carly abandoned the laundry and jogged out of the room with Lara, who headed for the closest side exit.

"I thought we shut down the FEMA broadcast?" Carly said.

"We did," Lara said. "Even before it got blown up. Whoever these people are, if they're here because of Karen's broadcast, they're three months late."

⊷━▌ ▐━▶

LARA REACHED THE Tower and found Danny at the south window on the third floor, looking out with binoculars. Carly had separated from her outside the hotel, making a beeline for the beach to gather up the kids and bring them back to the hotel. It was a system Will had put in place, and everyone knew their roles.

Lara snatched the spare binoculars off a hook and peered out across the lake at the marina.

Or what was left of it. Will had burned it down, along with a storage garage. He had also set ablaze the two-story house across a small inlet from the marina at the same time, leaving only old trampled hurricane fencing behind. There were exactly eleven vehicles in the marina parking lot at the moment. A few hours ago, there had only been seven.

She saw tiny black dots climbing out of the newly arrived vehicles, the figures gathering near the water's edge. She could tell they had spotted the Tower and Song Island by the glint of binocular lenses staring back in their direction.

"How many do you count, Danny?"

"Seven from the trucks, four out of the van," Danny said.

Lara swung the binoculars toward the beach, at Maddie on the roof of the boat shack.

On cue, her radio squawked, and she heard Maddie's voice: "What are we looking at?"

"Eleven people so far," Lara said into the radio.

"Any ideas what they want?" Carly asked from somewhere else on the island, likely the hotel where she, Blaine, and Sarah were guarding the girls.

"Not yet," Danny said. He glanced over at Lara. "What do you think?"

"Why are you asking me?" she said, meeting his gaze.

"Well, Will's not here, so that kind of leaves you in charge."

She stared speechlessly back at him.

Her face must have also looked stunned, because he grinned and said, "Oh come on, that's surprising to you? Look, I don't say this a lot, but Willie boy's really good at this sort of stuff. Me, I'm just a lover and a fighter. Got a farmer's daughter you want seduced? I'm your man. Need a way out of an Afghanistan mountainside covered in Taliban? Uh, ask Will. Failing that, ask Lara."

It took her a moment to answer, but when she finally found her voice, the only thing that came out was an almost disbelieving, "Since when?"

"Since Will left four hours ago."

Lara peered through the binoculars again, if just to hide her sudden—but quickly growing—anxiety. The idea of being in charge in

Will's absence terrified her. She was a third-year medical student, for God's sake. They taught her how to sew up wounds and take care of colds, not to make decisions that could, potentially, lead to other people's deaths.

"What do you think?" she asked uncertainly.

"We should at least find out what they want," Danny said.

"I think we know what they want."

"They're a little late for that."

"Which sort of makes it unlikely this could be a trap."

"You think?"

"Think about it. If they're collaborators, and this is some elaborate scheme to get back on the island, this is kind of...dumb, don't you think? Show up three months after the last radio broadcast?"

"That's a good point."

"Or I could be overthinking it," she added quickly. "I don't know what I'm talking about, Danny. Maybe we should radio Will back and ask him."

"Nah, I think you're on to something."

He said it with such absolute certainty she almost believed him. *Almost.*

"I'll take a boat over with Maddie and suss them out," Danny continued. "Can't very well just ignore them, can we?" He glanced at his watch. "Seven hours till sunset, give or take."

Lara nodded reluctantly. "Be careful."

"Don't sweat it, doc. What's the worst that could happen?"

"They end up being ghoul collaborators and kill everyone on the island as soon as they set foot on the beach."

"Sure, there's *that*," Danny said.

CHAPTER 5

GABY

SHE THOUGHT SHE would have gotten used to the smell after a few hours, but four hours later Gaby was still unable to fully breathe through her nose without feeling overwhelmed. It wasn't just the presence of forty bodies crammed onto one floor, because the tenth floor was certainly massive enough to accommodate ten times that number. There was something else about the place, about the whole hospital. Something in the air she hadn't felt in a long time, and it took her a while to remember what it was.

Desperation.

She didn't like how these people lived. Even before she found Will and Lara, Gaby had had a better existence than this. Sure, going from town to town, hiding in basements, didn't sound like such a great time, but when you compared it to hiding *(stuck)* on the tenth floor of a hospital, with ghouls waiting in the nine floors below, it was a hell of a better alternative.

This isn't a sanctuary. It's a prison.

To escape it, she went up to the rooftop. There were a couple of guys outside smoking cigarettes. One of them was Benny, who had learned his lesson and hardly stared when she came outside. Instead, he offered her a cigarette.

"I don't smoke," she said. "It's a filthy habit."

"Yeah, I know."

"So why don't you quit?"

"I guess I'm weak." He gave her a shy smile. "I'm Benny, by the way."

"Gaby," she said, shaking his hand.

She had thought he was in his twenties when she first met him earlier, but up close she realized he was just a nice-looking eighteen-year-old kid. He sported amusing facial hair that did more harm than good, and he had pleasant enough light-blue eyes. The other boy, Mack, gave her a brief nod and turned away.

Gaby walked to the edge of the north tower rooftop, while Mack and Benny stayed behind near the access building. She wasn't sure what their jobs were, exactly. Who was going to invade the building from the rooftop? The only danger came at night…

She looked off at the city around her. The domed building—some kind of basketball arena, probably—was visible across the street, along with the baseball and football stadiums to either sides of it. They were definitely in some kind of college town.

College.

She used to have plans for college. She'd had everything worked out, too. Good grades, after school programs, extra credits, stacks of college preparation books, and admissions forms from every school around the country.

What was that old saying? *"The plans of mice and men…"* Or something like that.

"There you are," a voice said behind her.

Gaby looked back at Amy, who walked over with two cans of diet soda.

Gaby took one. "Thanks."

She opened her can. There was no fizz, of course, and the taste was sludgy and warm, and she suddenly missed the freezer back at the hotel. She did her best to hide her disappointment and hoped Amy hadn't caught it.

"Jen says you guys have a freezer on the island," Amy said. "That would be nice right about now."

"Refrigerators in our rooms, too."

"So, ice and cold drinks?"

"Uh huh."

"I've forgotten what that's like." She took a sip from her soda and made a face. "Yeah, I could really go for a little ice right about now."

"Where's Jen?"

"Asleep in her room. She always crashes after every trip. I personally think she does it on purpose—keeps going out there to tire herself out, because it's so hard to sleep day after day in here. There's not a lot to do, and you know hospitals…"

Gaby replayed the faces of the people on the tenth floor in her mind. Droopy, sleep-deprived, and pale. It was a depressing thought, and she pushed it away.

"What's out there?" she asked instead.

"The University of Louisiana at Lafayette. Go Ragin' Cajuns."

"I've never seen a Ragin' Cajun before."

"They're like your average Cajun. Only ragin'."

"Ah."

They shared an awkward smile.

Amy took another sip from her flat soda and made another face. "Ugh. This thing tastes terrible. You swear you guys have ice over there?"

"Cross my heart and hope to die."

"Good enough for me."

"Are you going?"

"To Song Island?" She seemed to think about it. "If everyone's going, I guess there's no reason for me to stay behind."

"Jen doesn't seem to care either way."

"It's 'have helicopter, will fly' with her. I don't think she cares about anything else, to be perfectly honest."

"Was she in the Army, too?"

"She was the news chopper pilot for one of the local stations around here. You should have seen her at the beginning of all this. Ferrying people to the hospital like some kind of aerial avenger. It was beautiful."

Gaby took another sip from the soda, thought about spitting it out, but didn't want to hurt Amy's feelings, so she forced herself to swallow it instead.

"Can you hear it?" Amy asked.

"What's that?"

"The city."

Gaby thought that was a strange question. She tried to listen to the city, but she only heard the whistling of the wind, the occasional *flap-flap-flap* of trash moving around the street and the parking lot below them.

"I don't hear anything," Gaby said.

"Yeah," Amy said. "We heard them in the first few months. Dogs and cats. But we haven't heard a single one of them for months now. The only animals that are safe are the birds."

Gaby watched a flock of birds glide gracefully across the skyline in front of them, far from the reaches of the streets below...

SHE FOUND WILL in his room, next to hers along the north tower. There weren't nearly enough people for the tenth floor's 200 rooms, so they had their pick. She guessed Will had chosen two rooms within twenty yards of the stairs for the quick rooftop access.

"Hope for the best, prepare for the worst" was his and Danny's motto. They did almost everything with it in mind, something she had slowly begun to adopt. It was a new way of not just thinking, but living, and it took more effort than she had expected, mostly because Will and Danny made it look so effortless.

He stood next to his window, staring out through rusted rebars. Every room on the floor had the same long, rectangle windows that stretched almost the entire width of the back wall. Will had dumped his pack on an uncomfortable-looking pull-out sofa, and his beaten up M4A1 rifle lay across the patient bed behind him. The good thing about staying in a hospital was that every room had its own bed and bathroom. Unfortunately, the bathroom didn't have running water or working plumbing, but the bed was clean enough, if not entirely comfortable.

Will glanced over. "Settled in?"

"Lumpy bed, window you can't open, and the smell of desperation in the air. What's not to like?"

He chuckled. "What's up?"

"About Mike's people..."

"Close the door first."

She nodded and closed the door after her. "Are we taking them back with us?"

"Some. Maybe ten at first. See how that works out, then act accordingly."

"We could definitely use more guns."

He nodded. "You can never go wrong with more guns, as long as you can trust the finger pulling the trigger."

She stood next to him and looked out the window at the quiet, empty city below. It looked more dead from behind bars than it had from the rooftop. They didn't speak for a long time, something Gaby had become used to with Will.

"Thanks again for bringing me with you," she said after a while.

"I wouldn't have if I didn't think you could hack it."

A sudden flush of pride raced through her, and she did her best to not let it show on her face.

Instead, she reached through the bars, rasped her knuckles against the glass window, and got back a dull thudding sound. "Can they get through this?"

"Doubtful. Hospital windows are made to be permanently closed and nearly impossible to break."

"I didn't know that."

"It's to keep the patients from deciding to end it all when times get tough."

"That's a pleasant thought."

He glanced back at the door briefly, as if to make sure it was still closed. "They've been really lucky here so far. I think Mike knows it, too. That's why he's so desperate to get them to the island."

"There are a lot of long faces in those hallways."

"They look like good people, so there's that."

"Pretty decent, yeah."

"It won't hurt to bring them over. Mike would be a valuable as-set...with some sleep."

"And the others?"

"Danny and I have experience sanding down kids and turning them into decent soldiers."

She smiled. "Did Mike say what they're planning to do with the silver bullets we brought over?"

"There's an Archers Sports and Outdoors a few streets down with supplies he's been itching to get at. The last time he tried to take them was about three months ago, and they lost a couple of guys."

"So we'll be here for at least tonight."

"Homesick already?"

"Nah," she said. "Just missing that kitchen freezer, that's all."

Then she added, "And the cold drinks. And the ice. And the showers. But mostly the showers."

THERE WASN'T A lot to do until tomorrow, so after washing her face with warm bottled water in the bathroom, Gaby sat on the bed, stripped down her M4, and cleaned it piece by piece while she still had some light from the window. She took out a small pouch with cleaning solvents, an old toothbrush, lint-free cloth, and a bore brush for the job. It was the most basic cleaning kit they could put together using equipment available at the hotel.

She looked up when there was a knock on her door. "Come in."

A pair of familiar blue eyes and bad stubble peeked in at her through the open door. Benny shot a curious look at the pieces of the rifle spread out on the white bedsheet in front of her.

"You busy?" he asked.

"No. What's up?"

"We're about to have dinner. They wanted me to call you. Well, I volunteered."

"Where?"

"Huh?"

"Where do you guys eat?"

"Oh. At the central hub."

"Okay."

"Okay?"

"I'll be over when I'm done."

"Oh. Okay. I'll…" She thought he was going to stammer his way to something else, but he apparently decided to just leave instead.

Gaby picked up the bore brush and went back to cleaning the M4. The old Gaby wouldn't have had the patience for something so tedious, but that girl was gone. If the new her had learned anything from three months with Will and Danny, it was that no one was going to depend more on her gear than her.

Out here, the difference between life and death was a weapon that worked the way it was supposed to.

IF SHE THOUGHT the sight of the hospital's survivors was depressing, the dinner wasn't much of an improvement. Gaby spent the thirty minutes in the central hub listening to Will, Mike, and Amy talking, while people came and went in a never-ending stream. Although Benny told her it was dinner, it was really eat-when-you-feel-like-it time. Food consisted of canned meat, MREs, and bags of noodles washed down with warm soft drinks and water. Unfortunately, there wasn't a single can of fruit dripped in syrup to be found.

Even with the bright LED lights, the room looked and felt uninviting.

"There are others out there," Will was saying. "In other states. I'm not sure if it's anything resembling an organized resistance, but they're out there. We're not alone by any means."

"That's good to know," Mike said. "One of the disadvantages of locking ourselves in here is the lack of information. Even Jen hasn't really brought anything back about what's happening out there."

"Has she left Louisiana yet?"

"Not yet," Amy said.

"What are your immediate priorities?" Will asked Mike.

"Those supplies in the Archers, first."

"What are you running low on?"

"Everything. That's one of the reasons why I want to start shuttling people to Song Island. Starting with the women and children."

"I'll agree to that. What I don't want is for you to load everyone into a van and drive down there. We're not ready for that kind of influx."

"And you're right to be wary of that," Mike nodded. "We've been here for eleven months. Another month won't kill us."

"In terms of medical supplies," Amy said, "what are you looking for?"

Will took out a piece of folded paper and handed it to her. "A lot of supplies for everyday use and the occasional emergencies."

Amy scanned the sheet of paper, then nodded at Mike. "I can fill everything on here."

"So that's settled," Mike said. "When do you head back?"

"I'm not in any hurry," Will said. "If you want, I can help out with the Archers tomorrow."

"I'd be an idiot to turn down an Army Ranger's offer."

The two men shook hands.

AFTER DINNER, GABY walked back to her room. She saw a boy watching her from a partially open door. He had a pale face and hollow eyes, and for a brief instant she thought she was looking at a ghoul child.

The boy closed the door as she walked past.

She finally made it back to her room, feeling less than full after dinner. She hadn't wanted to say anything, because Mike and the others went out of their way to welcome them. The food wasn't bad, it just wasn't island food.

There was still enough light outside, so she decided to strip down her Glock and clean it, too, and was slightly annoyed when there was another knock on her door.

"Come in."

It was Will this time. He closed the door softly behind him.

"Thank God," she said. "I thought it was that Benny kid again."

"He likes you."

"He's a teenager, Will. He likes anything with tits and ass."

That got an amused grin from him.

"What's up?" she asked.

Will had a small bundle wrapped in red felt and tied with brown twine in his hand. He tossed it to her. "Happy early birthday."

"It's not—" She stopped herself.

Oh my God.

"I forgot," she said quietly. "I can't believe I forgot my own birthday."

"Lara didn't. Eighteen, right?"

"Nineteen."

"Right. Nineteen."

"Can I…?"

"Knock yourself out, birthday girl."

"It won't be official until tomorrow."

"Close enough."

Gaby pulled at the twine and it slipped effortlessly free. She realized she was trembling slightly when she peeled the felt wrapping to reveal a can of Dole Pineapple Chunks.

"It's the last can on the island," Will said. "Lara saved it two weeks ago to give it to you. She's been hiding it in the freezer without telling anyone, so…" Will put a finger to his lips. "Mum's the word."

"I don't know what to say."

"I told her we should have gotten you something else. Like jewelry. Teenage girls love jewelry, right?"

Gaby gave him a wry look before beaming. "This is great, Will. Thank you."

"Yeah?"

She smiled and nodded enthusiastically. "Yeah. I mean it. You guys are awesome."

"Glad to hear it." He fished a plastic spork out of his pocket and tossed it to her. "Go crazy, kid."

Gaby anxiously pulled the tab off the can.

Will headed for the door, singing badly off-key, "Happy birthday to you, happy birthday to you."

Gaby was too busy fishing out a chunk of pineapple dripping with heavy, artificially-flavored syrup to reply. She plopped it into her mouth and sighed with bliss.

AMY WARNED HER to keep her blinds closed at night, and she did. Even so, once darkness fell, Gaby heard them almost immediately.

She knew the ghouls could climb, and there were enough handholds along the sides of the hospital for them to use. Even so, she was stunned by the speed with which they appeared once the sun set. It had been so long since she was this close to a ghoul, she almost cringed at the realization that they were *outside her window at this very moment.*

She sat on the floor, back against the side of the bed, and listened to them moving. The M4 lay across her lap, the magazine in it, like the ones around her waist, loaded with silver bullets. They had stopped carrying regular ammo a long time ago. Silver killed a human being just as well as a ghoul.

The window blinds were made of thick, hypoallergenic fabric that did a tremendous job of reflecting sunlight in the daytime, and was just as effective at night against moonlight. She could barely make out the lone, thin figure clinging to the windowsill on the other side. She didn't have to see it to know what it was, though. There was nothing human about the way it moved, the thin, almost skeletal shadow it cast against the moonlight in the background.

How many were out there now, climbing the sides of the hospital? A hundred? A thousand?

Gaby swore she could hear them moving in the floors under her, too, scurrying about like cockroaches. She hadn't heard them earlier today, even though she knew they were down there the whole time. It was the night, she thought. They lived—they *thrived*—at night.

The ghoul outside seemed to be tapping its fists lightly against the window. She could barely make out the noise through the thick glass.

Tap-tap-tap. Tap-tap-tap...

She wasn't nearly as terrified as she thought she would be. Maybe it was her training, maybe it was all the days and weeks working with the M4 and the Glock that infused her with a surprising amount of courage.

The creature stopped its odd activity when it was suddenly joined by a second skeletal figure. This one looked even thinner than the first, with what looked like shadowed bones sticking out of its skin.

Gaby wasn't sure when she made the decision, but she was only vaguely aware of standing up and walking forward and reaching for the blinds' drawstring. She jerked it with one smooth motion, and the hypoallergenic blinds opened up in a loud rush.

The first ghoul had wandered off, leaving behind the new arrival to cling perilously to the windowsill. Hollowed eye sockets and something that might have been eyeballs peered back curiously at her from the other side. Moonlight reflected off its hairless, pruned skin, and its slightly upturned, almost impish nose flared at her presence.

She wondered if the creature could smell her, too. Probably not...

The creature opened its mouth, revealing devastated teeth jutting out from gums that were pink and black and oozing thick fluids. It might have been drooling, or maybe it was just bleeding. The bones of its left leg below the kneecap were sticking out from punctured flesh, matching bones protruding out of its ribcage. When the creature moved, it did so awkwardly, in a way that made her think it was in great pain—if they even felt pain at all.

Gaby leaned toward the window, ignoring the black eyes staring back at her, and looked down. She thought she was ready for what she would see, but she was wrong. The sight took her breath away.

They were everywhere, crawling up the side of the building. She imagined they must have looked like spiders scaling the brick structure, scurrying wildly from handhold to handhold like adrenaline junkies.

She looked to her left and right, and saw more of them.

Hundreds. Definitely hundreds.

Gaby walked back to the bed and sat down. She laid the M4 and Glock on both sides of her and stared back at the ghoul outside the window. There was movement, and a second ghoul appeared and joined the first.

A moment later, two became three, then four, crowding around the window, so many that one was knocked loose and fell, plummeting out of view. Not that it stopped the others. They kept coming, squirming into the small rectangular area, leaving sticky puddles on the glass.

They stared in at her as if they were deformed mimes incapable of speech, their nostrils flaring from time to time. She wondered what was going through their minds at the moment. Did they even still think? Or was it all instincts now?

"Dead, not stupid" was how Will described them.

Gaby picked up the can of Dole Pineapple Chunks off the floor next to her. She used the spork to fish out one of the half dozen or so remaining pieces and tossed it into her mouth. She chewed slowly, savoring the sweet syrup.

She watched the creatures watching her.

For the life of her, Gaby didn't know why she wasn't afraid. Not even a little bit.

CHAPTER 6

LARA

SHE SHOULD CALL Will. That was the smart thing to do. Will would know how to handle this.

So why hadn't she called him yet?

It was the way Danny had asked her about what they should do. They were friends, but there was more to the look he had given her. He actually *trusted* her. She didn't know what she could have done in the past to merit such commitment from him.

But it was too late to reconsider, and she was left to watch Danny approaching the marina in the pontoon through binoculars. Maddie stood behind him, steering the boat. They were a good 300 yards from the mouth of the inlet when the people at the marina saw them coming and pointed. She couldn't tell their reaction from this distance. Excitement? Suspicion? Alarm? That uncertainty sent a sudden pang of apprehension through her.

Call Will. He'll know what to do.

She looked back at the ham radio on the desk. It would be easy. It had only been an hour ago since she last talked to him.

Call Will. You are not ready for this.

The radio on her hip squawked, and she heard Danny's voice: "Five men and six women. Three children. Two boys and a girl."

"Weapons?" she asked.

"Armed to the teeth, but that's the fashion these days. Don't leave home without your AK."

"Be careful, Danny."

"Careful's my middle name. But don't tell Carly that. I told her it was Ronald."

"The boss lady means it, Danny," Carly said through the radio. She was at the beach with Blaine, standing on top of the boat shack. "You get shot and fall overboard, I'm not swimming over to get you. You know how much I suck at swimming."

"Yes, dear," Danny said.

Lara had grimaced a bit when Carly called her "boss lady."

Not her, too. Who do these people think I am?

She keyed the radio, meaning to say something profound to Danny—something Will would say—but she only managed, "Don't take any unnecessary risks, Danny. You too, Maddie. The first sign of trouble, get out of there."

Okay, not too bad.

"Will do," Danny said. "But it looks like we might not have too much of an issue."

"Why?"

"They're putting their weapons on the ground and stepping away from them."

She breathed a heavy sigh of relief. "That's a good sign, Danny."

"Or a trap," Carly said. "This whole thing smells like an ambush. Something an asshole collaborator would come up with."

"What's an ambush smell like, my dearest?" Danny asked.

"Pungent and acrid," Carly said without missing a beat.

She was describing the ghouls. Once you got a whiff of the undead creatures, it was difficult to forget. The memory was burned into your soul.

Lara looked over at the ham radio again.

Call Will. You're not ready for this. What are you waiting for?

She looked through the binoculars at the marina instead. Danny's pontoon was still moving up the inlet.

"Give me an update, Danny," she said into the radio.

"They're not shooting at me, which is a good sign," Danny said. "They also have an old woman with them. That's another good sign."

"I don't understand."

"It's the end of the world. No one lugs around an old broad unless they're really nice."

Good point.

Danny and Maddie were pulling the pontoon up alongside the marina as two men approached them with hands raised. Danny stood at the front of the boat *(What was that, the port? Starboard? Will would know…)* and was chatting them up. It seemed as if the conversation was going well, and soon Danny stepped off the boat and onto solid ground.

Her radio squawked, and she heard his voice: "They're willing to hand over their weapons. And they promise they don't have Dillingers hidden in inappropriate places."

"What's a Dillinger?" she asked.

"Uh, you know, those small handguns? Never mind."

Danny was wearing his old special forces comm gear, with the throat mic and earbud, so she knew she was safe to ask her next question: "Can we trust them?"

"I don't see why not." Danny had walked away from the others so they couldn't hear him. "Of the five *hombres*, only three are really worth being concerned over. One looks too friendly to have shot anyone, and the other two—well, I can keep an eye on them. Then there's a teenager and a kid who looks about ten."

"Will they let us frisk them?"

"That's a no-brainer."

"Okay, Danny. If you think we can trust them…"

"I don't think we can trust them," Danny said. "But I think we can manage them. The old woman and the girls look innocent enough. Tired and hungry. And like I said—there are only two guys I would have to keep an eye on."

"Can we leave those two behind?" Carly asked.

"That's not going to happen," Danny said. "They've survived together for a while. They won't abandon each other now."

"Just like we wouldn't abandon Danny, despite his god-awful jokes," Lara said.

"Oh, that's funny," Danny said.

Lara smiled. "It's your call, Danny."

"They won't be left behind, but maybe they're willing to part ways temporarily."

"You think they'll go for that?"

"Wouldn't hurt to ask."

"Okay. Do it."

She watched Danny walk back to the group. She could only imagine what he was saying to them: *"Good news and bad news! The good news is, we're going to let you guys on the island. The bad news is, we're going to have to give you a cavity search first."*

Knowing Danny, she was probably close.

LARA WAITED FOR Blaine to show up before she headed down the Tower, because someone always had to be on the third floor at all times. More standard operating procedure that Will had drilled into their heads.

When the big man finally arrived, Lara hurried over to the beach to join Carly, who was waiting on the roof of the boat shack with her Benelli shotgun slung over her back. Lara had her own Remington 870 with her. Like Carly, she was trained on the rifles, but being trained on them wasn't the same as actually hitting something with them. The shotguns, on the other hand, were harder to miss with.

Carly glanced down at her. "Hey, boss lady."

"Stop calling me that, please."

"What? You don't like it?"

"No."

"Oh, come on. With Will gone, you're our new fearless leader. Accept it."

Lara frowned. "When did you and Danny come to that conclusion?"

"Last night. We were hoping Will's leadership abilities had seeped into you by osmosis. You know, on account of how you guys have hot sex every night."

Lara smiled. "Is that what you think Will and I do every night? Have hot sex?"

"Just a little bit?"

"Maybe a tad."

She climbed up to the roof using a ladder in the back. The shack was a smooth concrete block, completely unappealing to the eyes, and used purely to store supplies and fuel. Even a hurricane probably wouldn't be able to lift the ugly thing, which was the size of a four-car garage.

Carly handed her the binoculars. "They're on their way back. I can't believe they agreed to bringing just the women and children first."

"They're desperate," Lara said. "You remember what it was like for us out there. I just hope we didn't make a really big mistake."

"I trust you."

Why? I don't even trust myself.

◄━━▌ ▐━━►

LARA WALKED UP the middle pier to meet the pontoon boat as it slowed, then drifted toward her. Danny stood at the front with his M4A1 rifle slung over his back. The carbine had been damaged during the attack on the island, but Danny had gutted parts from a couple of M4 rifles Tom had stored under the Tower to fix it.

Maddie was in the center of the pontoon, looking even smaller behind the big steering wheel. The boat was not built for speed, but it had plenty of space for the eight people crammed into it at the moment.

The fact that half of them were children, and the adults looked thin, helped to calm her nerves. Besides backpacks, the newcomers carried only luggage with them. Lara wondered if she had looked that way—somewhere between hopeful and very afraid it might all be too good to be true—when they first arrived on Song Island.

And did I ever look that thin?

Danny tossed a rope over to her, and Lara tied it around a metal anchor while Danny pulled the pontoon in by hand, stopping only when they were alongside. He quickly hopped out and wrapped the rest of the rope's length around the anchor before cinching it.

"Ladies and gentleman," Danny announced, "welcome to Song Island. Pictures are five dollars apiece and can be purchased at that delightful little concrete block at the end of the pier."

The newcomers consisted of four women, one elderly woman, and three children—two girls in their early teens and a boy. They stared at the island and its white beaches with a mixture of awe and barely-contained joy. The women looked on the verge of tears.

Please God, let this be the right decision.

One of the women was striking and tall, with auburn hair that looked red under the sun. She helped the older woman out of the boat. "Easy, Mae, don't rush it."

Mae looked to be in her sixties, brushing frizzled gray hair out of her face as she reached up and took the attractive woman's hand to be pulled up. Danny and another woman, a short blonde in her twenties wearing a slightly dirty sweater and cargo pants, also lent a hand. Lara was afraid the older woman might break under the three people pulling at her slim figure all at once, but she somehow got onto the pier in one piece.

"Just luggage?" Lara asked.

"The rest are back with the men," the tall woman said. She smiled and held out her hand. "I'm Bonnie." She pointed at the others. "This is Mae. That's Gwen and Jo, and the kids are Lucy, Kylie, and Logan. Thank you for letting us come here. We've been…looking for it for a long time."

Lara managed a smile back. "You guys must be hungry."

"Starving," a young woman with ash blonde hair, Gwen, said. She was short and barely went up to Bonnie's chest, but she made up for that with breasts that were twice the size of Bonnie's.

"Come on, we have some food at the hotel," Lara said.

"You have a *hotel?*" the younger brunette, Jo, said. Lara guessed Jo and Bonnie were related. They had similar prominent cheekbones and hazel eyes. Jo looked barely out of her teens but was already taller than Lara.

The women and the boy exchanged excited looks at the mention of "hotel."

She had to smile at that. "When was the last time you guys had cold water? Or ice in your soft drinks?"

"I…" Bonnie began to say, but couldn't get it out.

Jo laughed. "I think what Bonnie's trying to say is, it's been so long, we can't remember."

LARA AND DANNY watched the women and the boy feast on plates of fried, boiled, and baked fish in the big dining room next to the lobby. The unfinished room was massive, with a large marble table that seated twenty. The new arrivals didn't seemed to notice the lack of proper flooring or walls—or ceiling, for that matter—when the food was served.

Sarah and Carly brought out the dishes and the newcomers devoured everything put in front of them, probably a combination of real hunger and having to eat out of cans and bags for the last eleven months.

Ah, the good ol' days.

Danny tapped her on the shoulder and nodded toward the door. She followed him back into the lobby, then over to the front doors.

"So how'd I do, boss?" Danny asked.

"You did good, kid," she said, playing along. "I have a cookie here somewhere."

"Yum."

She put on her serious face. "What about the men?"

Danny looked back at the open dining room door, at the women inside. "It's still early. I'll let them stew in the sun for another couple of hours."

"That seems kind of mean."

"I want to see how they react."

"Meaning?"

"When I go back, I want to see their reaction. Are they agitated? Annoyed? Ready to shoot me between the eyes?"

"Sounds kind of dangerous."

"Will and I would never have let some guys we didn't know from Adam take you and Carly to an island while they left us behind. The fact that these guys did means they're willing to bend over backward to get here. You have to wonder why. And like I said, there are two guys back there that I don't really trust."

"You've said that before. What about them bothers you so much?"

"They have squirrelly eyes."

She smiled. "Squirrelly eyes, Danny?"

"Will and I had a CO back in the Stan. Guy had squirrelly eyes. One day, we were on assignment in the mountains and we walk right into an ambush. They knew we were coming, don't ask me how. Anyway, long story short, first thing our CO does is he bails. Just like that. Drops his rifle and takes off for cover, while his men are in the middle of the road with bullets flying everywhere." Danny smirked. "Moral of this lesson? You can't trust guys with squirrelly eyes."

"Okay, so guys with squirrelly eyes are bad."

"I'm not saying they're bad. I'm saying they're untrustworthy."

"Untrustworthy, then. But what if you're wrong?"

What if I'm wrong for even letting any of them on the island?

I should have called Will...

Danny looked back at the women. "That's been known to happen once or twice, sure. After all, I'm making assumptions based on a couple of minutes with them. But I bet those women know them more than we do. You can learn a lot about someone after spending months on the road with them."

"You think we should ask them?"

"Not 'we,' you."

"Why me?"

"You guys share similar sensibilities. By which I mean, you both have boobies."

"Nice of you to notice."

"I got eyes."

"Even if I did ask, how could I trust their answers? What if those two can't be trusted, but they feel a sense of loyalty to lie about them anyway? Like you said, they've been on the road together for months now. That kind of experience builds bonds, Danny."

"Call it a hunch, but when I saw them together, the women—especially the big redhead—seemed overly protective of the others."

"From you?"

Danny shook his head. "No. From the other two. The ones with squirrelly eyes. I got the sense she was happy to leave them behind back there at the marina. You gotta wonder why, after all this time on the road together."

Lara looked back inside the dining room at Bonnie. "You think we can trust her?"

"She's one of your species," Danny said. "You tell me."

"How would I even approach the topic?"

"Let her know she's safe now, that whatever happens, she and the others aren't going anywhere. That might get her to open up."

She smiled back at him. "For a guy who doesn't know anything about women, you sure know a lot."

"It's my secret weapon," Danny grinned. "How do you think I convinced Carly to do all the creative—"

"Enough," she said, pressing her palm against his mouth. "She's my little sister. I don't need to hear all the vile things you've been doing to her in bed."

▄◀█▌ ▐█▌▶

LARA EXPECTED THE two men Danny described as "squirrelly" to look, well, squirrelly. But apparently her definition of "squirrelly" wasn't quite the same as his, because the two men looked like cowboys, complete with jeans and Levi's shirts and empty gun belts, as if they had just returned from the range…in the mid-1800s.

One of the men introduced himself as Brody. He was in his early thirties, with one of those ridiculous jawlines she used to think only existed in movies starring action heroes from the '80s. He was well over six feet tall, and the only thing missing on him was a big Stetson hat. Instead, he wore a bandana around his neck to help soak up the sweat.

"Thank you for letting us on this island," Brody said, his thick *(exaggerated?)* Texas drawl coming through. He shook her proffered hand lightly, as if he were afraid he might break her. "You don't know what this means to us. It's dangerous out there."

Don't get ahead of yourself, buddy.

Brody's friend was named West. Like Brody, West looked as if he had just stepped out of an old-fashioned Western about righteous Texas cowboys who worked hard and played harder. When he leaned over to shake her hand, he towered over her like a giant. His hand felt rough, and the bright sun glinted off a gold watch around his wrist.

"I second what Brody said," West said. "You won't regret your decision."

"We'll see how it goes," Lara said. "Nice watch."

"Thanks," he smiled. "My dad gave it to me."

"Miss," a voice said.

Lara looked between the two cowboys at a third man. Compared to Brody and West, he was tiny, but he was actually about Will's height. He was wearing a sweat-stained white dress shirt and black slacks, as if he had just come from work in an office. She found that oddly amusing.

He leaned between Brody and West to shake her hand. "I'm Roy. Thank you for letting us on the island. I know it's not easy trusting complete strangers these days. This is Derek—" He pointed at a teenager standing awkwardly behind them, in jeans and a hoodie. It wasn't nearly cool enough for a hoodie, so she found that a bit strange.

"Hey," Derek said, lifting a half-wave.

"Hi, Derek," Lara said.

She hadn't failed to notice that Danny had strategically placed himself on the other side of the pier, behind the newcomers. He was holding a thick leather bag stuffed with weapons.

"Are you guys hungry?" Lara asked the men.

"Starving," Brody said.

"Whatever you can spare," West added.

She gave them her best hostess smile. "Follow me to the hotel. The women are already getting settled in."

"Wait, you have a *hotel*?" Roy said. "I was just hoping for a soft patch of ground to sleep on where I don't have to worry about bloodsuckers."

"We have a hotel," Danny said, "but only basic cable, so it's sort of like sleeping on dirt if you really think about it."

Roy glanced back at Danny, not sure how to take that.

"He's kidding," Maddie said, following them from the back. "He does that a lot. He's got an unlimited supply of jokes. Very, very bad jokes."

"You know you love it," Danny said.

"When do we get our guns back?" Brody asked Lara.

"Why? Do you need them back?" she asked.

He smiled widely. "We've depended on them for so long, we feel naked walking around with an empty holster. I'm sure you guys know what that's like."

"Like Roy said, trust is hard to come by these days. This is our house, so if you want to stay, you'll have to play by our rules. And right now, our rule is no guns until we decide we can trust you to have them back."

"That sounds fine with me," West said. "You, Brody?"

Brody shrugged. "Makes sense."

"So we're good, then," he said, smiling at her.

"It's not like we need them, right?" Roy said, sounding overly anxious. "The creatures, they can't cross the water. Is that right?"

"That's right," Lara nodded.

"Then we don't need our weapons," Roy said, and she thought that last statement was directed more at Brody and West than her.

Roy moved ahead of the others until he was walking beside her. He was carrying a backpack, as were the other three. She assumed Danny had checked their bags before letting them on the pontoon.

"Thanks again for letting us on the island," Roy said as they walked down the pier. "You don't know what this means."

"Like I said, let's not get ahead of ourselves. We'll see how it goes."

"Absolutely, I understand."

"Danny says you guys came all the way from Oklahoma."

"Most of us, except for Brody and West. We started out from Tulsa."

"I've never been up that far."

"It's a city of about 400,000 people, about two hours from Oklahoma City, give or take. Home of the Tulsa Hurricane."

"You get a lot of hurricanes there?"

He grinned. "No, the Golden Hurricane is the mascot of the University of Tulsa. I'm an alumnus."

"Oh. What did you major in?"

"Computer science. Basically, the most useless degree you can think of these days, and I have it."

"So you know how to fix computers?" Danny asked from behind them.

"Sure, I was an IT manager in my old job," Roy said, sensing the sudden interest. "Why? You guys have a working computer on the island you need fixing?"

"Not on the island, no," Lara said. "Though we do have a couple of laptops."

"Working laptops?"

"Well, we have power..."

"But no Internet, sorry, kid," Danny said. "You'll have to get your porn elsewhere."

Lara exchanged a brief look with Danny and smiled. She was pretty sure they were thinking the exact same thing at that moment: Harold Campbell's facility back in Starch, Texas, was still waiting for them to reclaim it. They had left so much behind, from the supplies to those ultraviolet lamps inside the Green Room that had saved their lives. If they only had the time and the right personnel to fix what was broken, the facility would make for an invaluable backup plan. Jen's helicopter was the key, though. Without it, braving the highways again was simply too risky.

"Hope for the best, prepare for the worst," as Will would say.

◀■■■■ ■■■■▶

DANNY STAYED BEHIND with the men as they took their turn in the dining room. Sarah and Carly had whipped up a new batch of fish and cold drinks. The men attacked the cold drinks even more ferociously than the food, which wasn't that surprising. Ice was the new currency in today's world.

While the men ate, Lara went to check on the women. As expected, they had grabbed rooms next to each other near the middle of Hallway A. It was instinct. When she, Will, and the others had arrived at the hotel, they had done the exact same thing.

So when Lara found Jo's room, she didn't have to go far to find Jo's sister, Bonnie, in the room next door. Bonnie's door wasn't closed, and when Lara leaned in, the older woman was pulling clothes out of her backpack. She had washed her face and hair, and she looked more stunning than when Lara had seen her earlier in the day. An open luggage stuffed with undergarments and personal hygiene products sat on the bed.

Lara saw a portable sonic toothbrush and toothpaste among Bonnie's things. "You too, huh?"

Bonnie looked over. "Which one?"

"Toothbrush."

"Oh God, I would end it all now if I couldn't brush my teeth at least once a day." She pulled out a fresh batch of batteries still in shrink wrap. "That's all these are for, you know. The toothbrush. The trick is finding enough toothpaste."

"You're in luck. We have boxes of the stuff in storage."

"You don't know how happy I am to hear that." She held up an almost empty tube of toothpaste. "I'm not kidding."

"I'll show you guys where to grab everything you'll need later."

"Thanks."

"You and Jo are sisters, right?"

"How did you know?"

"There's a resemblance."

"She's my little sister, yeah."

Lara closed the door behind her.

Bonnie stopped what she was doing and looked over. She must have seen the seriousness on Lara's face. "You have questions."

"I do."

"About the men."

Lara nodded.

Bonnie pursed her lips.

She knows what I'm about to ask. She's been waiting for it.

No, that's not true. She's been dreading it.

"Can I trust them?" Lara asked.

Bonnie sat down on the bed. She seemed to be thinking about her answer. Or maybe she was trying to decide how much to say.

Lara didn't push her, letting her take her time. There was a reason she had decided to trust Bonnie. She had seen how the other woman acted around Mae, and how she made sure Lucy and Kylie and the boy Logan ate while they were in the dining room. Once, Bonnie gave the last piece of a fish to Logan, and sat for ten minutes waiting for the next round of food to show up. All the while, she hadn't complained, hadn't made a scene, and simply kept the conversation going, laughing all the while, even though Lara could tell she was still hungry.

She's a good woman, Lara remembered thinking.

After a while, Bonnie met her gaze. "Roy's a good guy."

"What about the other two?"

"It was just Roy, me, and the girls in the beginning," Bonnie said.

Lara didn't interrupt. She understood; Bonnie was telling her this because she thought Lara needed to know the background, the context of what she would say next. So Lara stood against the wall and listened.

"It was hard," Bonnie said. "Roy's a really good guy, but you can tell by the way he dresses, this isn't his thing." She gave Lara a small but endearing smile. "It's not our thing either, but it's really not Roy's thing. He worked in an office fixing computers, you know. But we got by. Barely. We were skin and bones when we ran across Brody and West. Those two guys could have survived in the pioneer days. Me, Jo, and Roy, and the others? I don't know how long we would have lasted."

"Brody and West saved you."

"They did, yes. In the very real sense that we wouldn't be here without them. Roy pitched in whenever he could, but it was mostly Brody and West. They went out for supplies, came back with food, kept us basically alive."

"How did you guys meet?"

"They were heading up north when we crossed paths with them in southern Oklahoma. We were on our way down here after we picked up the radio broadcast. We convinced them to come down with us because we needed them in the worst way." Bonnie paused. She looked down at her hands. "From the very first week, we made an arrangement. It was between me and Gwen, and Brody and West. They agreed not to touch Jo or the kids. And they didn't."

Lara didn't have to ask what kind of "arrangement" Bonnie was talking about. "You did what you had to do," she said.

Bonnie nodded. "I know. And I don't regret doing it. I'm not going to be writing about it in my journal or anything, but it's a different world out there. You have to do things you might not otherwise have done before in order to survive."

"You don't need them anymore, Bonnie. You're not going anywhere. Neither are the girls, or the kids. But I need to know—can I trust them? Can I trust Brody and West to stay here on the island and not cause trouble?"

Bonnie didn't answer right away. She met Lara's eyes and held them.

"I don't think you should, no," Bonnie said finally.

"Are they dangerous?"

"They can be."

"Were they ever violent with you and Gwen?"

"Sometimes."

"I might have to eventually give them back their weapons."

"I wouldn't, if I were you. At least, not while they're still on the island."

"Why?"

"We weren't always alone on the road. The eleven of us. We met other survivors."

"What happened?"

"They had things West and Brody wanted. Supplies." She

paused. "One day, those supplies just showed up in the house we were staying in. I asked West where they got them, but he told me they found them."

"How do you know he lied?"

"When you met him earlier, did you see the watch West had on?"

"The gold one?"

"Yeah. It used to belong to one of the survivors we ran across."

"Did you ask him about it?"

"He said he traded for it."

"Could he have?"

"No." She shook her head. "When we first met the others, West asked about the watch, but the man who had it—he was young, in his twenties—said it was his father's. West kept pestering him to trade for it, but the guy wouldn't budge. Then one day we have extra supplies and West is wearing the watch."

"He killed a man for a watch?"

"I don't know for sure," Bonnie said. "Maybe the guy changed his mind." She shrugged. "I don't know for sure, Lara, you know?"

"How many people were in the other group?"

"Four. Two men and two women. One of them was just a girl."

They didn't say anything else for a while.

"Thank you, Bonnie," Lara said finally, and she turned to go.

"Lara." Bonnie was standing when Lara looked back. "Is Danny good with those weapons?"

"Danny was an Army Ranger. After that, he was a SWAT commando. Yeah, Bonnie, he's really good with those weapons."

"Then he should think about using them."

"What do you mean?"

"If Brody and West think they'll never get their guns back, that you'll never trust them enough to let them stay on the island, they might do something drastic. Something you won't like."

"What do you think they'll do?"

"I don't know," Bonnie said, the fear clearly visible on her face. "That's the problem. I don't know what they'll do if you push them into a corner. I just know that they're capable of anything in order to get what they want. After seeing what the island has to offer, I don't think they're going to want to leave. Would you?"

No. No, I wouldn't...

CHAPTER 7

WILL

"YOU SOUND BEAUTIFUL."

"Oh, you can hear that through the radio, can you?" Lara asked playfully.

"Only because it's you," Will said.

He was alone inside a small administrative office in the east tower of Mercy Hospital's tenth floor. It was almost dark outside, with maybe thirty minutes of sunlight left. Will could sense the falling darkness, draping over the city of Lafayette inch by inch.

"Tell me about the new people," Will said.

"Six women and five men, including two cowboys."

"Cowboys?"

"Bona fide Texas cowboys. You know how, when everyone thinks of Texas, they picture us all wearing giant belt buckles, ten-gallon Stetson hats, and boots?"

"Yeah."

"Well, they haven't called me 'ma'am' or 'darlin'' yet, but that's basically them. And minus the hats."

"So your biggest knock against them is that they look too much like cowboys?"

"That, and Danny says they have squirrelly eyes."

"Hunh."

"That mean something to you, too?"

"We had a CO in Afghanistan with squirrelly eyes."

"So Danny tells me."

She went quiet.

"What is it?" he asked.

"I asked one of the women about them. About the cowboys."

"I'm guessing she didn't have very good things to say."

"She told me we should only trust them as far as we can throw them. Like into the lake. She thinks we should walk them at gunpoint to the beach and just shoot them in the back of their heads."

"She said that?"

"Not in so many words. I inferred."

"Hunh."

"'Hunh'? Is that all you have to say?"

"Did you tell Danny what the woman said?"

"I discussed everything with him, Carly, Blaine, and Maddie afterward."

"What about Sarah?"

"She was busy in the kitchen."

"A woman's work is never done."

"Tell me about it."

He paused to think about what she had said. Then, "What did Danny say?"

"That we need to watch them closely."

"Okay."

"Okay?"

"Okay."

"Just 'okay'? That's it? I was hoping for something more profound. Or at least, more than 'okay.' What does that mean, exactly?"

"It means if they so much as look cross-eyed at you or Carly, or anyone else on the island, Danny will put a bullet in their heads."

Lara went quiet on the other end.

"Lara?"

"I'm still here," she said. "Would he really do that?"

"Yes."

"Because of what Bonnie told me?"

"That, but mostly because Danny will do what he has to do in order to keep you and the others safe. Just follow his lead when it comes to the gunplay."

"What about everything else?"

"Lara," he said.

"Hmm?"

"Just follow Danny's lead on the two cowboys."

"Okay."

He could hear something else in her voice, a slight hesitation. "What is it?"

"I miss you."

He smiled. "I miss you, too."

"Are there any hot women over there?"

"They're not much to look at over here."

"Meaning?"

"They've been hiding inside a hospital floor for the last eleven months. Think about it."

"That bad?"

"The kids are straight out of *Village of the Damned.*"

"What's that?"

"It's a movie. About this town where the kids are damned."

"Oh."

"You've never seen it?"

"No."

"When we get back, I'll bring over a Blu-ray and we'll pop it into the TV and watch together."

"You have a Blu-ray copy of a movie about creepy children in a village that's damned?" He could hear the amusement in her voice.

"What, you don't?"

She laughed. "I can safely say, no."

"You'll love it."

"I'm sure I won't."

"Lara," he said.

"What?" she asked.

"I love you."

"You sound so serious."

"That's because I am."

"You're alone over there, aren't you?"

"Of course not. There are a dozen guys just sitting around listening to me profess my undying love for you."

"Good. Because for a moment there I thought you were only doing the lovey dovey stuff because you were alone."

"What kind of guy do you think I am?"

"I know exactly what kind of guy you are. And I still love you, too."

"That took a while."

She laughed again. "I had to think about it."

"Damn, lady, you really know how to hurt a guy's feelings."

"I'm just messing with you. I didn't have to think about it for one second."

"Better."

"Okay, maybe half a second."

"Hunh."

"By the way, one of the newcomers is a computer guy. Danny and I were discussing how he might come in handy."

"The hydro turbine back at Harold Campbell's facility?"

"Exactly. Of course, we'll need Jen's helicopter. How's it coming, anyway? Is your charm offensive going as planned?"

"I'm working on it."

"Work harder. We need that helicopter."

"Yes, ma'am."

They spent another thirty minutes talking. By then, Greg, the guy whose job it was to monitor the radio, had returned from dinner, and he sat back behind a desk and picked up an old, heavily dog-eared novel he had been reading when Will first arrived.

"Be careful," Lara said, when he told her about helping Mike with the Archers raid tomorrow. "I hate the idea of you doing that, Will."

"It's a goodwill gesture."

"Like some macho male bonding?"

"Something like that."

He imagined her rolling her eyes on the other end.

"Just don't get dead," she said. "Isn't that what Danny would say?"

"Probably something like that. But then he would spell it out, and instead of saying d-e-a-d, he would spell it d-e-d."

"And that makes it funny?"

"It's Danny, Lara," Will said. "Jokes don't have to be funny when he's telling them."

TAP-TAP-TAP.

Tap-tap-tap...

It had been so long since he saw one up close, that watching it peering back at him from the darkness elicited a curious reaction from Will. He didn't know whether to draw his Glock and shoot it, or engage the thing in a kind of macabre staring contest.

He wasn't worried the glass window would give. Mike's people had been here for eleven months, and the ghouls hadn't gotten in yet. The fact that the creatures hadn't even attempted to do anything beyond patiently *tap-tap-tapping* the glass told him they were aware of its unyielding strength.

The one staring back at him now looked as if it had once been a woman. There were small bumps on its chest where breasts would have been. It was impossible to tell its age, and it had turned so long ago its skin, pruned and hairless, looked like plastic surgery gone wrong. Its eyes were dark and hollow, like two black voids staring back at him against the moonlight. Its upturned nose sniffed the glass pane.

There was a knock on his door.

"Come in."

Mike entered, a pool of dimmed LED light from the hallway splashing across the window. The ghoul turned its head toward the door, regarding Mike with similar muted curiosity.

"Don't let them get to you," Mike said.

"You're used to this? Seeing them out here every night?"

"Eventually, yeah. Come on," Mike said. "I got just the cure for insomnia."

BACK IN MIKE'S room, the former lieutenant opened a cabinet and took out a full bottle of Wild Turkey. He grabbed two plastic cups and pointed to an empty chair near the rebar-reinforced window. An LED lamp turned on low in one corner lit the room up just enough to navigate by.

Will sat down and watched Mike open the bottle and pour out a generous amount into both cups. Mike looked somehow even more weary than this afternoon, which was quite a feat.

"I had four of these the first week we came here," Mike said. "I've been steadily draining them for the last year. Finished the third bottle last night. I thought, hell, I'll save the final bottle for something special. I guess this is as good a time as any."

"Cheers," Will said, and touched plastic cups with the former officer. He took a sip of the bourbon and grimaced as the bitterness washed down his throat. It had been a while.

Mike smiled knowingly. "Not a bourbon man, I take it."

"Hard to afford them on an enlisted man's salary."

"Amy said you were a corporal. Where did you serve?"

"Afghanistan."

"I never made it in-country, even though I was supposed to go. After OCS, they gave me a second lieutenant commission and I spent most of my time waiting to pack my bags. Never happened, for some reason. After a while, my CO got pissed that I kept pestering him about it." He smirked. "Turns out, I didn't have to go overseas to see action."

"How'd it go down that night?"

"I was at the Lafayette army base doing field training exercises. At first we thought it was some kind of pandemic. No one knew what was happening. I tried getting orders from the higher-ups, but they didn't have a clue. No one did. I don't know how, but we managed to organize enough people at the base to make a stand, but by morning…" He shook his head. "All those people, jammed in there at night, gone. Just gone. Like that, it was a ghost town."

"How many men did you bring with you?"

"A couple, including Park. The rest scattered, went looking for their families in the city or out of town. Can't blame them. If I had family, I would have done the same thing. They might still be alive out there somewhere. Who knows? There were some good, very capable men in the bunch."

Mike looked out the window, as if expecting a ghoul to be there. There wasn't, though Will could still here the soft *tap-tap-tap* from other parts of the hospital.

They're probing for weaknesses. Relentless. Night after night.
Dead, not stupid…

"How active are they?" Will asked.

"They're erratic. Sometimes there are waves of them, so many you can't see the city in the background. Other times, it's like this—

they show up, look around, and then disappear just as quickly."

"They're smart."

Mike nodded. "They would have to be, wouldn't they? To pull off what they did?" Mike refilled their cups. "Down the hatch," he said, and drained his in one swallow.

Will winced for him, then sipped his. "Are you sure you want to hit that Archers tomorrow?"

"Why wouldn't I?"

"You said you were running out of supplies. Can you last another month without replenishing?"

Mike thought about it. "Maybe. But why should I do that? You said it yourself, I can't just put everyone into our cars tomorrow and drive down to Beaufont Lake. I need supplies until that happens." He grinned at Will. "Unless you're telling me you've changed your mind?"

"Not yet. Sorry."

"I understand." He leaned back. "Look, you have a good thing going there. Forty extra bodies is a lot. If I was in your position, I'd do the same thing."

"How are you handling who goes and who stays?"

"I was thinking about sending the kids and women first. We have a couple of fifty-somethings that would probably benefit from the fresh air. And they'll be able to contribute right away. One's an engineer, another's an electrician. Of course, you'll have to take their families, too. The electrician, Darren, has a fourteen-year-old girl, and the engineer, John, has a wife. I think she was a real estate agent, in case you were thinking about selling the island."

He chuckled. "Probably not."

"Well, I tried."

Mike took another emptying swig of the plastic cup, then quickly refilled it.

THE NEXT MORNING, Will learned how Mike and his people left the hospital for supply runs when they couldn't access any of the lower floors. Mike led him and Gaby up to the roof at an hour past sunup, and if Will thought Mike looked terrible last night, the man could have passed for a scarecrow in the morning light.

A few of Mike's people followed them up to the rooftop carrying large nylon bags, two of them wearing hard plastic shell helmets. Will heard *clinking* noises as the men tossed the bags down near the edge of the north tower and began pulling out rappelling equipment.

"Where'd you get these?" Will asked.

"Jen," Mike said. "When we realized we were essentially trapped on the tenth floor, we used her helicopter to make trips down to the streets for supplies. That wasn't going to work forever, though. Too much fuel and time. So we raided a surplus store and grabbed these. It's a pain in the ass, but it has an added benefit."

"What's that?"

"It keeps people from wandering outside the building."

Mike picked up a harness and stepped into it with practiced ease. Two men Will recognized from last night as Paul and Johnson were already doing the same thing. They slipped heavy-duty nylon webbing harnesses between their legs, then around their waists. There was nothing comfortable about the rigs, but they would hold.

Mike's people had drilled a half dozen anchor points along the rooftop about two meters from the edge, each one attached with a carabiner. The system had a three anchor point redundancy in case one of the anchors gave way. Not a bad idea. Will had seen plenty of rappelling falls, and they were never a pretty sight. Mike's people had also set up a pulley system where the group that rappelled down could later be pulled back up. He guessed that explained the presence of two muscular guys standing behind them, watching the show. The designated pullers.

"Strap in," Mike said. "You'll need to take off your belt."

Will unslung the M4A1 and took off his gun belt. He handed his rifle to Gaby and his belt to another one of Mike's men, who put it into a duffel bag already stuffed with supplies.

Gaby picked up one of the harnesses and offered it to him. "You sure you wanna be doing this, boss? Looks like a pretty steep drop."

"It's not too bad," Mike said. "Thirty-six meters, give or take."

"How much is that in feet?" she asked.

"Each floor is about twelve feet," Will said. "So ten floors is…"

"One hundred and twenty feet," Gaby finished. "That's a long way down. I would totally still respect you in the morning if you change your mind."

"I've rappelled from higher."

"Off the side of a hospital?"

"Once or twice." Will slipped on his harness and took a proffered shell helmet from one of the pullers. "How many supply runs do you do in a month?" he asked Mike.

"Two, three times, depending on what we need," Mike said. "We try to limit it. The creatures aren't the only problems out there, but you already know that."

"And you've never run across collaborators before?"

"Not yet, just your standard marauders. As far as I know, there are two, maybe three, other groups out there in the city, trying to take the same things we are. I lost a couple of men to them over the months, but I took a couple of theirs, too."

"We saw plenty of those kinds of people," Gaby said.

"It's inevitable," Mike said. "There will always be people trying to take advantage of a desperate situation."

Gaby handed Will his rifle, then a pair of leather gloves which he slipped on. "If you fall and break your neck, can I tell Lara I at least tried to stop you?"

He smiled. "Permission granted."

Will slung his rifle, made sure the gloves were tight, then joined the others taking their positions along four of the anchor points. Mike stepped off the edge first and Will followed, then Paul and Johnson dropped down after them.

It had been a while since he rappelled. Most of it was from his Army Ranger days, but there hadn't been nearly as much rappelling during his tour with Harris County SWAT. Still, as he went down the tenth floor, passing by a rectangular window, it all came rushing back. Controlling his descent was the hardest part, but muscle memory kicked in around the seventh floor, and the rest was easy.

He landed back on earth between some bushes and overgrown grass. They were at the front of the hospital, with the parking lot on one side and the lobby behind them. Will instantly detached himself from his rig and unslung his M4A1.

Mike did the same thing, unslinging a Mossberg 590 tactical shotgun. Will wished he had brought his Remington from the island. The spreading power of a shotgun always made clearing buildings so much easier.

Paul and Johnson came down on Will's right. Paul was a big man, and he landed with a loud *whump*, as if he were out of breath. Johnson was lighter on his feet, probably helped by the fact he was carrying fifty less pounds than Paul. They both unslung AR-15 rifles.

When they were sure there was no one to greet them but dead cars in the parking lot and empty streets to the left and right, Mike looked up and whistled. The men above lowered their weapons bag, tied to a rope.

Out of curiosity, Will moved toward the lobby's dirt-smeared glass windows and peered into the darkness on the other side. He couldn't detect very much, but there was the unmistakable hint of movement. The ghouls were creatures of habit, and though they were rarely active in the day, they could be easily awakened to movement.

"Can you see them?" Mike asked from behind him.

"I see some movement."

"There must be hundreds, maybe thousands, of them in there. It's a big building. Nine floors' worth of space."

"If they ever get onto the tenth floor..." Johnson said, but let his voice trail off.

"Enough chatter," Mike said. "Gear up. I want to be back here by noon."

Paul opened the duffel bag and pulled out their gun belts. Will slipped his on after prying himself from the harness. He always carried the cross-knife, and Mike and his people had their own recently made silver-bladed weapons in makeshift sheaths around their waists.

Will tossed his harness back to Paul, who stuffed it into the same bag. When they had all the rappelling equipment inside, Paul stood up and whistled, and the bag was pulled back up to the rooftop by a half-hidden figure high above them.

Mike unzipped his backpack, pulled out four empty gym bags, and handed them out. "For supplies."

A shadow fell over Will and he glanced up, saw Gaby looking back down at him over the edge. "Don't get dead!" she shouted down.

He gave her a brief salute.

"Let's get this show on the road," Mike said, and began moving out.

Will followed. "How far is the Archers?"

"Two blocks. The last time we tried it, there were less than a hundred undead things inside. If these silver bullets of yours actually work, we shouldn't have any problems clearing the place out."

"Sounds like you have it all figured out."

Mike grinned. "That's the trick, isn't it? Making the plan work without everyone getting killed."

WILL WAS INTIMATELY familiar with Archers Sports and Outdoors, a warehouse store that sold everything from fishing supplies to hunting gear and everything in-between. It was at an Archers in Houston where he and Danny spent the night after The Purge, making the very first batch of silver bullets. It brought back memories, along with the phantom smell of explosives, courtesy of Danny's C4.

"They're in the back," Mike said. "Away from the sunlight during the day. The last time we tried this, we got halfway inside before it became too dangerous. We did our best to stick to the light, grab what we could off the racks, but all the good stuff's in the back."

Will nodded. Mike was talking about the guns, ammo, and hunting supplies. The majority of the store's middle sections were reserved for clothes. With the windows mostly cleared of obstruction, sunlight filtered in across the long rows of cash registers and clothing racks visible from the sidewalk.

Mike moved toward the front door, shotgun in hand. "I'll go first. Will follows me, and the two of you watch our six."

Mike pulled the unlocked door open and slipped inside, shotgun moving quickly up to chest level. Will kept pace with him, allowing enough of a distance that Mike could turn a full 360 degrees if he needed to. He heard Johnson's footsteps behind him, followed by the loud, laborious squeaks of Paul's boots.

I'm going into a ghoul's nest with Paul Bunyan.

They turned right immediately after entering the store, and moved along the aisle with the cash registers to their right and clothing racks to their left. Someone had actually taken the time to empty a couple of the registers for God knew what reason.

The store, like all Archers, had smooth, tiled floors. There were old patches of faded blood, the color of dull brown scattered about them. The store's racks were still mostly intact, with surprisingly very few signs of having been plundered over the last eleven months. Up ahead would be the hardware aisles, with fishing supplies in the right corner and hunting gear to the left, farther up the store. They stuck to the pathway, away from racks with too much darkness underneath and shelves that were just a bit too high.

Soon, they turned left, and after a few more meters, Mike stopped.

There was only darkness in front of them, sunlight from the windows unable to penetrate this far into the building.

Mike gave Will a nervous grin. "Silver bullets, right?"

Will nodded. "Silver bullets."

Mike gave him an *"Okay, here goes"* expression and turned back around. He flicked on the flashlight taped underneath his Mossberg and—

Two ghouls, hiding in the darkness, were instantly illuminated by the bright light. They hissed and lunged at Mike, who fired instinctively, and the two ghouls were eviscerated in front of him. What was left of one creature flopped forward into the sunlight, its flesh vaporized into fine white mists on contact.

Mike took a quick step back, and so did Paul and Johnson behind Will.

The former army officer, breathing just a little too loudly, stared down at the white bones of the dead ghoul, the still-intact half of the creature lying in the shadows. Or mostly intact. The buckshot had torn its head clean off, leaving a decapitated body. The other one lay perfectly still in the shadows a few meters away.

Paul and Johnson leaned forward to look at the damage.

"Silver bullets," Mike said breathlessly.

"Silver bullets," Will nodded.

Mike gave him the strangest grin, then racked a fresh shell into the shotgun. "Let's go shopping."

CHAPTER 8

LARA

SHE SAT AT the table on the third floor of the Tower, staring at the radio. Will had signed off more than thirty minutes ago, but Lara hadn't been able to get up and leave yet. Maddie moved quietly behind her, shifting from one window to the next with night-vision binoculars. An LED lamp hung from the ceiling above them, keeping the darkness outside at bay.

"Are you going to stay here all night?" Maddie finally asked.

Lara sighed. "I don't know. If it keeps me from making a decision, I might."

"I'm sure you'll make the right one."

She looked back at Maddie. "Really? Because I'm not. Will wouldn't have a problem with this. He makes these decisions by morning."

"If it makes you feel any better, Danny, Carly, and everyone else won't second-guess you."

"Thanks. I think." She got up and stretched. "I'm going for a walk, try to clear my head. You good?"

"I'm good."

Lara left the Tower.

Nightfall brought surprising coolness to the island, and it made her shiver slightly underneath her T-shirt as she walked across the grounds. The solar-powered LED lampposts that traveled across the island with the cobblestone pathways had lit up a few minutes ago. There were lights on inside the hotel lobby and bright floodlights along the sides of the building's exterior.

"We're lit up like a Christmas tree" was an expression Will liked to use to describe how the island looked from land.

Instead of entering the hotel from the back, which would have been quicker, she circled it, using the time to convince herself that she knew what she was doing, that she was capable of this, even if every ounce of her screamed that she was deluding herself.

I'm a third-year medical student. What am I doing deciding who goes and who stays?

This is crazy. I'm not ready for this responsibility. I might never be ready.

Do I even want to ever be ready?

She spotted a lone figure on the front patio, and Lara recognized Mae leaning against the railing, looking off at nothing. No, not nothing. Back toward the shore. Mae had looked noticeably stronger throughout the evening, as if she were gaining strength with every minute on the island.

The older woman looked over at the sound of Lara's footsteps. "I never thought it would happen."

"What's that?"

"That I'd be able to stand out here, at night, and not fear for my life with every breath I take." She smiled and breathed in the cool air. "Thank you, Lara. Thank you for this island."

Lara felt slightly embarrassed and proud at the same time. "You're welcome, Mae. How are you settling in?"

"It's wonderful. This place is wonderful. It's more than we ever hoped for."

Lara climbed the steps and stood beside Mae. She thought she needed some alone time to think, but maybe what she really needed was someone to talk to. Someone who hadn't already put all their faith in her like Maddie, or Danny, or Carly had.

God knows why they think I'm capable of this.

"Are they out there?" Mae asked.

"They're out there," she nodded. "You can see them moving around on land, along the shores. It's impossible not to see the island, since we're the only artificial light for miles around."

Mae gave her a grateful smile. "I never thought we'd make it here. It was Bonnie's idea, you know. God bless her. She pushed us to come down here. There were so many times when we wanted to give up, but that girl...she kept pushing and pushing. Even when everyone wanted to quit, especially after we couldn't hear the radio broadcast anymore, she wouldn't let us. She was so determined. We argued about it. Over and over."

"Is that why it took so long for you guys to get down here?"

"Yes. Whenever we'd find a good spot—a safe place—West and Brody didn't want to leave. But she always managed to convince them. I don't know how she did it, but we always kept moving."

"She's a tough woman."

"She is. Especially considering what she did before all of this. She was a model, you know."

"I'm not surprised. She's very pretty."

"She's gorgeous, dear," Mae said. "Not that you're chopped liver."

Lara surprised herself by blushing a bit, and hoped Mae couldn't see under the floodlights. "Thanks."

"I bet all the boys turn their heads when you walk into a room."

"There's only one boy I care about these days."

"The mysterious Will. Oft-heard, but not yet seen."

"He'll be back soon. You'll like him."

"If he's anything like Danny, then I'm sure I'll like him. It's very easy to be fond of your Danny. All the girls are smitten, and they're heartbroken he's already taken."

"Carly will be happy to hear that," Lara smiled.

"It's fun, isn't it?" Mae said, sounding giddy.

"What's that?"

"To be able to talk about inconsequential things like this."

Lara nodded. "It is, isn't it?"

"What is?" a deep male voice said behind them.

They both looked back at West, coming out of the lobby. He had showered, slicked his hair back, and changed into a new pair of jeans and a long-sleeve shirt.

He smiled at them. "Am I interrupting something, ladies?"

"Girl talk," Lara said.

"What about?"

She shook her head. "Nothing important."

He walked to the railing and breathed in the air. "It's a hell of a place you guys have here, Lara. When I heard the creatures—what do you guys call them, ghouls?—couldn't get to it, I was skeptical. But it's true. Look at us, standing out here in the dark, in the open, talking like we're on someone's porch. It's amazing."

"It certainly is," Mae said. "I was just telling Lara that."

"Aren't you tired, Mae?" West said, looking over at the older woman. "You look tired. You should probably go get some rest." Then to Lara, as if to explain, "We had to push it this afternoon to get down here. We were so close the ladies couldn't wait. Heck, I think we almost ran out of gas. That right, Mae?"

Mae nodded. "That's right, West."

"You should go get some rest," West said again.

Mae looked at Lara almost apologetically. "I should go get some rest. Thank you again, Lara. This island…it's everything we dreamt it would be, and more."

"You're welcome, Mae. I'll see you tomorrow for breakfast."

Lara hugged her and was surprised by the strength in Mae's embrace.

"God bless you, dear," the older woman said, before pulling away and disappearing back into the lobby.

"I have to tell you," West said, looking after Mae, "there were times when we didn't think she'd make it. She's not exactly a spring chicken anymore."

"She looks pretty strong to me."

"Oh, don't get me wrong, they're a tough bunch. Brody and me didn't think some of them would make it during the trip down here, to be honest with you. You know, we almost turned back after we couldn't get your radio broadcast anymore."

It wasn't our radio broadcast, she thought, but said instead, "Mae says Bonnie wouldn't let you guys give up."

"Bonnie can be pretty persuasive." He smiled to himself, like he was reliving a private joke. "She's a tough one. But then, I guess you'd have to be to survive these days, right?"

"It doesn't hurt."

He looked around at the bright hotel grounds. "How many lights are on this island? I stopped counting after about twenty."

"There's a lot."

"And they're all solar-powered?"

"Yup," she said.

He must have sensed the lack of enthusiasm in her voice. "I think we might have gotten off on the wrong foot," he said, looking at her. He was so much taller, with broad shoulders, that she felt like a child staring back at him.

"What makes you say that?"

"I don't know, it's just a feeling that I got. Maybe I'm wrong."

"What's on your mind, West?"

"Brody and me, we're not bad guys. We'll earn our keep around here."

"I don't doubt that."

"I can't promise the same thing about the company we came with. But you're not going to have to worry about us. We're not afraid of hard work. Never were, and never will be."

"I believe you."

"So in case you have any doubts, don't. I get it, we need to earn your trust. And we will. You just have to give us a chance, that's all."

"We'll see," she said.

Lara gave him a smile that she hoped *(prayed)* was at least semi-convincing.

SHE HEADED FOR Danny and Carly's room, next to the one Vera shared with Elise. The conversation with West continued to gnaw at her, ten minutes after leaving him behind on the patio by himself. It wasn't just what he had said, but what he didn't say. There was a tone in his voice that she couldn't quite figure out.

Was he warning me? Or maybe threatening me?

She knocked on Carly and Danny's door. "You guys decent?"

"No, but come on in anyway," Danny called from inside.

Lara entered. Carly was folding freshly laundered clothes on the bed, while Danny was brushing his teeth in the open bathroom door, with only a towel around his waist.

He winked at her. "Hey, Lara, like what you see?"

"Oh, gross, babe, go finish your shower," Carly said.

"Shout if you want a piece of this," Danny said, flexing his biceps before disappearing into the bathroom. She heard the shower turn on a few moments later.

Carly looked over at her. "The love of my life, Lara. Can you believe how charming he is?"

"Mae says all the new girls are swooning over him."

"Of course they are. It's the blue eyes and California good looks. Why did you think I jumped his bones in the first place?"

"Oh, so the secret's out now."

"Was it ever in?" Carly picked up a stack of shirts and walked to a dresser. "You're worried about them."

It wasn't a question, and she didn't even have to elaborate on who "them" was.

Lara sat down on the bed. "Yeah."

"Did you decide what to do?"

"That's what I wanted to talk to you guys about."

"I think it's the right decision."

"I didn't tell you what I've decided."

"You don't think I can read you like an open book after all we've been through?"

"So you agree?"

"It's the only decision. The other girls are terrified of them, especially the younger ones."

"I didn't know that."

"Bonnie told you she's been able to keep the two of them away from the other girls and her sister Jo, right?"

"She did, but she didn't say anything about the others."

"She didn't have to. It's inferred, Lara." She cocked her head. "Is 'inferred' the right word?"

Lara smiled. "Close enough. Tell me what you mean."

"If you read between the lines, it means Brody and West have tried to do things with the other girls before. One of them is what, thirteen?"

Lara nodded. Lucy was fourteen, and Kylie thirteen. They were both pretty girls, and she saw how Bonnie, Jo, and Gwen protectively watched over them. She imagined it must have been the same with her and Carly, and the girls.

The shower turned off and a few seconds later Danny reappeared in the doorway, wearing the same towel around his waist, wet hair dripping onto the carpet underneath him.

"Lara and I were talking about that thing," Carly said.

Danny grinned. "I get to be in the middle."

"Don't be an idiot, babe. The cowboys."

"But we can still discuss the other thing, right?"

"Maybe later," Lara said. "What do you think, Danny?"

He shrugged. "Just call it *Brokeback Island.*"

"What does that even mean?" Carly said.

"You know, that movie? *Brokeback Mountain?*"

Carly and Lara exchanged a confused look.

"You know what he's talking about?" Carly asked.

"Not a clue," Lara said.

"Christ, how old are you two?" Danny grunted.

SHE BARELY SLEPT all night. The queen-size mattress felt too big without Will, and she kept turning over on her side to look across the bed, expecting him to be there. His presence was always such a soothing reminder that everything was fine, that if Will was sleeping soundly, it had to be safe for her to do the same.

She couldn't count on that tonight.

Instead, she lay awake, staring at the patio window. There was a nightlight in one corner, but most of the room was dark and she only had her conflicted thoughts to keep her company. It was cool outside, and she pulled the blankets up to her chest.

Will they fight?

Yes, they would fight. Brody and West were fighters. She knew that the second she laid eyes on them. The same trait that made them so valuable out there was what would make them a problem on the island. They were aggressive, daring, and most of all, willing to cross lines in order to get what they wanted.

Even so, she couldn't completely fight back the feeling of guilt about what she was about to do to them when the sun came up. Brody and West had saved the others. Bonnie admitted as much, regardless of what they may or may not have done to other survivors...

I can't risk it. If they did kill those other people...

I just can't risk it. Not with Elise and Vera, and the others...

She turned over onto her back and stared up at the ceiling. Dark patches of shadow danced above her, mocking her.

I can't risk it...

There was no decision here. There was only the one choice in front of her. It was obvious.

Wasn't it?

She told herself her experiences with the Sunday brothers had nothing to do with this. No, she wasn't punishing West and Brody because of what the Sundays had done to her all those months ago...

When her mind slipped—and it did, every now and then—she found herself reliving the days inside that cabin hidden in the woods. The Sundays. Life with the Sundays. They had kept her chained to the floor, and she could still smell the desperation, along with the filthy dress they forced her to wear because she wasn't deserving of decent clothing. She could still feel the cold, merciless bite of the metal collar around her ankle...

May you forever burn in hell, John Sunday. You and your brothers.

THE GUNSHOT WOKE her up. It split the calm, serene night air like lightning, shooting across the island and through every room and hallway of the hotel.

Lara was on her feet before the gunshot even finished its echo. She snatched up her Glock from the nightstand and scanned the room to make sure there was no one inside. She calmed her breathing, put the gun back down, and grabbed her pants and shirt and pulled them on, then spent more precious seconds struggling to shove her feet into socks and sneakers.

Footsteps raced across her door, then Danny's voice: "Lara!"

"I'm coming!" she shouted back.

The footsteps faded as Danny raced up the hallway. She listened to the direction he was heading.

North.

That meant the back of the building, which meant—

The Tower.

Then two more gunshots, this time coming in quick succession.

Shotguns.

Lara glanced at her alarm clock: 2:14 A.M.

Blaine.

Maddie had the night shift in the Tower, but Blaine would have already relieved her at midnight. He would be there now.

Lara threw her gun belt around her waist, slipped the Glock into the holster, then snatched up the Benelli M4 shotgun from the corner and ran for the door.

Carly was in the hallway in pajamas and a cotton T-shirt, standing just outside the girls' room with a Glock in her right hand. "Danny just went."

"Stay with the girls!" she shouted, and ran up Hallway A, following in Danny's footsteps.

She burst out of the hotel's back door, the cool air sending a thrill through her body. Or maybe it was just the adrenaline.

She ran as fast as she could, making a straight line for the Tower.

She was halfway there when she saw the door into the lighthouse had been thrown open, bright lights spilling out across the grass. She caught movement from the corner of her eye and looked up at the windows on the second and third floor, glimpsed movement along the second floor, just before Danny appeared in one of the openings.

He was scanning the hotel grounds when he spotted her. "Lara! Get down!"

"What?" she got out, just before a shot shattered the night air around her. She felt something fast zip past her head.

She threw herself to the ground so awkwardly that she lost the shotgun halfway down. It landed in the grass a few feet from her. Lara scrambled forward, snatching it back up and turning toward where she thought the shot had come from.

She heard two shots coming from behind her and looked back at Danny, who was firing from the second-floor window with his M4A1. She tried to follow where he was shooting, but even with the bright LED lights all around them, there were still too many patches of darkness where anyone could be hiding.

Lara scrambled to her feet and raced toward the Tower, even as Danny fired two more shots. The hidden shooter answered Danny's shots with two of his own, and chunks of the Tower's second-floor window—where Danny was standing—filled the air.

Danny stepped back a bit, but undeterred, kept returning fire.

When she was almost at the Tower, she stopped short at the sight of blood on the grass outside the door. There was more blood inside, a jagged line running along the floor and continued up the spiral staircase. She darted inside then hurried up the steps, listening to Danny shooting from above her.

She stuck her head carefully through the second-floor opening.

Danny was still at the window, peering out with his rifle. "Danny, what's happening?"

"Third floor, Lara," Danny said. "Blaine's hurt."

She climbed up onto the floor, then hurried over to the second set of cast iron staircases.

"Watch for the blood," Danny added, just as a shot dislodged a section of the window frame above his head. Danny took another step backward, before returning fire.

"Whose blood?" Lara asked.

"I don't know, a lot of bleeding going on up there." Danny fired again. "I have him pinned down behind one of the palm trees."

"Who's out there?"

"One of the cowboys. West. I think."

"You think?"

"Hard to tell who's up there with Blaine."

"Danny, what—"

"Upstairs, Lara," he said, cutting her off. "Blaine's kinda bleeding to death."

Lara hurried up the staircase, almost slipping on the fresh blood that covered the steps. She grabbed on to the railing to keep her balance, and pushed on toward the opening.

When she stepped up onto the third floor, she was greeted by another thick pool of blood right away. It was coming from a body. Brody. Or what was left of Brody. A shotgun blast had taken his head almost clean off, spraying chunks of it against the wall. A knife lay nearby, very close to his open hand. It looked like one of the knives from the hotel's kitchen.

Blaine sat on the floor across from Brody's lifeless body. There was another knife sticking out of Blaine's left side, and he was pressing his hand over the wound, his Remington shotgun resting in his lap. Three spent shotgun shells formed a kind of semicircle around him.

"Hey, doc," Blaine said. His face was covered in sweat despite the chilly night air. "Sorry about this. You must be sick and tired of keeping me from bleeding to death by now."

Lara made an effort to smile. She stepped over what was left of Brody's body, moving toward Blaine. "What happened?"

"They showed up and tried to get the drop on me. I managed to get one of them, but the other one split with the M4. Sorry, boss."

Two more shots rang out from below them.

Lara crouched next to Blaine and put down her shotgun. She eased his hand away from the knife to get a better look. "I'm going to have to cut off a piece of your shirt to see how bad it is."

"Go for it," Blaine said. He drew a big combat knife from a sheath along his hip and handed it to her hilt first.

She took the knife and started cutting. "Tell me what happened."

"One of them showed up and made small talk. Then the second one comes up from behind and I saw the knife in his hand and I shot him. But the first one tries to stab me. Well, not try. He actually did stab me. Then he grabbed the M4 and took off. I tried picking him off when he was running down, but I missed. I'm a lousy shot. Always have been, even with a shotgun."

She looked back at Brody's mostly decapitated body. "Brody would beg to differ."

"Lucky shot. He was close, and when he saw me catch him coming up the staircase, he sort of froze. I got real lucky tonight, doc."

"Why didn't West shoot you if he had the M4?"

"He was backing up when he tried, but I guess he was fumbling with the weapon, forgot all about the safety. What an amateur, as Will would probably say."

She smiled at that. Will would definitely have said that.

"Then he took off," Blaine continued. "I guess he thought he'd figure it out later."

They heard two more gunshots, this time coming from outside the Tower.

"I guess he's since figured it out," Blaine said. "Is it bad, doc?"

"Compared to when I first saw you? This is a cakewalk."

"Glad to hear it," he said, closing his eyes and leaning back. "I'm gonna go to sleep for a while, doc. Wake me up when it's over, will ya?"

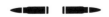

BLAINE WASN'T ENTIRELY a bad shot. Besides blowing Brody's head off, one of his other two shots had hit West, who bled all the way down to the first floor, and then kept on bleeding on his way out of the Tower. He had gotten halfway to the beach when Lara and Danny came out of the hotel. The M4 West had in his possession was equipped with the ACOG, which gave him an advantage over Danny during their back and forth exchange.

Danny, wearing night-vision goggles, had tracked West away from the hotel. "He's headed into the woods on the west side," Danny said over the radio. "Bleeding like a stuck pig, from the looks of it."

"Be careful, babe," Carly said through the radio.

"Careful's my middle name," Danny said.

"Since when?"

"Since I ran across this spunky redhead. She's got me all kinds of messed up these days."

"I love you, too," Carly said.

Until they could find West, Lara ordered the hotel sealed. The doors were closed and windows locked. She gave Bonnie and Roy gun belts with Glocks and told them to stay inside until it was over. She considered confining everyone to their rooms but thought better of it. Instead, she put them all in the lobby for the night with Carly so they would know where everyone was at all times.

Maddie had gone back to the Tower to keep overwatch. Will had drilled the importance of having constant overwatch in the Tower for so long, Lara wasn't surprised how effortlessly everyone responded to taking turns up there.

With the help of Bonnie and Roy, Lara carried Blaine back to the hotel manager's office behind the kitchen, where she had converted the room into a makeshift infirmary a few months back. It was just big enough for a couple of beds they had liberated from some of the unused rooms, and she had added a cabinet to hold extra medical supplies. Afterward, Roy wandered back out into the lobby to be with the others.

Bonnie didn't leave right away, but stood by quietly as Lara stitched Blaine's wound. The big man was asleep, snoring lightly under general anesthesia. He bled profusely when she had pulled out the knife, but thankfully the blade had missed his left kidney by half an inch.

When she was finished, Lara tossed the surgical latex gloves into a bin and washed her hands in the sink.

"I'm sorry," Bonnie said behind her.

Bonnie had been so quiet that Lara was actually surprised she was even still there. "For what?"

"This is my fault, isn't it?"

"I asked, and you told me the truth, Bonnie. You have nothing to be sorry for."

"Maybe I should have waited..."

"It wouldn't have mattered. Danny had doubts about them from the very beginning. It's a dangerous world out there, Bonnie. There are a lot of dangerous people. I—*we've*—encountered plenty of them since all of this began."

The Sundays...

May you all burn in hell.

Bonnie nodded. Lara couldn't tell if she was convinced. She hadn't known the woman long enough and there was an inherent sadness about Bonnie, despite the perfect everything, that told Lara the other woman had been through more than she was willing to share.

Bonnie finally looked down at the Glock holstered on her right hip. "Can I tell you something?"

"You've never used a gun before?"

"Is it that obvious?"

"Kind of. Will and Danny can teach you, if you want."

"I'd like that. Thank you. Roy wouldn't mind a lesson or two, either."

"I'll ask them—"

Two gunshots, in quick succession, interrupted her. It sounded far away, from the other side of the island.

Lara snatched up the radio from the counter. "Danny, what's happening?"

"Found him," Danny said through the radio. "I'm pursuing him through the woods now."

"Be careful."

"Will do."

Lara said to Bonnie, "Can you do me a favor?"

"Anything," Bonnie said.

"Stay here with Blaine in case he wakes up and needs something. He should be sleeping for most of the day, but he's stubborn, so you never know. After this is over, we'll issue you and Roy radios. Until then, Carly will be outside in the lobby the entire time." Lara picked up her Benelli and headed for the door, but stopped and looked back at Bonnie. "Hey."

Bonnie looked over.

Lara gave her a pursed smile. "Don't blame yourself. For any of it. You did what you had to in order to get here. What West and Brody did to Blaine wasn't your fault. They made their own choices. Okay?"

Bonnie nodded back. "Okay."

Lara hurried outside. "Danny," she said into the radio.

"Yeah," Danny said. She thought he might be whispering.

"I'm coming to you. Where are you exactly?"

"About thirty meters directly behind the power station."

"How many is that in feet?"

"Ninety-eight, give or take."

"Can you wait for me?"

"Sure, why not," Danny said. "The more the merrier. Bring pajamas. We'll have a sleepover."

CHAPTER 9

GABY

SEEING THE WORLD through a small red dot mounted on top of an assault rifle wasn't what Gaby expected to be doing a year after what was supposed to be her senior year in high school. Then again, she hadn't expected the world to end, either, so it wasn't as if she had control of anything anymore.

The sight on top of her M4 was a squat black tube, about five and three-quarters inches long. It allowed her to acquire and fire on a target without too much preparation. It was only capable of two-times magnification, so she wasn't going to hit anything long distance. She wasn't nearly good enough to do that, even with the ACOG in the Tower, but she was getting there.

One of these days...

She lowered the carbine and looked down at the sprawling parking lot on the north side of the hospital. So many cars. Sometimes she found herself wondering what had happened to their owners.

The two muscle-bound guys that came up to the rooftop with her this morning had wandered back downstairs to eat something. Benny and Tom had taken their place, and she could hear them moving around behind her, chatting about something pointless, when the sound of a gunshot from up the street exploded across the dead city.

Benny and Tom quickly rushed over.

"There they go," Benny said. "I hope those silver bullets work."

"They work," Gaby said.

The three of them stood at the edge of the rooftop and listened as the first gunshot faded. Moments later, shotguns and the cracking of a rifle rolled across the distance, one after another. The shooting went on for a while. Five minutes. Then ten... It was continuous, and for a time felt like it would never end.

Until, that is, it did stop.

As the last shot disappeared across the city, Benny said, "Sounds like they're done."

Gaby looked down at her watch. Will and the others had been gone for less than an hour.

"What's it like?" Tom asked her. "The island."

"There's a beach on the south side," she said. "It's long, with white sands. It was hot when we arrived, but it's cooled down with the weather."

"And you guys have a hotel?" Benny asked. "How many rooms?"

"Fifty completed rooms. Fully furnished. But there's plenty of space to build more."

"That's more than enough for everyone here," Tom said.

"And a lot of fish, right?" Benny said eagerly.

"A *lot* of fish," she nodded.

"I've always liked fish. My mom used to bake fish fillet with melted margarine, lemon juice, and paprika. You didn't think a simple dish like that could taste so good..."

"Did she ever bake fish sandwiches?" Tom asked.

"Nah," Benny said. "Good?"

"You put it between some crusty French loaf and add mustard, lettuce, and tomatoes, and it's probably the best thing you'll ever eat. My dad used to make them with chives, but I can't stand those. Cucumbers, now, that's another story."

"Yeah, not a big fan of chives, either."

"You guys have mustard over there?" Tom asked her.

"As long as you don't mind frozen packages from the freezer," she said.

"Better than nothing," Benny said.

"Definitely better than spoiled ketchup," Tom agreed.

The two of them went on like that, talking about fish and what condiments went better with which type of dishes. Gaby sneaked a couple of looks over at Benny, not that he noticed. He reminded her a little bit of Josh. They didn't look anything alike, but they were about the same age, and they both had that innocent, almost earnest quality about them.

She still remembered that night with Josh. Their only night, as it had turned out.

But Josh was dead, along with Matt and her parents. Her friends were probably long gone, too. People kept dying around her. Even Will might not make it back from the Archers raid. He was good, but he wasn't invincible. None of them were. They had the island, but how long would that last? It wasn't impossible that they could lose it tomorrow, or the next day, or the next month. The word "impossible" had ceased to have any meaning. Maybe it did, once, but not anymore.

She had gone to sleep last night as an eighteen-year-old and woken up a nineteen-year-old. What were the chances she would see her twentieth birthday? Maybe it was the state of the hospital, the poor souls on the tenth floor under her, but Gaby had never felt so depressed and mortal in her life.

She sneaked another look at Benny. He really was cute...

⬤▬▬▮   ▮▬▬➤

"SO, REALLY?" BENNY said.

"Yeah, why not?" Gaby said.

"I don't know. It's just kind of fast."

"We might die today. Or tonight. Or the next day. Look around you, Benny. All we have is today, right now." She shrugged. "Or I could go back up to the rooftop and bring Tom down here instead—"

"Fuck Tom," Benny said.

She almost laughed when he started taking off his clothes at a frenzied pace. She laid her M4 against the wall next to the bed inside her room and watched him struggling with his pants, before he realized removing his gun belt first was the way to go.

She actually smiled that time.

"What?" he said.

"Nothing. You're very cute."

He grinned. "That's good, right?"

"Better than the alternative."

He finally got his pants off, revealing brown boxers with Peanuts characters on them.

He saw where she was looking and blushed. "It was the only pair I had left that was still, you know, wearable."

"You guys don't do laundry around here?"

"Kinda hard without power."

"You could always hang them on the roof."

"Not a lot of water to spare, either."

"No wonder everyone stinks. When was the last time you showered?"

"I poured some water on myself last night. Does that count?"

"Not really, no."

He didn't really smell any better than when she had sniffed him yesterday, but she didn't feel like crushing that desperate-to-please look on his face at the moment. Gaby stepped out of her cargo pants and moved toward him in red silk panties. He stood perfectly still and stared at her. It was cute and charming, and she hoped he didn't have a stroke when she took off her shirt.

"You okay?" she asked.

"Yeah." He swallowed. "You're so beautiful."

"Thanks. Now come here."

He walked toward her. She put her arms around his waist and stood slightly on her tiptoes to kiss him. Benny put his arms around her waist and pulled her greedily against his mouth. He wasn't exactly the world's best kisser, but she had been attacked by worse.

She moaned against his mouth, and Benny, being a smart boy, rightfully took that as approval and cupped her breasts with both hands.

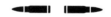

THEY STAYED IN her room long after, but since the bed was designed for only one person, she was forced to lay on top of Benny. What she really wanted was the bed all to herself, but kicking Benny out so she could catch up on some of the sleep she hadn't managed to get last night was probably too rude. Not that she didn't actually think about it really hard.

There was very little ventilation on the entire floor, and none in her room, so she wasn't sure if she was sweating from that or the sex. Maybe a little of both.

"That was awesome," Benny said after a while.

Gaby smiled. Men said the least creative things after sex. "How long has it been?"

"A while. Most of the girls here are already spoken for. It's mostly just jacking off, but even that loses its charm once you've done it a few hundred times."

"I didn't know that was possible with guys."

"Oh, trust me, it's possible. But anyway, you smelled really nice. Even down there."

Okay, that's a new one.

"You're not even wearing any perfume, right?" Benny asked.

"Not that I'm aware of."

"What's that smell, then?"

"Soap, Benny."

He laughed. "No kidding? It smells really nice. You're easily the best smelling boy or girl in this entire building."

No kidding.

"Thanks," she said, not sure what else to say.

"You guys have your own rooms and everything, huh? Back on the island?"

"Uh huh."

"Air conditioning, too?"

"We do, but we don't turn it on to conserve power. We might turn the heat on if it gets really cold down here, though."

"It doesn't get too cold, though."

"Then we probably won't turn the heat on."

"And you guys have a freezer."

"Yup."

"That means ice."

"Uh huh."

"Man, I haven't had ice in ages. I'd love to have some in a glass with some Coke." He licked his lips. "I'm drooling just thinking about it."

"When you get there, the first glass of ice Coke is on me."

"Sweet." He was quiet for a moment, then said, "You don't have a boyfriend back on the island, do you?"

I did, but he's dead.

"No," she said.

"I know this is too early and everything, and I don't want to freak you out, but would you consider me?"

He said it with such earnestness that she couldn't help but lift her head. He met her gaze and she thought he had the most puppy dog look she had ever seen. She almost laughed, but realizing that might hurt his feelings, she nodded instead.

"Sure," she said. "I'll give you a spin."

He laughed again. "Gee, thanks."

She sat up, and no surprise, his eyes went straight to her breasts. "Will and the others are gonna be back soon, but I can spare ten more minutes. What do you think?"

"Fuck yeah," he said without hesitation.

JEN LOOKED REFRESHED when she knocked on Gaby's door, then barged inside without warning. She caught Benny struggling to pull on his shirt next to the bed, while Gaby had already dressed.

"Oops," Jen said. Then she grinned at Gaby. "Fitting right in, I see."

"There's not a lot to do around here," Gaby said. She was surprised she didn't sound more embarrassed.

"I hear ya, sister. Come on, Amy's got those medical supplies Lara wanted."

Jen left, and Gaby looked over at Benny, who was stuffing his shirt into his pants.

He smiled at her. "You'll be around after today?"

"That's up to Will," she said, slipping the M4 over her shoulder.

"Will's going to let me go there, right? To the island?"

"Maybe."

He frowned. "Any ideas on how I can increase my odds?"

"Easy. Don't be a dumbass. He hates that."

"Oh, that's it?"

She smiled and he returned it. It was a nice moment, and she quickly hurried out of the room before he had the chance to ruin it, like by trying to kiss her.

Jen's long strides had already carried her down the hallway, and Gaby had to run to catch up. "You in a hurry?" Gaby called after her.

"Just trying to keep you on your toes, kid."

Kid. Right.

They turned a corner, where Gaby saw a five-year-old with a button nose and a face that probably hadn't seen water in a few days peering out at them from a slightly ajar door. Gaby smiled at the boy, who responded by running off to hide, leaving the door open behind him.

"How you like the hospital so far?" Jen asked.

"It's okay."

"Bullshit. It's depressing as hell. This is the kind of place that makes you think about your mortality and how shitty everything is. Hospitals already do that, but this place, at this time? This is fifty times worse."

Gaby didn't argue. How could she? Jen was right about everything.

"Why do you think I'm always flying around out there?" Jen asked.

"Do you ever think about not coming back?"

"Every time."

"But you do."

She shrugged. "God help me, I guess I've become fond of these people. Speaking of which…"

"Are we really going to talk about that?" Gaby said.

The older woman grinned. "Don't sweat it, kid. I've pretty much screwed every available guy in this place. If I didn't, I'd probably go nuts or try to kill myself. It's all so fucking depressing."

"Thanks for sharing."

Jen laughed. "Benny's a good kid, though."

"He's all right," Gaby said.

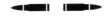

AMY WAS IN the east tower, packing medical equipment into bundles, with plenty of foam for protection against damage, before wrapping them up in thick coatings of shrink wrap. She had filled three gym bags when Jen led Gaby inside what looked like a large inventory room.

"Did Mike come back yet?" Amy asked.

"Not yet," Jen said.

"They should be back soon," Gaby said. "Will's got a scheduled call back to Song Island at ten. He wouldn't miss that."

"Well, until then," Amy said. She picked up a large bundle of gauze tape and shoved it into a gym bag, then zipped it up and held it out to Gaby. "I've filled about eighty percent of the list Will gave me. Gauze, IV drips, syringes, anesthesia, and pain killers. Since we're going to be partners for hopefully a long time, I included some of the good ones for goodwill. Vicodin, Percocet, and I even threw in some OxyContin, so you're welcome. I take it you guys have had past troubles? A lot of this stuff is shit-happens type of supplies."

"We've had our share of problems."

If you only knew half of it.

"What about the other twenty percent?" Gaby asked.

"Depends on how many's going back with you guys," Amy said. "It's mostly about rationing. Any ideas when you plan on heading back?"

"If I had to guess, it might be later today. Will wants to get this stuff back to the island as soon as possible."

"Do you guys have sick people?" Amy asked. There was a note of concern in her voice.

"He just likes being prepared. It's a Ranger thing."

"I guess we'll let the men hash it out," Jen said. "Us little women aren't smart enough for all that negotiatin' talk."

"It would be nice to sit on a beach sipping Mai Tais," Amy said with a smile.

"What's that?" Gaby asked.

"Mai Tais? Rum, pineapple, and lime in a highball glass."

"I don't know what any of that is. The closest I ever got to alcohol was a Budweiser."

"How old are you, kid?" Jen asked.

"I turned nineteen today."

"Holy crap. You look older."

"Thanks," Gaby said. "I guess."

Jen laughed.

"Happy birthday," Amy said. She picked up another gym bag

and handed it to Gaby. "Some rolls of gauze tape and IV bags. Don't say I never gave you anything."

"Oh, I think she already got something this afternoon," Jen said with a wink.

Gaby shook her head. "Nice. Real mature, Jen."

"Benny," Amy said knowingly.

"How'd you know?" Jen asked.

"Are you kidding? That poor kid's on the verge of quivering into bowls of jelly every time he's around her."

"Okay, okay," Gaby said. "Enough with the talking about my sex life like I'm not even here. It's becoming annoying."

"Only if you promise to tell us all the gory details," Jen said.

"Whatever," Gaby said, and headed for the door.

The two women grabbed a gym bag each and followed her.

"Did he take a trip down south?" Jen asked.

Gaby groaned. "Give it a rest."

They were almost at the door when a scream, followed quickly by a gunshot, ripped across the tenth floor. The gunshot was followed by a series of gunfire—the *pop-pop-pop* of a three-round burst—and Gaby knew right away that more than one person was shooting in different parts of the building at the same time.

They dropped the gym bags and rushed to the door, Gaby already unslinging her M4. Jen, with her longer stride, beat her to the door, and as the pilot threw it open, Gaby lunged outside and slid to a stop in the hallway, her boots battling against the slick vinyl.

She saw a man in a dull white tactical hazmat suit and gas mask moving away from her, stepping over a body lying prone on the floor. The suit was thin, one of those Level B hazmat suits. The man was wearing boots, and as he stepped over the dead man, she could see blood on his soles. She recognized an M4, identical to her own, in the man's hands. As soon as the shooter heard the sound of the inventory room door opening behind him, he stopped and turned around.

Gaby glimpsed dark black eyes behind the gas mask's single face covering, a stunted one-piece air purifier jutting out from underneath.

The man started to lift his rifle, but he hadn't gotten it halfway

up before Gaby shot him in the chest. She fired without thinking—
"muscle memory" Will would have said—and was momentarily stunned
by the sight of the man collapsing in front of her. The bullet had
drilled into the thin fabric of his suit, and it didn't look as if there
were any blood at all. But of course, she knew better. The suit kept
the blood inside, leaving behind a small hole in its wake.

Just like that man in Beaumont, Texas…

Jen and Amy stumbled out of the room behind her. It didn't
occur to Gaby how vulnerable the two women were. They were both
unarmed, and they gasped at the sight of the dead man in the hazmat
suit lying near one of their own.

"Oh my God, Dan!" Amy said, rushing forward.

She hadn't gotten more than a few yards when gunfire ripped
over her head and shredded a large painting hanging on the wall
beside her. Amy instinctively fell to the floor headfirst, sliding
comically along the smooth tiles with her hands thrown over her
head, as if that would somehow protect her from bullets.

Gaby turned to her right, looking down the hall as another man
in a hazmat suit moved toward them, also armed with an M4. The
man was taking aim at Amy's scrambling form when Gaby fired at
him. Her first shot missed, but her second shot hit the man in the leg
and he stumbled, then turned and hobbled desperately behind a
corner.

She heard gunfire from other parts of the hospital, and Gaby
desperately longed for a radio. Will insisted everyone on the island
carried one, but Mike didn't have that kind of system in place.

God, they're so unprepared. How did they survive for so long?

She stopped thinking when the same gas-masked face peered out
from behind the corner down the hallway. She snapped a quick shot
in his direction, and the man jerked his head back behind the wall as
her bullet tore a big chunk off the corner.

Gaby kept her rifle on semi-automatic. She wasn't worried about
ammo. She had two magazines for the rifle around her waist and two
more for the Glock in her pouches. She had even more in her
pack…*back in her room.*

She risked a quick look behind her, and saw Jen helping Amy up
from the floor, shouting, "Come on, we can't do anything for him

now!" Then she looked back at Gaby. "We have to go!"

"Go where?" Gaby shouted back. "They're all over the floor! Listen!"

The two women stopped their frantic movements and listened. Gaby saw their faces go from pale and confused to horrified.

The screaming, the gunshots—it was coming from all around them, as if they had just stumbled into the middle of a war zone.

And this day started off so well, too...

CHAPTER 10

LARA

SHE DIDN'T KNOW how Will wore his communications rig all day. It was cumbersome and unwieldy, and she thought the plastic mic around her throat was going to choke the life out of her with every step she took. The thing was supposed to work on bone vibrations, or something like that. The earbud didn't look like it would stay in her ear, though when she purposefully moved around like a spastic, it refused to dislodge.

She was wearing the assault vest Will had designed specifically for her a month ago. She remembered almost swooning. How many girls got custom-made assault vests? It was a slimmed-down version of the kind he and Danny wore, with pouches for equipment, such as the radio connected to the throat mic and earbud. It was a lot more convenient than holding the radio with one hand, especially when she was moving.

An hour after kneeling on the wet ground inside the woods in the western half of the island, the Benelli shotgun had begun to feel almost weightless leaning against her knee. The first signs of sunup appeared in the distance, casting the kind of glow across the sky that still took her breath away many mornings later.

Danny was somewhere to her left, hidden among the foliage. The woods were brightening around her, slivers of the clear sky coming through where it was pitch dark moments before. Every now and then she heard movement that prompted her to tighten up, get ready to spring into action. The paranoia was justified, because he was out here somewhere.

West.

He and Brody had done exactly what Bonnie had predicted they would do. She chastised herself for not seeing it sooner. Thank God they had padlocked the Tower basement, where all the weapons were stored. She didn't want to think about what would have happened had both West and Brody gotten to their rifles while the rest of them slept, with only Blaine on the third floor to stand in their way.

This wouldn't have happened if Will was here.

The thought popped into her head every few minutes, twisting her into knots, and confirming what she already knew: She wasn't ready for this. Not even close. So why did the others think she was? Whatever possessed them to put so much faith in her judgment? She wasn't ready—

She was startled by a *clicking* sound in her right ear, before Danny's voice came through a second later to soothe her nerves: "Look how pretty the sky is. Makes you appreciate all the finer things in life, doesn't it?"

"Like what?" she whispered.

She had learned a few hours ago that even when she barely whispered, Danny could hear her just fine.

No wonder Will loves these things.

"Girls," Danny said. "Fresh air. Girls. Walking around the woods at night. Girls."

"You forgot girls."

"Oh, right, girls."

She smiled despite herself. "Where are you now? I can't see you."

"Your eleven o'clock."

"I don't know what that is, Danny."

"Imagine the hands on a clock."

"Okay…"

"Now imagine where eleven o'clock is."

"So, to my left?"

"Close. Northwest of you."

"Couldn't you have just said that in the first place?"

"Sure, but it's cooler this way."

Snap!

She shot up to her feet and spun around, the shotgun rising, her forefinger slipping into the trigger guard—

"Don't shoot!" Roy shouted.

He stood twenty yards behind her, hands trembling in the air.

"What are you doing here?" she hissed.

He hesitated, as if trying to decide if he should turn back around or proceed forward. She took pity on him and motioned for him to join her. He rushed over, making so much noise that she now understood what it was like for Will and Danny whenever they had to deal with her and the others.

You have the patience of a saint, Will.

Roy crouched next to her and looked forward. She glanced over and was surprised how young he looked. Maybe it was the water and shower, wiping the grime from his face; she'd had him pegged as being in his late twenties when they first met, but that couldn't have been right.

"How old are you, Roy?" she whispered.

"What?" he said, straining to hear her.

"How old are you?" she said, raising her voice just a little bit.

"Twenty-eight. Why?"

"Are you sure?"

He gave her an amused look. "Pretty sure, yeah."

"You look younger."

"I have one of those faces. My friends used to make fun of me. When I was an infant, I looked like an egg, they said."

She smiled.

He saw it and looked pleased. "You're pretty when you smile."

Uh oh.

"I'm taken, Roy."

"I know. I just had to say it."

They sat in silence for a moment. Of course, it didn't last, just as she knew it wouldn't.

"So, this Will guy…" he started.

"What are you doing here, Roy?" she said, cutting him off. "You should be back at the hotel with the others."

"I didn't feel right letting you chase West out here alone."

"Danny's doing most of the chasing. I'm just backing him up."

"I know, but what happened to Blaine was our fault. I keep wondering if I could have warned you sooner that Brody and West were dangerous. I should have told you about the watch…"

"The gold watch that West wore?"

"You know about that?"

"Bonnie told me. She said she wasn't sure, but she thought that maybe West killed the guy who owned it."

"He did," Roy said.

She looked over at him. "What are you saying, Roy?"

"I wasn't there when they did it or anything, but they told me about it afterward. Brody was gloating about how they got the drop on them. Jesus, one of them was just a kid..."

"It's okay, Roy. Bonnie warned us. She warned *me*. It's my fault for not acting on it earlier. I should have—"

"Ahem," Danny said in her right ear. "I don't mean to cut in on your little chat with Geek Wonder over there, but I can hear you all the way across the island."

"Sorry," she whispered.

"For what?" Roy said.

She started to answer, but shook her head and put a forefinger to her lips instead. He nodded, understanding.

Another *click,* and Danny said, "Lara and Roy, sitting in a tree, k-i-s-s-i-n-g."

She sighed. This was going to be a long morning.

ROY WAS GETTING antsy next to her, shifting back and forth, going from one knee to both knees, then back again. The last two times she had ordered him back to the hotel, he'd insisted on staying with her. His version of gallantry, she supposed. Not that she needed him. He was more of a burden at the moment, but she couldn't help but feel slightly impressed with his stick-to-itiveness.

Salvation finally came in the form of a *click* in her right ear, and Danny's voice: "He's moving. Push ahead and cut him off. Fire three shots into the air."

"Stay here!" Lara said sharply to Roy, lunging up to her feet and racing away before he could respond.

She fired one shot into the air, heard the echo, then fired a second and a third time.

She was still moving when she heard gunshots in front of her.

Not too far away, but far enough that she didn't have to dive for cover. She heard footsteps, threw a quick look over her shoulder, and saw Roy giving chase. He was surprisingly fast for a former tech geek.

She heard two more shots in front of her, then nothing.

Lara slid to a stop, and Roy almost crashed into her. He was breathing hard, out of breath. She had to wonder how Roy had managed to survive so long when he was so clearly out of shape.

Click. "Forty meters," Danny said. "Your twelve o'clock."

"Danny," she said.

"Sorry. Directly ahead."

She looked over at Roy and nodded, and they both climbed back to their feet and began jogging forward through the brush. Roy was already huffing and puffing again by the time they reached a clearing.

Danny was sitting on a boulder, facing West, who sat slumped against a tree trunk. There were bullet holes in the tree over West's head, though at the moment those were the least of his worries. West was holding on to his right side, where he had been shot. His right thigh, where he had caught some of Blaine's buckshot from last night, was covered in mud and pieces of his shirt that he had been using as a tourniquet. The stolen M4 with the ACOG scope lay a few yards beyond his reach.

Danny was chewing on a twig. "West decided he'd like to give up."

"Is he armed?" she asked.

"Not anymore."

Lara turned to Roy and handed him her shotgun. He took it hesitantly. She also drew her Glock and handed it to him as well.

"I need to take a look at that wound," she said, walking toward West and crouching in front of him.

He looked tired, his face a mess of mud and blood and dirt. He had been running around the woods all night, trying to stay one step ahead of Danny. It showed in his hollowed eyes and all over his slackened, beaten body. He was barely breathing; whether from his tired condition or a lack of desire, she didn't know and didn't particularly care at the moment.

Lara took a handkerchief out of her pocket. "I'm going to remove your hand. Don't fight me."

He didn't say anything. Instead, he continued to watch her curiously.

She ignored his stare and pulled his hand away from his side. Blood oozed out, and she quickly pushed the handkerchief against it. The orange fabric turned dark red and West flinched a bit, though he was clearly trying not to show it.

Tough guy, huh? Not tough enough.

"I need to get you back to the hotel and sew this up, or you're going to die," she said.

West's eyebrows furrowed. "I thought that was the plan. Letting me die."

"It was never my intention to kill you or Brody."

"Sending us back out there is the same thing."

"Not to me. You have no future on this island, but you have a chance out there."

He snorted. "I don't have a shit ounce of chance out there. Especially not now, without Brody watching my back."

She met his eyes with her own harsh glare. "You should have thought about that before you tried to murder Blaine last night."

He looked away, but Lara didn't feel the flush of triumph she had expected. If anything, there was just overwhelming sadness. For him…and for herself.

She looked back at Roy. "Give the weapons to Danny, then I need you to help me get him back to the hotel." While looking straight at West, she added, "Danny, if he tries anything, you have my permission to end his miserable life."

<hr/>

THERE WERE NO holding cells in the hotel, but there were two extra beds in the makeshift infirmary. She had Danny zip tie West's hands and legs down on one of the beds while she kept him from bleeding to death. Blaine was snoring lightly on the next bed over, oblivious to West's presence. Just to make sure West behaved, Danny, eating breakfast, stood watch as she worked.

West was already developing an infection along his thigh thanks to the buckshot Blaine had put into him back in the Tower, something he further inflamed by spending the night in the woods rolling around in dirt and mud. The wound on his right side, courtesy of

Danny's rifle, was fresh, and it only required cleaning and dressing.

West didn't say a word as she worked on him, and she couldn't summon the strength to care.

She sent Roy, Bonnie, and the girls down to one of the supply rooms in the back of the hotel, past the laundry room, to clear it out. They didn't leave until the room was just concrete walls and a floor. Then Roy came back, and with Danny, they carried West—still strapped down to his bed—over to the same supply room and laid him in the center.

As Danny cut his zip ties, West looked at her from across the room. "So how is this going to work? You can't keep me in here forever."

"I'll let you know when I figure it out," she said.

West sat up gingerly and rubbed his wrists and ankles. "You haven't thought this through, have you?"

"Like I said, I'll let you know when I figure it out. Until then, sit tight."

She waited for Danny to come out, then closed the door and locked it, putting the key into her pocket.

Danny was leaning against the wall ten feet up the hallway, watching her.

"Go ahead, say it," she said as she walked past him.

He fell in beside her. "Say what?"

"That I'm weak. That I'm not cut out for this whole leadership thing. That Will would have put a bullet in him back in the woods. Or last night. Or when he saw them at the marina. Say it, Danny."

"I wasn't thinking any of those things."

"Then what were you thinking?"

"Handcuffs."

"Handcuffs?"

"Yeah. The old-fashioned kind. With a key, that we can reuse over and over."

She gave him a wry look. "You really think we'll have that many prisoners, we'll start needing reusable handcuffs?"

"Who says they're for holding prisoners?" Danny said. "Do you have any idea what kind of kinky stuff Carly's into?"

IT WAS TEN in the morning, and she sat in front of the ham radio and waited, but didn't hear Will's voice from the other end. For the fifth time in as many minutes, she made sure the dial was set to the correct frequency.

Lara passed the time by looking down at the floor. They had wiped the floorboards clean of Brody's blood and scraped his brains off the wall. Mostly. There was still plenty of evidence, but she had gotten used to the sight of dried blood.

She glanced down at her watch again. Five minutes after ten.

She wasn't the only one who had noticed the silence. Maddie was standing overwatch at the south window. "What time is Will supposed to call in?" she asked.

"Ten," Lara said.

"What time is it now?"

"Five after ten."

"Maybe he forgot?"

"Maybe…"

"Did you get any sleep last night?"

"A little bit. Why?"

"You look tired."

"I do?"

"You could definitely use a little more shut-eye."

"We all could."

"We all could, yeah, but you more than most," Maddie said. "You should go take a nap."

"Maybe later."

"Well, if you're not going to go to bed, then try the radio again. All this waiting is getting on my nerves."

Lara gladly picked up the microphone and clicked the transmit lever. She took a breath, then leaned toward it: "Mercy Hospital, come in, this is Song Island. Over."

She waited, but there was no response.

"Mercy Hospital, this is Song Island. Can you hear me? Over."

Again, there was no response.

"That's not good," Maddie said.

"No," she said softly.

That's not good at all…

Lara checked the piece of paper with the list of frequencies taped to the tabletop next to the radio. She spun the dial over to the one for Jen's helicopter, then pressed the transmit lever.

"Jen, this is Lara from Song Island. Can you hear me? Over."

She released the lever and waited, but there was no response.

"Jen, this is Lara from Song Island. Tell me you're receiving this. Over."

Nothing. Not a damn thing.

Please, someone, answer...

She was about to press the transmit lever again when the radio squawked and she heard a male voice—thick, guttural, deep, and definitely *not* Jen: "Who is this?"

Lara leaned into the mic: "Who is *this?*"

"I asked you first," the man said.

Lara glanced back at Maddie, just to be sure she wasn't the only one who had heard the voice. Maddie was watching with concern. There was something about the voice that bothered her, and Maddie too, from the look on the other woman's face. It was too cavalier, like this was all a big joke, like the man was *enjoying* himself.

"I'm looking for someone at Mercy Hospital," she said into the microphone.

"You're a little late," the man said.

"Why's that?"

"I'm afraid no one at Mercy Hospital is currently available to take your call right now. They're too busy being dead."

She couldn't speak immediately, as a variety of scenarios—good and bad and terrifying—whipped across her mind with dizzying speed. It was all she could do to hold on to the mic, her other hand clutching the edge of the table without realizing it.

"Who *is* this?" she said into the radio.

"I'm the guy who just took over Mercy Hospital," the man said. "That's who the fuck I am."

CHAPTER 11

WILL

IT TOOK THEM almost an hour to clear the entire Archers. Once Mike, Paul, and Johnson realized the silver worked as promised, Will could feel their unrestrained enthusiasm as they went through the store aisle by aisle, like wild men on a blood hunt long denied them. He almost felt sorry for the creatures that got in their way.

Will was more than willing to let them do the bulk of the work. By the time they were done, the tiled floor was slick with sticky congealed ghoul blood, splattered flesh, and shattered bone. He walked in black ooze, the *clump-clump-clump* under his boots not nearly as disturbing as the smell. He thought he would have gotten used to the stench of dead ghouls by now, but he was very much wrong.

While Mike and his men filled up on what they came for, Will wandered over to the shoe aisle. He maneuvered by flashlight and located the women's section. Locating the right shoes in the right size took another few minutes. He grabbed two pairs, one in white and one in black, and stuffed them into his gym bag. Her birthday was coming up, and she had been wearing the same pair for the last few months.

I'm shopping for Lara now. Danny would definitely have a field day with this.

He went looking for Mike, finding the former lieutenant behind the gun display on the other side of the store, the glass counter dripping with thick black blood. Mike had turned on an LED lamp to see with and was tossing boxes of 9mm, 5x56mm, and shotgun shells into his already overstuffed bag.

"You might need another one," Will said.

Mike grinned and produced a second bag from his back pocket. "The good thing about an Archers? Plenty of bags to go around. Where did you wander off to?"

"Shoe aisle."

"What's over there?"

"Shoes."

"Boots?"

"No, just tennis shoes."

Mike gave him a curious look.

"It's for Lara," Will said.

"The girlfriend?"

"She's more than that."

"Say no more. What's it like over there? The island?"

"What do you wanna know?"

"Jen made it sound like paradise." He gave Will a skeptical look. "Is it paradise? Between the two of us. Man to man. Grunt to grunt."

Will grinned. "That's the first time an officer's ever referred to himself as a grunt in front of me. But yeah, it's pretty damn close to paradise."

"How's the fishing?"

"You fish?"

"Every now and then."

"You know how when you go fishing, sometimes you catch something and sometimes you don't?"

"I know that feeling too well. Mostly the latter."

"You won't have that problem on the island. You could dip a bucket into the lake and you'd scoop up enough fish to eat for a week."

"You're not fucking with me, are you?"

"Not even a little bit."

"Damn. I could get used to that." He held up a box of bullets. "You need some for that rifle?"

"Nah, I stocked up before I left the island."

"What's that, M4A1? That thing looks like it's been through the wringer."

"It's been with me since Afghanistan."

"No kidding. How'd you get Uncle Sam to let you keep it?"

"I know a guy who knows a guy, who made it happen."

Mike chuckled. "Say no more." He finished up and walked out from behind the counter. The soles of his boots squeaked, leaving bloodied prints in his wake. He sniffed himself. "Jesus, they smell. I had no idea they smelled worse when they're dead."

They could hear Paul and Johnson farther back in the store, making a ruckus, and what sounded like something falling down from a high place on a shelf and crashing.

Like going shopping with Paul Bunyan and Babe the Blue Ox.

"I wish we could lock this place up," Mike said.

"Your private stash?"

"Something like that." He shook his head. "It's not just the ghouls we have to worry about coming back here tomorrow night. Those marauders I told you about. I wouldn't be surprised if they heard all the shooting. With the city this dead, you'd probably be able to hear a fart from a mile away."

"Good to know," Will said. He glanced at his watch. "It's early. You can come back for more later. Bring more people."

"I might have to seriously consider that."

Johnson appeared in the aisle behind them, flashlight bouncing wildly. He was carrying two gym bags.

"We good?" Mike called over.

"We good," Johnson called back.

"Where's Paul?"

"He's on his way."

They headed toward the front of the store, Paul appearing out of nowhere and falling in behind them along the way. He was hauling two bags too, though they looked like toys against his huge frame.

"I want to be back at the hospital by nine," Mike said. He looked over at Will. "When's your next scheduled call with Song Island?"

"Ten," Will said.

"Must be nice to have a woman waiting for you on an island. That sounds like the plot of a bad romance book."

Will smiled. "There's nothing bad about it."

THEY HADN'T GONE more than half a block when they heard the

first series of gunshots. The sound exploded across the city like a flash of lightning, one after another.

Instantly, Will knew they had come from the hospital.

Before Mike could say a word, Will was racing up the sidewalk, easily outpacing Mike's people. He was one and a half blocks away from the hospital, listening to the low, rumbling booms of gunshots as if they were coming from right across the street. He knew it was just the stillness of the city. Sound traveled these days, and the hard, violent cracks of gunfire moved with startling intensity.

Will didn't slow down until he was half a block from the hospital. He spotted movement along the rooftops. There had to be at least half a dozen figures, and there was something very wrong about their shapes…

He was jogging at a much slower pace as he approached the parking lot. He could hear Mike coming up behind him, gasping for breath. Will looked back, saw that Mike had dropped one of his gym bags. Even just hauling one bag, Mike still look badly winded. Will looked past Mike at Paul and Johnson, a good fifty meters behind them. They were also just clinging to one bag apiece now, and looked even more out of shape than Mike.

"How are you not breathing hard?" Mike gasped at him.

"I haven't spent eleven months inside a hospital," Will said.

They reached the end of the parking lot, keeping an eye on the cars in front of them and the rooftops of the hospital's visible three towers on the other side. The figures he had spotted earlier seemed to have disappeared, and that set off alarm bells inside Will's head.

But he couldn't stop. Not now. Not with gunfire still echoing from *inside* the building.

Gaby…

Mercy Hospital was only ten floors, but it looked much bigger from ground level, though it could just be the building's odd four-sided tower construction playing tricks with his eyes.

"Marauders?" Will asked.

"Maybe," Mike said between breaths. "If it is, then it'll be the first time. They've never been this bold before. Even if they waited for us to leave, they would have to know I've got more men up there."

"But how did they get *up* there?"

"I haven't a fucking clue," Mike said.

They reached the edge of the parking lot and were slowing down even further, the ringing inside Will's head increasing in volume.

The figures on the rooftop. Where did they go? Where—

He hadn't finished his thought when he saw a head pop up from the north tower rooftop.

"Sniper!" Will shouted.

Mike darted left and Will darted right as a man, wearing a white Level B hazmat suit, stood up and opened fire down on them. Will slid behind a parked white Ford as the vehicle's dust-covered windows shattered, the *ping-ping-ping* of bullets punching into doors. He kept low, taking into consideration the sniper's high angle that gave the man maximum coverage of the area.

No, not sniper. Snipers.

There were more than one. He could tell that just from the torrent of bullets raining down on him and Mike. From the sounds of it, they were shooting on three-round bursts, which accounted for the continuous *ping-ping-ping!* all around him.

Will glanced over at Mike, who had his back against a black Mercedes, the vehicle's windows shattered, glass fragments scattered on the parking lot around his boots. Mike's eyes were locked on something in front of him, back toward the street.

Will followed Mike's gaze over to Paul and Johnson, lying in the street, blood pooling around them. Johnson had fallen over his gym bag, while Paul was crumpled up like a marionette. Will couldn't tell how they had been shot. Not that it mattered. Dead was dead.

Gaby…

"Mike!" Will shouted over the gunfire. "We can't stay here!"

Mike looked back and nodded.

"Start running on three!" Will shouted. "One, two—*three!*"

Will spun around, slid the M4A1's barrel over the hood of the Ford, and fired three quick rounds up at the roof. In the split second that he fired, he spotted five figures on the rooftop, all wearing Level B hazmat suits with gas masks clipped to their waists. Three of the collaborators scurried away from the rooftop edge on instinct, but the remaining two turned toward him and opened up.

Will fired off five more rounds, not expecting to hit anything, before turning and running.

Bullets *zip-zip-zip!* past his head and played havoc against the concrete around him. One came dangerously close to taking off his right ear.

Mike had stopped in the middle of the street and was firing up at the roof with his Sig Sauer 9mm. Will almost laughed, but of course he knew why Mike was using his handgun. It was either the Sig Sauer or the shotgun, and at this range, he might as well be throwing salt at the snipers. Not that the Sig Sauer came even remotely close. But of course, the idea wasn't to hit anything on the rooftop, it was just to draw their fire away from Will.

"Go!" Will said just as he reached Mike.

Mike turned and ran, while Will stopped, spun around, and fired up at the rooftop again. He took a couple of chunks off the side of the north tower and sent another sniper scurrying for cover. The last man refused to budge, though, and continued firing down at him.

Ping-ping-ping! as bullets scraped the street dangerously close to his feet.

Will turned and ran, making a beeline for Mike, who was already hidden behind the side of a Starbucks across the street.

A bullet screamed as it tore through the gym bag slung over Will's back. He waited to feel the pain, but there was none.

So he kept running, jogging across the street with his head kept low.

He slid behind the Starbucks, adrenaline pouring through him. He unslung the gym bag and saw a hole in one side and out the other. He opened it and took out one of the shoes he had picked up for Lara. The bullet had gone clean through it.

Mike was reloading his Sig Sauer next to him. "You think we got any of them?"

"No."

"Figures."

Gunfire and a half dozen rounds pelted the Starbucks, obliterating the front windows. A couple of bullets fell short and dug divots in the concrete sidewalk.

"Sorry about Paul and Johnson," Will said.

Mike looked at the two bodies lying up the street. "Yeah. They were good men."

Will looked past the parking lot and up at the hospital rooftop. The hazmat-clad figures were standing and one of them was peering through a riflescope down in his direction, but the man didn't fire for some reason.

"Who the hell are those guys?" Mike asked. "What the hell were they wearing? Those looked like hazmat suits."

"Level B hazmat suits, yeah."

"Why the hell are they wearing those?"

"Remember those ghoul collaborators I told you about? That's them."

"Shit. How the fuck did they get up to the roof without my guys seeing them?"

"It's your hospital, you tell me." Will glanced at his watch. "And there's no other way into the building?"

Mike shook his head. Will could see he was fighting back emotions, trying desperately to process the loss of Johnson and Paul, and the very real possibility of losing Mercy Hospital.

"If I knew of one, do you really think we'd be rappelling up and down the rooftop?" Mike said.

A rifle shot took a big slab out of the Starbucks wall in front of them.

Will peeked out from behind the building and saw figures emerging out of the hospital lobby. "We gotta go."

Mike looked out and saw the same thing. "Where?"

"This is your city, you tell me."

Mike thought about it. "Come on," he said, and hurried toward the back of the Starbucks.

Will glanced out from behind the wall one last time and saw white-suited men, gas masks tapping against their waists, moving across the parking lot toward them.

He pulled his head back and followed Mike.

Hold on, Gaby. Hold on…

THERE WERE FOUR of them, moving from building to building, employing something that could, from a distance, be mistaken for tactics. They advanced up the street with two up front and two bringing up the rear.

The gunfire from Mercy Hospital had stopped a while ago. That was the bad news. Silence meant the battle was over and that the hospital had fallen. However the attack had gone down, it was obvious now that the collaborators had taken the place by surprise and with overwhelming force. If they could afford to leave that many on the rooftop, there were probably more inside the tenth floor itself.

Will lifted the M4A1 a couple of inches as he heard the sounds of boots scraping against hot asphalt. They were surprisingly quiet for a bunch of a civilians. Of course, in the stillness of the city, even breathing was too loud.

The closest man was twenty meters away when Mike finally made his move. As planned, he popped up from behind a dumpster next to a McDonald's and opened fire with the Sig Sauer. Will heard those same boots scrambling for cover, M4s firing back, and the *clink-clink-clink* of empty casings raining down on the street.

Will slipped out from behind the parked minivan and scanned the road. A figure in a hazmat suit made the mistake of running toward him for cover. Will came out from behind the vehicle, saw the man's eyes go wide as he started to lift his rifle.

Will shot him in the right eye.

Even as the man was dropping, Will was already turning slightly to his right, aiming down the street.

The remaining three were too busy firing back at Mike to notice him. Which was the idea. One of the men was hiding in an alleyway between a Barnes & Noble bookstore and a Mexican restaurant, his white hazmat suit like a beacon against the darkened mouth of the alley. The other two were using a parked police car as cover, popping up one at a time to return fire. The dumpster up the street was pockmarked with bullets, but Mike had ducked behind the squat object to reload.

Will shot the man in the alleyway in the abdomen. The man seemed to grope for the bullet hole, stumbling out onto the sidewalk before falling on his stomach.

Will was already moving as the two remaining collaborators turned in his direction and returned fire. He darted back behind the minivan, heard windows breaking around him, the *ping-ping-ping* of bullets tearing into the parked vehicle on the other side. There was a loud popping noise next to him as the right rear tire was punctured.

Then Mike was shooting again, and immediately the gunfire directed at the minivan stopped as the men turned their attention back up the street.

Will laid down against the hot sidewalk and peered underneath the vehicle at the two men, thirty meters away, crouched behind the back bumper of the police car. One was reloading while the other was firing off one three-round burst after another.

Will took two quick steps backward and slid the M4A1 underneath the minivan. It was a tight fit, so he had to aim with the rifle lying on its side. Tricky.

His first shot hit the side of the squad car two meters from the head of the closest man. The man flinched, then scrambled to reload faster when he figured out where the bullet had come from.

Will moved the rifle a bit to the right and shot again, this time hitting the man in the chest. The man in the hazmat suit seemed surprised for the brief half-second he was still alive. Then he crumpled forward and lay still.

The last man got up and scrambled down the street. Will hurried back up to his feet and stepped forward, took aim at the running figure, and shot the man once in the thigh and watched him twist slightly, as if he had tripped on something, and fall to the street in a ball of tangled legs and arms.

Mike was already running toward them, never breaking stride even as he snatched up one of the fallen rifles from a dead body. The man in hazmat suit had managed to pull himself up to his feet and was dragging himself desperately down the street. Mike easily caught up to him and smashed the stock of the rifle into his back.

Will jogged over to the first man he had shot and picked up his rifle. He collected two spare magazines and a radio, then salvaged another carbine from another dead body before joining Mike, who stood over the last surviving collaborator.

The man lay bleeding and hyperventilating, eyes looking desperately up at an unsympathetic Mike. "Don't kill me. Please, God, don't kill me. I don't want to die. I didn't want to do this. I swear to God, they made me do this."

Then the man threw up.

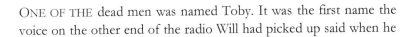

ONE OF THE dead men was named Toby. It was the first name the voice on the other end of the radio Will had picked up said when he called over:

"Toby, give me a sitrep. Are they dead? What's going on over there? Someone answer me, goddammit."

"Who was that?" Will asked.

The collaborator wiped at strings of what looked like eggs and bread with the sleeve of his hazmat suit. The lower half of his face was covered with dry vomit. It smelled, and Will alternated between breathing through his nose and mouth. And he thought the dead ghouls were tough on the smell factories…

"Please, can I have some water?" the man asked. He looked on the verge of tears.

Mike shoved the barrel of his shotgun into the back of the man's neck. "Answer the question."

"Kellerson," the man said. "His name's Kellerson."

"He's in charge?" Will asked.

"Yeah."

"How many of you are there?"

The man didn't answer right away. He seemed to be counting. "Sixteen," he said finally.

"Counting you and the other three on the streets?"

"Yeah."

"So there are twelve left at the hospital," Mike said.

"Yeah," the man said.

"What's your name?" Will asked.

"Jones," the man said.

They were a block away from the ambush site, inside a Subway sandwich shop. The building was tiny and easy to miss, but it gave them a perfect view of the streets while staying out of sight. Jones sat in a booth, hands on the tabletop. Mike kept vigil behind the nervous man, while Will stood slightly to his right, so he could see the street at the same time.

"How did you get into the hospital?" Mike asked.

"We climbed up," Jones said.

"How?"

"Through the ventilation shaft."

"Bullshit. We checked. The shafts are too small for anything to climb through. Even those bloodsuckers."

"No, not the main ventilation system," Jones said. "There's an older one that's been out of service that Kellerson found on a blueprint of the place. It goes straight up along the north side, then loops around the roof. It comes out of a sealed grate in the rooftop stairwell. The guys who went up there had to remove the grate, but since there was no one inside the stairwell, I guess it wasn't too hard. From there, they were supposed to open the other stairwell door and let the others in."

Mike's face had grown paler. The idea that he had missed something so vital, that had now come back to take the lives of his people, was playing havoc with his mind. Will felt sorry for the guy. Eleven months, and they hadn't realized there wasn't one, but two ventilation systems. Mike was the leader. What had just happened at the hospital, ultimately, was on him.

"What's the plan?" Will asked Jones. "For the floor. Are they going to kill everyone?"

Jones didn't look anxious to answer.

Mike shoved his shotgun against Jones's neck again. "Answer the man."

"Just the adults," Jones said. "They want the kids."

"'They'?" Mike asked, though Will thought the former officer already knew the answer before Jones even replied.

"Yeah, them," Jones said. *"Them."*

"Why do they want the kids?" Will asked.

"I don't know."

"For the blood?"

"Maybe. I don't know."

"What else would they want the kids for if not for their blood?"

Jones looked hesitant. "I heard stories…"

"Go on."

"The creatures, they have a plan. It involves the kids. I don't know any more than that. Just that they're concentrating on the kids now, for some reason."

"What about the adults?" Will asked.

"They're too hard to control. The kids are…easier."

Will glanced briefly at Mike, expecting him to pick up the interrogation, but Mike's mind wasn't there at the moment. It was up the street, back at the hospital.

"Where were you taking the kids?" Will asked Jones.

"I don't know. That's Kellerson's job. He knows all the details." Then he added, quickly, "I'm just a grunt, okay?"

"Are they on the tenth floor now? The bloodsuckers?"

"No, it's still too bright. They don't like to risk the sunlight, and the guys don't like having them run around. It's...creepy. They won't flood the floor until nightfall. We were supposed to be gone by then."

Mike glanced reflexively down at his watch. Will didn't have to. It was noon outside. He had been fleeing the sun long enough that he could tell the hour from the feel of the warmth against his skin.

"What do you mean by 'adults'?" Will asked.

"What?" Jones said, not comprehending.

"How old."

"Over sixteen, I guess. Basically, anyone with a gun. They don't want anyone who resists. They just want the kids."

Gaby turned nineteen today. And she's certainly as hell going to resist.

"Is it over?" Will asked. "Did you kill all the adults? I don't hear anymore shooting."

"Last time I checked, there were a couple unaccounted for. They're still looking for them."

Gaby?

"Why are you doing this?" Mike asked. He had been so quiet for so long that his sudden voice made Jones jump a bit.

"What do you mean?" Jones asked, turning to look back at Mike.

"Why are you betraying your own kind?"

"I..." Jones's mind seemed to be working overtime, probably trying to come up with an answer that would keep him alive. "To survive," he said finally. "Isn't that what we're all just trying to do here? I'm just trying to survive like everyone else."

"That's it?"

"I'm not proud of it, but I don't have a choice."

"You had a choice," Mike said. "You just chose the wrong one."

Jones opened his mouth to answer, but thought better of it.

Mike looked at Will. "You wanna ask him anything else?"

"How many did you kill on the tenth floor?" Will asked Jones.

Jones shook his head. "Wasn't my assignment. Me and the other three guys that chased you had the lobby. I didn't even kill anyone."

"Not for lack of trying."

"I'm just following orders," Jones said defensively.

"Now where have I heard that before?"

Jones didn't answer. He looked away instead.

"Anything else?" Mike said.

Will shook his head. "I'm done."

"Good," Mike said, and blew Jones's head off with the Mossberg from less than a foot away.

CHAPTER 12

GABY

I JUST TURNED nineteen, and I've already killed three men.
Happy birthday to me.

Eleven months ago, she was trying to decide who to let take her to the senior prom. After a lot of debate and conversations with friends, her choices had come down to two likely candidates—Trevor and Scott. They were both cute boys, and she knew Scott from tenth grade when they dated for half a year before calling it quits. Trevor was new in town, but he had the bluest eyes, and she had always been a sucker for blue eyes.

She wondered where Trevor was now. Maybe hiding in a basement. Or inside a building with friends. If he was lucky, he would have found some people to travel with. That was the only way to survive these days. You couldn't do it on your own. She remembered those months when she stayed behind in whatever basement they had found while Josh and Matt went out to search for supplies.

Had she been scared back then? No, not really. Thinking back, she was never really scared. She just deferred to the boys because they were *boys*, and she was a *girl*. She didn't know any better.

She felt like laughing as she thought about the Gaby from a few months ago.

She might have actually laughed, or made a noise, because Jen glanced over. "What's so funny?"

"Nothing," she whispered back. "Just thinking of an old joke."

"Really? Now?"

They were squeezed inside a small, six-by-seven room in the back of the nurses' lounge. It would have been pitch black if not for a few slivers of sunlight poking through the edges of the closed door. The lounge had a north side-facing window with raised blinds that looked out at the parking lot.

The room had once been a bathroom, judging by the big toilet in the back and a porcelain sink somewhere on her left, poking into her rib cage at the moment. The nurses had pushed a refrigerator over one side of the door and covered up the other half with a big poster boasting Mercy Hospital as one of the Top 50 Best Reviewed Hospitals in America. Mike's people had discovered the room a while back, but never did anything with it. There wasn't any point with so many rooms to choose from, and she guessed they never expected to need an emergency hideout.

Will would have put it to use 'just in case.'

She wasn't alone in the room. Besides Jen, there was Amy, who was the one who had remembered the room and led them here. It was only a couple of turns from where they had been when the attack began. Along the way they had run across Benny, running with the button-nosed boy Gaby had seen earlier, both of their eyes wide with fear.

Benny sat directly behind her now. Amy was in the back with the boy in her lap. The kid was strangely quiet, though he was clearly terrified, the large whites of his eyes staring back at her in the semidarkness. All four looked stunned and bewildered by what had happened. She didn't blame them. The attack had been swift and brutal. The four of them were probably thinking of all the friends they had just lost. She knew how that felt, too.

The five of them packed into the small bathroom was tight enough, but they also had to battle the bags of medical supplies for the limited space. Amy and Jen had wanted to leave them behind, but Gaby wouldn't let them. She and Will had come all the way here for them, and she'd be damned if she was going to abandon them now. She liked to think Will would have done the same thing in her position.

"What now?" Benny whispered, leaning forward until the cold barrel of his AR-15 poked into Gaby's back, causing her to wince a bit. "Sorry."

For the longest time, they heard gunfire and screaming. When it was finally over, they heard sniffling and crying, and she knew without actually seeing that the men outside were taking the children. Amy told her there were eleven kids in the hospital, not counting the one with the button nose.

What are they doing with the children?

They weren't shooting them; she was certain of that. They shot everyone else, though. The adults and some of the teenagers. She remembered the sight of Tom, Benny's friend, lying around a corner with a bullet hole in his forehead. The men in hazmat suits hadn't shown any mercy.

She saw and heard them entering the lounge twice in the last hour. They had looked around before moving on. The sight of the gas masks reminded her of Beaumont, but she did her best to push those memories into the past where they belonged and focused instead on the moment, the here and now, on trying to stay alive *today*.

One of the collaborators had actually walked over and opened the fridge, looked in at the bottles of warm water and Gatorade inside, before slamming it shut and leaving. He may or may not have taken a bottle with him. She had a limited view of the lounge through the small slivers in the uncovered parts of the doorframe.

Sometime between the start of the attack and when she heard the last gunshot, Gaby swore she could hear gunfire from above her, on the rooftop. It seemed to go on for a while, and she immediately thought, *Will and Mike are back. They're firing on Will and Mike.*

The fact that the gunfire went on for some time told her it hadn't been a massacre, so that was a good sign.

Hopefully.

Then it was quiet. Very quiet.

Now, Gaby looked down at the glowing hands of her watch: 12:13 P.M.

"We can't stay here forever," she whispered.

Jen nodded. "I know."

"Why not?" Amy whispered behind them. "Why can't we just wait them out? They have to leave eventually."

"Not before they open the doors to the ghouls," Gaby said. "By nightfall, this entire floor will be filled with them. You think they're just going to lock everything back up when they go? That's not how this works."

Amy didn't answer, and Benny seemed to be breathing a little harder than before.

"So what now?" Jen asked.

For some reason, the pilot's eyes were focused on Gaby's when she asked the question.

Seriously? I'm nineteen years old. Why are you looking at me?

But she knew why. Mike had let them down. Jen, Amy, Benny, and the kid. He hadn't prepared them for this. It was only Amy's quick thinking that had saved their lives. The hazmat suits were everywhere, in every hallway, and moving through all four towers of the hospital, looking for targets. Neither Jen nor Amy had any idea how they had gotten in.

They're so unprepared. Will would never have let us be such easy prey.

"We have to get out of here," Gaby said.

"How?" Benny whispered.

"The helicopter," Gaby said. She looked at Jen. "You have the keys with you, right?"

"Keys?" Jen said.

"To the helicopter."

Jen looked a bit confused. "It's a Bell 407 model. It doesn't have keys."

"So how do you keep people from stealing it?"

"What, the helicopter?"

"Yeah."

"Gaby, who would steal a helicopter? It's not like stealing a car. You actually do need to know more than where the gas pedal is to fly one."

"So if we get to the rooftop, you could just hop in and fly us out of here?"

"Pretty much, yeah."

"How are you for fuel?"

"I'm down to eleven gallons."

"Could you get more?"

"There's a private airport about ten miles from here. It's my primary refueling depot."

Gaby nodded. "So we just need to get up to the roof."

"Gee, that's it?" Benny said.

She gave him an annoyed look, and Benny turned away. The nineteen-year-old girl in her felt bad for her quick-tempered reaction, but the survivor part of her, who had struggled to survive Will and Danny's crucible on the island over the last three months, was glad he was embarrassed.

"All I know is we can't stay in here forever," Gaby said. She looked down at her watch again. "If we're still here when it gets dark, we're never leaving. Not as ourselves, anyway. I don't know about you, but I'd rather eat a bullet than become one of those things."

She looked back at their faces. Even the kid with the button nose seemed to grasp the gravity of what she was telling them. Or maybe not. For all she knew, he probably didn't speak English.

"What's your plan?" Jen finally asked.

"I think Will's out there," Gaby said. "Maybe with Mike and the others. The shooting we heard earlier, I think that was them."

"We could wait for them," Benny said. "Mike wouldn't leave us."

"No, he wouldn't," Amy nodded certainly.

"And Will wouldn't leave me, either," Gaby said. "But they would be on a timetable just like we are. Will especially would know it'll be too late if they don't do something by nightfall. We have to let them know there are still people in here to help."

"How do we do that?" Jen asked.

Good question...

SHE WAITED UNTIL one in the afternoon before acting. She wasn't entirely sure what she was doing, but spending the next six hours stuck in the bathroom, waiting for the inevitable nightfall, didn't strike her as a very good plan. The old Gaby might not have been so assertive, but she hadn't been her old self in a while, thank God.

Jen argued briefly, and Benny gave her a horrified look when she told them her plans. He spent the next twenty minutes trying to talk her out of it. She wasn't sure if he was afraid she would get them caught, or if there was something more. The truth was probably somewhere in-between.

"I'll be fine," she said. "Just wait for my signal."

"What kind of signal?" Jen asked.

"I don't know yet."

"That's comforting."

"Hey, you got any bright ideas?"

"No..."

"So okay, then. Wait for my signal."

Using the slivers in the doorframe, she looked into the nurses' lounge and saw no one. She listened, and heard nothing. The men in hazmat suits were all wearing combat boots, and they weren't shy about stomping back and forth. She could usually feel the ground vibrating slightly whenever they approached or walked past the lounge.

The bathroom door opened inward, so she had to move back a bit, bumping into Benny in the process. He struggled to give her space, and she swung the door open, revealing the dust-covered poster that had saved their lives. Gaby pushed the lower half of the glossy sheet forward, gently, and was thankful the top half was held in place by thumbtacks. It fluttered a bit as she slipped outside, and she heard the door instantly closing back up behind her.

She pushed the poster back into place, rubbing down the bottom edges as best she could until it stopped moving. She unslung her M4 and moved toward the open door, then leaned against the wall next to it.

She heard voices in the hallway and the loud crunch of footsteps moving around. There hadn't been any additional gunfire since around noon, which meant the attackers had completely taken over the hospital. She tried not to think about how many people were already dead out there. She had seen four on the way to the lounge, and the look frozen on their faces said it all—they never saw it coming.

Gaby tried to picture the hospital's layout in her head. They were in the north tower, and the rooftop access was to her right, around a couple of turns, then at the very end. There had to be men on the rooftop, so even if she could make her way up there, she had to expect an additional fight.

What the hell am I doing? Is this what Will would do?

She glanced back at the long window behind her, the parking lot visible below. She looked for a bit, but couldn't detect any signs of movements. There had been a gun battle out there not all that long ago. Will and Mike, she was sure of it. Definitely Will. Sound traveled, and he would have heard the attack all the way at the

Archers a couple of blocks away.

If only Mike had been smart enough to issue radios to his people…

Gaby turned back toward the door for a moment. From her angle, she only had a limited view of the hallway. The sounds of footsteps from earlier were gone, along with the voices. How many of them were still out there? It wouldn't have taken very many to secure the floor. Mike's people were shockingly unprepared, and most of them were women and children. As for the men, she only saw about a dozen that could have really put up a fight.

She moved to the window and put a palm on it. Thick glass, like in the patient rooms. Knocking on it produced a dull, thudding sound. No wonder the ghouls couldn't get inside. It would have taken an entire magazine just to make a dent in it.

She peered out at the parking lot below, then along the streets, trying to catch sight of something she could use. Would Will be out there now? He had to be. If he knew the hospital was under attack, he would try to get back in, find out if she was still alive. She knew him. You didn't eat and sleep on the same patch of dirt with someone in the woods for two weeks without a shower and not know how he would respond in a crisis.

Will wouldn't leave me.

So where the hell is he…?

Unless he thought she was dead. Will might head back to the island if he believed that. Will wasn't cold-blooded, but he was extremely practical. Maybe—

Gaby froze.

There!

She saw it near an alleyway to the left of the parking lot, across the street and between a couple of orange buildings. It looked like a reflection.

Sunlight glinting off metal?

No, not metal. Glass.

Gaby focused on the glinting object.

She was sure of it now. It wasn't something natural, because the reflection wasn't constant. It was there one second and gone the next. Then it was there for a good five seconds, then disappeared for two more, before flickering again. Like it was trying to get her attention.

Will?

A single gunshot echoed directly above her, from the rooftop. The reflection vanished as small pieces of the orange building flicked into the air.

I guess I wasn't the only one who saw that.

The loud sounds of heavy footsteps in the hallway snapped her back to the lounge.

Gaby hurried to the door and pushed against the wall. She glimpsed two figures in hazmat suits walking awkwardly across the open door. One of them was carrying a crate of canned food, while the other was lugging a familiar green ammo can.

That's ours, asshole.

They passed by without bothering to look into the lounge.

She heard another man coming down the hallway trailing the first two, already fading as they got farther away. Her mind's eye flashed back to the man in Beaumont and how he had worn his gas mask. She remembered only his eyes and the bridge of his nose, but no real details about his face because it was hard to see what he really looked like under the gas mask.

That's it. That's the way out of here.

Just as the third man reached the lounge, Gaby picked up a ceramic black mug—World's Best Nurse was written on the side—from a nearby table and tossed it to the floor. The mug cracked, revealing stained black insides.

The man stopped in the hallway and stepped into the lounge, his rifle in front of him. Gaby watched him walk past her and noticed he was about her height. He moved carefully inside, before stopping when he saw the broken pieces of the mug on the floor.

He might have sensed her, but before he could turn, Gaby jammed the barrel of her M4 into the back of his neck. "Put the rifle on the floor."

Her voice was amazingly steady.

Why aren't I afraid? I should be afraid, right?

The man did as she ordered, bending slowly at the knees. He might even have been shaking a bit inside the suit. Gaby reached back with one hand and closed the door behind them.

"Benny," she called. "Get out here."

She heard the bathroom door opening, then the poster fluttered as Benny hurried out. "This is your plan?"

"This is it."

"So now what?"

"Put your gun on him."

Benny aimed his rifle at the man in the hazmat suit while Gaby freed his sidearm from a holster, then unsnapped the gas mask from his belt.

The man looked to be in his mid-thirties, with the kind of face that made her think he might have been an accountant in a past life. She knew the type. Her father was a taxman, and he'd had the same pudgy and pale complexion from working in an office for most of his life.

"I need your suit," Gaby said.

◄▬▮ ▮▬►

THIS IS STUPID.

I'm an idiot.

This will never work.

I'm going to get killed.

God help me, I'm going to get killed.

Those were some of the thoughts that raced through her head as Gaby walked down the hallway in the hazmat suit. She was at least comforted by the fact that the suit's original wearer wasn't fat despite his slightly pudgy face, and the suit wasn't too big for her. With the gun belt strapped around her waist and the M4 in her hands, she could almost pull it off.

Hopefully.

Benny gave her an 'okay' nod when she asked him how she looked, but she could tell by his eyes that he was scared. Not for himself, but for her. Which was both sweet and worrisome. Was he scared because he liked her and didn't want her to get hurt? Or frightened because she didn't look convincing in the suit?

She couldn't tell how she looked, and frankly, she didn't want to. She concentrated instead on how she felt, which was surprisingly calm. With the combat boots on, she wouldn't necessarily look out of place. And the gas mask hid most of her face, if not the blonde ponytail.

They're going to see the ponytail...

But not if she kept in front of them. It was hard enough to see the eyes of someone wearing a gas mask; maybe they wouldn't notice what was behind her, either.

This is the dumbest thing I've ever done.

I am so going to die.

She kept walking, because if she stopped for even a second she might change her mind and run back to the lounge. And then what? Hide in the old bathroom? Sure, that might work for a while…until nightfall. Then the ghouls would be all over the tenth floor, and the idea of being surrounded by those things, with just a fridge, a poster, and a flimsy door as protection made her skin crawl.

She made it halfway to her destination without meeting another person on the floor, though she saw plenty of bodies. Some of Mike's soldiers, but a lot of the civilians, too. Men and women, some still in their teens. Blood smeared the walls and open doors, and the entire floor had the thick aura of abandonment and death.

She turned another corner and slowed down.

The rooftop access door was at the end of the hallway, and there was a man in a hazmat suit standing in front of it, eating from a can of beans, his gas mask hanging off his web belt. But it wasn't the man that startled her. It was the door to the man's right, the one that accessed the other nine floors of the hospital. The lumber that had been nailed across the door, keeping it barricaded, had been pried loose and was piled nearby on the floor.

The door was open.

She could see blackness inside the stairwell door, and it was…*moving.*

Quickly, she checked the windows along the hallway. The blinds were pulled up and sunlight filtered in, illuminating large swaths of the tiled floor. That was why the ghouls hadn't come out of the stairwell yet. Still too much sunlight. She wondered if the men in hazmat suits had left the windows uncovered intentionally.

Maybe they're still human, after all.

She was halfway to the man when he finally looked up. He licked at brown stains around his lips, before saying, "What are you still doing up here?"

"Are we leaving already?" she asked.

My God, how is my voice so calm?

"You didn't get the signal?" the man asked. "That's what the radio's for, genius."

Gaby looked down at the radio clipped to her hip. "I think mine's dead. Where is everyone?"

"Downstairs, loading up the Humvees." He glanced down at his watch. "We got five hours to bag all the supplies before this place goes dark. I don't know about you, but I don't wanna be here when that happens."

Gaby was thirty yards away now. She moved her head around to purposefully avoid looking him in the eyes because she could see him trying to get a better look at her. He had also subtly let his right hand drift toward his holstered handgun. His rifle, another M4 *(Where did they get all the M4s?)*, rested on the wall behind him.

"That's you, right, Janice?" the man said, peering at her. "I thought you were on the roof."

"I was," Gaby said. "I came down for some food."

Keep walking. Don't stop.

Keep walking…

"You're supposed to be on the roof," the man said. Then a flicker of alarm crossed his face. "Bullshit. You're not Janice."

The man reached for his handgun, dropping the can of beans at the same instant.

Gaby had been walking with her rifle in her arms the entire time, and all she had to do was lift it and shoot the man in the chest. She was so close—less than fifteen yards away—that it wasn't much of a shot and she barely had to aim or use the red dot sight.

It was the sound of the gunshot that startled her. It was *too loud*.

The man slumped against the wall and slid down to the floor. He sat awkwardly with his head hanging against his chest, as if he were asleep. A small, thin trail of blood dripped out of the white hazmat suit.

Gaby looked back down the hallway, hoping Jen and the others had heard that. Of course they had heard that. *Everyone* must have heard that shot.

She moved toward the dead man, saw the darkness shifting in the open stairwell door to her left, just barely visible out of the corner of her eye. She could feel the intensity growing, the sudden squirming of bodies jammed inside, the almost palpable vibe of growing *excitement*.

Ignore them. They can't come out.

Ignore them!

She looked away as the radio clipped to her hip squawked, and a man's deep voice came through: "What the fuck was that? Where did that shot come from?"

A female voice answered, "That's from the tenth floor."

"Gary," the man said. "Come in, Gary." When no one answered, the man said, "Mark, are you there? Where the fuck are you guys?"

Mark and Gary. Probably the man with the pudgy face whose suit she was wearing, and the dead man in front of her. Not that it mattered.

She ripped the gas mask off and tossed it, then glanced back down the hallway, expecting to see Jen and the others charging toward her at any second.

But there was no one back there except an empty hallway.

Come on, guys.

She waited.

Seconds felt like hours, and her heart beat erratically against her chest.

Come on, dammit.

What if Jen didn't think the gunshot was the signal? She couldn't really blame them. She didn't even know what the signal would be. What if they were still back there, hiding inside the bathroom? What if—

She heard feet pounding down the hallway and spun around, lifting her rifle.

Jen, taking the corner, slid to a stop, the pudgy man's rifle gripped tightly in her hands and the big medical supply bag jutting out from behind her back. "It's just us!" she shouted.

Benny, shouldering the other medical bag, turned the corner so recklessly he almost crashed into Jen. Amy was behind him, holding the kid, whose arms were wrapped tightly around the former Army medic's neck, his face buried in her shoulder.

Gaby waved them over. "What happened to the other guy?"

"I hit him with my rifle," Benny said. "I think he's unconscious. Or dead. I'm not sure."

"Good enough."

A loud burst of gunfire tore through the air outside the building, making all five of them—including the kid—jump. The *pop-pop-pop* of automatic rifle fire seemed to fill every inch and space of the world around her. They were coming from below and behind and above them all at the same time.

The radio on the floor squawked, and she heard the same man with the deep voice, this time the unmistakable quiver of fear coming through in every word he shouted:

"We're under attack! I repeat, we're under attack!"

CHAPTER 13

WILL

NINE.

That was how many times he thought Gaby would tell him she was through, that she was done with the training, the scars, the bruises, and the waking up with every inch of her body aching, where even breathing hurt.

Nine times.

The first week was the hardest, because it had to be. It would get easier if she stuck with it, but he had to know what kind of fortitude she had, what kind of quit she had in her, if any. His version of Basic Training was quick and painful and soul-crushing. It was difficult, but nothing compared to what he and Danny had gone through. They squeezed in Basic along with Ranger discipline, with half of her days spent on building up her stamina and the other half on weapons training.

And she stuck with it.

They told her she could quit any day. Every day. They told her when they started at the beginning of the day, and later when she was done at night. They pushed her. She complained often and loudly, but she never quit.

After a while, she even stopped complaining.

And she was a natural shooter. He hadn't expected that. Under Danny's tutelage, she flourished, and he gave her more time in the Tower with the ACOG to get her used to the riflescope. In time, he had no doubt she would surpass him, and maybe even Danny.

He remembered his conversations with Lara about Gaby. Lara's problem was that she still thought of Gaby as a kid, a little sister, and wasn't convinced turning her into a soldier was the right path. Not that she could have stopped the teenager. They weren't the girl's parents, and she was eighteen. In post-Purge years, that was plenty old enough.

"What if she gets hurt?" Lara had asked. "People get hurt during Basic Training all the time, don't they?"

"Of course they do," he had answered. "That's why you're here."

"I'm just a third-year medical student, Will."

"So hopefully she'll only have a third-year medical-student-type accident."

"Not funny."

"She'll be fine."

"She's just a kid."

"She's eighteen going on thirty."

That led to Lara's theory that Gaby was throwing herself into training so she wouldn't have to think about Josh, the kid who had died under Will's watch. Maybe. Probably. It wasn't his job to dig under Gaby's motivations. He only cared that she *had* motivations.

It didn't really hit him just how young she really was until they spent two weeks together in the woods. The exercise was simple—live and survive off the land, eating only what they killed, and using only what they could scavenge. Roots, plants, bugs, and animals.

Over a campfire one night, he saw her smiling to herself.

"What's so funny?" he had asked.

"I was just thinking how funny all of this is," she had said. "I'm camping in the woods, eating plants and bugs. This isn't exactly my thing, Will. I'm not sure if my friends would be horrified or impressed if they saw me today."

"You're surprisingly good at this."

"That's a compliment, right?"

"Lara wasn't sure Danny and I should be pushing you this hard."

"Lara's sweet. She's the big sister I never had."

"I told her you could handle it."

"Thanks."

"Nine times, you know."

"Nine times what?"

"That's how many times I thought you would come and tell me you were quitting. All of it in the first month."

She had laughed. "Nine sounds a little low. I was thinking more around thirtyish."

"But you didn't quit."

"No..."

"Why not?"

"I'm good at this. God knows I had no idea I would be. But I am. Go figure, right?"

"This is just the beginning."

"What, it gets harder?"

"A lot harder."

"Oh." She had picked up a stick and was poking at the fire. "But you and Danny will be there, right?"

"We're not going anywhere."

"Good." Then she had smiled across the fire at him. "Then bring it."

GABY.

He smiled when he saw her in his binoculars, looking out from one of the windows along the north face of Mercy Hospital. She was scanning for something among the cars in the parking lot below her.

Will leaned farther out from behind a big orange building across the street and to the left of the parking lot. In a bit of a twist, he had a better view of the snipers on the rooftop than they did of him. They had the better vantage point from high up, sure, but it was easy to avoid them if you chose the right angles.

He lowered the binoculars and glanced back at Mike, crouched behind him. "It's Gaby. She's alive."

"The teenager?"

"Looks like she found a place to hide during the attack. Maybe she managed to save some of your people, too."

Mike fished out a pair of binoculars from his pack and leaned out from behind the building and looked through them.

"Four windows from the left," Will said.

"That's the nurses' lounge," Mike said. "There's an old, unused bathroom in the back." Mike lowered his binoculars. "You're right, she's probably not alone. Most of my people know about that bathroom, so someone must have taken her there."

Mike moved back behind cover, stuffing the binoculars into his pack. They had returned to the Archers after interrogating Jones, exchanging the bulky gym bags for tactical packs made of heavy-duty nylon. They had brought back with them only what they needed for the assault on the hospital, to make sure there were no survivors left to save. Neither one of them was willing to leave until they had made absolutely damn sure.

Will searched inside his pack and pulled out a small mirror housed inside a pouch. It was a part of a baton kit, but right now he only needed the mirror. He leaned back out, made sure Gaby was still visible in the window, then stuck the mirror into the open and flicked it back and forth to catch the light.

"What are you doing?" Mike asked behind him.

"Trying to get her attention."

"Morse code?"

"I don't think she knows Morse code. At least, I never taught her. It's just to let her know she's not alone up there."

"And then?"

"She's a resourceful kid. If she knows she has help down here, she'll act accordingly."

"Jen's helicopter is still on the roof," Mike said. "If Jen's still alive, they could use it to escape. But that'll mean taking out the snipers on the rooftop first."

"One thing at a time," Will said.

He heard the gunshot a split second before the piece of brick a few centimeters from his face cracked and showered the air with a fine orange clay cloud. He pulled his head back as a second shot broke another brick in half.

"You hit?" Mike asked.

Will brushed flecks of powder out of his hair. "I'm fine. You ready?"

Mike unslung one of the M4s he had taken from one of the dead collaborators. He had a second one for backup, and had ditched his shotgun. If this was going to work, they couldn't be seen. They were already outnumbered, so they needed every advantage they could get.

Will made do with his M4A1, but he had loaded on extra magazines. He nodded at Mike. "Stick to the plan."

"I have a choice?"

"Not really, no."

He grinned. "You know, I outrank you. I should be the one giving the orders."

"Yeah, but I've been at this longer than you."

"Can't argue with that. I'll see you when I see you, then."

Mike jogged off, keeping low and behind the other orange building. He was safe, unless the snipers on the rooftop could see through brick walls.

Will watched him go for a moment, then stuck his head back out of the building to look at the rooftop. He pulled it back just before a gunshot sent another flurry of orange into the air around him.

THERE WERE FOUR military Humvees in desert camo parked in a line in front of the hospital's front lobby outside the north tower. They hadn't been there this morning. All four vehicles looked well-worn, their tires covered in mud, and flying insect carcasses splattered across the back windows facing him.

Men in hazmat suits and gas masks were leading a couple of kids toward one of the Humvees. There were already other children inside two of the vehicles. The other hazmat suits stood guard with M4s. Will counted four, not including the two in the process of shoving the kids into a Humvee. He was too far to hear anything, but some of kids were crying, their tear-streaked faces glancing around in terror, clear as day through his binoculars.

He remembered what Jones had said: *"They don't want anyone who resists. They just want the kids."*

He hadn't heard a single thing through the radio clipped to his hip. He was surprised by that. Whoever was in charge—maybe this Kellerson that Jones had mentioned—wasn't stupid after all. They knew Will and Mike had probably procured radios from the four men they had killed earlier, so it was possible the collaborators had switched to a different frequency. That level of tactical thinking already made them more dangerous than the ones he had run across in Dansby, Texas.

Even their human minions are getting smarter.

Will skirted the parking lot, easily avoiding the rooftop sentries. He moved as quickly as he could up the empty street, until he was safely pressed up against the side of a brown low-to-the-ground building on the outskirts of the parking lot. It was some kind of auxiliary building, with a small flight of stairs leading to a side door.

He leaned around the corner and did the numbers in his head.

Four Humvees. Six men outside the lobby. Two more on the rooftop that he could see, probably more that he couldn't. He and Mike had already killed four, and Jones said there were sixteen in all. That left four unaccounted for. Maybe one of the men standing around the Humvees was Kellerson himself. Will would have loved to take out Kellerson first.

Cut the head off the snake and the body falls.

He pulled back and waited. The building's wooden wall felt flimsy behind his back. It wasn't going to provide him with a lot of protection when the bullets started flying, but at least they couldn't see him from either the front driveway or the rooftop.

Any time now, Mike.

The former lieutenant had been careful to make his way down the street before looping back toward the hospital so that he couldn't be seen. He was now perched on a big billboard fifty meters from the end of the parking. The sign featured a man in a suit and tie smiling brightly, holding a wad of cash, with the caption "The Lafayette Hammer."

Will didn't have to wait too long before a gunshot split the calm afternoon.

Mike's bullet may or may not have hit anyone. Will couldn't see and didn't care to look. Mike was firing on semi-auto, spacing out his ammo and trying to distract the guards on the ground and on the rooftop in equal measure. Almost instantly, there was return fire. Will didn't worry about those, either. The distance was too vast, and unless someone up there had a long-distance riflescope, Will didn't think they had a snowball's chance in hell of actually hitting Mike, and vice versa.

He slipped out from behind the building and took another look at the men gathered outside the hospital lobby. The ones at the Humvees had moved into defensive positions behind the heavy vehicles, while the children inside smartly made themselves small.

The men in hazmat suits weren't shooting back yet, probably because they couldn't locate Mike's position.

Will took aim, raising the rifle slightly over the roofs of cars in his way, and shot the first man in the left hip. The man jerked, stunned, and turned around, presenting his entire body. Will shot him again in the chest.

He immediately swiveled his rifle, picking up another man in a hazmat suit, this one standing farther away from the Humvee than the others. The man saw his comrade go down and turned frantically in Will's direction. Will shot him in the face, shattering one of the gas mask's lenses. The man's head jerked back and he crumpled to the driveway.

The others reacted as Will slipped back behind the side of the building. They opened fire in his direction and predictably, the wall didn't stand a chance. Chunks of cheap wood chipped and came undone as Will began moving away from the corner. Then one of the snipers on the rooftop joined in, his bullets punching through the wall and digging into the concrete walkway.

Two down. Ten to go.

When the building he was moving across began chipping at a faster rate, Will picked up his speed toward the other end before slipping around to the back. He leaned out to gauge what was ahead of him.

There was nothing between him and the main hospital building except for sixty meters of open driveway and some trees. A few trees. So few, it was pointless to even spend a second counting them. As far as he could tell, there was absolutely nothing to keep him from being seen and shot at.

This is gonna suck.

He unclipped the radio from his hip. "Mike."

"You ready?" Mike said through the radio.

"No, but count it down anyway."

"Good luck," Mike said. "On the count of three. One, two—*three.*"

There was a hellacious spurt of gunfire as Mike switched his rifle from semi-auto to full-auto and unleashed on the building. Will counted to two, then began darting across the open ground, praying Mike's fusillade would do what it was supposed to—keep the rooftop snipers from looking down at him.

Will had gotten ten meters into the open when he risked a glance up and saw the closest man on the rooftop crouching, firing back in Mike's direction. Mike's bullets were speckling the north tower and falling short.

By the time Will was halfway to the west tower, the men gathered outside the lobby had spotted him and turned their guns on him. Bullets slashed through the air around him, tore chunks off the concrete driveway, and shredded the branches of a tree over his head. Will kept as low as possible, zig-zagging, making himself into an erratic target. A couple of bullets came dangerously close, but he was getting by.

That is, until he felt a sharp pain in his left arm, just above the elbow, as a round finally found its mark.

He had left a bloody trail behind him by the time he reached the west tower, sliding against the rough brick wall and moving away from the edge just as it was obliterated by gunfire.

He was separated from the north tower by only thirty meters, and the bullets were coming fast and furious as everyone on the ground concentrated their fire on him now. They must have also realized Mike had no chance of hitting them from his location. Soon, they were going to come charging, taking advantage of their number. They had to know it was just him by now against—how many were left?

Still too many.

He grabbed a black handkerchief out of his pack and wrapped it tightly around his arm over the squirting hole. Blood seeped out as he tightened the fabric and winced. Good enough for now.

He had been listening, but hadn't heard any sounds of approaching footsteps, even though Mike had stopped firing by now, either to reload or switch weapons. At least, Will hoped that was what Mike was doing at the moment. The lack of noise coming from Mike, either through the radio or from his rifles, made Will slightly nervous.

Don't die on me yet, Mike. I still need your diversion.

A sudden and eerie silence fell over the city as everyone seemed to stop shooting at almost the exact same time. It was so quiet Will didn't have any trouble picking up the unmistakable noise of a Humvee's engine roaring to life, followed by thirty-seven-inch military-grade tires spinning against concrete.

Oh, hell.

He leaned out from behind the corner and saw what he expected to see—one of the Humvees coming right at him, two of the hazmat suits racing behind it, while a third man was emerging out of the rooftop opening, where a gun turret was supposed to go. Now that he was looking at the Humvee from the front, Will saw that it had two thick sheets of metal soldered onto the grill, like the wedge on a snow plow.

The third man hanging out of the Humvee's rooftop saw him and opened fire with an M4.

Will pulled his head back as a section of the corner shattered near his head. He took off along the length of the west tower, wondering how pissed off Lara was going to be when she found out he got killed going up against a Humvee.

Because he was fucked. He was truly and royally *fucked.*

Whose bright idea was this again? Oh, right, yours.

To add insult to injury, Mike was probably dead. Or dying. Or wounded. Either way, he was on his own.

Will was still ten meters from the other side of the tower—and elusive safety—when the Humvee appeared behind him, its tires sliding to a stop with a loud, menacing crunch. Will spun, lifting his rifle. He hadn't turned all the way around when he heard two quick shots and—turning fully—saw the man in the turret opening disappear back into the Humvee. Will didn't know what had happened, or why the two men in the back of the vehicle were shooting, except not at him. They were shooting *up at the rooftop.*

He pushed aside the questions and fired at the front windshield of the Humvee, aiming over the metal wedge and at the figure behind the steering wheel. It took nearly half of his magazine on full-auto before his bullets punched through the spiderwebbed glass and reached the driver, who seemed to flinch in his seat before slumping forward violently. The man must have also stepped on the gas in death, because the vehicle lurched right at Will.

He dived out of the way, flattening his back against the tower wall as the Humvee blasted past him, stopping only after it had rammed into a Toyota Camry parked along the curb, the metal wedge eviscerating the smaller car's side like it was a plastic toy.

Will expected to see the two men running behind the Humvee take their shots at him, but they were nowhere to be found. He hurried away from the wall, glanced up at the rooftop, and saw a solitary figure looking back down at him, waving.

Gaby.

He waved back, though he swore she was wearing one of the hazmat suits. Or was he seeing things?

A moment later, Gaby disappeared back behind the edge of the rooftop, and Will jogged to the corner, reloading as he went. He looked out and glimpsed the backsides of the two hazmat suits racing back to the north tower and the remaining Humvees.

He shot the closest one in the back, but before he could take down the second one, the man darted behind a supporting column.

Two of the remaining three military vehicles had come to life and were already moving slowly down the driveway, picking up speed with every second. The man who had hidden behind the support column rushed forward and threw open one of the doors, diving inside. Will saw children in the backseats of the Humvees, flailing against the window, screaming silently back at him.

He watched helplessly, feeling about two feet tall, as the fleeing vehicles circled the driveway, turning into the street, and disappearing like ghosts.

Suddenly he was alone on the hotel grounds, surrounded by empty cars and bodies.

Will unclipped the radio. "Mike, come in."

He waited, but there was no response.

"Mike, come in."

Nothing.

"Mike, talk to me, man. You still there?"

Shit.

The man he had shot moments ago hadn't moved from the spot, gas masked face turned on its side. Will searched his pouches and collected spare magazines, before moving toward the front lobby, watching for signs of movement from the left-behind Humvee. When he was sure there was no one there, he turned his attention to the hospital doors.

The front driveway curved slightly to the right and toward the front doors before curving back left again. Will stepped over the bodies and spent a few seconds looking in at the remaining Humvee, then at the tire tracks of the two that had fled. Fresh motor oil stains on the driveway and the familiar scent of spilled diesel remained in the air.

He wasted another second staring into the lobby, at the creatures he knew were inside, even if he couldn't see them. They were watching him back, waiting, because that was what they did best.

And why not? They had all the time in the world.

Will turned and kicked something on the ground. He looked down at a dirty, ragged pink Hello Kitty plush doll. Will picked it up and stuffed it into his pack without thinking.

Above him, the familiar whine of a turbine engine started up. Jen's helicopter.

Will glanced back across the parking lot in the direction the Humvees had gone.

"The creatures, they have a plan," Jones had said. *"It involves the kids. I don't know any more than that. Just that they're concentrating on the kids now..."*

CHAPTER 14

GABY

IT SOUNDED LIKE a war was raging outside the building. Not that Gaby had time to process what was happening beyond the hallway of the tenth floor. There were more pressing matters, such as the heavy footsteps approaching the other side of the rooftop stairwell door.

Gaby didn't have to wait for very long before the doorknob began turning.

She strafed the door from left to right on full-auto, then just for good measure, from top to bottom. She didn't stop firing until she had emptied the entire magazine. She heard the sound of falling bodies on the other side of the door, the clattering of weapons against solid concrete.

She took two steps away from the door, moving sideways in case someone fired back, then calmly ejected the magazine and slapped in a new one without thinking about it.

Shoot, reload, and repeat.

Then she waited for a reply of some kind. Bullets. Gunfire. Screams.

There was nothing.

Behind her, the others shuffled nervously. They were farther down the hallway, but they might as well have been standing an inch behind her because they were making so much noise. Or maybe that was just her imagination. Her senses were heightened beyond belief.

She couldn't make out anything through the two dozen or so

holes she had put into the door, only the dull, gray wall in the background. So that was a good sign. If anyone were still alive, she would have seen movement flitting across the holes.

The radio clipped to the dead man in front of her squawked again, and she heard the same deep male voice: "What the hell was that? Where did that come from? Gary? Janice? Someone answer me!"

Muffled gunshots, like firecrackers, echoed from the other side of the radio.

Then Benny was suddenly crouched next to her, breathing too hard. "Now what?"

"I need you to open the door."

He gave her a terrified look.

"Just throw it open and step out of the way," she said.

Benny summoned his courage, slung his rifle, and moved toward the door, stepping over the dead body from earlier. Gaby glanced back at Amy, Jen, and the kid with the button nose, keeping low to the ground twenty yards behind her. They were watching her closely, waiting.

She looked back at Benny and gave him the go-ahead nod.

He began counting down to himself, then grabbed the doorknob and pulled in one quick motion.

Gaby's finger tightened against the trigger, but she didn't have to press it. There were two bodies in hazmat suits crumpled on the stairwell landing before her, blood dripping from holes in the fronts of their uniforms. She had put almost as many bullets into the two bodies as she had the brick wall behind them, and there was a fine white concrete cloud hovering inside the LED-illuminated room.

Gaby stood up and looked back at Jen. "We have to go up."

Jen grinned back at her. "After you, G.I. Jane."

"G.I. what?"

"*G.I. Jane.* That movie with Demi Moore?"

"Who's Demi Moore?"

Jen shook her head. "Never mind. Let's go."

Gaby looked at Benny. "You okay?"

He nodded. "Rooftop?"

"Yeah. While they're still busy with whoever is out there. Maybe Will. Maybe Mike. Or both."

"Let's do it, then," he said.

She could almost believe there was some bravado in there somewhere, if she didn't know for certain he was scared out of his mind. She didn't blame him. To Benny, Jen, and Amy, this was probably the first time they had actually seen combat, before or since The Purge. It hadn't been quite as uneventful for her.

"Stay behind me, okay?" she said.

"Don't have to tell me twice," he nodded back.

Gaby stepped into the stairwell, rifle at the ready in case someone poked their head down from the top of the stairs. There was no one, so she continued toward the first step and went up. Benny's labored breathing followed closely behind. She wished he wasn't moving so close to her. If she turned around now, she would crack his skull with the rifle. Didn't he realize that? Probably not.

Amy and Jen entered behind them with the kid.

She made it all the way up to the door without encountering resistance, probably because whoever was up there was too busy shooting at someone else. How many were on the rooftop right now? Definitely more than one, because the shooting never stopped. The only way that could be possible was if someone else was firing while another person reloaded.

She looked back at Benny, still standing too close behind her. "I need you to open the door for me again."

He nodded, then moved forward and gripped the door handle. The door opened outward, so he would have to push out. It was hot in the stairwell, and Benny's face was already slick with sweat. She could feel her own perspiration running down the sides of her face.

"Try to stay to the side," Gaby said. "Don't move into my line of fire. Whenever you're ready…"

Benny turned back to the door and began counting to himself. Then, taking a deep breath, he opened the door, rammed his entire body into it, and stumbled outside, losing his footing on the loose, graveled rooftop along the way. He was still carrying the medical supply bag, and its weight probably hadn't done him any favors.

Gaby rushed past Benny. She saw wide open skies, but no one in front of her. The door had opened up into the center of the rooftop, and the first thing she saw was Jen's helicopter, sitting where she had last seen it.

Loud, booming gunfire erupted from behind her on the other side of the stairwell access building.

She turned to her left and navigated as fast as she could around the building. A woman standing at the edge of the rooftop wearing a white hazmat suit turned in response to the sound of Gaby's boots.

Janice, I presume.

The woman hesitated, just as Gaby assumed she would. Even without wearing the gas mask, the fact that she was still wearing a hazmat suit caused the woman to waste precious seconds processing the information. While she was doing that, Gaby shot her once in the chest, and because she couldn't be sure, shot the woman a second time even as she was going down.

She heard gravel shuffling loudly and swiveled to her left, seeing a man in a hazmat suit standing on the other side pointing his M4 at her. She stared into the barrel of the man's rifle, while her own was still in the process of coming up, knowing, but unable to accept, that she was too late, she was dead—

She flinched at the loud sound of gunfire and waited for the pain. Except there was none. Instead, Gaby watched the man crumple in front of her as two bloody dots spread across his chest like bright red watercolor.

Gaby looked over and found Benny standing on the other side of the rooftop access building, numbly lowering his AR-15. He looked almost stunned by what had just happened, his eyes glued to the dead body in front of him.

There was a loud roar from below them and Gaby snapped out of it first, hurrying to the edge of the rooftop and looking down. There were four military Humvees parked in front of the lobby, and one of them had made a wide U-turn and was picking up speed. There was a man poking his head out from a circular hole in the roof while two others jogged behind the vehicle, using it like some kind of moving shield. They were making a beeline toward the west tower.

She ran back, passing Benny, who still looked stunned, then Jen and Amy farther back. Jen shouted something at her, but Gaby was too busy concentrating on the Humvee below, tracing its progress by sound. She turned right and ran down the length of the west tower rooftop, just in time to see the Humvee taking the corner below her.

And there, a figure moving away from the charging Humvee. She couldn't tell if it was Will or Mike, or someone else, because she could only see the man's head. But the people in the Humvee were collaborators, and that was all she needed to know.

The man standing out of the hole in the Humvee's roof was taking aim at the running figure when Gaby fired down at him. Her first shot missed, hitting the desert camo rooftop instead, but it startled the man enough that he abandoned his target and looked up at her. Her second shot hit him just above the right eye, and his lifeless body slipped back through the hole.

The two men running behind the Humvee opened up on her. Gaby dived backward, falling to the gravel floor as bullets tore at the rooftop edge, sprinkling her with chunks of loosed brick. She didn't know how long the gunfire went; it might have just been a few seconds. Her heart was pounding in her chest, making telling time difficult.

Then the shooting stopped, and she heard what sounded like a car crash in the distance.

She pulled herself back up and moved slowly back toward the edge. It was so suddenly quiet that she couldn't help but feel as if she was being lured into the open. She cautiously peered down one more time and saw the man she had saved, looking back up at her.

Will.

She waved down at him, and he waved back.

Gaby backtracked and hurried over to another section of the rooftop. She glimpsed the two men in hazmat suits fleeing back toward the front driveway. She lifted her rifle, but they were moving too fast and she was at the wrong angle. She heard a gunshot and one of the men stumbled and fell, but the second one managed to slip behind a support column and take cover.

A moment later, two of the Humvees roared to life and took off. She watched them go, winding around the driveway, picking up speed as they drove through the parking lot. She was glad to see them retreating, glad it was over, until she saw the small faces pressed up against the back windshields.

No. No...

Then they turned into the street and was gone, the loud sounds of their heavy engines fading up the road. She didn't know how long she stood there and listened, but it seemed like hours. Or maybe that was just her mind reliving the sight of the small faces in the back of the Humvees.

The children. Where are they taking the children?

IT TOOK JEN a while to find a safe place to land the helicopter. She hovered over the parking lot, then tried the side streets, but there were always too many cables, cars, or trees in the way. Finally, she found a mostly empty parking lot in a strip mall half a block away and touched down.

Will was moving under them the entire time. Gaby, sitting in the cockpit's passenger seat, spotted him climbing up, then down, a billboard between where they eventually landed and the hospital parking lot.

Gaby hopped out of the helicopter before the rotors stopped spinning and jogged over to meet Will halfway. He had a black military-type backpack slung over his back.

"Where's Mike?" she asked.

Will shook his head.

Gaby looked back at Jen, Benny, and Amy as they climbed down the helicopter. The kid stayed behind, looking out the back window, button nose pressed against the glass.

"Where's Mike?" Jen asked as soon as she reached them.

Will pointed back at the billboard he had climbed earlier. "He was covering me from there. One of them must have gotten in a lucky shot."

"Are you sure?" Amy asked.

"He's still up there."

The three of them hurried past him and toward the billboard.

Gaby stayed where she was. "The other two guys?"

"Snipers on the roof took them out when we were coming back," Will said. "What about everyone inside?"

She shook her head. "There's no one left. They killed everyone."

"Not everyone. They took the children."

"I saw them in the Humvees. Why did they take the children, Will? For the ghouls?"

"Mike and I captured one of the collaborators. He told us the ghouls had some kind of plan for them. Their orders were to kill the adults and anyone who fought back."

"That doesn't make sense. Don't they need every ounce of blood they can get? There's not exactly a lot of us still running around."

"Apparently not anymore."

He looked back at the billboard, at Jen and Amy as they climbed up to the scaffolding while Benny waited at the bottom.

"Your arm," she said, noticing the bloody handkerchief around his left arm.

"It's fine. Just a scratch."

"I grabbed the medical supplies Amy put together for us. They're in the helicopter."

"Good. At least we won't be going back empty-handed."

"Are we going back to the island?"

"I don't know yet." Will looked down at his watch. "Those Humvees…"

"Tell me we're going after them," she said, surprised by the conviction in her voice. "We can't just let them take the kids, Will."

"It's not entirely up to us."

Jen, Amy, and Benny were already walking back toward them. Amy had an M4 rifle slung over her shoulder, and Benny was carrying a pack similar to Will's. They look sullen, like relatives at a funeral. Which, she guessed, wasn't too far from the truth.

"Should we bury him?" Jen asked, when she finally reached them.

"We can," Will said. "Or we can go after the Humvees. They left with the kids inside, and they have a thirty-minute head start on us."

"What are we going to do?" Benny asked.

"It's your call," Will said. "The three of you. It's your friends up there in the hospital. If you want to chase them and get the kids back, Gaby and I will come with you. Or you can cut your losses and come back to the island with us."

The three of them exchanged a look, and Gaby was happy to see the strong resolve in Amy's and Jen's faces, though Benny didn't look completely sold on the idea. He looked even younger than his eighteen years at that moment, bad facial hair and all.

"We can't just let them get away with it," Jen said.

"Those were our friends," Amy said. "Those kids…we knew their parents. They're our families, too."

"What about you?" Will asked Benny.

"How would we even find them?" Benny said.

"Look around you," Jen said. There was a look of determination on her face, maybe even anger. "This city's dead. If they're on the road, we'll find them, because they'll be the only things moving for miles."

"COMM'S DOWN," JEN said when she saw Will putting on his headset.

"What happened?" Will asked.

"See for yourself."

She had discovered it back on the rooftop—someone had put a bullet through the box that controlled the helicopter's communications system. The damage had been limited, and according to Jen, everything she needed to fly was still intact.

Will put down the headset and glanced back at her. "You didn't grab the ham radio too, did you?"

"It didn't occur to me, sorry," Gaby said. "Should we go back for it?"

"No, it'll take too much time, and the attackers already have too big a lead on us. We can always come back for it later."

Gaby nodded, even though the idea of returning to Mercy Hospital made her squeamish. After the gunfight on the rooftop, she had raced back downstairs for her pack, in her room, which thankfully the collaborators hadn't bothered to raid. That had meant running through the bloodied hallways, and she didn't feel like doing it all over again.

"Let's go, Jen," Will said. "We're burning daylight."

Jen lifted them back into the air and angled the helicopter north. Benny, sitting next to Gaby, was staring out the window, looking back at the hospital. She could only imagine all the emotions going through him at the moment. Tom was back there, along with all of his other friends. Dead now, all of them.

Nothing lasts forever out here. I learned that with Matt and Josh.

"Will, your arm," Amy said, leaning forward in her seat, her movements constrained by the kid in her lap. "Let me look at it."

"It's fine, just a scratch," Will said.

"Are you sure?"

"Yes."

Will picked up his pack from the floor and put it on his lap, then took out a bottle of water. He unwound the bloodied handkerchief from around his arm and poured water over the wound, then wiped it down with a new, clean handkerchief.

Gaby leaned forward. "Will, I have the medical supplies back here."

"We might need them later."

He disinfected the wound, then wrapped gauze tape tightly around it, before shoving everything back into the pack. It didn't look like much of a dressing at all, but Will didn't seem bothered by its lack of aesthetics.

They didn't know where the Humvees were going, but using their last known direction, Jen guessed they were heading toward Interstate 10 about two miles north. The highway was still the fastest route in and out of the city, but the Humvees weren't exactly made to travel in heavy, unmoving traffic. Gaby wondered how they expected to maneuver through the car-strewn roads.

They found out when they saw cars along the thicker parts of the highway stacked up along the sides, where they had been pushed to clear a path for a Humvee-sized vehicle to move through freely. The attackers were heading east on I-10.

"Humvees can do that?" Gaby asked.

"No, but the ones I saw had thick sheets of metal soldered onto the front grills," Will said, "like you'd see on snow plows. It looked like they've been using that method for a while."

"So they're literally just pushing cars out of their path."

"Looks like it."

"Makes it easy to track them," Jen said.

"In the city, yes," Will said, "but once they reach the country-side, they wouldn't need to push cars around anymore."

"I guess we better catch them before then."

Gaby sat in the back with Amy, Benny, and the button-nose kid. The Bell 407 helicopter was designed for two in the cockpit and three in the back. The two gym bags filled with medical supplies, along with her backpack, were on the floor around their feet, further limiting their ability to move around. Benny was in the middle between her and Amy, his rifle between his legs.

She leaned against her window to get a better look at the high-way stretched out below them, straining to see what lay ahead. The wall of vehicles pushed to the sides went on endlessly, and she wondered how far they could have gotten in the forty-minute head start they had on the helicopter.

"Any ideas where they might have gone?" Will was asking Jen.

"I-10 joins up with I-49 in about a mile," Jen said. "If they keep straight after that, it's sixty miles to Baton Rouge, the closest big city."

"What if they turn off I-49?"

"Alexandria is the first big city, about ninety miles up the Interstate, and lots of smaller cities in between. There's also Sandwhite Wildlife State Park."

"What's there?"

"About 15,000 acres of state-run woods, give or take."

"So they're probably not going there."

"Who the hell knows. I didn't even know these people existed until two days ago."

Gaby looked over at Benny. He was staring straight ahead, trying to concentrate on something outside the cockpit window. Maybe the bugs hitting the glass. He looked so young and unprepared for all of this, but she had to remind herself that he had saved her life on the rooftop.

He's full of surprises.

She put her hand over his. He flinched at the surprise contact, then softened when she gave him her most comforting smile. She leaned over and kissed him on the cheek. When she pulled back, he was blushing.

"You'll love the island," she said.

"Does this mean you're taking me there?" he asked, grinning awkwardly back at her.

"One hundred percent." Gaby looked across Benny at Amy. "Does he have a name?" she asked, nodding at the boy.

"Freddie," Amy said.

"Hey, Freddie," Gaby said to the boy.

He looked over at her for a moment, seemed to think about responding, but decided against it and looked back out the window instead.

"I've tried all day," Amy said. "Nothing."

"What about his parents?"

Amy shook her head. She didn't have to elaborate, because they both knew what that meant.

"The loop's up ahead," Jen announced.

They were coming up to the intersection of I-10 and I-49, which, according to a big sign, met at a large loop called the Marabond Throughway. They saw right away that the trail of vehicles pushed to the sides didn't continue along I-10, but instead moved toward the curving ramp that joined up with I-49. Because the off-ramp was a tight squeeze, some of the cars had been pushed off the highway completely and were now scattered along the ground below.

"I-49," Will said. "They're heading north."

"Looks like it," Jen nodded.

"The closest big city is Alexandria?"

"Yeah."

"How many people?"

"Two hundred thousand, give or take."

"A lot of people means a lot of ghouls," Will said. Then, "How are you for fuel?"

Jen checked her gauges. "If we catch them before Alexandria, I should be fine." Then Jen saw something else outside the cockpit window: "Do you see that? Is that one of the Humvees we've been chasing?"

Will leaned forward to get a better view.

"How many did you see take off?" Jen asked.

"Two."

"Could that be one of them?"

"It's possible."

Gaby leaned against her window, trying to spot the Humvee among the cars. Instead, she caught a glint of something metallic— and a man leaning out the open side hatch of a parked van on the highway below them. He was wearing some kind of camouflage uniform and had something that looked like a long, green tube resting on his right shoulder. He was pointing it up at the sky—*right at them.*

"Will!" Gaby shouted. "Down there!"

Will glanced back at her, saw where she was pointing, and looked down and immediately saw the man. "Rocket launcher!" he shouted. "Jen, evasive maneuvers!"

Jen jerked reflexively on the control stick and the helicopter banked left just as Gaby saw a rocket slash across the sky, trailing white smoke behind it. She looked over and saw Benny staring back at her, eyes wide with terror. On the other side of Benny, Amy was clutching the boy.

The helicopter kept turning, and though Gaby had no idea what a helicopter could and couldn't do, she had a feeling this wasn't something it was *supposed* to do.

"Hold on!" Will shouted from the cockpit. "Everyone hold on to something!"

Gaby grabbed Benny and he reciprocated, clutching on to her so tightly she almost couldn't breathe. Then her world shook as something violently slammed into the helicopter and there was a loud, strange scream—not human, but more like metal cutting metal.

In the part of her mind where logical thought was still possible, she guessed that the rocket hadn't landed a direct hit, because she was still alive and not incinerated. But it was close enough that the helicopter was spinning out of control and was clearly falling out of the sky. She had the strangest feeling of being weightless.

The helicopter was now emitting a loud, screeching noise around her. Or maybe that was Amy screaming. Benny's grip on her was so tight, almost cutting off her oxygen, that she wasn't entirely certain if everything she was hearing was coming from outside or inside her head.

She looked over her shoulder and back at the window just in time to see the rotor blades—still spinning at impossible speeds—plummeting out of the sky alongside them. It had come completely detached from the helicopter and was engulfed in flames…

BOOK TWO

GIMME SHELTER

CHAPTER 15

LARA

SHE SPENT MOST of the afternoon trying to ignore the fact that she couldn't reach Will at Mercy Hospital. Or reach anyone there at all. The only time she made contact was through Jen's helicopter, but the man with the deep voice who answered hadn't picked up the second time.

Her last contact with Mercy Hospital had been two hours ago.

Lara paced the Tower's third floor, looking at the ham radio every few minutes. She willed it to squawk, for Will's voice to come through. If not Will's, then Gaby's or Jen's. She would have settled for just about anyone at the moment.

But there was nothing.

What the hell is going on over there?

Either they had turned off their radios, or they were purposefully ignoring her call. Neither answer made any sense. Had she allowed Will to walk into an ambush? Will was certain Jen could be trusted, and Lara had learned to trust his instincts. There was nothing "squirrelly" about Jen. Will would have noticed, just as Danny noticed it from West and Brody in the first few seconds after meeting them. The two of them just *knew* when something wasn't right.

There had to be another explanation.

What the hell is going on over there?

"Still nothing from Mercy Hospital?" Danny asked, coming through the door behind her.

She shook her head and continued pacing.

"Nothing," Maddie, standing at the window, said.

"What about our designated emergency frequency?" Danny asked. "If Mercy Hospital's MIA, Will or Gaby would be using it to try to contact us."

"I tried that, too," Lara said, grinding her teeth. "Nothing."

Maddie and Danny exchanged a brief look that they were probably hoping she didn't catch.

"What's going on?" she asked Danny.

"You've been up here for two hours," he said. "Go back to the hotel. Go eat something."

"Soon."

"When?"

"*Soon*, Danny."

Maddie put a comforting hand on her shoulder. "He'll be fine, Lara. It's Will. He's pretty good at being fine."

"I know," she said, smiling. She hoped it was at least semi-convincing.

"Come downstairs and get something to eat with me. Danny will call if he gets anything on the radio."

Lara nodded. "I'll be right down."

Maddie gave her a pursed smile that said she didn't entirely believe her, but the smaller woman left anyway. Lara waited until she couldn't hear Maddie's footsteps before looking over at Danny. He was watching her closely.

"He's in trouble," she said.

"What else did the guy say?"

"That was it. He cut the connection and hasn't picked up again. No one has. Someone *should* have, Danny."

"It doesn't mean Will's in trouble."

"Then why hasn't he called back? He knows we'd be monitoring the emergency frequency by now."

"Maybe he doesn't have access to the building anymore. Or a radio."

"That doesn't make any sense."

"Last night he said he was going to help this Mike guy clear out an Archers early in the morning, right?"

"Yeah, so?"

"So maybe he wasn't at the hospital when everything went bad, when this dickhead you talked to took over the place. Or so he says."

"He sounded pretty damn certain."

"Look, if this was Joe Blow we're talking about, I'd be worried. If it was Joe Blow's ex-military badass brother-in-law, I'd still be worried. But it's Willie boy, so I'm not all that worried."

"What about Gaby? I haven't heard anything from her, either."

"If Will's around, he'll look after her. And vice versa."

"She's just a kid…"

"She's eighteen."

"Nineteen."

"Nineteen? When did that happen?"

"Today. She turned nineteen today."

"Huh. I guess I gotta get her a present when she comes back."

If *she comes back.* If *they come back.*

"Go get something to eat," Danny said. "You haven't eaten since last night."

"That's not true."

"It's not? Then what did you eat this morning?"

"I…" She shook her head. "I was too busy helping you catch West all night."

"And West has been caught. So go down to the kitchen and eat something. It'll make you feel better." He unclipped his radio and held it up. "I'll give you a ring if something comes through. Promise."

She hesitated.

"*Go,* Lara," Danny said.

◄━━▌ ▐━━►

FOOD HELPED, BUT it didn't keep her from thinking about Will. Or Gaby. Or about what was happening eighty miles away in Lafayette that very moment. But at least it kept her from fainting, because she had felt lightheaded on the walk over, and for a moment didn't think she would actually make it.

Mae had become a fixture in the kitchen along with Jo, Bonnie's eighteen-year-old sister. Sarah was more than happy to spread the work around, and although Mae brought some cooking experience, Jo was clueless but, according to Sarah, anxious to learn.

Bonnie found Lara while she was finishing up a plate of foil-baked crappie outside on the patio, watching Lucy, Kylie, and Logan racing around the expansive grounds of the hotel, while Vera, Elise, and Jenny chased them. She wished she could be more like them, allow herself to forget what was happening out there. With Will, with Gaby…

What the hell is going on out there?

"Still no word from Will?" Bonnie asked.

Lara shook her head. "Danny's keeping an eye on the radio."

"From what I hear, Will's extremely capable."

"He is."

"Then he should be fine."

"I hope so."

"You were lucky to find him and Danny."

I wasn't always so lucky.

"I was," she said.

Bonnie leaned against the railing and watched the kids. After a while, she said, "I've missed that."

"What?"

"Children laughing. Not that we've had a lot to laugh about, but they've persevered. God knows how, but they never once broke down during all those miserable days and nights hiding in basements and homes."

"Kids are adaptable. We don't give them enough credit for it." She looked over at Bonnie, who looked preoccupied with something. "What is it?"

"This whole thing with West and Brody… I'm sorry."

"You don't have to keep apologizing. It's done and over with."

"I know, but I still… God, I never wanted it to be like this."

"As Will would say if he was here now, it is what it is."

"You love Will."

"A lot," she said without hesitation.

Bonnie smiled. "That's bad news for Roy. He's been trying to enlist me into talking him up to you."

She couldn't help but smile. "He doesn't give up, does he?"

"He can be very stubborn. Roy was the one who kept us alive before we ran across West and Brody. We lost a couple of people during that time, and I think he blames himself. I've tried to tell him he shouldn't, that he did his best."

"If it makes him feel any better, the old me would have totally swooned over him."

"Missed his chance by that much, huh?"

"Yup."

They looked back at the kids. Bonnie's girls had tired themselves out and were resting in the grass, while Vera, Elise, and Jenny ran rings around them.

Her radio squawked, and she heard Maddie's voice: "Lara, Danny, we have a problem."

So what else is new?

She unclipped the radio. "What's going on, Maddie?"

"It's West."

Next to her, Bonnie tensed at the name.

"What about him?" Lara asked.

"He's gone," Maddie said.

"GWEN DISCOVERED IT when she brought his lunch over," Maddie said. "She came and woke me from my nap because my room was closest, and I called you guys."

"When was the last time someone came to see him?" Lara asked.

"Four hours ago," Sarah said. "Around eight in the morning, when I had Bonnie bring him his breakfast."

Bonnie nodded. "He was in there when I brought it over."

The tray still sat on the bed, a used plastic spoon and crumbs of bread left behind on a Styrofoam plate.

"So he could have gotten free any time between eight and now," Lara said. "Four hours."

"Who had the key?" Bonnie asked.

"I did," Lara said, pulling the key out of her pocket. "Not that he needed it, apparently."

She pulled the door toward her. The deadbolt was still in place, but someone had used a prying bar to break the door open at the strike plate. There was a big crater left behind in the doorframe. The wood around the area where the lock would be had caved in.

"Where's Roy?" Lara asked.

"He's on the beach," Maddie said.

Lara nodded. "How old is Derek?" she asked Bonnie.

"Fourteen," Bonnie said. "Why?"

"He's a pretty big kid for fourteen. I thought he was sixteen when I first saw him."

"I guess."

"Where is he now?"

"You think…?"

"It's not one of the girls, I know that much. You need a lot of strength to do this to the door."

"Oh, God," Jo said quietly.

Lara looked over at her. "What is it?"

Jo turned to Bonnie, as if asking for permission. Bonnie nodded.

Jo looked at Lara. "Derek always sort of looked up to Brody and West. You can't really blame him," she added almost defensively. "They're big and tough guys. Kids like Derek are impressionable, and whatever we thought of them, we couldn't have gotten here without those two."

"Where is Derek now?" Lara asked.

◄▬▬▮   ▮▬▬►

DEREK WAS EXACTLY where Bonnie said he would be—in his room, still wearing the same hoodie from yesterday. He sat on the end of his bed, hands in his pockets, as if he had been waiting for them and was relieved when they finally showed up.

"You found out, huh?" he said.

Bonnie exchanged a look with Lara.

"Where is he?" Lara asked him.

"I don't know. He said it was better if I didn't know, so you couldn't force me to tell you. I told him to take me too, but he wouldn't, that it was better for me to stay here. Are you going to kick me off the island now?"

Lara didn't answer him. She turned to Bonnie. "I need to talk to Danny about this."

"I'll stay here and talk to him for a while," Bonnie said. "If I find out anything, I'll come get you."

Lara nodded. She left Derek's room and stepped back into Hallway A. Maddie and Jo were waiting for her outside.

"God, he really did do it," Jo said, looking sick to her stomach.

"Like you said, he's impressionable." She started up the hallway, the two women falling in behind her. Lara said into the radio, "Danny."

"So, go West, young man rides again?" Danny said through the radio.

"Can you see anything from up there?"

"I'm scanning every inch of the island, but if he's back in the western half, we're probably going to have to do this the old-fashioned way...again."

"Lock the door to your floor, just in case."

"Will do, boss."

She sighed. She still hated that title.

"Roy," she said into the radio. "Where are you?"

"On the beach," Roy said through the radio. "You need me somewhere else?"

"No. Stay where you are. Radio immediately if you spot him. He might be going for the boats, and if he does, let him. Don't try to stop him."

"You mean just let him go?"

"Yes. At this point, if he wants to leave the island, he'll be doing us a favor."

"Okay," Roy said.

She looked over at Maddie. "Go back to the lobby, just in case he shows up there."

Maddie nodded and jogged off, one hand on her holstered Glock.

Jo moved up alongside her. "Can he get his hands on any weapons? Besides the knives in the kitchen, I mean?"

"No, we have everything locked up in the Tower basement as a precaution."

"So he probably only has that prying bar..."

"Probably."

"He's still hurt. Maybe he won't try anything."

"Yeah," Lara said, though she didn't believe it.

What was that Will always said? *"Hope for the best, prepare for the worst."*

She looked over at Jo. "Tell me the truth, Jo. Will he hurt the kids?"

Jo shook her head. "Brody, maybe, but I don't think West would. He's really not that bad of a guy, honestly. He might have hit Bonnie once or twice, and he got aggressive when he wanted her to, you know, do things that she didn't want to."

She doesn't know about West and Brody killing the other survivors for their supplies and the gold watch. Bonnie and Roy never told her.

"But, I don't know," Jo continued, looking very uncomfortable. "I don't think he would stoop to hurting the kids, but I could be wrong."

"Go bring the girls into the hotel anyway, just to be safe."

Jo nodded and hurried off.

Lara stopped at her room and went inside. She hadn't completely lied to Jo. Most of the weapons were in the Tower, just not all of them.

She closed the door and walked straight to the nightstand. The sight of the soft, comfortable bed reminded her that she hadn't slept in a while, ever since waking up in the middle of the night to chase West. She thought about lying down for a moment to catch that nap Maddie had suggested. What would it hurt?

An hour. Maybe thirty minutes?

That'll have to wait.

She opened the nightstand drawer and froze.

The spare Glock she was looking for wasn't there.

She was still trying to process that when she heard the closet door opening behind her and reached for the Glock in her holster— a split second before she felt the cold barrel of the missing gun pressed against the back of her neck.

"I figured you might have a spare piece or two in your room," West said behind her. "Is it yours or the boyfriend's?"

"Does it matter?" she asked.

She was surprised she wasn't more afraid, that her voice didn't break slightly or tremble when she responded. Why weren't her legs shaking? A man had a gun pressed into the back of her neck. She should be scared right about now.

"Not really," West said.

"Don't do anything stupid, West."

"Shut up, Lara. You don't get to tell me what to do anymore." He pulled the other Glock from her holster. "Now, be a good girl and keep your trap shut for once, or I might just put a bullet in you out of pure spite."

"West, don't—" she started to say.

He grabbed her by the hair and pulled back so hard she almost screamed. Somehow, she managed to stop herself. Instead, her mind raced, looking for a way out of this that would keep them both alive. That would keep *her* alive.

He pushed himself up against her. She imagined he had to lower himself quite a bit, given how much taller he was, to whisper menacingly against her ear. "This is where you beg me not to kill you."

"*Are* you going to kill me?" she managed to say, despite the pain pulling at her scalp.

"I haven't decided yet."

West must have sensed her lack of fear, because he let go of her hair and moved back. She let out a relieved sigh, then turned around to face him. He gestured for her to sit down on the bed. She did, watching him the whole time. He leaned next to the closet door.

Reminder to self: put locks on all the doors.

All the hotel doors were equipped with keycard locks, but there hadn't been any need to keep the doors locked when it was just them. Now, with Bonnie's group on the island, it was something she should probably bring up to everyone. Of course, to do that, she had to survive this encounter with West first.

Oh, that's it? Easy peasy, then.

West had her other Glock stuffed in his front waistband. He was wearing the new pants and shirt she had sent over to him earlier this morning, and he was still favoring his right leg from his wounds. She wondered if it hurt him just to be moving around even a little bit.

Maybe he's not as strong as he looks...

"I was going to let you go," she said. "After you healed up. I would have given you supplies, weapons, and let you take your chances out there."

"I won't have much of a chance out there on my own."

"I thought you were a tough guy."

He chortled. "I'd be tougher with Brody."

"It's not my fault you and he decided to try to kill Blaine last night."

"Yeah, well, it was a good idea at the time."

"So that was the big plan?"

He sighed almost wistfully. "It wasn't a bad plan. Once we were armed, we could renegotiate our stay on the island. But, unfortunately, things went sideways."

"It doesn't have to go further than this. You haven't hurt anyone yet. This situation is still salvageable, West. Right now the only thing you've damaged is that door down the hall, and maybe my closet. Give me the gun and I won't count this against you."

He smirked. "I'm the one with the gun, Lara."

"And I have people with guns out there, too. They outnumber you, the last time I checked."

He narrowed his eyes at her. "You're not scared at all, are you?"

"Should I be?"

He was right, though. She wasn't scared at all. Not even a little bit. If anything, she was just annoyed. At her own stupidity, at her inability to predict his movements, at her unwillingness to let Danny end it all earlier this morning.

I'm not Will. And I'll never be Will.

He lowered the gun to his side, grimacing slightly from the effort. "I was hoping for a little bit of fear. Just a tiny bit? Now I don't know what to do with you if you're not going to play along."

"There are only two ways out of this, West. Give me the gun and I forget this ever happened. I let you rest, heal up, and then I put you back on land, just like I originally planned. The other option ends with you dead."

"And who's going to do the shooting?"

"Maddie. Carly. Or Danny. It doesn't matter. The second option always ends with you dead. I'd rather not see you dead, West."

"It's not fair, you know," he said, almost pathetically, and for a moment—a split moment—she nearly felt sorry for him. "We brought them here. If it wasn't for us, they wouldn't have made it. We did that. We did a lot of things for them they couldn't do on their own. You think it was easy?"

"I know it wasn't easy. I've been there."

"Yeah, I forgot. You were out there, too. So you know how hard it was. And then we get here, what's the first thing they do? They turn on us. Those bitches."

"They told me what I asked them. The truth. That's all."

"Danny. The blond California surfer. He had it out for us from the word go, didn't he?"

"Danny was born and raised in Texas."

"Bull."

"It's true."

"Hunh. He looks like a California surfer."

"That's what everyone says."

He walked across the room to the patio window. She noticed that he was moving gingerly. He brushed back the curtain and looked out. "Nice view you got here."

"Give me the gun, West."

He looked back at her and grinned. "What's to stop me from taking what I want? Including you. I'm going to die anyway. Either here on this island, or back there on land. Maybe I should take some treats before I go. My reward for having to put up with this garbage. Sounds fair, don't you think?"

He walked back and stood in front of her. He still held the gun at his side, almost casually, as if it were a can of beer instead of a deadly weapon.

"You're pretty, Lara," he said. "I can see why Roy gets all hot and bothered whenever he's around you."

He touched her hair, then caressed her cheek, before sliding his fingers under her chin. She forced herself not to flinch. She didn't want to give him the satisfaction, even if the touch of another man's hand other than Will's brought back bad memories.

May you forever burn in hell, John Sunday.

"This boyfriend of yours," West said. "What's his name?"

"Will."

"What do you think he'd do if he found out what I'm thinking about doing to you right this moment?"

"You don't want to know."

"Big tough guy, huh?"

"Big and tough enough."

"Ah, hell, I'm not gonna do anything." He let out a frustrated sigh. "I like my woman with more meat on her bones anyway. Now Bonnie... Damn, that woman. I always knew she might be the death of me. The way she—"

He stopped suddenly when they both heard footsteps moving down the hallway outside the room. West turned his head toward the door on instinct—

Now!

—and Lara launched herself off the bed and tackled him, catching him mostly in the ribs. He grunted with pain as she jolted his still fresh wound, and her momentum drove them into the closet door. He smashed into it, cratering the door and stumbling to the floor, putting up so little fight for a man of his size that she was momentarily stunned.

But he was still moving, and he still had the gun.

Lara reached for the closest weapon she could find—the radio clipped to her hip—and pulled it free. She swung it as hard as she could and hit West across the side of the head. He fired the Glock in her direction—or where he thought she was—but he hadn't turned his head and was shooting blind.

He missed her by a good solid foot.

Before he could squeeze the trigger again, she smashed the radio into the side of his head a second time—then a third time, and finally, a fourth time.

West's gun hand dropped weakly to the floor and she wrestled the Glock from his pliant fingers, then used her feet to turn him onto his back and pulled the other Glock out of his waistband. He was bleeding again, blood seeping through the front of his shirt, and his temple was a bloody mess. He groaned on the floor, eyes closed in obvious pain.

Her door burst open and Maddie and Carly ran inside, their guns drawn.

"Holy shit!" Maddie said, seeing West on the floor.

Lara tossed one of the Glocks on the bed and holstered the other one. She picked up the remains of her radio. Most of them were sprinkled along the floor around her.

"I need a new radio," she said quietly.

"Damn, girl, that's the understatement of the century," Carly said, and started laughing.

After a moment, Lara started laughing with her, and then Maddie joined in.

CHAPTER 16

WILL

HEAT. PAIN. AND Lara in his mind's eye.

Her blonde hair, so bright under the sun. Crystal-blue eyes like the clear water of Beaufont Lake. The early morning walks on the beach, and all their private moments, even before the others woke up. Listening to her soft heartbeat against his, a reminder of why he lived, fought so hard, and strived to always come through alive. The taste of her lips, sweet and addictive. Her smell, like roses. The feel of her skin, soft and delicate.

Lara.

He opened his eyes to twisted and smoking wrecks around, below, and above him. He knew he was bleeding *(again)* without having to actually see it. His face throbbed, and he could feel the bruises and cuts without having to see them. Predictably, every inch of him hurt like a sonofabitch.

He grunted through the aches and tried to move his arms and legs. There was a sharp stabbing pain from his right leg, but his left seemed fine. The operative word being seemed. His arms were mostly okay, and happily, the bullet wound from this afternoon had numbed, probably because the rest of his body was making up for it.

He was still fastened to the passenger seat by the seatbelt, which was a minor miracle. Rays of sunlight filtered in through the cracked windshield, so that was a good sign. Sunlight meant day, and day meant time. He lifted his left arm, shards of glass and tiny pieces of steel and aluminum falling free every time he moved any part of his body.

3:14 P.M.

A couple of hours since the helicopter had come down. That explained the lack of roaring flames around him, except for those still lingering over pieces of wreckage scattered about the hard concrete highway. The other good news was that he couldn't smell burning flesh or singed hair, which meant he wasn't currently roasting to death inside the carcass of the destroyed helicopter.

The bad news was everything else.

He couldn't see behind him, so he didn't know where the others were, or if they were even still inside with him. He couldn't hear anyone other than himself moving, and despite the stillness of the city, the only breathing he could detect was his own. Jen was nowhere to be found, and her pilot's seat was raised at an odd angle; it had probably overturned during the crash. The seatbelt hung upside down and was slashed near the middle. There were thick patches of blood against her side of the windshield. That wasn't good.

The air around him was hot despite the cooling September breeze. The cockpit passenger door was gone, leaving a big, gaping hole exposing the sight of overturned vehicles piled on top of one another. The result was something akin to a makeshift tunnel extending from the open door to freedom, with broken glass and sharp metal lining his path.

He turned his head slightly to the left. When he couldn't turn just his head far enough, he twisted his body slowly, carefully, in case he was impaled on something. Fortunately, he was able to turn a solid sixty degrees to look into the backseats. He wished he hadn't.

Amy was still fastened to her seat, with the boy clinging to her chest, his arms around her neck. Her head was slumped forward, and Will was glad he couldn't see the boy's face because there was a large slab of metal jutting out from his back. He thought at first it was a piece of the rotor, but no, it was too jagged, too rough around the edges. The metal had pierced the boy first, then continued into Amy and exited the back of her seat. A large pool of blood gathered under them on the seat and the floor. The metal must have missed him by mere inches.

There were no signs of Gaby or Benny, though he spotted an AR-15 *(Benny's)* lying on the floor, the barrel bent, with metal shrapnel sticking out of the side between the ejection port and magazine slot. More blood on the seats, but not enough to convince him Gaby or Benny were bleeding to death somewhere. They had either been thrown clear in the crash, or they had crawled out.

Will turned back around, pain shooting up from his right leg, where he had felt the first stinging sensation earlier. He finally looked down, saw a piece of glass—probably from the cracked windshield— three inches of it visible above the fabric of his pant leg. He guessed there were another two inches under there, embedded just deep enough that he felt it every time he moved a little bit. It hadn't hit anything vital, he was sure of that, and it had missed the bone entirely.

"Will," a voice said from outside.

Will looked to his right and saw Gaby kneeling on the other end of the vehicle cocoon. There was a nasty gash across her forehead, covered in a thick layer of drying ointment. Her chin and cheeks were scratched up, and her neck was purple and bruised.

"You gonna sit there all day, or you want us to pull you out?" Gaby asked.

"'Us'?"

"Benny's out here with me."

"You guys okay?"

"I've looked better. Benny's limping around a bit." She frowned at the shard of glass sticking out of him. "How bad?"

"It didn't puncture anything major. I should be fine."

"Right. Fine. When aren't you fine?"

He ignored her comment, said, "Jen?"

Gaby shook her head. "You don't want to know."

"That bad?"

"Worse."

"Shit."

They were both silent for a moment.

Then Gaby asked, "Can you move?"

He looked down at the glass. "I'm going to have to remove it first."

Gaby winced. "Are you sure?"

"I can't crawl out with this, Gaby."

She nodded. "The medical supplies are all across the highway. We gathered up as much as we could find. Found your pack, though, with all the ammo still in it."

"I need a first aid kit. Or if you can't find one, a towel, water, gauze, duct tape, and antiseptic."

"I'll be back," Gaby said, and disappeared.

Alone again, Will took inventory.

His left arm was fine. Well, not fine, exactly, but workable. The wound was bleeding again, but it wasn't too bad. Eventually, he would have to suture it to make sure he didn't bleed to death later. His legs weren't broken, which was very good news. He wouldn't have gone very far with broken legs. It was a simple matter of removing the glass shard, then cleaning the wound in his right leg. Disinfectant would keep out infection, and he could stitch it the same time he did his arm.

Doable.

He freed himself from the seatbelt, then reached down and touched the glass with a finger and tried pushing on it. Stabbing pain. He grimaced through it.

Gaby came back, knees scraping against the highway. "Ready?"

He nodded.

Gaby rolled the water bottle first. Then a fresh rag, the edges taped into the middle. He opened it, taking out a white packet, gauze in shrink wrapping, and a roll of gray duct tape.

"You sure you don't need a hand?" she asked.

"I'll manage."

Will slid the cross-knife out of its sheath and sliced his pant leg open around the embedded glass, careful not to cut too wide, but enough to see—and eventually get at—the wound underneath. Surprisingly very little blood, but that was going to change when he pulled the glass out.

He laid down the knife and opened the water bottle, then set it back down. He picked up the rag with one hand, took hold of the shard of glass with the other. He didn't think about it, just pulled it out with a grunt. Blood spurted and he quickly shoved the rag down against the opening, pressing down hard.

"How's Benny?" he asked.

"Hobbling around," Gaby said. Her eyes were glued to his leg.

"Any threats out there?"

"None that I could see. The Humvee that we saw earlier is gone. What was that, some kind of rocket launcher?"

"M72 Law anti-tank rocket launcher, yeah. I guess it works just as well on helicopters. We were lucky."

"You call this lucky?"

"The M72 is unguided. If he had something more sophisticated, we wouldn't be having this conversation."

"Where the hell did they get something like that, anyway?"

"Army base would be my guess. Louisiana has plenty of them around. They probably looted them about the same time they picked up the Humvees and all those M4s. Those are military grade stuff."

Will lifted the rag and peeked at the wound before pouring water over it. The warmth helped him with the pain. He wiped at the wet blood, clearing it from the opening, then used his teeth to tear the package and squeezed out the antiseptic ointment that he then spread liberally over the hole.

"Weapons?" he asked.

Gaby didn't answer right away. She was too busy staring at the blood.

"Gaby, weapons?" he asked again.

"I still have my M4, and another one the others took from Mike. Also, all the magazines in my pack and yours. Found mine about twenty yards up the highway."

Will pressed the gauze over the wound, careful to position it under the pant leg, then wrapped the whole thing with two revolutions of duct tape.

"Did you find my rifle?" he asked.

"It's behind you. I remember stepping on it when I was climbing out earlier."

"Catch," Will said, and tossed the duct tape back to her. Then he drank what was left in the water bottle and sat back for a moment to catch his breath.

"You okay?" Gaby asked.

"I'll be fine. Get ready to move."

She nodded and disappeared from the opening again.

Will turned around in his seat and saw the barrel of his M4A1 behind him, amazingly still in one piece. From Afghanistan, to Harris County SWAT, to the end of the world. And now to this.

Will wasn't a superstitious man, but if he were…

THERE WAS A certain order to the destruction when viewed from inside the wreckage. It was a much different story on the outside.

Pieces of the helicopter were strewn across nearly a 200-meter length and along both sides of the highway. Two of the rotor blades were buried in the thick concrete not far from the main bulk of what was left of the fuselage. The landing skids, in four sections, had ripped through a dozen cars and impaled a minivan's engine block. There were little impact craters everywhere.

Will climbed down from the police cruiser, wincing a bit as his right leg touched down.

Benny had seen better days, too. The kid's face, like his and Gaby's, was bruised and cut, and he had a large scar across one cheek that he had treated. All the first aid they had wasn't much help for a broken leg that made him limp everywhere, though Gaby had made a splint for him using two pieces of wooden sticks cinched in place with duct tape. He remembered teaching her that during one of those two weeks they had spent together in the woods back on the island.

Benny stood gazing off at the highway, Mike's M4 and a bag only half full with the medical supplies they had managed to salvage slung over his shoulders. He moved with the help of a makeshift crutch—a wooden baseball bat with the headrest from a car seat duct taped to the top. Again, another impromptu creation by Gaby.

It had taken Will longer to crawl out of the wreckage than he had anticipated. It was already 4:11 P.M. by the time he emerged and looked up at the sky. Late September in Louisiana meant 7:00 P.M. sunsets, give or take.

Gaby walked over to him, carrying her pack and rifle. "Do we go after them?"

Will shook his head. "We'll never catch them on foot. Not in our condition."

"What about the kids?" Benny asked.

Will didn't answer right away. He looked up the highway, in the direction the Humvees had gone. Then glanced back at Benny, limping on a makeshift crutch, and at Gaby, her face a mess of bruises and cuts. All three of them looked like hell, and there wasn't an inch of him that wasn't in pain at the moment.

"We can't do anything for them now," Will said after a while. "Right now, we need to find shelter. We have three hours before it gets dark."

"The closest off-ramp is back there," Gaby said.

"Take point."

She headed west, and they followed on foot. There wasn't any need to weave around vehicles abandoned eleven months ago because the Humvees had done such an efficient job of clearing everything to the sides, creating a single, almost-perfect lane to drive—or walk—through.

Will found that if he focused on something else, like Lara's image in his head, or the lake breeze around the island, he could *almost* ignore the stabbing pain in his right leg. Thank God for the numbness in his left arm. He wasn't sure if he could fight through both wounds at the moment.

He caught up with Gaby, who was moving slowly—on purpose for their benefit, he guessed. "How far?"

"Half a mile," she said.

"That's too far." He glanced at his watch, then looked up at the sun for confirmation. "We need to pick it up."

"Your leg and Benny's..."

"We'll be fine. It'll be worse if we're caught out here at night."

She nodded and began moving faster.

Will waited for Benny to catch up. "Lean on me, Benny."

Will took his crutch and slipped his left arm around Benny's waist. He used the crutch for himself, and surprisingly, with Benny on one side and the crutch on the other, he walked relatively pain-free.

Or at least, that's what he told himself. The trick to ignoring pain was conviction.

Yeah, that's the ticket.

◄━━▌ ▐━━►

IT TOOK THEM nearly thirty minutes to reach the off-ramp, which was much too long. They stuck to the shoulder to maneuver around the parked vehicles frozen in their lanes, dried blood clinging to dashboards and steering wheels and seats baking in the sun.

With the help of gravity, it didn't take them nearly as long to reach the bottom of the off-ramp. As they were walking down, Will scanned the feeder road, looking for buildings they could use. Gas stations, strip malls—nothing that made him happy. There was a motel about half a kilometer up the street, but just walking there would easily take them another half an hour. They didn't have that much time.

"Gaby," he said, "the gas station."

"Are you sure?" she asked. "It doesn't look that safe."

"We just need one room that can be defended."

She jogged on ahead toward a Valero gas station, and Will followed with Benny. They passed a red Chevy waiting in line at the pump, and Will skirted around a white, overturned Bronco in the parking lot.

The Valero, like most gas stations, had glass windows, so he could see into the store before they ever reached the front doors.

"Silver ammo?" he asked Gaby.

She nodded back. "Nothing but."

"Give me a moment." Will sat Benny down on the curb outside the store. "Stay here. We'll clear the store, then come back for you."

"Take your time," Benny said. He looked over at Gaby. "Grab me a bag of Funyuns, will ya?"

"They're probably all stale by now," Gaby said.

"Just as good."

"I'll see what I can do."

Will unslung his M4A1 and walked over to Gaby, who was already waiting for him at the doors. He nodded, and she pulled the door open. Will slipped inside first, rifle raised. He glimpsed the aisles, then stopped and listened for noises. There was very little chance the ghouls would be using the gas station as a nest. It was too small and too inconvenient; they preferred bigger places with thick walls *(like Mercy Hospital)*.

Will nodded right, and Gaby disappeared down the aisle. He took left.

After about ten minutes of going from aisle to aisle and looking through an employee lounge in the back and a bathroom next door, they met up again at the front. Gaby had grabbed a bag of Funyuns sometime during the trip back.

"Stale?" he asked.

"Expired eight months ago. Maybe he won't notice the difference."

"Must be love," Will teased.

"He did save my life on the rooftop."

"That always helps, sure."

BENNY DIDN'T SEEM to mind the expired Funyuns, digging into the bag as if he hadn't eaten in days. Will left them in the employee lounge, a big block of concrete with some Brad Pitt movie posters and old hunting magazines stacked on a flimsy fold-out portable table. The only other furniture was an old lime-green couch.

The good news was that there was only one way into the lounge—through a sturdy steel door that had been painted over at least four times in its lifetime, judging by the eclectic mix of colors visible underneath the peeling paint.

Will grabbed a couple of plastic bags from behind the front counter and filled them with water bottles from the freezers, all the beef jerky he could find, and five cans of Vienna sausages with pull tabs from the shelves. The sun was already starting to fall outside, casting an orange-red glow across the highway as Will walked back to the lounge.

He handed Gaby the bags, then went through the gym bag they were hauling around and pulled out what he needed.

"You need a hand?" Gaby asked, looking worriedly at him.

"I'll call if I do." He pulled out a bottle of Vicodin and handed it to Gaby. "Give Benny two, and don't let him move around on that leg."

"What about you?"

"I'll take some tramadol."

"That's it?"

"We have to stay awake, but Benny doesn't have to."

She nodded, and he had to remind himself that even scratched up, bruised, and cut, she was still just a kid.

Back outside, he used the fading daylight to take off the gauze from around his left arm. He washed the wound again, disinfected it, then took out the needle and medical suture and went to work. When he was done, he snipped the thread and wrapped it back up with a new layer of gauze.

Working on his right leg was trickier. He had to unwind the duct tape along with the gauze, which was of course wet and sticky with blood. He pulled off his pants and sat in his boxers with his leg propped up on the counter. He had to wash and disinfect the wound again before he could finally start suturing it. He thought about Lara, her lips, kissing those lips, the feel of her skin, and was able to get through it with minimal pain. By the time he was finished wrapping it back up with more gauze and fresh duct tape and had pulled his pants back on, the windows had almost completely faded to gray.

Will took out the bottle of painkillers and chewed on a couple, then gave them a few minutes to do their job. Afterward, he gathered up the bloody items from the floor and tossed them into a bag before heading back to the lounge. He tied up the bag and tossed it into a corner, then made sure the door was locked. There was a deadbolt, but that was it.

"Gaby, give me a hand with the couch."

They moved the couch over, stood it on its side, then leaned it at an angle against the middle of the bigger door. He stood back and gave it a look.

"It'll never hold," she said.

"No, but it's better than nothing." He looked back at Benny, sitting on the floor with his back against the wall, head lulling to one side and struggling to keep his eyes open. "Push comes to shove, we can always use him. He's what, 200 pounds?"

"One fifty, tops."

Will grinned. "We'll be okay."

"Yeah? What makes you say that?"

"I have faith."

"In what, this ugly couch? Or this twenty-year-old door?"

"Both."

"This is all for my benefit, isn't it?"

"Yup."

"Swell."

They sat down on the floor, backs against the far wall, and laid their rifles across their laps.

Will dug out a couple of water bottles and handed her one. "You did good out there."

She smiled, pleased. "Yeah?"

"Yeah."

"Thanks."

"Don't let it go to your head."

"Perish the thought," she said. "But just between you and me. I'm a better soldier than Danny, right?"

"Without a doubt," he smiled.

"Good. I'm going to rub it in his face when we get back. Assuming we survive this."

"We'll survive this."

"Is that just for my benefit, too?"

"Yup."

She smirked. "You know, it would work better if you didn't automatically tell the truth once I pressed you on it."

"Oh yeah, sorry about that."

◄▬▬▮ ▮▬▬►

BENNY WAS SNORING long before nightfall. They moved him into the corner so he wouldn't accidentally topple to the floor and hurt himself.

They didn't see the night coming outside the door, but they could feel it. Will's internal clock buzzed and screamed and rang when his watch ticked to 7:10 P.M. The temperature dropped noticeably about thirty minutes later. That was good, because he was afraid of suffocation by heat inside the room.

Gaby's eyes, like Will's, never left the door, even as visibility dropped to almost nothing.

"Should we pop a glow stick?" she asked.

"There's too big a slot under the door and around the frame. They'll see the glow if they look into the store for longer than a few seconds."

"So we're just going to sit here in the pitch dark, then?"

"Pretty much."

"Romantic."

"Uh huh. Beef jerky?" He offered her one from the bundle he had shoved into his pack earlier.

"Don't mind if I do."

It took only a few minutes until they were completely engulfed in darkness, and his only clue Gaby was even sitting next to him was the sound of her chewing. Benny, somewhere in the corner, was snoring, though not loudly enough for Will to be too concerned.

"I liked Amy and Jen," Gaby said quietly.

"I did, too."

"And they took the fucking kids, Will."

"Yeah."

"We couldn't even save the one kid. Amy said his name was Freddie."

Gaby didn't say much after that.

"Go to sleep, Gaby," he said after a while.

"What about you?"

"I'll wake you around three."

"Okay."

He heard her repositioning her rifle in her lap, then the rustling of clothes as she folded her arms across her chest against the growing chill.

Will leaned his head back against the wall, keeping his eyes on the door in front of him. Despite the darkness, the door stood out, the slivers along its frame giving it the impression of being some otherworldly portal.

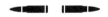

SOMEWHERE AROUND MIDNIGHT, he heard them moving around the store outside the lounge. One of them appeared in front of the door and jingled the doorknob, its shadow moving in that staccato, unnatural gait that they possessed.

He gripped the M4A1 in the darkness.

Gaby was sleeping quietly next to him, while Benny snored softly in the corner. Still not too loud, but just loud *enough* to make him nervous. He was struck by how much more of a soldier Gaby was compared to Benny. Hell, compared to all of Mike's people. He always knew he and Danny had done a good job with her, but to see her in action was impressive.

The creature finally grew bored of playing with the door. It turned and scampered off.

But it wasn't alone. There were more movements outside, and shadows flitted across the crevices around the door.

These other creatures, though, didn't bother to stop and inspect the back room.

The hive mind. One knows, so the others know, too.

Dead, not stupid.

An hour later, the last of the noises faded into the background, and Will felt comfortable enough to close his eyes.

He thought about Lara. About their mornings on the beach and their nights in bed. He could almost hear the rise and fall of her heartbeat, and it made him smile. He wondered what she was doing right now, and if she missed him nearly as much as he was missing her...

CHAPTER 17

LARA

SHE WAS TIRED, and she wanted nothing more than to just lie down and close her eyes and go to sleep. But while Lara felt mentally fatigued, West actually looked the part. His face was black and bruised, his temple bearing the stitches from a couple of hours ago. His eyes were glassy, his nose partially broken, and he looked like a hospital patient who had stumbled out of bed after surgery.

"This is a death sentence," West said as they approached the marina.

He sat up front facing them, with Lara in the back and Danny in the middle. His hands were zip tied in front of him, not that he looked like he was in any shape to fight at the moment.

"You know that, right?" West said.

She didn't answer.

Danny steered them into the mouth of the inlet, then glided up toward the marina. It had been a while since she left the island, and just stepping into the boat felt terrifying, as if she would never be able to return.

She glanced over at the blackened property to their left. It looked miserably bleak, which, she guessed, was the point. It was the same with the marina. There used to be a garage near the water's edge, but it, too, had been burned down. The marina itself was still in one piece, since it was a little difficult to burn down an asphalt parking lot. The area around it was nothing but towering fields of grass as far as the eye could see.

"Are you listening to me?" West said.

"I heard you," she said. "It won't change anything, so you can stop wasting your breath."

"You're a doctor, for God's sake."

Third-year medical student, actually.

"I gave you every chance in the world," she said. "This is all your doing."

"Keep telling yourself that, and maybe one day you'll believe it."

She should have let Maddie come instead. Or any of the others. But she hadn't passed off the responsibility to them, because she needed to do this, because it *was* her responsibility.

I made the decision. Now I have to stare it in the face.

Danny eased up on the boat, then angled it toward one of the boat ramps. The front of the boat slid gently up the sloping concrete, until it came to a rough, grinding stop.

"This is where you get off, Kemosabe," Danny said, pulling back on the throttle.

West stood up and sought out her eyes. She wanted desperately to look away, but Lara forced herself to stare right back at him.

"Look, I'm sorry about this afternoon," West said. "About everything. But this isn't right. You know this isn't right. I'm going to die out here. I don't stand a chance."

"You'll stand a chance if you're smart," she said.

"You know that's not true. You *know* it."

She ignored his plea and said, "Danny."

Danny drew his cross-knife. "Hands."

West held out his zip tied hands and Danny cut them free. West towered over Danny, but at the moment she had never seen such a tall man look so small. At first she thought it was an act, an attempt to garner sympathy.

But no. This was the real thing. West was *terrified.*

"I'm sorry," she said.

That seemed to utterly deflate him, stripping him of whatever last vestige of hope he had been clinging to that she would change her mind.

"Turn around," Danny said.

West obeyed. "Please…"

"And don't forget the battery."

West picked up a car battery at his feet, then clumsily climbed over the side of the boat. He stumbled most of the way, trying to fight the slight rocking of the boat while clinging to the heavy burden in his hands.

"Try not to get it wet," Danny said.

West barely made it to the angled ramp, sacrificing his pant legs as they dipped into the cold water of Beaufont Lake. He scrambled, fighting against the sloping concrete, and finally pulled himself up onto the dry parking lot with a lot of effort. He dumped the battery on the ground and immediately—desperately—searched out her eyes again.

"Please, Lara. You can't do this. You know this isn't right. Whatever I did, I don't deserve this. You know that. *Please.*"

She stared back at him.

This is where I change my mind. This is where I let the squishy woman in me take over and allow him back on the island. This is where I prove to him that I have no killer instinct.

This is where he's wrong.

She picked up a gym bag and threw it onto the marina ten feet from where he stood. The bag was stuffed with his rifle and a shotgun, knives and ammo, canned goods and bottled water. All the supplies he would need to survive—for a while, anyway. It was everything she thought she owed him and nothing more.

"Don't touch the bag until we're out of sight," Lara said. "Danny will shoot you if you do. Trust me, he's a better shot than you are."

"Catch," Danny said, and tossed West a key. "The blue Tacoma. There should be some gas left. Not a lot, mind you, but we took it out a week ago, and there might be half a tank if you're lucky. Swap in the battery and you're good to go. Well, goodish, anyway."

"Drive north as fast as you can," Lara said. "You don't have a lot of time."

West blinked nervously up at the sun.

"Do yourself a favor," Danny said. "Don't be here when we come back. I see you, I'm shooting first, and it's never mind the questions."

Lara didn't wait for West to respond. "Let's go, Danny."

Danny made a U-turn, and when he had the boat facing the lake again, he stepped aside for her to take over the steering wheel. Danny unslung his M4A1 and looked back at West in case he went for the bag.

"Do us both a favor," Danny shouted. "Go for the bag. Pretty please?"

West didn't go for the bag.

"You're no fun," Danny said.

She guided the boat out of the inlet and back onto the lake. It was like driving a car, only each slight jerk of the steering wheel was more dramatic. She could almost feel West's eyes on her back, but she never turned around.

"You did the right thing," Danny said behind her. "Don't beat yourself up over it. If Will was here, West would never have survived the woods. The idiot doesn't know it, but he's lucky he got to deal with you instead."

"Thanks, Danny," she said quietly.

ONCE THEY WERE back on the island, she waited for Danny to return to the Tower to relieve Maddie before calling him on her radio. It was the longest, most excruciating ten minutes of her life.

"Anything from Will?"

"Nothing, sorry," he said.

Dammit, Will, where are you?

"Get some sleep, Lara. I'll send Carly to bang on your door when Willie boy calls. And he will. Have faith."

Faith.

Yeah, I'm finding a shortage of that lately, Danny.

She ate dinner with everyone in the dining room, trying her best to engage in their conversation. Sarah was in the Infirmary with Blaine and had been since Lara left them a few hours ago. Sarah would probably be there all night, since Mae, Bonnie, and Gwen had taken over the kitchen. The food, a bit spicier than Sarah's, was still delicious, though about halfway through Lara realized she was more tired than hungry.

After dinner, she took her half-empty dishes into the kitchen, where Bonnie was pouring Coke from a two-liter plastic bottle into a dozen tall glasses on a tray. Each glass was topped with ice, and by the time Bonnie finished pouring, there was more ice than Coke in each glass.

"Got enough ice there?" Lara smiled.

Bonnie laughed. "When you've been drinking warm soda for as long as we have, you can never get enough ice."

Bonnie handed her one of the glasses and Lara took it gratefully. "Mae said you were a model before all of this."

Bonnie looked embarrassed. "Talk about a useless career, huh?"

"Oh, I don't know. I was thinking about opening an island magazine, call it *Island Breeze*, or something like that."

"Are you saying you're looking for a model?"

"That depends. Are you expensive?"

"I had a pretty lucrative career. Did you used to read a lot of fashion magazines before all this?"

"Did the *New England Journal of Medicine* ever put out a fashion issue?"

"I'm going to go out on a limb and say no?"

"Figures. My roommate used to buy stacks of them, though."

"Is she...?"

"I'm not sure. I don't know what happened to her."

Bonnie nodded. Lara didn't have to say anything else. They all knew people who either didn't make it or were unaccounted for.

"I guess I was lucky," Bonnie said. "With Jo, I mean. So many people have lost so much, and somehow we still have each other. You were lucky, too."

"I was?"

"You found Will. Treasure that, Lara. This kind of thing was a rarity back when the world made sense, but now, it's a miracle."

Lara nodded. "I guess you're right. It's good to be reminded of that every now and then. Thanks."

"Glad to do it."

"Anyway," Lara said, brightening up. "How much would it cost to book you for a fashion shoot?"

Bonnie laughed. "Since I know you, I'll cut you in for a discount. Give me your cell and I'll get my people to call your people and we'll work something out."

They talked for a bit longer, before Bonnie finally had to take the drinks out before the ice melted.

Lara walked through Hallway A by herself. Her joints ached and she had difficultly trying to keep her mind focused on one thing. By the time she reached her room, her body was already half asleep.

Seconds after lying down on the bed and closing her eyes, she didn't even remember if she had closed the door behind her. She realized she didn't really care either, and went to sleep, her last jumbled thoughts of Will.

CHAPTER 18

GABY

THE WARM MORNING sunlight on her face was somehow more soothing out here, beyond the safety of the island. She guessed it had something to do with the precarious nature of their situation. Out here, beyond the white beaches of Song Island or the purview of the Tower's watchful eye, there were no guarantees.

Benny hobbled out of the Valero behind her. His face remained scratched up and bruised, but he had lost the pale, hollowed look of yesterday. She hoped she was equally improved, but had been too scared to actually glance at anything too shiny for fear of seeing the truth.

"Hey there, gimpy," she said.

"Funny," Benny smirked back. "Let's see you break a leg and not gimp around." He sat down and leaned back against the store, then opened a gym bag and took out a long Slim Jim stick. "Breakfast?"

"Whatcha got?"

Benny tossed her a bag of Jack Link's turkey-flavored jerky. "Where's Will?" he asked. "He wasn't in the lounge when I woke up."

"He'll be back soon."

Benny opened a bottle of water and poured it over his head, then dabbed his face with a rag from the store's racks, wincing with every contact.

"Did they find us last night?" he asked.

"Will said they searched the gas station, but didn't try to break down the door. I wouldn't know. He didn't wake me up last night."

"He probably thought you needed the sleep."

"We all needed the sleep. He was just being Will."

"I don't know what that means."

She shrugged, but didn't feel like explaining. Instead, she walked over and sat down next to him and dug out a bottle of water from her pack, then wet a towel with it to clean her face. Unlike Benny, she was more careful and managed to clean up most of her face without too much pain. She fought the urge to look at herself in the glass window behind her.

"What now?" Benny asked.

"I don't know."

"Will didn't say?"

"No."

Benny looked toward the highway. Gaby knew he was trying to locate the remains of the helicopter. She had done the same thing when she first emerged from the store earlier.

"I'm the only one left," Benny said quietly. "Out of forty people. Mike, Tom, Amy... I'm the only one left. Crazy how it worked out. I wasn't even supposed to be alive, you know." He shook his head and looked as if he were on the verge of laughing. Or crying. "When it happened... I didn't know what to do. I was lucky Mike and the others were there. They took me in and taught me how to fend for myself. And now... God, I'm the only one left, Gaby."

"You'll like the island," she said. "White beaches. Nice breeze. More fish than you can eat."

"And you."

"We'll see."

"But you're not against it?"

"We'll see," she said again.

◄━━ ━━►

WILL CAME BACK a few minutes later. He wasn't hobbling quite as much, even though she knew the strongest painkiller he took last night was some tramadol. Benny, who took the same pills this morning, wanted something stronger, but they couldn't afford for him to fall asleep in the daytime. That, and neither she nor Will felt like carrying him more than they already had.

They headed west on foot along the I-10 feeder road, back in the direction of Mercy Hospital and, beyond that, Song Island. There was no point in chasing Kellerson or his collaborators. Not on foot, anyway. Even if they could find a ride, the Humvees were long gone, and it would be difficult—if not downright impossible—to locate them once they left the city, and there were no longer cars pushed to the sides of the road to track by. Kellerson had also proven that he wasn't a total idiot. Leaving the man with the rocket launcher behind to ambush them was proof of that.

As much as she hated to abandon the chase—and the kids— Gaby didn't have to look any farther than Will and Benny to know that they were in no position to keep going. Even so, the decision to head back made her feel empty and dirty, as if she were betraying not just those kids but herself as well.

"What about all the cars?" Benny asked after a while. "Shouldn't we be looking for a car that'll run?"

There were a lot of cars along the streets. Sedans, trucks, semi-trailers, and a dozen others. Most of them still had keys stuck in the ignitions.

"Waste of time," Will said. "Batteries don't work after eleven months. Gas is another issue. Better to just look for something else, like a bicycle."

"A bicycle?" Benny sighed. "I'm not sure I could even pedal on this leg."

"Better than walking on that leg."

"At this rate, it'll take us most of the day to reach Mercy Hospital. Then what? Are we staying at the hospital? I'm not sure I want to go back there after what happened."

"Less talk, more walk."

"I'm just saying…"

"Say less, walk more."

Benny sighed again.

Gaby gave him a disappointed look. She accepted that he was injured, but so was Will. She had seen Will pull a chunk of glass out of his right leg, for God's sake, but he wasn't being nearly as dramatic about it as Benny. She felt growing irritation and did her best to temper it. Telling herself that Benny was new to all of this helped a little bit, but it was difficult to reconcile this whiny Benny with the same one who had saved her yesterday on the rooftop.

They hadn't gone more than five minutes when Will stopped in the middle of the road and snapped, "Cover!"

Gaby unslung her M4 and rushed behind a red Camaro, sliding up against the driver's side door. She looked back and was horrified to see Benny standing out in the open, frozen in place.

"Benny!" she hissed.

He snapped out of it and hobbled over to her. "What's going on?"

"Get down!"

She glanced over at Will, crouched behind a white pickup truck. He was peering over the hood at something up the road. She followed his gaze and saw a figure standing on the rooftop of an auto body shop. The figure had binoculars and was looking in their direction. It was a man, but he was too far for her to make out any details. Something that looked like a rifle was slung over his back.

She looked back at Will, who seemed to be considering his options. Then, finally, he made a decision and slung his rifle and looked back at her.

She surprised herself by knowing exactly what he was going to do, and nodded back at him.

"What's going on?" Benny asked.

"I'm going to cover Will," she said. "Stay down and don't do anything, okay?"

"What's he going to do?"

"Just stay down, Benny," she said, putting just enough annoyance in her voice to get through to him.

Will stood up and walked out from behind the pickup truck. The figure on the rooftop watched him curiously, perhaps trying to guess Will's intentions. The man hadn't reached for his rifle yet, which she took to be a good sign.

Gaby kept her M4 at the ready anyway. She guessed her target was maybe 100 yards, give or take. Will and Danny could probably hit someone from that distance, but her best shot had come at just under eighty. She was at least somewhat comforted in the knowledge that if she couldn't hit the guy, maybe he couldn't hit her or Will, either. Of course, all that went out the window if the guy was a really good shot.

"Don't shoot!" Will shouted.

His voice echoed up and down the feeder road. Birds perched on top of the highway's concrete barriers burst into flight.

She watched the figure on the rooftop carefully, waiting for signs—any signs at all—of aggression. But the man hadn't moved from his spot and hadn't gone for his rifle. Maybe the guy understood what Will was doing. Or maybe he was a decoy, and there were other men hiding up the street, waiting for Will to get closer so they could take a shot—

She gripped her rifle tighter, her legs a bundle of energy, ready to spring up from behind the Camaro and start shooting.

Be ready. Be ready…

"I have two more people behind me!" Will shouted, stopping twenty yards up the street.

Why had he stopped? Had he spotted something?

She waited for him to look back at her, to give her some kind of signal. But he remained fixed on the man on the auto body rooftop.

"What—" Benny started to say beside her.

"Shhh!" she snapped before he could get another word out.

They waited for what seemed like hours, though it was probably only a few seconds, before the guy finally shouted back, "What do you want?"

"Just passing through!" Will shouted. "We're trying to get home!"

"Where's home?"

"South!"

"There's not much down south!"

"There is if you know where to look! We're just passing through! You don't try to shoot us, and we won't shoot you. Deal?"

The guy hesitated for a moment, then shouted back, "Deal!"

Will looked back at Gaby and nodded.

She relaxed her grip on the rifle and stood up. Benny struggled back up to his feet next to her, groaning like an old woman who had sat down for too long.

HIS NAME WAS Nate and he had short blond hair, though it was hard to tell the color since he had almost completely shaved it off, leaving behind just a small, ridiculous looking Mohawk in the center. He was armed with a gun belt and a bolt-action hunting rifle.

"We heard the helicopter coming from a distance," Nate said. "You guys flew right over us. Then there was a loud boom, but by the time we came outside, we could only see fire and smoke. We thought about coming to help, but you know how it is. We didn't want to get in the middle of whatever was going on between you and the other guys. We only checked it out this morning, when it was safer."

"You went to the wreck?" Will asked.

"For supplies, yeah. We picked up some things, lots of pill bottles. Since it's yours, we'll give it back."

"We have everything we need. You can keep them."

Nate nodded gratefully. "You were in the Army?"

"Yeah. You?"

"I was in ROTC at Lafayette University."

"Good. That means you haven't been tainted by Officer Candidate School yet."

Nate grinned. "That's one way to put it."

He finally looked over at her. Like Benny, she had kept quiet as Nate and Will talked. Now, facing his pale blue eyes, she was suddenly very self-conscious about her appearance. The gash in her forehead, not to mention the cuts and bruises along every inch of her face and neck. She wanted to shrink away and hide, but willed herself to stand perfectly still and stare back at him instead.

"I'm Nate," he said, extending a hand to her.

"I heard," Gaby said, shaking his hand. "This is Benny."

"Hey," Benny said, offering up a half-wave.

"Hey," Nate said, before looking back at her. "That's a pretty wicked gash."

"I ran into a door," she said.

"Must have been a pretty big ass door."

"It was oak."

"Ouch." Nate looked back at Will. "So what's down south?"

"You know where Song Island is?" Will asked.

"Never heard of it. What's so special about Song Island?"

"That depends."

"On?"

"What kind of transportation you have, and whether you're useful to me or not."

Nate didn't look fazed. "The answer to those two questions depends on two things. One, what's so special about this Song Island, and two, what are the chances you'll take us with you?"

***

"US" WAS NATE and five others. They were staying in the basement of a house half a block from the feeder road where they had met Nate. The house was just one of many in a neighborhood with fallen-down picket fences, overgrown lawns, weed-covered gardens, and dirt-strewn streets. Curtains covering broken windows blew in the breeze around them, with a museum of cars frozen along curbs and driveways.

All five of Nate's people had come outside to meet them. Nate had called ahead on a radio, proving to be more tactically sound than Mike, who had been a former Army officer. Nate reminded her of Will; they were about the same height and build. Except for the silly Mohawk on top of Nate's head, the two of them could almost pass for brothers.

They gathered in the driveway while Nate introduced everyone.

Kendra was a black woman in her thirties. She had a son, Dwayne, who looked all of twelve, though the kid was already as tall as his mom. Gaby guessed he was going to sprout like a beanstalk by the time he hit puberty in a few years. Like Nate, Dwayne was carrying a hunting rifle that looked almost as big as him. His mother looked tired, as if she hadn't slept in a while.

The other two were a Hispanic couple, Stan and Liza. Stan looked at least twenty years older than Liza, who was about Lara's age. Liza could only speak Spanish, so Stan translated everything for her.

The fifth member of Nate's group was a teenage girl named Mary, who had possibly the largest eyes Gaby had ever seen on someone who wasn't a cartoon character. Mary stood silently next to Nate, clinging to his arm with both hands.

"What's your transportation look like?" Will asked.

"It's not much to look at, but she'll run," Nate said.

He led them to a beat-up black Dodge Caravan parked nearby. He was right; it didn't look like much at all. It was long, with four doors—two front doors and two rear ones that slid backward. The backseats could be folded down to accommodate more people.

"Gas?" Will asked.

"Stan topped her off three days ago when we settled down here," Nate said.

"She's not exactly a speed demon, but she's comfortable," Stan said. "Well, for six people, anyway. I don't know about all of us. Might be a bit of a tight squeeze."

"Are we leaving?" Mary asked anxiously.

"Maybe," Nate said. "It depends on what they have to say. Apparently they have an island."

"An island?" Dwayne said. "Seriously?"

They stayed outside in the sun as Will told them about Song Island.

"It sounds wonderful," Mary said enthusiastically. "We're going there, aren't we, Nate?"

"I don't know," Nate said. "That depends on what Will decides."

"There's plenty of room on the island," Will said. "All we need is a second vehicle."

"It'll be tight, but we could probably fit everyone into the minivan."

"I don't like having that many people in one vehicle. We need a second one, just in case. Battery's still good?"

"Definitely. I turn on the engine at least once a day even if we're not going anywhere, just to keep it running."

"Spare gas?"

"Two extra cans for emergencies."

"Smart."

"We weren't always this smart, but we learned as we went."

"You wouldn't happen to have a ham radio on you, would you?"

"No. You need one?"

"I need to contact Song Island. Let them know we're coming back."

"I know where you can get one. There's a pawnshop about two blocks up the street. I saw a shelf full of them on the counter when I was window-scouting earlier yesterday."

Will looked over at her. "Gaby, find a vehicle that we can use. A truck, preferably, while Nate takes me to go get the radio."

"I should go instead," she said. Then added quickly, "You could use the rest."

"I'm fine."

"Bullshit. Your leg's killing you, and you barely slept last night because you didn't wake me up like you promised. Besides, it's a radio, Will. I can go get a damn radio."

He sighed. "All right. Be careful."

"SILVER?" NATE SAID.

"Yeah, silver," Gaby said.

"Didn't know that."

"No one does. We wouldn't even know about it if not for Will and Danny."

"Silver crosses, too?"

"Yeah."

"That has to be some kind of a sign, right?"

"Will doesn't believe in signs. He thinks it's all coincidence."

"I have to admit, I'm not religious either, but that was before these things crawled out of the pits of Hell and tried to eat me."

Nate walked quietly beside her. Despite the fact that he wore thick combat boots just like her, he barely made any noise. He had a smooth walking motion that was not quite swagger, but came dangerously close. She also noticed the way he kept looking around them. It wasn't paranoia, it was alertness of his surroundings. Will did that, too.

They had been walking for close to thirty minutes before they finally reached their destination. The strip mall didn't look like much as they walked across its parking lot.

"So you were in the Army?" she asked.

"Sort of. I was still in ROTC in college. Reserve Officers' Training Corp."

"Then you were supposed to go into the Army?"

"Uh huh. I was supposed to get a commission as a second lieutenant and go to the branch of my choice. That's the idea, anyway. They say, though, that mostly you go wherever they need you."

"Where were you going to go?"

"I always wanted to become a Ranger."

"Will was a Ranger."

"No shit?"

"Yeah."

"He didn't mention that."

"He wouldn't."

"I can dig it. Badass guys don't need to tell people how badass they are."

She smiled to herself, deciding that she liked the way he put things in perspective without making a big deal out of it. It was too bad about the Mohawk, though. What the hell was that about?

"Where's this pawnshop?" she asked.

"There," he said, pointing to a place called Leroy's Stuff, squeezed between a Subway sandwich shop and an AT&T outlet store.

There were bigger stores in the strip mall, but Leroy's managed to stand out because of its burglar bars over its glass wall and front door.

"See them?" Nate said, pointing at a shelf behind the counter inside the store.

Gaby saw a large selection of radios and recognized a couple that looked like the ham radio they had back in the Tower on Song Island.

"How are we going to get inside?" she asked, looking at the burglar bars. "Can you squeeze through?"

"Are you serious? I'm bigger than you."

"You're taller, but you're not bigger."

"I'm at least fifty pounds heavier. What are you, a hundred soaking wet?"

"In your dreams."

"I could probably bend the bars back far enough to slide under."

She put a hand on his right bicep and squeezed. "With what? This little thing?"

He snickered. "That's a challenge if I ever heard one. Step back."

He crouched and used the butt of his rifle to break the glass window near the bottom. He then used the barrel to knock loose the glass shards still sticking along the frame.

"Why a bolt-action rifle?" she asked. It had been on her mind ever since she saw it.

"I don't know, really, I grabbed it when all of this was happening. I never thought much about trading up. Why the M4?"

"I learned to shoot with it."

"Yeah? You good with that thing?"

"I could probably shoot a target from eighty yards."

"That's not bad for a civilian."

"Gee, thanks."

He chuckled, then cracked his knuckles. "Moment of truth."

"Fair warning: if you hurt yourself, I'm heading back without you."

He gave her a wry look. "You don't have to be such a bitch, Gaby. I'm just trying to impress you here."

She smirked. "So shut up and impress me already."

IT TOOK NATE almost an hour to bend the bars back, creating a makeshift entrance near the bottom to crawl under. Before he could slide under the bent bars, she handed him her Glock. Nate carried an M1911 Colt .45 loaded with regular ammo, and her spare magazines weren't going to fit his weapon.

The building was brightly lit by sunlight up front, but the back was pitch-dark. Gaby didn't think there was anything back there because the pawnshop gave off that undisturbed vibe, but she didn't feel like taking the risk anyway.

When he was inside, she followed, moving on her belly to slide under the bars.

He pulled her up from the floor. "I think we're safe. No monsters. Or what do you guys call them?"

"Ghouls."

"Interesting name."

"Will's idea. I used to just call them 'bloodsuckers.'" She looked around the interior of the pawnshop. It looked a lot more claustrophobic now that she was inside. "Look for something we can use and I'll grab the radio."

"Who put you in charge?"

"Just do it, will you?"

"Yes, *ma'am*," he said, snapping her a mock salute before disappearing into the back with her Glock.

Gaby, safe in the sunlight, went behind the counter and looked over the radios. She grabbed a couple, choosing the newest looking ones. She found bags, but they looked too flimsy. There were backpacks hanging from hooks nearby, and she brought a couple over and stuffed two of the radios into one bag, then grabbed unopened battery packs from a rack. By the time she was done, the backpack with the batteries was at least twice as heavy as the one with the radios.

"Nate," she called.

"Yeah?" he called back. She couldn't see him in the shadowed parts of the store.

"Find anything?"

"Junk. Lots and lots of useless junk."

"It's a pawnshop, not the Sharper Image. Let's go, Will's waiting."

"What's the hurry?"

"We haven't been in contact with Song Island for two days now. They're probably worried sick about us."

"Coming…"

While she was waiting, she grabbed some silver jewelry from the glass counter and tossed them into a backpack, then snatched up some silver pens and cutlery, too. She looked up as Nate walked back over to her, twirling a machete in one hand. With the Mohawk, he looked like some bad extra from a post-apocalyptic movie.

"Check this out," he grinned.

"It looks good on you."

"You think?"

"Sure. Now all you need is some face paint."

"Don't tempt me, because I will do it."

"Somehow, I believe you," she said, tossing him the heavy backpack with the batteries.

WHEN THEY GOT back to the house, she knew something was wrong when the first person she saw wasn't Will, but Benny. He was waiting for her next to the Caravan, the minivan's hood propped open and jumper cables dangling from it.

"Where's Will?" she asked.

"He's gone," Benny said.

"Gone? What do you mean, 'gone'?"

"He took off about thirty minutes ago."

"How the hell did he do that?"

"He found a motorcycle in the garage next door. He charged the battery with the minivan's, then took off."

"Where did he go?"

"After that Kellerson guy."

Gaby looked in the direction of the highway. She tried to see if she could hear the sound of a motorcycle, but couldn't.

"By himself?" she asked.

"Yeah," Benny said.

"What about the island?" Nate asked.

Benny took out a map from his back pocket and laid it across the minivan's driver seat. "He showed me how to get there. It's pretty much a straight shot down south. He also jotted down the radio frequency to contact the island."

Gaby didn't pay attention to what they were saying behind her. Her mind was elsewhere.

Of course Will would go after Kellerson. It wasn't just that Kellerson murdered Mike's group; he also took the children. Will knew, more than anyone, what the ghouls did to people they captured. He had seen the blood farms up close, something she had only heard about but never witnessed.

She wasn't even sure if she could blame him. The image of those kids, pressing their faces against the back windshield, still gnawed at her core.

"Gaby?" Nate said behind her. "He's got a motorcycle. You'll never catch up to him."

"Benny," she said, ignoring Nate, "I need you to take them to Song Island." She pulled one of the radios out of the backpack, along with a handful of batteries. "Contact Lara before you get there, let them know you're coming so they can come get you at the marina."

"You're not coming?" Benny asked.

"I'm going after Will."

"You'll never find him, Gaby. He's got a thirty-minute lead on you."

"Will thinks he can find this Kellerson asshole, or he wouldn't have gone. Maybe I can, too."

"That's a lot of maybes," Nate said.

She continued to ignore him, and said to Benny, "I'll follow you down to the island with Will as soon as I can."

"This is nuts, Gaby," Benny said, frowning miserably at her. He looked so young, so out of his element. "Come with me. *Please.*"

This time she ignored Benny and looked over at Nate. "I need a car. Can you find me something I can use to get through all the traffic? Maybe something small?"

"Are you seriously going after him?" Nate asked.

"Yes. Now, can you help me or not?"

He shrugged. "I saw something that might work, back in the auto body garage."

"Thank you."

"Are you kidding me?" Benny said, his face turning slightly red with frustration, though directed at Nate this time. "You're going to help her?"

"She wants to go, I'm not stopping her," Nate said. "It's her choice."

Nate walked over to the hood and detached the jumper cables, then slammed the hood down and climbed into the driver's seat, tossing the cables to the floor. The key was already in the ignition.

Gaby hurried around the hood to the passenger side, where she looked back across at Benny. "Don't stop for anything, okay? Just keep going south, and radio Lara when you're almost there."

He opened his mouth to say something, but she was already climbing into the passenger side as Nate fired up the minivan. They drove off, leaving Benny to stare after them in the side mirror, his mouth still hanging open in disbelief.

Nate turned up the street, moving around a couple of over-turned vehicles. "You might need some help," he said.

"I don't."

"Tough girl, huh?"

"Tough enough."

"All right then. I'm volunteering."

She gave him a quizzical look. "Volunteering for what?"

"To go with you."

"I don't need you to come with me."

"Doesn't matter. That's why they call it volunteering."

"What about your people?"

"They'll be fine with Benny. According to the map, it's a straightforward trip down south and they should get there by this afternoon. Besides, Stan's pretty good in a pinch, and Dwayne isn't bad with the rifle."

"The kid?"

"Yeah."

"He's just a kid."

"So are you."

"I'm nineteen."

"Yeah, well, still a kid. Anyways, we'll go pick up the car I mentioned and come back and give them the van. Sound good?"

She looked forward. "Your funeral."

"You ever heard of the power of positive thinking?"

"Is that how you've survived this long? Positive thinking?"

"Sure," he said. Then added, "That, and hiding. That works pretty well, too."

CHAPTER 19

WILL

IT WAS EASY to track the Humvees—at least for a while. All he had to do was ride the Triumph Bonneville through the clearing they had carved out of the highway traffic. He picked up the trail along I-10 before taking the ramp at the Marabond Throughway onto I-49 and continuing north.

As soon as he left the city and its stalled traffic behind, things got more iffy. There were signs here and there that the Humvees had come through, mostly the occasional vehicles pushed to the sides, their doors bearing the aggressive markings of contact with the Humvees' makeshift V-shaped steel plows. After a while, traffic thinned out so much that he went for whole kilometers without seeing a single confirmation he was on the right path. His only hope was that Kellerson's destination was still far off, which would allow him to pick up the trail farther up the highway.

Without traffic, he made good time, reaching the small city of Harvest within an hour of leaving Lafayette behind. The I-49 had gone flat to the ground a few kilometers back, and he was able to scan the sides of the highway for a gas station when the Triumph's fuel gauge dipped dangerously close to 'E.'

Harvest, Louisiana, was a city of about 5,000 people, and was oddly spread out almost entirely on the left side of the highway. There was a Holiday Inn near the feeder road, and across the street a sprawling Walmart with a parking lot teeming with vehicles.

And there, a Shell gas station two streets up from the Walmart.

Will slowed down, then turned off the I-45, rode across a small strip of grass down to a frontage road, before turning right into the Shell. There were already two vehicles waiting in line—a red Chevy station wagon and a white Mazda with red trimmings, both occupying separate gas pumps. He wasn't going to get the pumps working, not without electricity, so he eased the bike alongside the Chevy and parked, removing the motorcycle helmet and hanging it on one of the handlebars.

He pulled out a clear siphoning hose from his pack. Nate had placed a box full of them in the back of the Caravan. The kid was well-prepared, which was more than Will could say for a lot of survivors he had met along the road. That included Mike, unfortunately.

Will took a moment to look at his surroundings before getting to work pulling the fuel pump nozzle out of the station wagon's gas tank. Leaning down, he took a whiff. Not much. Gas in car tanks could sometimes last up to a year, so he was hopeful to find something to refuel the Triumph with. He moved on to the Mazda and did the same thing and got better results this time. He moved the Triumph over, then dipped the hose as far down into the Mazda's tank as it would go. He sucked on his end until he saw gas flowing, then slipped the clear plastic hose into the Triumph's open gas tank.

He sat down on the curb between the pumps and took out the bottle of tramadol from his pack. He swallowed three pills, then hunted for some food. Two strips of Jalapeno-flavored Jack Link's beef jerky tasted better than anything he had ever eaten before, which was an obvious indication he was starving. He chased them down with warm water, wishing badly for the cold drinks of Song Island.

As he was rummaging in the pack for more beef jerky, he touched something soft and pulled it out. It was the plush Hello Kitty doll from Mercy Hospital. Will stared at it for a moment, unable to recall when he had decided to hang on to it.

But he wasn't here because of the doll. It was the picture of the family whose house Nate's people were staying in that convinced him he couldn't let it go. There was no way in hell he could just let Kellerson run off with the kids from the hospital. That picture showed a nice-looking family: nice-looking parents and their nice-looking children. Two girls and a boy. They looked happy, innocent, and wide-eyed with hope. He was already considering it when he woke up this morning, but that picture, staring back at him in the living room...

Lara would understand why he couldn't go back to Song Island. At least, not yet. Not until he knew for sure.

She'll understand...

The sound of dripping water got his attention. He got up quickly, dropping the Hello Kitty, and grabbed the hose and pulled it free from the Triumph's tank as gas spilled. He jerked the hose out of the Mazda and dropped it to the ground, then screwed the lid back over the tank.

He wiped his gas-slicked hands on his pant legs and was about to climb back on the bike when he remembered the doll. Will leaned down for it when he heard the *crack!* of a gunshot and a bullet *zipped* past his head and drilled into the gas pump in front of him, shattering the glass display and scattering shards into the air.

He dove off the Triumph and darted between the pumps as two more shots smashed into the machines behind him. A fourth shot buzzed past his right ear and hit the glass door of the Shell. Will made a quick left turn as the gunshots came faster, shattering the gas station windows one by one by one.

He found salvation by lunging behind an ugly green dumpster at the end of the parking lot. It was stained and smelled, but it was also six cubic yards of fourteen gauge steel. Immediately, the sharp *ping-ping!* of bullets peppered the other side of the dumpster, vibrating across the metal and through his body.

Will almost laughed when he realized he had held on to the Hello Kitty the entire time.

God bless you, Hello Kitty.

He stuffed the plush doll back into his pack and unslung the M4A1.

As the last gunshot faded, he waited for more, but there weren't any.

Silence, as the shooter—or shooters—stopped firing.

Will reached into his pack and pulled out the baton and mirror kit. He snapped the metal rod to its full sixteen inches, then attached the mirror to the end with a solid *click*. Careful not to show himself, he stuck the baton, mirror-first, out the side of the dumpster, keeping it low enough to the ground to avoid detection.

First, he made sure no one was moving in on his position, which was his first worry. If there were more than two, he was in trouble. Two, he could probably handle. More, and they could come at him from multiple angles.

When he was certain a forward charge wasn't coming, he moved the mirror back to the highway to study the vehicles, in case the shooter was hiding behind one of them. Because the I-49 was flat to the ground, he could easily see the other side.

He glimpsed a row of buildings, including what looked like an auto body shop next to a school. The buildings were all one story, so he concentrated on the roofs because that was where the sniper—or snipers—were likely to be. A high vantage point was always the key to a successful ambush.

He picked up a structure in the distance, jutting up from the ground, and looked like some type of water tower. A lot of small cities like Harvest had their own water towers, and this one was bright white and tall. It would have made for a terrific shooting spot if it wasn't way back on the other side of the city—more than half a kilometer—and the chances of someone shooting from that distance were dismal.

He spotted another possibility, this one closer to the highway. Not the buildings that were low to the ground, but rising steel struts that went high up. He angled the mirror to get a better view, revealing a giant billboard advertising something called the Sandwhite Wildlife State Park. Cute cartoon animals poked their heads out from behind bushes, and a family of four smiled back at him as they set up camp for a picnic.

He saw a metallic reflection along the length of the billboard scaffolding, about the same time a gunshot interrupted the calmness and a bullet slammed into the concrete floor just three inches from the mirror.

Will quickly pulled the baton back.

He took a moment, gauging the distance between him and the sniper—120 meters, give or take. That meant two possible scenarios—the man was either a really good shot, or he had a nice riflescope on top of what sounded like an M4 doing most of the aiming for him.

Another M4? Same as the guys back at Mercy Hospital...

He moved to the other side of the dumpster and slowly eased

the baton out again. He immediately angled it to get a better view of the billboard, and could just make out a figure lying on top of the metal scaffolding. There was only one man up there, but he seemed pretty comfortable. The guy was patient, too, which was another potential problem. He couldn't make out a whole lot of details on the shooter, but it was easy enough to see the long barrel of the man's rifle. The sun also glinted off a riflescope resting on top of it.

Just my luck, it's probably an ACOG.

If the guy did have an ACOG, that meant he didn't have to be a great shooter. The rifle scope was good for two, maybe 300 meters in the hands of an amateur. A pro like Danny could stretch that out to 800 in optimal conditions. At a distance of a hundred and change, the shooter had the advantage. Even a blind man could hit him from that distance, given enough time and a steady enough target.

Will pulled the mirror back and considered his options.

There was no way around it. He was pinned. There were no places to hide between him and the shooter. No buildings, or raised highway structures, or even a decent natural defilade to shelter behind. He wasn't getting anywhere near the guy without being picked off first.

Which left him with…what?

There's always an option. Always…

He glanced down at his watch: 10:13 A.M.

He had plenty of daylight to come up with something. That was the only good news.

He could make the Shell next door easily, but then what? The Triumph was on the wrong side of the gas pumps and he wouldn't last more than a few seconds out there trying to climb on top of it, much less start it. And he wasn't going to hit anything from this distance with the M4A1's red dot sight. Maybe if he had an ACOG of his own, things would be different.

Yeah, and if wishes were assholes…

◄▬▮ ▮▬►

TEN MINUTES PASSED, and Will was surprised the sniper hadn't called in reinforcements yet. It made him wonder if Kellerson and the others were too far away, or if the sniper was even a collaborator.

He hadn't seen any signs of a hazmat suit, but then again, the sniper might have taken it off, including the gas mask, to aim better. That made sense. The hazmat suit was essentially a uniform—to distinguish them from other humans and to each other, and of course, to the ghouls. There would be no reason for the sniper to wear it here.

If, that is, the man was even one of Kellerson's people. For all Will knew, this could be a lone nutter. A survivalist who didn't like people trespassing through his domain. But that wouldn't explain why the man would take a shot at him. A survivalist would do all he could to avoid interaction with other people, including sniping at random passersby.

But if the sniper was one of Kellerson's men, how many of them were out there? Maybe Jones had lied to him about their number. Or maybe Kellerson had already gotten reinforcements.

A lot of possibilities, and none of them did him any good at the moment.

Will slipped the baton outside again, angling it to get another look at the billboard. Almost instantly, he heard the *crack!* of a shot and a bullet chopped into the concrete parking lot a foot from the mirror.

He pulled the baton back quickly.

Will looked over at the Triumph, leaning on its kickstand. Impossible to get to, which further limited his options. He could retreat in the other direction. He could make it to the Shell easily, and from there, the Walmart next door. The sniper couldn't hit him from that distance. He could gradually move back even farther and look for shelter.

Then what?

Will sat on the ground and took out another strip of Jack Link's beef jerky. He ate slowly, in no real hurry, breathing through his mouth to keep out the rank stench of the dumpster behind him.

The sniper wasn't going to attack. Why should he? He had the dominant position and was in total control of the situation. Attacking would be giving up his one major advantage. It was obvious now that it was just one man up there. Harvest, Louisiana, was as dead as you could get, and Will could hear almost everything, including debris scattering along the highway. The crunch of boots rushing him would be like firecrackers in this serenity.

He washed the jerky down with warm water and wished he were

back on Song Island, walking on the beaches with Lara.

Lara… If I die now, she's going to really be pissed.

He was thinking about how best to apologize to her when he heard the sound of a car engine. It was still distant, but approaching fast.

Alarms went off inside his head and he thought the car was reinforcement for the sniper, but he realized it was coming from the *wrong* direction. It wasn't approaching from the north, where Kellerson would have vanished, but coming up from the south, from Lafayette.

Will scrambled up and inched toward the edge of the dumpster. He didn't have to lean out completely to see the highway, or the green Volkswagen Beetle doing around forty miles per hour up the road. Out here, it was easy to get careless with speed; the lack of vehicles lulled you into a sense of safety that could be snatched away at any moment by just about anything, like debris, a pileup…or a sniper perched on a billboard.

The Beetle was still over 300 meters away…

Then 250…200 …

…150…

Will glanced toward the billboard. He saw sudden movement as the man shifted his position to pick up the Beetle.

…100 meters now…

At about seventy meters, Will heard the first shot from the M4, then brakes squealing and tires sliding desperately against the smooth highway. He leaned out a bit further and watched the sniper firing at the Beetle in three-round bursts.

The Beetle had come to a complete stop in the middle of the highway about fifty meters away, and Will watched a figure scramble out of the front passenger seat. Then a second later, another figure crawled out the same door, even as the sniper put round after round into the Beetle's windshield and front hood and sides. The man seemed to be spraying and praying.

Then Will glimpsed a blonde ponytail.

Gaby.

What the hell was she doing here?

He sighed. She was following him, of course. It was the same reason why he had left before she had come back, because he knew she would argue and eventually decide to come with him. She was stubborn that way. It was the same trait that helped her to persevere and overcome.

He slipped out from behind the dumpster and ran across the parking lot. His thigh throbbed, reminding him he wasn't 100 percent. Not even close.

He got twenty meters and was already crossing the feeder road and moving through the overgrown grass before the sniper remembered he was still around. The man shifted on the scaffolding and began shooting at him.

A bullet came close to putting a hole in his right arm, to match the one already in his left. Thankfully, he was able to find shelter behind a Chevy truck parked on the northbound lane. The windows above him shattered, and he heard the *ping-ping-ping!* of bullets going into the hood and the side of the truck.

He looked down the highway, in the direction of the Beetle.

Gaby was crouched behind the green vehicle, staring back at him. The guy crouched next to her looked familiar, and although Will thought it was Benny at first, he realized it was actually Nate, the twenty-something ROTC college student. The dumbass Mohawk gave it away.

Will caught Gaby's eyes over the distance and held up his left hand, with all five fingers extended. Then he began to count down.

Four...three...

She nodded back, understanding. She said something to Nate, who then scooted over to the back of the Beetle and stopped next to the back tire.

When he got to *one*, Gaby and Nate stood up in unison and began firing back at the billboard sign. They were close enough that they were hitting the billboard, and Will could hear the bullets that didn't puncture the big sign ricocheting off the metal struts around the sniper.

He waited, and only dove out from behind the Chevy when he heard the sniper firing back at the Beetle. He kept an eye on the billboard, on the cute creatures and family of four welcoming him to visit Sandwhite Wildlife State Park, as he moved across the flat highway lanes, doing his best to ignore the stabbing pain from his leg. He hit the median about four seconds later and rushed across overgrown grass that looked more like jungles.

By the time the sniper realized he was moving again, Will was on the southbound lane and already too close. He saw the man clinging low to the scaffolding, Gaby and Nate still firing at him, their bullets perforating the billboard. Every time the sniper tried to get up, another bullet came close to taking his head off.

Will stopped and took aim and fired, hitting the metal tubes just under the sniper. The man flinched as sparks flickered at his face. He scrambled up to his knees to get a better view.

Big mistake.

Will fired—and *missed.*

His bullet hit the billboard behind the man's head, but it must have come pretty close, because the sniper twisted around involuntarily, lost his balance, and fell about fourteen meters to the ground—and landed in a thick bush that hadn't been pruned in eleven months.

Gaby and Nate stopped shooting as Will jogged across the highway over the southbound feeder road and approached the sniper. He spotted a hand reaching out from the brush, groping for a Beretta M9 in a hip holster.

Will stepped on the arm and the man screamed. He bent down, pulled out the Beretta, and shoved it behind his back.

The man had a thick red beard and was wearing some kind of camo uniform. He glared up at Will with dark, bloodshot eyes, grimacing in pain, but looking, miraculously enough, still in one piece.

"How many lives you got?" Will asked.

"Seven, give or take," the guy said.

Will grinned back at him, and looking up at the billboard, saw the rifle still up there. "You forgot your rifle."

"You wanna go get it for me?" the guy said.

"Well, since you asked so nicely…"

Gaby and Nate had run over. They were out of breath, though he guessed it was less from the short jog and more from the adrenaline.

"Friend of yours?" Gaby asked.

"Not quite," Will said.

"Who is he?" Nate asked. "And why was he trying to kill you? Us?"

"I don't know," Will said. He looked back down at the man. "He's either one of Kellerson's, or some random asshole that likes shooting people for fun. So which one is it?"

The sniper said nothing.

"Kellerson?" Nate said.

"He's in charge of the collaborators I told you about," Gaby said. "The ones that attacked Mercy Hospital."

"Look around for his vehicle," Will said. "It should be around here somewhere."

"What about you?" Gaby asked.

Will looked up at the billboard. "Watch him for me. He was using an ACOG, and it's still up there."

"Sweet," Gaby said.

IT WAS SWEET, until he climbed all the way up and saw the M4 carbine with a big piece of metal sticking out of its side. There was another, smaller piece sticking out of the front lens of the scope mounted on top of it.

The sniper was sitting on the curb with his hands draped over his knees when Will climbed back down. Gaby stood in front of him, almost daring him to try something. He was smarter than he looked, though, and didn't.

"Where's the ACOG?" Gaby asked.

"It's broken. Along with the rifle."

"Of course. Why should we get any luck, right?"

"Did you find his vehicle?"

"Behind the school. Nate's bringing it over now." She looked at the man. "You killed a lot of people back at Mercy Hospital."

"I didn't kill anyone," the man said. "I was downstairs in front of the building the whole time."

"So you are one of Kellerson's men," Will said.

"I'll talk to the girl over here—I've always been partial to blondes—but you can kiss my ass."

"Did you find out where Kellerson went?" Gaby asked Will.

"I bet my friend here knows," Will said. Then he shifted his attention over to her. "What are you doing here, Gaby?"

"I could ask you the same thing," she said, staring back at him defiantly.

"You know what I'm doing here."

"Asked and answered, then."

"I left before you came back for a reason."

"I know. You tried to ditch me. That wasn't very nice."

"You shouldn't be here."

"And where should I be?"

"Back on Song Island."

"Benny's taking the others there. He doesn't need me to ride shotgun."

He sighed.

"Look," she said, showing no signs of giving in, "I can't just let you chase after Kellerson and those kids by yourself. Besides, that dick killed Amy and Jen. I liked them, Will. I liked them a lot, and I'm not going to let him get away with it."

They heard a car coming and looked over as a white truck appeared from behind the auto body shop, driving through the grass before easing onto the road. Nate was behind the wheel.

"I know your story," Will said. "What's his? He voluntarily left his group to come chasing me, too?"

Gaby actually blushed a bit. "I guess he likes me."

"And that's the only reason he came?"

"He's a guy, Will," she said, as if that should explain everything.

He smiled. He guessed it did. "What about Benny?"

"What about Benny?"

"I thought you liked him."

"Give me a break. It's the end of the world. I get to pick whoever the hell I want to hang around with. Even if that someone is your dumb, suicidal ass."

"Fair enough."

"Besides," Gaby said, "I figured, with the three of us, there's a better chance you'll come home alive, and I won't have to explain to Lara why I let you run off to get yourself killed. Tell me I'm wrong."

He didn't, because she wasn't wrong.

Three against Kellerson was better odds. It still wasn't *great* odds, but it was a hell of a lot better than it had been an hour ago when he rode out of Lafayette.

CHAPTER 20

LARA

SHE OVERSLEPT AND woke up with a hangover. It wasn't quite the pounding-in-your-brain type of hangover she had endured a couple of times in college, when she couldn't pull herself away from a party fast enough. Lara was always good at either resisting or dodging peer pressure entirely, but there were only so many times you could tell your friends you didn't want to drink with them before they took it personally.

She sat up in bed and grimaced at the sunlight splashing rudely across her face. She had slept in her clothes, but had somehow managed to kick off one shoe during the night. Not soon enough, as it turned out, because the bedsheets were covered with crumbs of dirt and dried mud.

She stumbled to her feet and into the bathroom for a hot shower, spending the full five minutes to gather herself. Afterward, Lara dressed in fresh cargo pants and a long-sleeve shirt, then grabbed her gun belt. All the while, she stepped over pieces of the broken radio and closet door she hadn't gotten to yesterday.

She picked up a new radio from the nightstand and debated whether to call Danny, who would already have been in the Tower since five this morning. With Blaine still in the Infirmary, Carly had pitched in, taking over Blaine's shift in the evenings. Soon Lara would have to start assigning Bonnie, Roy, and the others their own duties. But that could wait, maybe until after Will got back.

If he's still alive...

She had overslept her eight o'clock shift on the beach, which meant Roy had either failed to wake her up or had decided not to. If it was the former, she had cause to be worried; she needed people she could trust to do what they promised. But if it was the latter, and he purposely didn't wake her because he thought she needed the extra sleep, then she would have to thank him.

SHE FOUND BONNIE in the kitchen, helping Sarah and Jo fix breakfast for everyone.

Breakfast, unlike lunch and dinner, didn't involve fish. There were plenty of freeze-dried breakfast items in the freezer, enough to feed, according to Sarah, an army for a few years. That was an exaggeration, but not far from the truth. There were stacks of frozen biscuits, sausage patties, bacon strips, pancake batter, waffles, oatmeal, French toast sticks, popcorn chicken, and a hundred other items she didn't even know came in frozen form. Sarah had begun to catalog everything—something that was never done when Karen ran the island—and was still going through the shelves three months later.

"Where's Roy?" she asked them.

"He went to bed about two hours ago," Bonnie said. "I found him snoring on top of the boat shack this morning. Poor guy, he wanted to stay up there until you came to relieve him. I put Gwen in his place with the binoculars, if that's okay."

She nodded. "That's fine. The beach is just a precaution, anyway. She has a radio?"

"Danny assigned everyone radios this morning."

"Why didn't anyone wake me?"

Sarah gave her a sympathetic smile. "Everyone agreed you need-ed the extra sleep. Besides, Carly and Danny are around. Nothing happened, and you got your rest. Everything's fine, Lara."

Lara smiled. "So, Roy was snoring on top of the shack?"

"More like snorting," Jo said, and the girls laughed.

Lara left the kitchen, imagining Roy with his boyish blond hair snoring on the roof of the boat shack in the morning hours.

She made her way across the hotel grounds, watching and enjoying the sight of Lucy and Kylie giving themselves a tour of the island. Derek, the teenage boy who had let West out of his makeshift jail cell yesterday, was with the girls, along with the younger boy, Logan. When they saw her, they waved—all except Derek, who looked away, whether out of anger or embarrassment, she had no idea.

Adapt or perish, kid.

She crossed over to the Tower and climbed the spiral staircase, the sound of her boots *click-clacking* against the cast iron metal. She was halfway up the second floor staircase when she heard voices floating through the open door above her.

Danny, talking to a second, muffled voice.

The radio.

She hurried up the last dozen steps and burst onto the third floor. Danny was leaning over the ham radio at the table.

"Will?" she asked.

He shook his head. "Someone else, but here's a kicker—it came through our emergency frequency."

"Then it has to be Will and Gaby."

"That's what I figured." He turned back to the radio, pressed the transmit lever. "The boss just showed up. You'll want to talk to her."

Lara took the microphone from him. "How long ago?" she asked him.

"A few minutes."

She turned to the mic and pressed the lever. "This is Lara. Who am I talking to?"

"My name's Benny," a male voice said.

"Benny, how did you get this frequency?"

"Will gave it to me."

Will. Oh thank God.

"Is he okay?" she asked, somehow managing not to scream the question through the radio. Not that it stopped her heart from racing noticeably inside her chest.

"Last time I saw him," Benny said.

"He's not with you?"

"No."

"What about Gaby?"

"She went to find Will."

"What does that mean, Benny?"

"Will sent her to find a ham radio, but before she came back, he took off. Gaby decided to go after him, and Nate went with her."

"Who's Nate?"

"The guy leading this group I'm with now."

"Wait, you're not all from Mercy Hospital?"

"No." He paused for a moment. "The hospital was attacked. Most of the people there are dead. I think I might be the only survivor."

Lara exchanged a worried look with Danny. This explained so much. Why Will was out of contact, and who the man with the deep voice was that had answered when she called Jen's helicopter yesterday.

"They killed everyone?" she asked.

"I think so, yeah," Benny said. Then he added, "Except for the children."

"What about the children?"

"They took them," Benny said. "The ones Will called collaborators. That's where Will went. To get the children back."

<hr>

OF COURSE WILL would try to get the children back. Will was practical to a fault, but there was a streak of righteous decency in him that she admired and loved. So *of course* he would decide to go on a fool's errand to save children he had never met, whose names he probably didn't even know. Because there was a chance he could succeed, and a chance was good enough for Will.

If you get killed, I'm going to kick your ass, Will.

Knowing why he was doing what he was doing didn't make it any easier to accept. But she understood it. God, did she understand it. She might have even done the same thing in his position, though she was sure her chances of success would be far less.

"That's Will for you," Danny said. "Personally, I think he's just going after this Kellerson guy because he's bored."

She stood at the window next to him, looking out at Bonnie's girls gathered near the edge of a nearby cliff, throwing rocks at the lake below. Even Derek seemed to have come out of his shell and was skipping his share of pebbles.

She was still trying to digest what Benny had told her a few minutes ago. Will, Gaby, and Mercy Hospital. Most of all, she couldn't quite wrap her head around the collaborators deciding to kill everyone except the kids.

"Why did they take the children?" she said out loud.

"I'm just a grunt, doc," Danny said. "You tell me."

"They have a plan."

"Collaborators?"

"No, the ghouls. They keep pressing forward, building on what they've done. The Purge, the blood farms. The one we saw in Dansby was just the early stage. The one Blaine saw in Beaumont was another one, but further along. Now they're taking children and killing the adults. Before, they took the adults, too. But that's changed. Why?"

"I get the feeling Will's thinking the same thing. I wouldn't be surprised if that's one of the reasons he's not back here yet."

"I don't understand."

"*Know thy enemy,*" Danny said. "Willie boy really takes that motto seriously."

BENNY AND THE others reached Beaufont Lake around four in the afternoon. They arrived on a single tank of gas, and Benny radioed ahead when they were halfway down Route 27. Lara remembered when they had originally come down the same stretch of road. It had seemed as if the drive would never end.

Danny, with Bonnie, took the pontoon boat back over to the marina to get the new arrivals. Bonnie volunteered, and Lara was more than willing to accept. She had more questions for Benny—about Will, about Mercy Hospital, about what had happened to everyone there—but she needed them to rest up first.

With six new people now on the island, Lara spent the next couple of hours with Carly in the hotel arranging living quarters for them. They needed five rooms for one couple, a mother and her teenage son, a teenage girl, and Benny. They had to bring fresh bedsheets, blankets, and pillows from the supply closets in the back. Eventually, Lara knew they would have to start prioritizing the rooms when the island's population increased. She had already begun keeping a ledger, noting everyone's room number, as well as writing down the names of the room's occupants on the doors themselves using large white envelope labels she had found in one of the offices.

It was mundane things like that that kept her from spending every second worrying about Will and Gaby. They were out there, in God knew how much danger, chasing men who had already tried to kill them.

If she didn't keep her mind constantly occupied with something else, like the tedious running of the island, she was almost certain she would go insane.

IT WAS ALMOST five when everyone was back on the island and she could breathe easier. Sending people on land always left her anxious, especially to a launching point as obvious as the marina. You never knew who could be lurking in the grass, harboring ill-intentions.

Like West…

She let Benny and the newcomers eat first. They were tired from the long drive, from being squeezed into a vehicle for most of the day. She remembered how that felt, too.

She asked Roy, who had woken up, to go back to the beach and stay on the boat shack. Afterward, she went to the third floor of the Tower and sat down at the table with the radio. She had renewed hope that Will would contact them, because the first thing Benny had told her when they met was that Gaby had taken a second radio with her.

That was the good news.

The bad news was that she hadn't heard from them yet. The fact that they had a radio and hadn't contacted Song Island introduced a whole new set of possibilities, each one more confusing than the next.

Had Gaby even managed to find Will? According to Benny, Will had an hour's head start on her and Nate. If they hadn't caught up to him yet, it explained a lot. Moving by himself, on a motorcycle, Will would be able to travel faster on the highway. Gaby and Nate, on the other hand, had left in a Volkswagen Beetle.

She waited with Maddie in the Tower, staring at the radio and willing it to make a sound, but the damn thing refused to obey her mental commands.

"How long are you staying up here?" Maddie asked after a while.

"Why? Are you tired of me already?"

"Not at all, boss. Just wonderin'."

"I'm waiting for Benny."

"Speaking of which, what do you think of them?"

"Stan's an electrician, so he's going to be invaluable. And Kendra was a gardener at Home Depot, so she'll come in handy when we start growing things around here."

"It would be nice to have some fruits and vegetables to go along with all the fish," Maddie said.

Lara heard footsteps on the spiral staircase and looked over as Benny poked his head up through the opening. His face was covered in sweat from the climb and he looked older with the stubble, though she guessed he was only eighteen or nineteen. He had dimples that reminded her of a boy she used to like back in middle school.

"You guys could use an elevator in this place," Benny said as he climbed up onto the floor. "I thought I was going to have a stroke halfway up."

He was breathing hard and moving on a crutch—really, a baseball bat with a car seat's headrest duct taped at the top. One of his leg was encased in splints made from two pieces of wood, with more duct tape wrapped around them.

"How's the leg?" she asked.

"Hurts."

"But you're not in any major pain?"

"I pretty much loaded up on painkillers on the way over here, so it's mostly numbed over, thank God."

"I'll look at the leg later, then get Danny to make you some proper crutches."

He nodded gratefully. "You're a doctor, right?"

"I'm just a third-year medical student."

"Three more years than I got."

She smiled. If she had a dime every time someone said that to her...

"Sit down, Benny."

She gave him her chair. Benny sat down and glanced up at the glass skylight.

"You knew Gaby, too?" Lara asked.

"Yeah, we—" He stopped short, then actually blushed a bit. "Yeah, we got to be pretty good friends."

Lara and Maddie exchanged a knowing look.

"So you wanted to ask me some questions?" Benny said.

"Tell me what happened at Mercy Hospital," Lara said.

"What do you wanna know?"

"Everything. The men that attacked the hospital. What did they look like. How many were there. How Jen died. Everything you can tell me, Benny."

Benny nodded. He took his time, gathering his thoughts.

"They came out of nowhere," he began. "One moment they weren't there, and the next they're all over the tenth floor. It was bloody. It was so bloody…"

CHAPTER 21

GABY

GABY BELIEVED IN a higher power, that there was a God out there somewhere watching over her and her friends. But she'd be damned if she didn't think she was listening to God himself as Will crouched in front of Kellerson's sniper and talked to the guy.

"Here's the deal," Will began. "I was with Harris County SWAT before all of this happened. Before that, I was an Army Ranger and I served in Afghanistan. I won't bore you with the details, but I wasn't building roads or schools or holding anybody's hand when I was in-country. They sent me to kill people, because that's what I do. I'll admit it, I did it—and I still do it—very well."

The guy's face hadn't changed since Will started talking, and the only time he moved at all was to pick pieces of dried grass out of his thick red beard.

Will continued: "So when I tell you that I have absolutely no desire to hurt you, but that I will if you don't tell me everything I want to know, you should take it as gospel. I would have done this to you before the world went to shit if you had something I needed. Now, after everything that's happened? The whole end of the world stuff? The lying in wait to put a bullet in my head? I will hurt you—and hurt you badly—and I won't lose a single second of sleep over it."

The man finally looked Will in the eyes.

"Do you understand me?" Will asked.

The guy nodded. "Yeah, I understand you."

"Do you believe me?"

"Yeah, I believe you."

"So tell me about Kellerson."

"What do you wanna know?"

Gaby exchanged a look with Nate. *That was easy.*

The man leaned back tiredly against the tire of the Saleen sports truck he had been using, trapped between Will in front and Gaby and Nate on either side. Not that he noticed Gaby or Nate. His eyes—even if he pretended otherwise—were firmly focused on Will.

"What's your name?" Will asked.

"Harris," the man said.

"Where is Kellerson, Harris?"

"Sandwhite."

"Sandwhite Wildlife State Park?" Nate asked.

"Yeah. Just like on the billboard."

"What's he doing there?" Will asked.

"That's where the nightcrawlers told him to take the kids."

"Where in the park?"

"I don't know. We usually just deliver them to the main parking area and the others come and get them."

"Others?"

"Others like us."

"Collaborators."

"Yeah, I guess."

"Nightcrawlers?" Gaby said.

"It's what we call those things," Harris said. "Why? What do you call them?"

"Ghouls."

Harris shrugged. "Good name as any, I guess."

"So there are ghouls—nightcrawlers—in Sandwhite, farther up the road," Will said.

"I guess so," Harris said. "It's dark in there. There are parts of the place where sunlight doesn't even reach. They might have been there all this time, I don't know, we never stuck around long enough to find out."

"Who told Kellerson to take the kids there?"

"Them."

"Who is 'them'?"

"One of them had blue eyes…"

Blue-eyed ghouls.

Gaby had never seen one herself, but Will had. So had Lara, and Blaine, and Maddie. She wasn't sure if she wanted to see a blue-eyed ghoul; the black-eyed kind was disturbing enough.

"He's right," Nate said. "The trees grow pretty big in there."

"You know the area?" Will asked.

"I grew up around here. Used to go to Sandwhite every now and then for camping and hunting."

Will said to Harris, "What are they doing with the kids in Sandwhite?"

"I have no fucking idea," Harris said. "We just drop them off and leave."

"Where were you headed after Sandwhite?"

"I dunno. Kellerson didn't say. Probably to pick up more men. You guys—back there at the hospital—did a pretty good number on us."

"How many are left with Kellerson now?"

"Just me and Danvers. You killed the rest."

"So Kellerson isn't at Sandwhite right now?"

"Probably not. He went on ahead of me yesterday."

"And left you behind. Why?"

"In case there were more of you Mercy Hospital guys chasing us. He got spooked when you showed up with the helicopter yesterday. We saw it a mile away, on our ass."

"That was his idea? Using the Law?"

"Yeah."

"Where'd you get something like that?"

"We raided Fort Polk. Kellerson's got all kinds of hardware stashed around the state."

"Fort Polk is in Vernon Parish," Nate said. "About 180 klicks from Lafayette."

"What else does he have?" Will asked Harris.

"Everything," Harris said. "We raided the armory."

"Is that where you got all the M4s?"

"Yeah."

"Where's your base?"

"Tatum Golf and Country Club."

"Near Oden Lake?" Nate asked.

"Yeah."

"Country club?" Gaby said.

"Clean living," Harris said. "Greens as far as the eye can see. And you can catch fish at the lake nearby."

"Yeah, but who cuts the grass?" Nate smirked.

"Who cares. We didn't go there for the golf."

Will stood up. Harris tensed, then looked over at Gaby and Nate. She could guess what was probably going through his mind at the moment: *"Now what?"*

"Do we just…leave him here?" she asked Will.

Will didn't answer right away.

That, more than anything, unnerved Harris. "Leave me here," the man said. "I told you everything you wanted to know. You promised."

"Did I?" Will said.

Harris opened his mouth to protest, but stopped short. It was true. The only thing Will had promised was pain if he didn't talk. Other than that, she didn't remember anything about letting Harris go.

"Look, I was just following orders," Harris said.

Will ignored him and glanced down at his watch before looking over at Nate. "What's the word on the Beetle?"

"There are at least four bullets in the engine block," Nate said. "It's not going anywhere."

"Transfer everything you have over to the Saleen."

"Now?" Gaby said.

Will nodded.

Gaby took the hint and started off, but noticed Nate wasn't following. She glanced back at him. "Nate, come on."

He hesitated, before grudgingly leaving with her.

They walked along the feeder road for a moment, then crossed over to the highway's southbound lane, back to the Beetle farther down the I-49.

Nate kept glancing back at Will and Harris. "Is he going to kill that guy?"

"I don't know," Gaby said. "Maybe."

"Should we stop him?"

"Why?"

"It's murder, Gaby."

"He was trying to murder us."

"It's not the same thing."

"Isn't it?"

"If we killed him during the gun battle, that's fine. I won't lose sleep over it. But this…this is murder."

She gave him a sharp look, ready to get pissed at him, but saw the very real conflict on his face. He looked so young, even with that Mohawk.

"When did you get so soft and gooey?" she asked instead.

He chuckled. "Is that what I'm being? Soft and gooey? Just because I don't want Will to murder some guy?"

"You really think he wouldn't do the same to us if the shoe was on the other foot?"

"I'm sure he would. But we're better than him. He and this Kellerson guy. These collaborators. That's what sets us apart from them."

Gaby didn't reply. She didn't really know how. Maybe he was right. The old Gaby would have jumped at the chance to agree with him. But she had seen too many things, faced too much ugliness from her fellow man, and lost too many friends to just forgive Harris for "following orders."

When she didn't answer, Nate said, "Gaby?"

"What?"

"Nothing. I expected you to say something."

She shrugged. "What do you want me to say?"

"I don't know. That you agree with me would be nice."

"I don't."

"You don't?"

"No. Why do you find that so hard to believe?"

"I thought—" He paused. "I just thought you would."

"Well, I don't."

"So you're fine with Will shooting Harris in cold blood?"

"I'm fine with whatever Will decides to do with him."

"You trust him that much?"

"I trust him more than I trust you. You're cute and all, but you haven't been through the shit me and Will have been through."

He grinned crookedly at her. "You think I'm cute?"

She gave him a wry look. "Really? From arguing for Harris's life in one breath to grinning like an idiot over me calling you 'cute' in the other? Classy, Nate, real classy."

"Hey, a guy's gotta make some points where he can. Girls like you don't come around very often, you know."

"I have bruises and scratches all over my face, and my forehead looks like someone cut it open with a hammer, then poured dirt into it."

"Scars heal and bruises fade, but you'll always be beautiful."

"Wow. That was almost...sweet."

He laughed. "I get some brownie points for that, right?"

"I'll think about it," she said.

GABY WAS AMAZED they had survived the ambush unscathed, given the state of the Beetle. It was almost completely destroyed, every single window shattered, even the back windshield. The doors were covered in bullet holes and the car seats and dashboards were shredded. The man had really unleashed on them, but then again, given how much ammo he was carrying inside the Saleen, she guessed he wasn't exactly trying to conserve bullets.

Before she left Benny, Gaby had taken some of the emergency supplies from the gym bag they were hauling around, giving Benny the bulk of it to take back to Lara. The ham radio she had brought with her was in pieces in the back of the Beetle, with a nice big hole in the center.

They grabbed their packs and headed back to Will.

"RADIO'S KAPUT," GABY said.

Will nodded, keeping one eye on Harris, who was still seated on the curb in front of him. As she expected, Will didn't look all that torn up about the loss of the ham radio.

Of course not. He left before I came back for a reason...so he wouldn't have to explain to Lara why he isn't coming back to the island yet.

Slick, Will, real slick.

Next to them, Nate was busy taking inventory of everything from inside Harris's truck, including one of the green ammo cans that had been stolen from Mercy Hospital. The bullets inside were 9mm and 5.56x45mm silver rounds, not that Harris had cared or noticed. There was also a white Level B tactical hazmat suit in the backseat, along with a spare M4 rifle, a backpack, gas mask, and a crate of food.

"So what're we gonna do with this asshole?" she asked Will.

Harris narrowed his eyes at the insult.

"We'll leave him here," Will said. "If he survives the day, fine. If not, that's his problem."

Gaby glanced over at Nate to see his reaction. He looked satisfied with the compromise.

"I can live with that," Nate said.

"What about my suit?" Harris asked.

"What about it?" Will said.

"I need it."

"That's too bad, because we're taking it, too."

Harris didn't bother arguing.

She left Will and Harris and climbed into the front passenger seat of the truck.

Nate settled down behind the steering wheel, moving his butt around the luxurious leather sports seat and whistling his approval. "I could get used to this."

"Considering the fates of every vehicle I've been in lately, you probably shouldn't."

"Oh come on, your luck's changing."

"What gave you that crazy idea?"

"You met me, didn't you?"

"Unbelievable," she said. "We're probably going to die soon, and all you can think about is getting into my pants."

"Is it working yet?"

"You're not even at the belt."

"Damn," Nate said.

She watched Harris outside the window, looking forlornly back at them. He hadn't bothered to move from the curb, probably realizing there was nowhere to run anyway.

Will soon showed up, riding his Triumph motorcycle across the flat highway lanes over to them. He stopped next to Harris, who remained seated like a kid sent to the corner as punishment.

"What's the point?" Harris asked. "So you save a couple of kids.

Then what? There are hundreds—*thousands*—of people out there. You'll never be able to save them all. Why even bother?"

"How many did you personally hand over to the ghouls?" Will asked.

"Enough."

"Maybe you can explain to them how loyal you've been when you see them tonight."

Will gunned the motorcycle and shot forward, up the southbound lane, before switching over to the northbound. Nate eased the truck back onto the road, then increased speed as they hopped the lanes. Will had slowed down for them to catch up before increasing speed again.

They drove past a sign that read, "Sandwhite Wildlife State Park. 29 Miles."

Gaby looked in her side mirror, back at Harris. He was still sitting on the curb, watching them go.

"How long do you think he'll last out here by himself?" Nate asked. "Without food, weapons, or the hazmat suit?"

Gaby remembered the kids, their faces pressed against the rear windshield of the Humvee, looking back at her, horror frozen on their tear-streaked faces.

"Gaby?" Nate said. "How long do you think he'll last out here?"

"I couldn't give a shit," she said finally.

SANDWHITE WAS ONLY twenty-nine miles from Harvest, but as they approached the five-mile mark, Will slowed down and pulled over to the side, motioning for them to drive up next to him.

Gaby glanced down at her watch: 11:55 A.M.

Nate pulled up alongside Will and put the truck in park.

Will flicked up his helmet's visor. "How big is Sandwhite?"

"It's big," Nate said. "About 10,000 acres the last time I was there. The state might have expanded it since."

"Ten thousand is massive," Gaby said.

"Yeah, it's pretty big. Some rich family originally owned it before gifting it over to the state. It's essentially halved—one for the hunters and the other for campers. It's got trails, but honestly, it's a good idea not to get lost inside at night."

"What kind of wildlife?" Will asked.

"Squirrels, rabbits, wood ducks, and large herds of deer. And oh, woodcocks."

"Woodcocks?" Gaby said doubtfully.

"Yeah, you know, small birds with long, skinny beaks?"

"You're making that up."

"No, I'm serious. They're called woodcocks."

"Trails?" Will asked.

"About twelve miles in all, mostly used by hunters. We used to notch some nice trophy bucks from those woods."

"What's the plan?" she asked Will.

He glanced at his watch. "What are you loaded with, Nate?"

"I have Harris's 9 mil Beretta, and I swapped my rifle with his spare M4. Thought it'd be more appropriate if we run across this Kellerson asshole."

"I reloaded all the mags with the silver from the ammo can," Gaby added. "Just in case."

Will looked forward. "If Harris was telling the truth, then Kellerson will have already delivered the kids and left yesterday. You said there are places in the park where the sun doesn't reach?"

"A lot of places," Nate said.

"This is where I give you the option of turning back," Will said. "Gaby—"

"Forget it," she said, cutting him off. "The only place I'm going is wherever you are."

She thought she was in for an argument, but instead he looked at Nate. "What about you, ROTC?"

"Hell, I came this far," Nate said. "Why the hell not?"

"You could die."

"Yeah, well, I could die tomorrow. Or the day after that. If I am going to die, I might as well do it for a good cause. And rescuing some kids is as good as any."

Will nodded. "Harris said they drove to the main parking lot and waited for the others to come get the kids. You know where that is?"

"There's only one main parking lot, in the center of the park. I know where it is."

"All right. You take point."

Will flicked his visor back down and waited. Nate pulled on

ahead, and Will followed behind them.

Gaby glanced over at Nate. "Are you doing all of this just for me?"

He gave her a serious look. "Maybe. I don't know. But I wasn't lying back there. I don't like the idea of kids being hand-delivered to those things by other human beings. It makes my skin crawl."

"Yeah, me too."

He drove in silence for a while, before asking her, "How good is Will? Tell me the truth."

"He's really good. Just do what he says and follow his lead, and our chances of coming out of this alive are decent."

"I was hoping for more than decent."

"Yeah, well, hope springs eternal, Louisiana."

◄━━▌ ▐━━►

NATE PULLED OFF I-49 five miles later, taking a small two-lane road for the next ten minutes.

"Sandwhite?" she asked.

Nate nodded. "This is the main entrance. From here, we'll go to the main parking, which is exactly in the middle of the park for easy access to all the other areas."

They passed large sections of undeveloped land, broken up by the occasional wall of trees to the left and right of them. There were buildings and small businesses, but no houses or farms that she could see. It was quiet, almost serene, but Gaby couldn't shake the feeling there were things inside the woods watching her.

Eventually, Nate slowed down and took a right onto another two-lane road. It went east for about five minutes, before curving left for another two, then arching back right again. They passed more thick trees, so many and so tightly packed together that it was impossible to see slivers of sunlight between them.

Gaby shivered slightly at the thought of being lost in there. It would take days, maybe weeks, to find her way out. That was, if she survived the first night...

"You okay?" Nate asked.

"Yeah, I'm fine. How much farther?"

"One more mile."

They passed a group of tanned buildings. There were three similarly colored trucks parked in front of them, but she didn't look quickly enough to catch the sign up front.

Then there were more trees. Everywhere. She had never seen so many trees in her life.

Ten thousand acres. Twelve miles of trail. Where do we even start?

She was about to give up ever reaching anything resembling civilization again when Nate slowed down and pulled onto an asphalt parking lot. It wasn't nearly as big as she had expected, given the size of the park. There were about thirty to forty vehicles already inside, with plenty of empty slots for at least a hundred more. The wall of trees made it look foreboding, like the green scenery could collapse in on them at any moment.

"I thought it'd be bigger," she said.

"Most of the hunters like to park around the area so they can reach their favorite hunting grounds faster. The people who park here are mostly campers and hikers. There's a bayou about a mile's walk where you can do some fishing."

"You do come here a lot."

"What can I say? I'm easily bored. Hunting and fishing take up a lot of time."

Will pulled up ahead of them, sliding his motorcycle into one of two open spaces flanked by a white and a red truck. They were both much bigger than the Saleen and swallowed up the sports truck as it eased into the empty spot next to Will's bike.

Will was already off the Triumph with his M4A1 in his hands by the time she and Nate climbed out with their packs and rifles.

The air around them was thick with the sound of animals. There was more wildlife here than she had seen or heard in a long time, though they were all either perched on branches or high up in the trees. Land animals, like in the cities, didn't last very long these days.

"Nate," Will said. "What's the highest point in the park? Some place where we can get a good look at what's around us?"

Nate thought about it. "Trail #8 takes us north to Sandwhite Point. It's a hill and should give us our best view of the surrounding area."

"There was something that looked like official buildings about a mile back, with some trucks in front of them."

"Game warden's office."

"All right. If anything happens and we get separated, we fall back to those buildings to meet up. Whatever happens, the two of you stay together. Understand?"

Nate and Gaby nodded.

"Lead the way, Nate," Will said.

Nate headed off across the parking lot, she and Will following.

The animal noises seem to increase in intensity as they neared the wall of trees, as if they knew humans were approaching. Her chest tightened as she took her first step inside the woods, the almost-choking chilly air wrapping around her fingers.

God help me to survive this place...

CHAPTER 22

WILL

WILL SPENT MOST of his career moving across hot deserts and rocky mountainsides before trading it all for hard concrete and steel jungles. There were woods in Afghanistan, but they were nothing like the thick, deep canvas of Sandwhite Wildlife State Park.

Nate was up front, keeping to Trail #8, with Gaby behind him. They were both moving at a fast clip while maintaining complete silence. Will kept them within range while drifting behind a bit, watching for signs of movement around them. The last thing he needed was to get outflanked in here.

Squirrels raced along branches above his head, and woodcocks fluttered when they got too close.

The trail was essentially a dirt path, approximately two meters wide. He saw old tracks—truck tires and faded shoe prints, some trampled over by much fresher prints. Bare feet.

Ghouls.

They were, without a doubt, moving behind enemy lines.

After about twenty minutes on Trail #8, Will caught up with them. "How far to Sandwhite Point?"

"Maybe another ten minutes," Nate said.

"You sure?"

"Pretty sure," he said, pointing at a sign about ten meters ahead that read, "Sandwhite Point" with an arrow pointing up the trail.

"Good enough," Will said.

They continued up Trail #8.

There was supposed to be a massive deer population in the park, but so far he hadn't seen a single one. Except for the birds and animals high above them, it seemed as if they were the only living beings moving on the ground.

They walked for another fourteen minutes before they finally reached Sandwhite Point. It wasn't much—a wide, circular clearing with a cliff at the end. Four wooden picnic tables were spread across the grounds, faded trash bins on opposite sides, and a couple of crushed beer cans half-buried in the dirt. There was an opening at the top of the clearing, which allowed sunlight to pour through. They had been moving through heavy canopies for so long that finally feeling heat against his skin again brought an odd sense of comfort.

"Sandwhite Point," Nate said.

"It's not much," Gaby said.

"Nope. But it's the highest point in the entire park." He started toward the cliff, Gaby and Will following. "We're still at the northern edge of the 10,000 acres that make up the park. Won't be able to see everything from here, but we'll be able to see a lot of it."

Will glanced down at his watch: 12:45 P.M. "If we don't find anything in two hours, we need to start heading back to the vehicles and looking for shelter for the night."

"I don't mind telling you, I'm looking forward to that," Nate said. "This place gives me the creeps."

"But you've been here before," Gaby said.

"Yeah, but it was never like *this*. Quiet and empty, and…"

"Dead," she finished.

"Yeah."

Nate and Gaby reached the cliff first, when Nate suddenly went into a crouch, grabbing Gaby's arm and pulling her down with him.

Will followed suit, his rifle raised, searching the area behind them. "What?"

"Oh my God," Gaby said, her voice breathless. "Will, come see this."

When he was sure there was no one behind them, Will hurried over, keeping low. He crouched next to Gaby and peered over the cliff.

Where he expected to see a valley teeming with nature, there was instead a large, ragged man-made clearing at least half a kilometer in diameter. It was a camp, filled with gray, beige, green, and camouflage tents. He was looking down at a sea of thick, heavy canvas spread out to accommodate a large population that didn't belong among the greens and trees that surrounded it.

Will had begun counting, starting at the south end, only to stop when he hit fifty tents and realized he wasn't even close to the middle yet.

He fished out binoculars from his pack and peered through them.

It was impossible to miss the large blue tent in the center. It looked like some kind of grand circus tent, and was literally and figuratively placed—purposefully, he assumed—in the very center of the camp. A long stream of people moved in and out of it, including men in white Level B hazmat suits, the sunlight glinting off the lenses of gas masks either over their faces or hanging from their waists.

"Collaborators," Gaby whispered.

"Not all of them," Will said.

There were at least two, maybe three hundred people for every collaborator he spotted. Regular people. Men and women, boys and girls, old and young. They moved between tents, reminding him of homeless refugees saved from some disastrous, unwinnable war.

Maybe not so far from the truth...

"What the hell is going on?" Nate whispered.

It was a good question, because the people down there didn't look afraid. He saw small circles of people gathered around camp-fires, and smelled the very strong aroma of smoked meat filling the air. The voices drifting up from the camp were not dripping with mortal terror. If he didn't know better, he would think he was looking at some kind of mass cookout.

There was hurricane fencing around the camp, and a group of twenty to thirty men were swinging axes at the north side, felling trees to make more room. A couple of men in Level B hazmat suits stood watch, though there was an easiness, a sense of familiarity and cooperation between the two groups that was obvious even from this distance. They looked more like friends instead of captors and captives.

There were vehicles on the other side of the fence—trucks, mostly. He counted thirty to forty in all, including a half-dozen green military five-ton transport trucks he hadn't seen since his days in the

Army.

"I've seen this before," Gaby whispered.

"Where?" Nate asked.

"Back in school. During our World War II phase of world history. This reminds me of concentration camps."

"Is that what this is? A prison for human survivors?"

"I think we're looking at something else," Will said, lowering the binoculars.

"Like what?" Nate asked.

"Like what the ghouls have planned for us. First The Purge, then the blood farms, and now this."

"Yeah, but what is 'this'?" Gaby said.

"You're right, it's some kind of camp," Will said. "But I don't think it's a concentration camp. Maybe the better analogy would be an internment camp."

"What's the difference?"

"FDR illegally detained over 100,000 Americans of Japanese ancestry during World War II. They weren't harmed, and they were fed and allowed to work, but they were still captives. It's one of the biggest black stains in American history, but people survived it, and they were eventually freed and allowed to return to society."

"They look almost...content," Gaby said, staring down at the camp.

"Blaine said there were thousands of people in the Beaumont mall when he showed up, and by the time he left, they were gone. Where did they go?"

"You think they were brought here?"

"Maybe not here specifically, but maybe a place like this one."

Will shook his head, processing the information.

What the hell have you been doing out here, Kate?

"I think we're looking at the next phase of whatever final solution the ghouls are moving toward," he said. "This...is something new. Something we haven't seen before. And it's big, so it has to be a pretty significant part of their plan."

Gaby shivered next to him, though she did her best to hide it. "What now?"

"The blue tent."

"What about it?"

"It might be worth seeing what's going on inside. It's the center of whatever's happening here, literally and figuratively."

"You mean you want to sneak in there?"

"The suit," Will said. "The one Harris wore. It's still in the truck?"

Nate nodded. "We left it in the back seat."

"Will," Gaby said, "you're not seriously thinking about putting that suit on and going *in* there?"

"That blue tent," Will said. He couldn't look away from it. "The answer is in there."

"There has to be another way."

"I'm open to suggestions."

She struggled for an answer, and finally said, "I don't know."

"There's no reason why they wouldn't think I belong if I wear the suit. Especially with the gas mask on."

"You hope," she said.

"Yeah," he nodded.

He tried to eyeball the size of the blue tent. It had to be at least fifty meters in diameter, easily half the size of a football field. What the hell was going on in there? What would they need something that big for?

"How many hazmat suits did you see?" Nate asked.

"About thirty, give or take," Will said.

"How many people do you think are down there?" Gaby asked.

"A thousand?" Nate said.

"Maybe," Will said. "A lot, in any case." He glanced down at his watch again. "Let's head back to the vehicles. I want to get in there and out before it gets dark—"

Snap!

Will was already rising and spinning, the rifle lifted, before the sound of snapping twigs had even run its course.

He stared across the clearing at a figure in a white hazmat suit. The man stared back at him with light blue eyes, gas mask clipped to his hip.

No, he was wrong. It wasn't a man.

It was a *boy*.

A teenager. Sixteen, maybe even younger than that. *(Fifteen?)* The gun belt was too big around his slim waist, and the holstered handgun hung too loosely from his hip. He looked like a boy wearing his father's uniform.

And there was something else: the hazmat suit had a name tag, and the word "Ray" written across it. Nothing fancy, just an envelope label with the name scribbled on it in black marker. It was the first time Will had seen the collaborators putting any identifying marks on their uniforms.

Ray the teenager had curly brown hair, and he was holding an apple near his mouth. He had taken a bite, and was in the process of chewing when he saw them. Or more specifically, looked into the barrel of Will's M4A1.

Gaby and Nate had both turned at his point and taken aim at the kid with their own weapons. The teenager gawked at them, the apple absurdly poised in front of his mouth, as if he didn't know whether to drop it or continue eating it.

"Oh, shit," Gaby whispered.

There was a radio clipped to the teenager's hip, and Will watched—and wished he wasn't seeing it—as the kid dropped the apple and reached for the radio.

"Don't," Will said.

The kid looked at him, then down at the radio, then back up at Will again. Blue eyes trembled, and the kid's lips quivered.

"No, don't," Nate said. "Don't do it, kid, just don't do it, for Christ sake."

Ray unclipped the radio and lifted it to his lips.

"Don't," Will said again, louder this time.

"No, please, don't," Gaby said.

The kid pressed the transmit lever and said, "Intruders—"

Will shot Ray in the chest.

The gunshot shattered the stillness, the loud boom like thunder flashing across the entire park. Birds took off in sudden flight, the sound of hundreds, maybe thousands, of flapping wings almost as loud as the gunshot.

"Go!" Will shouted.

They broke off into a run.

Will snatched up the dead teenager's radio almost at the same instant it squawked, and a man's voice shouted through: "Ray, was that you? Ray!" Then, when Ray didn't answer, the man shouted, "Converge on Trail #8 now! Trail #8!"

Gaby, running at a full sprint up ahead, looked back at him. "Where are we going?"

"The truck!" he shouted. "Get to the truck and get out of here!"

"What about you?"

"I'll be right behind you!"

They hadn't been moving for more than ten seconds when a white hazmat suit stepped out of the tree line ten meters in front of them. Will opened his mouth to shout a warning, but he didn't have to. Nate, who was setting the pace up front, shot the man from nearly point blank range, his sprinting taking him almost on top of the figure when he fired.

Gaby smartly veered around the collapsing body so she wouldn't have to slow down. The man had dropped an Uzi submachine gun as he fell. By the time Will recognized the weapon and its value, he had already leaped over the body, and kept running.

The radio in his hand squawked again, and another voice, this one female, said, "Barnes, where's the truck? Where's the goddamn truck?"

A man who Will guessed was Barnes replied, "I'm close!"

Will looked down Trail #8 and for the first time realized how wide it was. He remembered the faded tire prints from earlier.

He glanced back about the same time he heard the roar of a truck behind him, still hidden by the turn farther down the trail.

"Gaby! Nate!" he shouted. "We have to split up! Whatever you do, make your way to the truck and get out of here!"

"Will—" she began, but stopped when the truck appeared out from the turn behind them, forty meters back. There was a man in a hazmat suit behind the wheel and two more in the back with assault rifles. "Shit!" she finished.

"Now!" Will shouted, and darted right.

He looked back briefly and saw Gaby and Nate jumping out of the trail and into the woods, going left. He hadn't turned his head completely back around when the rattle of gunfire filled the woods. Tree branches splintered and snapped, tree barks exploding under a torrent of bullets that seemed to be coming from every direction.

Will pushed his head down as low as he could and still maintained his speed, pushing hard through the woods, ignoring the slapping tree branches, the ground crunching under his boots, the sound of gunfire everywhere.

A man shouted through the radio he was still holding: "They're in the woods! They're in the fucking woods!"

"Where?" the same woman from earlier shouted.

"Off Trail #8, north sector! I got two heading west and one heading east!"

"Converge!" another man shouted through the radio. "If you're in the woods, I want you to converge on them now!"

"What about the camp?" someone else asked.

"Stay back! If you're not already in the woods, maintain your positions! I repeat: do not leave the camp unprotected!"

"Motherfucker, they killed Ray!" someone else said.

"We'll box them in," the woman said. "They're not getting out of here alive!"

SEEN FROM THE wrong angle, the branches of oak trees could look like the spindly arms of some angry demon emerging from the darkness to snatch a child from his bed. To a grown man, they looked like shelter, hiding him from men in hazmat suits. If he couldn't see them, then they couldn't see him. Of course, he could *hear* them, but that was only because they were big and clumsy and loud.

His watch ticked to 1:15 P.M.

Six hours, give or take, before sunset. He had to be out of the park by then. If he was caught in here, among these trees, he was a dead man. Or worse. He didn't particularly feel good about the worse part, and the dead man part didn't sit all that well with him, either.

Lara would be so pissed at me right about now.

He was crouched behind a large oak tree, one of thousands in the area, indistinguishable from a thousand others. He had been in the same spot, in the same position, for the last few minutes, listening to the men moving around him.

Three of them. Heavily armed and moving with all the subtlety of civilians in combat boots, lugging around assault rifles they weren't trained for.

He had turned down the radio to almost a whisper, and he lifted it to his ear whenever it squawked, which translated into soft vibrations against his palm. He got a squawk now, and raised it to his ear.

"Give me a sitrep," a male voice said.

"I got nothing," another man answered.

"Givens, is that you?"

"Yeah."

"Where is he?"

"I dunno," Givens said. "We thought we had him a moment ago, but he's gone again. Donner lost his track a few minutes back."

"Hey, I didn't say I could track," Donner said defensively.

"Keep looking," the first man said. "He couldn't have gotten very far."

"What about the other two?" Givens asked.

"Don't you worry about them. You just catch your guy."

Easier said than done.

Footsteps were approaching from behind him. Boots moving loudly over dry grass and brittle twigs. He lost the initial pursuit about twenty minutes back, but he knew eventually they would get close again. He didn't plan to keep running, but he needed a distraction. Some kind of camouflage…

What's going on in that blue tent?

The good news was that there was just one man close enough that Will could hear his loud, laborious breathing. The bad news was that there were two more somewhere nearby.

Will turned off the radio and clipped it to his belt, then slipped his rifle's strap over his shoulder. He reached down to his left hip and slid the cross-knife soundlessly out of its sheath.

The man walked past him, sticking to the other side of the giant oak tree.

Will stood up and maneuvered around the large tree trunk, moving right, continuing until he had performed a full ninety degrees and could see the back of a white-clad figure walking ahead of him. Ten meters between them.

He switched the knife to his right hand and took the first step toward the figure in front of him. The man didn't hear Will coming until he was almost on top of him, and even then, the man only stopped to listen, cocking his head curiously to one side.

Will slipped his left hand around the man's face, clasped his palm over the mouth, and drove the point of the cross-knife into the back of the neck, pushing it in deep until the body went slack against him and collapsed like a marionette with its strings snipped.

He caught the man halfway, then lowered the lifeless body all the way to the ground like precious cargo, careful not to get any blood on the plastic, shiny white hazmat suit.

CHAPTER 23

GABY

NATE WAS SHOT. Gaby had no idea how or when it had even happened. He had been running in front of her the whole time ever since they abandoned Trail #8, but somehow he had ended up getting shot anyway, while she remained unscathed.

The bullet had gone through his left arm, somewhere between his elbow and shoulder, and he was wincing as he ran, keeping his other hand pressed against the wound to slow down the bleeding.

When they had finally put enough distance between them and their pursuers, she felt safe enough to force him to stop next to a big oak tree, while she pulled out the first aid kit from her pack and stopped the bleeding, then wrapped gauze around the wound.

"You've done this before," he said, watching the woods with the Beretta in his good hand.

"I've had practice."

"You think Will made it?"

"I'm sure he did."

"I don't hear them."

"We might have lost them a few minutes ago, unless they followed your blood all the way to us."

He gave her a crooked grin. "Sorry about that."

"When did you get shot, anyway?"

"I don't remember."

"Weird."

"Yeah," he said.

She finished up with the gauze around his arm before stuffing the roll back into her pack. The result wasn't much to look at, but he wasn't bleeding anymore and that was all that counted.

Gaby snatched up her rifle and looked around. "How far did you think we ran?"

"No idea. I was too busy hauling ass."

She nodded.

"What are you thinking?" he asked.

"We were running away from the camp, and Will was running in the other direction to split up the chase. So that means he was running toward the camp."

"You think he did it on purpose?"

"I know he did it on purpose."

"So now what?"

She shook her head and thought about it. Nate leaned against the tree trunk to rest, looking a lot paler than when they stopped a few minutes ago, though his eyes seemed alert enough.

"He'd want us to leave, regroup at the game warden's place," she said.

"And are we going to do that?"

"He'd want us to do what he said."

"That never stopped you before."

She looked at him again, this time with a more critical eye. He was hurt and bleeding, trying to fight through the pain. Could she drag him back there to find Will? If it were just her, it would have been an easy choice. She would never leave Will behind, because Will would never leave her, even in a hospital full of gunmen. With a healthy Nate, it might have been a no-brainer. But she didn't have a healthy Nate...

Goddammit, Will.

"He's your friend," Nate said. "It's up to you."

"He's more than that."

"The big brother you never had."

"Or wanted," she smiled.

He smiled back. "I wouldn't leave him behind, either."

"Even if it means dying in here? In this place?"

"Eh. I always figured I'd end up somewhere like this."

"In a state park filled with traitors to the human race?"

"Okay, not exactly *like* this, but close."

"Thank you," she said.

He nodded. "You're welcome. So, should we—"

The loud *crack!* of a rifle cut him off, just before a bullet slammed into the tree two inches from Nate's head and showered him in bark.

Gaby spun, lifting her rifle, and even before she saw what she was aiming at, squeezed the trigger again and again and again.

Two men in hazmat suits were simultaneously stepping out of a bush and diving in separate directions. They fired back wildly as they ran for cover, bullets splintering tree branches over her head.

Nate grabbed her wrist, pulling her behind the big oak tree as bullets smashed into it and peppered her face and clothes with tiny pieces of bark. As soon as she made it to the other side, Nate let go of her and took off. She followed without hesitation.

Bullets pecked the ground around her, throwing dirt and grass into the air.

Nate wasn't running straight, she realized; he was starting to curve right—taking them back south, then southwest.

He's leading us back to the parking lot. Back to the truck.

Away from Will...

They ran nonstop for almost five minutes, and Gaby thanked God she was in the best physical shape of her life, thanks to training with Will and Danny on the island. It had been almost three minutes since she last heard gunfire, but Nate didn't seem anxious to stop, so she didn't, either.

After awhile, though, she started to gasp for breath and finally risked a glance over her shoulder, seeing no one behind them.

How long had they been running? Five minutes had felt more like five hours.

"Nate," she said. "I think we've lost them. Slow down."

Nate slid to a stop behind the trunk of another giant oak tree, taking up position with his carbine. Gaby did the same on the other side, both of their weapons pointing back in the direction they had come. She was out of breath, gasping for air. Nate was breathing just as loudly on the other side.

"See anything?" he said softly, keeping his voice down.

"No," she said, matching his pitch. "Are you okay?"

"I have pieces of trees in my hair, and I'm pretty sure some got into my eyeballs."

"I don't think that's possible."

"No?"

"No."

"Never mind, then. I'm probably fine."

"Probably?"

"Arm's throbbing like a sonofabitch, though."

"Are you bleeding again?"

"No. It just hurts."

"Yeah, well, you were shot. It should be hurting."

"Makes sense, then."

They both shut up when a man in a hazmat suit emerged out of the woods in front of them, moving in an unhurried trot as if he were jogging in a park. He was out of breath, and he stopped dead in his tracks the instant he saw them looking back at him. For a second—just a split second—he stared, brown eyes widening in an *"Oh, shit"* moment.

She flashed back to Ray, the young collaborator Will had shot earlier. This man wasn't a teenager. He was in his thirties and old enough to know better. Like Ray, the man had his name ("David") scribbled in painfully perfect letters on an envelope label over his left breast.

David started to lift his rifle, and she and Nate fired at the same time. The man slumped to the ground.

"Go!" Nate shouted.

Gaby took off running through the woods again, legs pumping, rifle swinging back and forth in front of her. She was only vaguely aware that she was purposefully keeping to the same southwest angle Nate had set for them earlier.

Toward the parking lot…farther away from Will…

She looked back at Nate, running after her, face constricted in pain, blood dripping from his left arm through her lousy-looking tourniquet. He tried to grin back at her, but he barely had the strength to make it convincing.

THEY RAN FOR another fifteen minutes, stopping to rest every five, before continuing again, when Gaby looked back and saw Nate's face. It was flushed and covered in sweat; he looked as if he was straining badly with every step.

She slowed down before coming to a complete stop next to another oak tree. She imagined what a nightmare it would be to get lost in here. Every tree looked like the 5,000 other trees around it. Turning left or right, south or north gave her no directional markers, because one side of the woods looked the same as the other three. There was only the sun to lead her southwest.

She put her hand on the tree trunk, the other holding the M4 against the ground like a crutch. Nate was gasping for breath next to her, his blinking eyes scanning the area.

"Do we keep going to the parking lot?" he asked between desperate, hard-fought gasps.

"I'm not sure."

"It's your call."

She thought about it for a moment, even looking back west. Not that she could see Will, or the camp. But he was back there, somewhere…

"We should go," she said finally.

"Are you sure?"

"Yes."

"Gaby…"

She picked up her rifle and began walking. "Come on, we'll retreat back to the game warden's office and wait for Will there, just like we planned."

Keep moving. Just keep moving…

THEY REACHED THE parking lot thirty-nine minutes later, walking at a brisk pace. Nate had used the time to get stronger, helped greatly by not having to overexert himself. She didn't know how they had managed to lose their pursuers, but they hadn't seen or heard anyone since they had shot the man named David.

They crouched near the edge of the parking lot, where the grass met the asphalt, and peered out. She didn't believe for a second that the bad guys wouldn't have the place covered. It would have been the first place they looked. Unless these people were total idiots—

and they had done nothing to show her that they were—the parking lot would be the perfect place for an ambush.

So where are they?

She couldn't see anything that wasn't here when they first arrived. They had emerged out of the woods at about the same spot where they'd entered, and she had a decent view of the gray Saleen sports truck about forty yards away. On the other side would be Will's Triumph, though Gaby couldn't see it from her crouched position.

"See anything?" she whispered.

Nate shook his head. It wasn't an enthusiastic *"No."* It was more of a cautious, *"No, but that's what worries me."*

"You're thinking it too, right?" she asked.

He nodded. "They should have figured out by now where we parked. It's a no-brainer."

"So where are they?"

"Exactly. Where are they?"

She looked out at the parking lot again, trying to see it from a different perspective.

After about a minute, she gave up.

"What do we do?" she whispered.

Nate thought about it, then said, "We might have to risk it. It's either that or take our chances back there."

And by "back there" he meant the woods, where every tree looked the same, and every patch of ground looked like the last patch. It was either that, or risk running for the truck and hoping no one was waiting behind one of the other thirty or so vehicles scattered around the parking lot. Neither option was very appealing to her.

Like we have a whole lot of choices...

She looked over at Nate again, saw him watching her back intently. "What's the plan?" he asked.

"You're asking me?"

"You seem to know what you're doing."

She looked back at the parking lot. "What choice do we have? We can't run around in here forever. Sooner or later, it's going to get dark."

"Yeah."

"We don't have any other, better choice. Right?"

"I don't see any."

She sighed. She hated this. It was stupid, reckless…and they had no choice.

Will would have figured out another way.

Too bad he's not here…

"On five, then?" Nate said.

"How about three?"

"Just three?"

"I don't like to count all the way to five," Gaby said. "I get anxious around two."

"Okay, on the count of three."

"Together, right?"

"Together, yeah."

"No bullshit." She fixed him with a hard look. "We step out together on three and make a run for the truck."

"Agreed. Ready?"

"Okay."

"One, two…*three.*"

Nate moved first, jumping out into the open.

She sighed, and got up to follow him.

Nate hadn't gone more than a few feet when the gunshot exploded across the parking lot, so loud that it startled and made her jump a little. The bullet went through Nate's left shoulder, exited his back, and kept going, clipping the tree branch over her head with a loud *crack*.

He fell backward and Gaby moved on instinct, dropping her rifle and lunging out into the open. She managed to slide under him, catching Nate as he fell. He was heavy and he pushed her down with him, her knees scraping against the hard asphalt through her pants.

Nate was already bleeding badly, warm blood pumping out of him and spilling over her clothes. Gaby shoved her hand over the wound, before her brain caught up with her and told her he was bleeding on *both sides* of his body because the bullet had gone right through him. She reached down with her other hand, digging underneath his heavy body, and cupped the other side of the bullet hole, too.

Her mind spun as panic fought for control over her senses.

Her pack! She had the first aid kit in her pack!

Gaby pulled her hands away from his wounds and ripped the

pack free, unzipped it, and pulled out the roll of gauze, pressing it against the hole in his back to stifle the bleeding on that side. Almost instantly, blood soaked through the cotton material, making it heavy. She kept it pressed against him anyway, using her other hand to wrap it around his body over his clothes. She was covered in blood, and she realized she was doing a terrible job of stopping his bleeding, but she couldn't think of anything else to do.

Nate's eyes shifted from the sky to her. His lips quivered and he seemed to be out of breath, fighting to get out every word. "Gaby...are you...crazy...*run...*"

She shook her head.

"Gaby...stupid...*go...*"

He was right. She knew it was stupid, and every part of her brain screamed at her to get up and run. Or at least reach for her weapons.

She did neither.

She had already abandoned Will, left him out there on his own. How long could he last by himself? Soon, he could be another casualty for her to add to her growing list. Right alongside her parents. Her friends. Poor Matt. Even Josh.

And she was supposed to let Nate just lie here and die, too?

No!

She wrapped up his shoulder again and again until she had run out of gauze. He grunted against her, his face a mask of pain. Her hands were slick with blood, but she didn't care. She wiped them on her pants and didn't give them another thought.

The sound of heavy boots rushing in her direction momentarily distracted her attention from Nate's face. Men were coming out of the woods around them, some appearing from behind parked vehicles. They were moving cautiously toward her, probably wondering what the hell she was doing with Nate. She wondered if she looked like a crazy woman in their eyes. A crazy woman covered in blood.

She saw flashes of hazmat suits. Gas masks. Assault rifles. White label strips with names written in marker. One of the men had a large hunting rifle with a big scope on top.

She thought about running. Dragging Nate back into the woods. *Too late. Too late for that now.*

She looked back down at Nate instead. His face was so pale, and he felt simultaneously heavy and lifeless in her lap. At least he had stopped bleeding, though it was hard to tell because they were both covered in blood.

The barrel of a rifle poked her in the shoulder. It didn't hurt, but it was annoying, forcing her to look up into an old face, gas mask perched on top of his forehead. The man had an AR-15 aimed at her face and was saying something, though she couldn't make out what. She didn't know why, but it was difficult to hear anything at the moment. The man's name tag, written in cursive handwriting, read, "Barton."

Barton seemed to finally give up communicating with her. He reached down and pulled the Glock from her holster, then scooped up her M4 and stepped back.

Another man in a hazmat suit did the same to the Beretta in Nate's holster, then picked up his M4. Nate stirred, but didn't fight.

The man with the hunting rifle ("Wilson" was written in careful lettering across his left breast) moved closer and casually aimed his weapon at her from point-blank range, eyes calmly watching her from behind the clear lenses of his gas mask. He was the only one still wearing his gas mask, she saw; the others had theirs hanging off their hips.

She stared back at Wilson. If she was going to die, she would look into the eyes of her killer. At least she could do that much.

Wilson matched her gaze, and his finger tightened around the trigger—

"Stop!" a voice shouted. "I said stop, goddammit!"

Wilson lowered his rifle reluctantly and looked back. "Orders were to shoot on sight," he said, his voice muffled by the gas mask.

"They weren't *my* orders," the voice said. It sounded equally distorted.

"I didn't know you were in charge now."

"You don't know a lot of things. That's the point."

The men gathered around her and Nate began to part, and a new figure in a hazmat suit and gas mask appeared. The others reacted strangely to his arrival—as if they didn't care for him, but felt the need to obey him anyway.

The newcomer was the only one without a name tag over his hazmat suit, which made her think he didn't really belong here. Maybe he was just passing through, or maybe he was part of another group, like Kellerson and Harris and the men who had attacked

Mercy Hospital. She didn't remember a single one of them wearing labels, either.

He looked down at her and Nate, and by the way his eyebrows raised, he seemed to be focusing on the way she held Nate's limp body in her lap.

"Who is he?" the man asked. "Why's he so important to you?"

That voice!

Even muffled by the gas mask's breathing apparatus, there was something familiar about the voice now that the man was closer. She couldn't quite place it, though. It was a maddening feeling, especially because she thought the voice belonged to someone who was, at one point, very important in her life.

But that couldn't be, could it? That man was...

"They killed Ray," Wilson said. "And David, too."

The newcomer ignored Wilson, and his eyes remained fixed on hers. "What are you doing here?" he asked. "You're not supposed to be here."

That voice! I know that voice!

When she didn't answer him, the man pulled off his gas mask.

Gaby stared into brown eyes she hadn't seen in months, belonging to a man she thought she would never see again.

But it was impossible.

The man *(the boy)* those soft, gentle brown eyes belonged to was dead. He had drowned in a lake. She knew this because Will had told her so himself. He had seen it happen. Blaine and Maddie had seen it happen, too.

That was over three months ago.

You're supposed to be dead!

"Answer me, Gaby," Josh said. "Who is this guy? Why is he so important to you?"

CHAPTER 24

WILL

GETTING INTO THE camp was easy once he put on the hazmat suit and gas mask. They belonged to a man named Givens, according to the label taped over the suit, which was a good fit if a bit loose around the midsection where Givens had stretched it out. Clasping on the gun belt fixed that.

The camp was much more encompassing when viewed at ground level. He was surprised by the breadth of it, along with the human congestion, and had to actually stop and take it all in. It was, in many ways, a self-contained city built from the ground up, even though there was a temporary vibe to it.

"How many people do you think are down there?" Gaby had asked.

"A thousand?" Nate had answered.

He was close. If there weren't a thousand people down here, mingling around the campfires and the hundreds of tents of every shape, size, and color, it was pretty damn close.

Now that he was seeing it from up close, the hurricane fencing around the camp looked haphazardly installed. He got the impression it was a minor inconvenience, a fait accompli with the people it was supposed to be holding in. Their acceptance of the situation was what kept them here, not a fence that looked as if it could be toppled by a five-year-old leaning against it. Certainly, the thirty or so collaborators he had spotted around the place weren't enough to keep this many people in line.

Will entered the camp through one of the gates interspersed every fifty meters or so. The gates had latches and coiled steel cables with padlocks, though none were being put to use. It was just another sign that this was less an internment camp as he had surmised from Sandwhite Point, and more of a voluntary way station of sorts.

As he walked through, the people didn't seem surprised or scared of him. Some nodded and moved on, and others—mostly children—looked on with what Will thought was admiration. That was disturbing, but he had to remember that the hazmat suits were essentially uniforms, and children, regardless of the situation, were naturally inclined to be wowed by a spiffy uniform—even if it happened to be something as aesthetically unpleasing to the eye as a Level B hazmat suit. Of course, in the eyes of a child, a chemical suit might have looked pretty impressive.

Directly ahead of him and impossible to miss was the blue tent. It reached so much higher into the air than the others that it almost looked like a mountain. Will walked toward it, maneuvering around the tents, campfires, and people in his path. He walked as if he belonged, unhurried, meeting every eye that bothered to catch his.

Then he saw something he didn't think he would ever see again: *a pregnant woman* sitting under a small pup tent. She was eating beans out of a can, while a young boy in an LSU Tigers T-shirt chewed on a stick of beef jerky next to her. They sat on the grass, so immersed in their surroundings that they were oblivious to him when Will stopped and stared. The woman was in her late twenties and looked at least a few months along. There were futons lying out on the grass in the tent behind them.

Will moved on just as the woman felt his stare and glanced up.

He hadn't gone another few steps when he saw *another pregnant woman.*

Then another one, and another…

What the hell is going on here?

They were everywhere. Two pregnant women came out of a beige canvas tent talking and laughing about something. They saw him and nodded, continuing on their way. One of the women looked further along in her pregnancy, while the other had a barely-there bump.

He walked on, doing his best not to stray, not to stop and stare, but feeling dazed by what he was seeing. There was something wrong here. Something *not right*. One pregnant woman would have been extraordinary, but two, or three, or a *dozen?*

What the hell is going on here?

He must have been walking in a fog, trying to process the incongruous appearances of the pregnant women around him, because suddenly he had arrived at the blue tent and didn't recall how he had actually gotten there.

The tent was octagonal, the flat sides extending eight meters high all around and held in place by thick beams of extruded aluminum alloy. He eyeballed the structure's span at sixty meters, held together by PVC-coated polyester textiles. It looked very much like a mini version of a sports dome, with multiple, unguarded tunnel entrances/exits jutting out along the sides.

He watched people moving in and out of those tunnels for a moment, before slipping in among one of the lines going in. Like with the rest of the camp, the sight of men in hazmat suits around the blue tent was apparently so common that no one gave him more than a couple of glances, if they even bothered at all.

Alarm bells went off when he spotted the shoulder of a man in a hazmat suit standing guard at the end of the tunnel.

Will kept walking, moving steadily but in no hurry. He casually lowered one hand toward his holstered Glock, then moved forward until he was walking behind a pregnant woman who was waddling more than she was actually walking. By the size of her bump, he guessed she was even further along in her pregnancy than the ones he had seen outside. She was leaning on a young woman's arm as they moved through the length of the tunnel, which extended for about five meters. The women were talking about clothes.

The three of them finally reached the end and stepped out into the main housing area. As he expected, the hazmat suit standing guard was just for show; the man was reading a magazine, paying zero attention to anyone coming or going. His rifle was slung over his shoulder, and his gas mask hung loosely around his neck.

Will let the women continue on, then he turned left and continued walking for a bit. He finally stopped and took a moment to orient himself with the scope of the blue tent's interior.

There was really just one vast, open room. The height of the tent, with its upwardly extended middle, gave the place the feel of being cavernous. Hundreds of civilians took up space among the grass floor, which was divided into two sections—a smaller area filled with cots, the type he had slept on in the Army, with the bigger area dotted with mats. The cots looked as if they were reserved almost exclusively for the women.

More pregnant women.

If he thought there were a lot of them outside, there were even more of them in here. There were, as far as he could tell, about one hundred cots, though only half of them were filled at the moment. The others, he assumed, were outside the camp walking around.

The mats were occupied by a more varied group of people: girls, women, men, and boys. There didn't seem to be any real organization to where they sat, though they all looked as if they were resting. There had to be over 300 mats spread out around the tent, almost all of them occupied with a warm body either lying down or sitting and chatting casually with the person next to them.

Will started moving through the tent, ignoring the voices buzzing and overlapping all around him. Hundreds of people talking at once, without a care in the world.

As with the campers outside, the ones in here barely gave him a second look. Their acceptance of his presence—or more specifically, the hazmat suit he wore—bothered him tremendously.

There were others moving through the tent—men and women in blue, green, and white hospital scrubs. He counted two, maybe three dozen in all. They were moving efficiently through the throng of bodies, dispensing everything from water to pills to medical advice. The bits and pieces of conversation he could overhear were overwhelmingly about the pregnancies.

Jesus Christ. This is a maternity ward.

"You," a female voice said behind him.

Will looked back at a woman in her early thirties, wearing a white doctor's coat. She had long blonde hair in a ponytail and was eyeing him with light green eyes. She had one of those envelope labels over her right breast pocket, with the name "Zoe" written on it. A stethoscope was draped around her neck, and she was holding a young pregnant woman's arm, apparently taking readings while talking to him.

"What are you doing, Givens?" the woman asked.

"Givens?"

Right. Givens. The dead guy.

"What do you mean?" he said.

"You're just walking around. Is that in your job description? Walking around?"

Will didn't quite know how to answer that, and felt a little bit like a kid who just got caught in the hallways trying to skip school.

"Well?" she said.

"Well what? You need something?"

"Yes, I do. Where are my cots? I have more patients than I have cots."

Cots. Right.

"Who did you talk to about that?" he asked.

"How the hell should I know. Half of you guys don't even wear name tags. I can't keep track of how many of you breeze through this camp in a given day."

Kellerson and how many others?

"How many more cots do you need?" he asked.

"Eleven—" She stopped, then corrected herself. "Twelve, since this morning. You wanted preggos, you got preggos."

Preggos?

"Right. I'll see what's keeping the cots," he said.

"You do that."

He turned and started to walk away.

"Givens," Zoe called after him.

He looked back. "Yeah?"

She gave him a pursed smile. "I didn't mean to put it all on you. We're both just trying to do our parts here, right?"

"Right," Will said, and gave her a smile back behind the gas mask, before realizing she probably couldn't see it since his mouth was entirely hidden. He said instead, "I'll see what I can do."

"You in a hurry?"

"No, why?"

"I got that list your boss wanted."

"Okay…"

Zoe turned to the young pregnant woman whose hand she had been holding, and gave her a friendly, reassuring smile. "You're coming along just fine, Anne. Just keep doing what we discussed, okay? No deviating."

Anne, the young woman, nodded gratefully. "Thanks, doc."

"Lay down and rest."

Anne did as she was instructed. Will thought she couldn't have been older than seventeen.

Zoe stood up and began walking off.

Will briefly considered continuing on and ignoring her, but thought better of it and followed her instead.

"Where's your boss?" Zoe asked. "I haven't seen him all day, and he promised to come talk to me before we start the next transport."

"What are we transporting?"

She stopped and looked back at him, eyes narrowing a bit. "What is this, some kind of game to you, Givens?"

She doesn't know who Givens is. Use that.

"I'm new here," Will said. "I'm just trying to get caught up."

She chewed on his excuse for a moment, then continued leading him through the blue tent. "The next transport scheduled to leave for the town. This new group is further along than the last one, so you guys need to bend over backward to make them more comfortable."

She led him to a small grouping of tents near the back. There were a dozen lined up. She slipped inside one of them and he followed. Inside was a small cot next to a portable fold-out desk and a stack of worn clothes.

Zoe walked over to her fold-out table, picked up a piece of paper, and handed it to him. "Here's the list your boss wanted."

"What's it for?" he asked, taking the list.

"The names of everyone that'll be on the next transport, organized by need."

Will unfolded the paper and glanced at it. It was a long, handwritten list of about 200 names, some with a check mark next to them. "What're the check marks?"

"The pregnant ones," Zoe said. "You guys need to put them in their own separate trucks and not stuff them in with everybody else like the last few times. You need to keep in mind you're dealing with pregnant women here. They're fragile."

He pocketed the paper. "Is that all?"

"How long have you been here?"

"Just a few days."

"I didn't know they were still bringing in new people." He heard the suspicion in her voice. "Is Givens your first or last name?"

"Does it matter?"

She shrugged. "Just curious."

"You're a doctor, right?"

She smiled. "Lucky guess." She walked over to a cot and sat down heavily. "Can I ask you a question?"

Why the hell not, it's not like I can stop you.

"Sure," he said instead.

"What's with the gas mask? I know, you wear it at night so the creatures steer clear of you. But why do you guys insist on wearing it in the daytime, too? I've always been curious."

He couldn't tell from the sound of her voice if it was just curiosity or something more.

"Habit," he said.

"It can't possibly be comfortable."

"You get used to it."

That seemed to strike a chord with her. "I guess we've all had to learn to get used to things, haven't we?"

He wondered if she was still talking to him or herself. Zoe was kneading her forehead with her fingers, like someone with the weight of the world on her shoulders.

"You okay, doc?" he asked.

She glanced up. "Yeah, why?"

"You look tired."

"How could you tell? Is it the wrinkles or the crow's feet? I'm pretty sure I've aged a year for every week I've been in this place."

"Why don't you leave?"

Damn. Did I just say that?

Instead of flashing him another one of her suspicious glances, she smirked at him instead. "I could ask you the same thing."

"I'm just a grunt. I follow orders."

"Isn't that what the Nazis said during World War II?"

"We all do what we have to in order to survive."

"I guess so." She sighed and stretched out on the cot, putting her hands on top of her forehead and closing her eyes. "Sorry about shitting all over you, Givens. That was unfair."

"No worries."

She smiled at nothing in particular. "You can go now."

"Right."

He stepped out of Zoe's tent and kept walking, glad to be out of there.

One thing she had said stuck in his head: *"The next transport scheduled to leave for the town."*

He was right, after all. The camp was just a way station to someplace else—a final destination.

"The town."

People were being relocated there from here, including the pregnant women. *Especially* the pregnant women. So what were the people sitting on the mats, the men and boys and women who weren't pregnant, doing inside the big tent?

He walked past young men and women—teenagers—pushing carts through the mats and cots, offering up fruits and vegetables, but also more meat and venison on cheap plastic plates. Everyone seemed to be doing their part, though it was obvious the doctors—or the ones in the scrubs, anyway—were paying more attention to the pregnant women.

It didn't escape him that he hadn't seen a single baby, toddler, or infant. That told him all these pregnancies had occurred *after* The Purge. The furthest along, as far as he could tell, was six months. He wasn't entirely sure what that told him, if anything. For the most part, the majority of the women looked newly pregnant.

By the time he reached the end of the tent, he had walked the entire length of the place and there wasn't a whole lot more to see, except for an entrance tunnel that joined another, smaller tent on the other side. But this entrance had two hazmat suits guarding it, and unlike the others, these looked alert. He glimpsed people lying down in cots inside the connecting tent, their arms hooked up to tubes that were connected to red bags.

No, not red bags. Clear bags with *red liquid* inside.

Blood. They're drawing blood.

He had trouble making out the size of the second tent through the tight opening. It looked big, though of course nowhere near as large as the blue tent. There were nurses inside, walking along the cots and checking the tubes connecting the arms and blood bags. People who were coming out of the tent looked noticeably tired and dazed, some moving on wobbly feet. Almost all of them went straight to the mats to sit or lie down.

Will thought about getting a better look at the other tent, maybe even trying to access it, but he decided against it. It was too risky, and the two men standing guard were too alert. Right now, his greatest asset was his ability to go everywhere as long as no one paid attention to his face. All it took was one hazmat suit to realize he wasn't Givens, and he was screwed. The prospect of having to shoot his way out of the camp, with its large population of pregnant women, made him queasy.

He walked on through the tent instead, slipping into a line of people exiting out a tunnel that didn't have any guards in front of it.

He stepped back outside and blinked in the sun, before glancing down at his watch: 2:11 P.M.

Plenty of time.

Will walked through the camp again, passing a group of men laughing around chunks of freshly killed deer meat sizzling on a grill. The rest of the animal was in a cooler, one man tasked with fanning it to scatter the flies every time they opened it for another piece of meat. The men were drinking beer. Warm beer, but he guessed they had gotten used to that from the sounds of the drunken voices.

One of the men noticed Will and speared a thick piece of meat with a cooking fork, then got up and walked over. "Wanna grab a piece of this? We have plenty to go around. More than plenty, actually."

"Where'd you get it?" Will asked, remembering the dearth of deer—or any animal life moving on the ground at all—that had crossed his path as he moved through the woods.

The man looked confused by the question. He was in his early forties, with a thick brown beard, and had the type of world-weary eyes Will would expect from a resistance fighter, not someone enjoying the company of his captors.

"Your buddies bring them over every morning," the man said, "for old farts like me who can't stand to eat out of cans anymore. You new to this camp?" he asked, switching topics with surprising dexterity. "I haven't seen you around before."

"You know everyone in camp?"

"Not everyone, but most of you guys. It's not like there's a lot of you."

Will nodded. "I just came over a few days ago."

"Ah, that explains it." The man offered up his hand. "I'm Jenkins."

Will shook it. "Givens."

"I know, it says so on your label thingie there," Jenkins grinned. Then he nodded at the campfire. "You wanna join us? Plenty of room. I've never been much of a deer man myself, but it's surprisingly good."

"How long have you been here, Jenkins?"

"You mean this camp?"

"Yeah."

"Just a little over a week now." He glanced around. "It's a lot bigger than the last camp I was in, and also a lot more organized."

"How many camps have you been in?"

"Counting this one? Three."

Jesus, how many of these places are out there?

You really have been busy, Kate.

"All in Louisiana?" Will asked.

"Yup. Though I hear there's one in Texas that's four times the size of this one. You seen it?"

"No. Just the Louisiana camps so far."

Then Jenkins leaned in a bit, as if he was going to say something important that he didn't want anyone else to overhear. "The guys and I were wondering. You know when they're gonna relocate us to the towns?"

Again with the towns.

"The next transport leaves tomorrow," Will said. "Why, you anxious to get there?"

"Sure, why not. I mean, I don't mind living out of a tent and eating deer meat, but it'd be nice to get back to civilization. Or as close to one as you'll get these days, anyway."

"How long have you been going from camp to camp, Jenkins?"

"Ever since I knew there was a choice."

"What choice is that?"

"You know, run around out there, or come here."

He means surrendering. Giving up.

Jenkins gave him a half-hearted smile. "You can only fight for so long, you know? And I'm getting old." He glanced around the camp. "It's good here. I think I made the right decision. Still, it would be nice to finally get to one of these towns I keep hearing about. Get on with living."

"You've never been to one of these towns before?"

"Nah. I've just been shuffling from camp to camp. Sure are a lot of pregnant women here." He whistled. "I don't think I've ever seen so many pregnant women in one place in my life."

"Neither have I."

"By the way, you know anything about all the shooting in the woods? You guys having trouble or something? There are plenty of boys here who wouldn't mind lending a hand if you need it."

Will shook his head. "We're fine."

"What was all that shooting about?"

"Don't worry about it. We've dealt with it."

Jenkins was about to ask something else—the man had a thousand questions, apparently—when he stopped and stared over Will's shoulder instead. He followed the older man's gaze and saw a group of six hazmat suits moving through the camp. They had two figures between them, leaning against each other.

Will casually walked away from Jenkins and out of the open, slipping behind one of the tents. Not that anyone noticed, including Jenkins. Every set of eyes in the immediate area was too busy watching the new arrivals, which included a tall blonde girl covered in blood.

Aw, shit.

Will watched Gaby shouldering Nate, who was moving with some difficulty alongside her. Nate looked shot—at least twice—with almost one entire shoulder swaddled in bloodied gauze. And although she was covered in almost as much blood as Nate, Gaby didn't actually look wounded; she seemed to be more tired than anything.

Nate's blood.

As Gaby and Nate were led past the tent he was standing behind, Will pulled off the gas mask and tried to catch Gaby's eye. She was looking around her, taking in the camp with an expression he imagined he must have had himself when he first saw the place up close.

Just as the group was about to pass him completely, Gaby glanced over and they locked eyes for a brief second. Her eyes widened just a bit, but then she quickly looked away, though he thought he saw a ghost of a smile cross her lips.

That's my girl.

CHAPTER 25

GABY

JOSH WAS ALIVE!

She didn't know how that was possible. It shouldn't be. But Josh was here, walking in front of her. He wasn't just one of these people, he was *leading* them.

Her mind spun, trying to process the information. At first she thought she was still lightheaded from watching Nate get shot and then trying to keep him from bleeding to death, but she realized now that it was more than that.

Josh was alive!

"Josh," she said, trying to get his attention.

She struggled to hold on to Nate as they were led through the woods. Gaby spent almost as much time swatting branches out of her face as she did trying to keep Nate upright. Somehow, though, he was keeping up with her. She couldn't fathom how he was doing it. She held on to Nate with both arms, his feet moving alongside her, his eyes were closed as if he were asleep.

"Josh," she said again, louder this time.

He finally looked back at her, his hair long and shaggy. She remembered all the times she had cut his and Matt's hair while they were hiding together for eight months after the world ended. But the brown eyes that looked back at her now were different. The same, but not quite. He wasn't as skinny anymore, and even the gun belt around his waist seemed to fit better.

He didn't say anything, and instead waited (forced) her to continue.

"Why aren't you dead?" she asked. "Will told me you died. You fell into the lake and you drowned."

"Will was wrong," he said. It was his first words to her after they had left the parking lot.

She waited for him to continue, but he didn't.

"So you *didn't* die that day?" she said.

"Gaby, I'm here, walking in front of you, aren't I? How could I do that if I died that day?" He chuckled, and for a brief moment, she saw the old Josh again.

Gaby looked around at the men walking with them. They didn't seem to be paying attention. Or care.

She repositioned Nate's body against hers with some effort. Nate groaned, but his eyes remained closed. He was painfully pale and sweat dripped from his face. She still couldn't understand how his legs were moving.

"Josh, please slow down."

Josh did slow down, and as he did, the others followed suit without a word.

Josh looked back at her again, and his eyes drifted to Nate. "Who is he, Gaby?"

"I told you, he's a friend. His name's Nate."

"Just a friend?"

"Yes. Just a friend. We only met this morning."

That seemed to satisfy him, and his eyes softened a bit. "Do you want some help? He looks heavy."

"No, I'm fine." That wasn't true, but she didn't want him to know that. Didn't want *them* to know that. "Josh, how are you still alive?"

"I fell in the water, but someone fished me out." He grinned. "Literally. They used this big fishing hook thing." He mimed it for her. "I guess I just wasn't ready to die yet."

"Just like that?"

"You think it should be more dramatic?"

"I guess."

"It wasn't." Then he frowned at her. "You guys killed some of my people, Gaby."

"I didn't know they were your people," she said, doing her best not to say the word "people" in a way that might be interpreted as anything other than a simple statement of fact. Even though the idea of Josh being one of these people sent a chill up her spine, to hear him actually call them *his people* was somehow a thousand times worse.

"Who was out there with you and...what's his name again?" Josh asked.

"Nate."

"Who was out there with you and Nate? They said there was a third guy."

"Henry," Gaby said without hesitation.

"Do I know him?"

"No. He came to the island after...you left."

He was reading her face carefully, trying to catch her in a lie. She looked back at him, doing her best to sell the untruth.

Apparently satisfied, Josh said, "What were you guys doing out there?"

"Some col—" She stopped herself, and said instead, "—of your guys raided a hospital in Lafayette. They took some kids, and we were trying to get them back."

"Are you talking about Mercy Hospital?"

"Yes."

He shook his head. "I didn't have anything to do with that. I'm only responsible for the camps and the towns. But I heard about it." He looked a bit sad—or was that just an act? "You were there?"

"We were trading with them."

"Just you and this Henry guy?"

"There were a few others, but they died at the hospital during the attack."

"Oh, I'm sorry about that."

You're sorry *about that?*

Instead of allowing her emotions to explode on him, she forced them down and concentrated on keeping her lies straight. Josh had always been a smart kid, and it wouldn't have taken much to slip up. He was probably keeping track of everything she had already told him so far.

Or maybe she was reading too much into it. Maybe, under that new, harder exterior, it was still just Josh, the boy who doted on her, who shook and shuddered and whispered "Thank you" when she finally made love to him that first night on the island.

"What about Will and Danny?" Josh asked. "They didn't come with you?"

"No. Just us."

"That's kind of dangerous, isn't it?"

"We had a helicopter," she said, thinking that he probably knew about that part.

"A helicopter," he said, almost wistfully. "I haven't seen one of those in a while."

"Neither had we. It belonged to the people at the hospital. They picked us up, brought us over. That's why Will and Danny didn't feel the need to come along. There was me and Henry and two other guys. We thought we were just coming to trade, but then your guys attacked."

"Not my guys, Gaby," he said, sounding almost annoyed at the accusation.

"One of these guys, then."

He sighed, but let it go. "So, this Henry guy. He's the one going around killing my people?"

"I don't know. Maybe. We got split up."

"I have an MIA. His name's Givens. You know anything about him?"

"No."

"Maybe this Henry took him."

"Maybe. I don't know. I told you, we got split up. I don't know what Henry's up to. He's smart, so he probably took off. That's what Nate and I were trying to do when you ambushed us in the parking lot."

He gave her that annoyed look again. "Like I said, I'm sorry about what happened at the hospital, but I had nothing to do with it. And as for your friend Nate, well, my guys were just shooting back. You attacked us first."

"My guys."

"Us."

Who are you, Josh?

"What is this place, Josh?" she asked instead. "What's this camp?"

"It's just temporary. From here, we take people to their final relocation spot. It's nice, Gaby." He beamed like a proud father. "It's a real town, and they're free to come and go, but most of them stay for obvious reasons."

"You have a fence."

"The gates aren't locked. They can leave any time, but they don't. Some do, but most don't. They know what's out there. It's safer in here. It's even safer in the towns."

"What are these towns?"

"We've taken over some of the smaller cities, resettling people in them."

"Resettling?"

He grinned at her, and the brash Josh, the one who always knew he was smarter than most of the kids around him, shone through again. "I'm at the ground floor on this, Gaby. She came up with the idea, but I'm the one making it happen. She's good at this, selling dreams to people. They call this Phase Three. We're almost at the end."

"We." He said "we" instead of "them."

"You're with them now," she said.

He started to answer, but stopped and seemed to consider his response more thoroughly before finally saying, "It's complicated."

"How complicated is it, Josh?"

"More complicated than you think, Gaby."

They finally stepped out of the woods and back onto a muddy dirt road. She saw a gate in front of them. It was wide open, inviting. He was right. The fences and the gates were just for show. They weren't going to keep anyone in who didn't want to stay.

And beyond the fencing was the camp.

Here we go…

◄▬▮▮ ▮▮▬►

WILL!

She saw him out of the corner of her eye, wearing a hazmat suit and watching them from behind one of the many tents sprouting up from the ground around her. Her eyes met his, just long enough to let him know she had seen him, before she quickly looked away.

Josh was moving slower in front of her as they serpentined their way through the camp. He had moved farther ahead of the group, apparently not interested in engaging in small talk with her anymore.

People stared as they passed. Not that Gaby blamed them. She was very aware of the scabbing gash in her forehead, along with the scratches and bruises that still adorned her face and neck from the helicopter crash. Her hair was a mess, and she hadn't showered since leaving Song Island two days ago. Her clothes—cargo pants and a long-sleeve button shirt—were covered in Nate's blood and dirt and God knew how many layers of sweat.

She discovered that she didn't care about the curious stares. She had nothing to be ashamed of. Certainly not to these people, who had given up everything to come here, to be a part of this. Whatever the hell *this* was.

The sight of pregnant women made her look twice, though. By the time she saw the second, third, and tenth one, she stopped doing a double take.

She remembered what Will had said back on Sandwhite Point: *"I think we're looking at the next phase of whatever final solution the ghouls are moving toward. This…is something new. Something we haven't seen before. And it's big, so it has to be a pretty significant part of their plan."*

Nate was groaning against her, and he was moving much slower than before, his feet dragging against the ground noticeably now.

"Josh," she said.

He didn't hear her, and kept walking.

"Josh," she said louder.

He glanced back. "Hmm?"

"Do you have a doctor? I don't think Nate's going to make it."

He stopped, and everyone stopped with him. "You, you, and you," he said, pointing at, from what she could tell, three random men, "take him to see a doctor. I want two people with him at all times."

The men grabbed Nate and pulled him roughly from her. Nate groaned as he was yanked away, and she helplessly watched them move toward the blue tent that rose from the campgrounds like some kind of plastic castle.

"You're not going to hurt him?" she asked Josh.

"He'll be fine," Josh said. "What happens after that is up to him."

"What does that mean?"

"We'll talk about it." He looked at the others. "You can go, I got her."

The others faded away, but Wilson hesitated. "Are you sure?"

"She's unarmed. I got it."

Wilson shrugged and wandered off after the others.

Josh took her gently by the arm and led her through the camp again, but it wasn't in the direction of the big blue tent. Gaby let him lead her, mulling over her options.

They were limited. The fact that she was unarmed was a problem. They had taken her rifle, her Glock, and her knife. They had even taken her pack. The only thing she had left was an empty gun belt and pouches, which felt so light without her sidearm and spare magazines that she almost forgot she was still wearing them.

"It's okay, Gaby," Josh said.

"Is it, Josh?"

"Yes. I'm here. I'll make sure you're safe." He smiled at her. "That's why I did all of this, you know. It's for you, Gaby. This is all for you."

JOSH'S TENT HAD a grass floor like all the others, with a small cot in one corner. The only other furniture was a fold-out table with a portable LED lamp and laptop on top.

"Laptop?" she said. Somehow the fact that Josh had a working laptop at the end of the world didn't surprise her at all.

He grinned. "I know, right? So cliché."

"How do you power it?"

"Rechargeable batteries. I got the idea from Will. You know those Army Rangers, always prepared. I'm trying to get everyone here into more of a battalion mentality. You should see the people running the other states, Gaby. They have no clue what they're doing. Compared to them, we're on the cutting edge."

He's so proud of it.

Josh must have seen the dubious look on her face, because he walked over and put his hands on her shoulders and squeezed. The Josh she remembered, who smiled a lot and always wanted to please her, seemed to return again in that instant.

"Gaby, I did all of this for you," he said, the earnestness in his voice almost cracking, as if he was *willing* her to understand.

"How is all of this for me, Josh?"

"They gave me a choice…"

"Who?"

"The blue-eyed ghoul. She said her name was Kate."

Kate? Will's Kate?

"They have names?" she said instead.

"The blue-eyed ones do."

"How many of them are there?"

"I've met ten so far, but there are more, spread out. Most of them are assigned to specific states, but there are a few that float around, doing what needs to be done. You have no idea how organized they are, Gaby. You would think with so many of them— *billions*—that they couldn't possibly be organized, but you'd be wrong. They have some kind of mental link, this hive mind, that lets them communicate. It's remarkable. I've learned so much in just three months. Imagine what I could learn in three years."

She tried to smile, but she knew it came out wrong even before she saw him frown back at her in response.

"What's wrong?" he asked.

"What's wrong?" My God, Josh, how could you even ask me that? Everything *is wrong.*

"You're working for them," was all she could manage. "You're one of them now. A collaborator."

"No, no, no." He walked away for a moment, before looking back at her with renewed focus. "You don't understand, Gaby."

"Then make me understand."

"I did all of this for you."

"You keep saying that."

"Because it's true."

"How is it true?"

"We can't fight them, Gaby. There are too many of them. Even if Will and Danny found a thousand more just like them—a *million* more—it still wouldn't matter. There are just too many of them. We can't win this war." He paused, seemed to gather his thoughts. "They gave me the opportunity to save you. To save everyone. Why did you think they left the island alone all these months? She could have kept throwing people at it if she wanted to, but she didn't."

"Because of you?"

"Yes, Gaby. Because of me. See, it was always my intention to come back to you. That's what all this is about, that's why I'm doing this. Everyone here will be taken to a town and allowed to live out the rest of their lives. They'll grow old, have children, and die of natural causes. Don't you want that?"

She didn't know how to answer. She had so many questions, but many of them, she knew, would sound like accusations if she voiced them.

Don't antagonize him, but find out what you can. That's what Will would do.

"Why are there so many pregnant women here?" she asked. "I haven't seen a pregnancy since all of this began."

"It's part of the deal."

"What deal?"

He walked over to a cooler and opened it, took out a can of Coke. "Want one?"

She shook her head. "What kind of deal did those women make, Josh?"

He took his time. Walked back to her, cracked open the can, and took a sip of warm soda. Then, wiping at his lips with the back of his hand, he shrugged. "The ghouls need live bodies. They need a continuous supply of blood. Human beings, in other words."

The blood farms...

"It's part of their plan," Josh continued. "The Purge, the blood farms, the relocation camps, and now, the towns. It's all part of a grand, ambitious plan, and it's up to people like me to make it happen. But don't worry, they're not going to extinguish the human race. They can't. They need us. They need humans, but *controlled* humans. Future generations of humanity that understand and are willing to do what needs to be done in order to coexist. They just want to share the planet."

"Are you saying those women out there are pregnant on purpose?"

"Yes. It's the entire basis of the agreement."

"The babies...?" she said, barely able to get the words out.

She remembered the Mercy Hospital children looking out the back window of the fleeing Humvee at her with tear-streaked faces, an image she would never be able to forget for as long as she lived.

"Oh, no, they're not going to *give* the babies to the ghouls," Josh said, and he almost laughed. "No, no, nothing like that. Don't be morbid, Gaby."

Morbid? This whole thing is morbid, Josh.

"Those babies will all grow up into healthy boys and girls," he continued. "The ghouls *need* us, Gaby. Animals won't do it. Yes, they can drink animal blood, and they have been, but it's not the same. They were always going to do this. This was always the plan all along. They just didn't really know *how* to go about doing it."

"That's where you come in…"

"That's where Kate and I came in, yeah. She used to be human—still is, for the most part. The trap on Song Island? That was her idea. All this? Her idea. I just added in the little details, made sure everything was working in the daytime. The less she and the other ghouls show themselves around the people, the easier it is to control them, to convince them that this is for their own good."

He motioned for her to follow him outside. She did, and stood next to him as he gestured at the people in tents, the ones walking around, the men ripping cooked meat with their teeth around the campfires.

"Look around you, Gaby," Josh said. "This was my idea. I showed these people there's nothing to fear. We let them go if they want, but the vast majority of them stay." He gave her that eager to please smile again. "We're giving them food, a place to live, and they don't ever have to fear the night again."

"What happens at night?" she asked.

"Nothing. Nothing happens at night. That's the point."

"What about blood…?"

"We have that taken care of, too." He looked over at the blue tent. "There's another, smaller tent behind that one. People give blood there. That's what we give to the ghouls. They don't *need* to suck it out of you, they just want the end results. It's like donating blood. Painless." He smiled again. "This is good for us, Gaby. That's why I'm so glad you're here."

"Why is that, Josh?"

"Because I get to see you again, that's why!"

He laughed and moved toward her, but Gaby took a quick, involuntary step away from him before she even realized what she was doing.

He froze, then frowned. "But you don't believe me."

"I don't know what to believe, Josh." *Find a way to salvage this.*

"You were supposed to be dead, then it turns out you're not. Three months, Josh. *Three months.*"

His frown eased, and she saw a hint of regret.

There. Keep going...

"And then you show up and tell me you're in charge of these collaborators?" she continued. "Not just that you're one of them, but you're actually *in charge* of them?"

People were stopping to look at them now. For the first time, she saw Josh feeling less than in charge. He reached for her arm, but stopped himself in time.

"Let's go back inside," he said quietly, almost meekly.

She followed him back into the tent.

"I should have contacted you sooner," he said. "I really wanted to. God, you have no idea how much I wanted to. I've missed you so much, Gaby. Every day I think of you, about that night we spent together."

His shoulders slackened, and he was suddenly the eighteen-year-old boy she had lived out of basements with all those months, always worried about when he went searching for supplies with Matt, and had been so happy to see when they came back safe.

Josh, are you really still in there?

"Please, don't be angry with me, Gaby." His voice almost pleading now. "You know how I feel about you. I love you. I've always loved you. I did all of this for you. Please, can't we just..." He paused. Then, softly, "Can't I just hug you? Please? It's been so long, and I've missed you so much..."

At that moment, he sounded like the same Josh, the awkward boy in love with her, who followed her around and sneaked looks at her in school when he didn't think anyone was watching. She threw herself into her training with Will and Danny in part to forget about him, to push away the hurt of losing him. And it had hurt. Not because he was the great love of her life, as he wanted so desperately to be, but because she liked him. Truly, truly liked him, and though she hadn't felt it yet, she was certain she could have grown to love him too, if they had only spent more time together.

Then he was gone, taken away in a hail of bullets.

Only to resurface now, so different, and yet...so much like the same Josh.

He looked as if he was about to cry, when she rushed forward and into his arms. She pressed her head against his chest and he wrapped his arms so tightly around her that she couldn't breathe for a moment.

"Gaby," he whispered. "God, it's been so long. I've missed you so much. You don't know how much I've missed you."

"Me too, Josh, me too," she said, forcing back tears.

In the back of her mind, one thought kept going around and around:

Can I kill him? If I have to—and God, I might have to—can I kill Josh?

BOOK THREE

TOWNIES

CHAPTER 26

WILL

JOSH WAS ALIVE. That shouldn't have been possible, but there it was. In living person. Flesh and blood. He was still Josh. Eighteen years old, with longer, shaggier hair than Will remembered, but still the same kid.

Will remembered watching him drop into the water, the urge to jump in after him overridden by the sight of the collaborator boat bearing down on them. At that moment, he had been forced to make a decision—save himself, Blaine, Maddie, and Bobby, not to mention the supplies they had come for, or risk everything for one kid.

He liked Josh. He did. But Josh was one life, while there were many more, including Lara, on the island. He wished he could say it was a difficult decision, but it wasn't.

Just when you think everything was starting to make sense, the world reminds you that you don't know Jack shit.

He stood next to Josh's tent and listened to the conversation inside. He moved slightly backward and out of view when Josh led Gaby out. When Josh told Gaby there were no reasons for the people to leave the camp, Will couldn't disagree. The kid was right. These people didn't want to leave. And why should they? They had it good here. Too good.

Will remembered what Kate had once said to him: *"But then again, I was always good at selling dreams to desperate people."*

And that was exactly what this was. A sell job. Where Kate began, Josh continued. Giving people a place to call their own, safety, and the ability to live and love and die of old age was a damn fine offer, especially given the alternative. No wonder most of the people around him now—the laughing kids, the smiling pregnant women, the gruff men gathered around campfires cooking fresh meat—thought this was better than running and hiding and constantly fearing the night.

Because, in so many ways, it was.

Josh and Gaby went back into the tent, where they continued their conversation. He could tell by her questions that Gaby was trying to squeeze Josh for information, to keep him talking.

Smart girl.

He glanced at his watch: 2:45 P.M.

Plenty of time, but it wouldn't last. He would have to do something sooner rather than later. Either rescue Gaby and Nate, or at least one of them. Eventually someone would notice the "Givens" on his chest. He couldn't remove it, either, because everyone here had a label—with the exception of Josh. Will guessed that was due to Josh's rank, his ability to come and go as he pleased.

Maybe that was it. Josh. Maybe that was his way out with not just Gaby, but Nate, too.

Doable.

Will walked around the tent and slipped inside the open flaps.

Josh looked up, clearly annoyed at the sight of him. "What is it?" Then Josh saw the gun in Will's hand. "What—?"

Gaby turned, saw Will, and recognized him instantly even behind the gas mask. "Thank God you're alive. They took Nate."

"I know," Will said.

"Gaby?" Josh said. "You know him?"

Will pulled the gas mask up, perching it on his forehead.

"Will," Josh said, frowning slightly.

"How you doing, kid?" Will said.

"I'm…fine."

"I can see that. Gaby," Will said, and nodded at Josh's handgun.

Gaby quickly pulled it—a 9mm Glock—free and slipped it into her own empty holster.

Josh's eyes snapped to her. "What are you doing, Gaby?"

"You know what I'm doing, Josh." She opened the pouches along his gun belt and stuffed his spare magazines into hers. "How did you think this was going to end?"

Josh's face seemed to crater. Will almost felt sorry for the kid. "You don't believe me," Josh said. "After everything I've told you, you still don't believe me."

"I believe you think you're doing all this for me. But it's bullshit, Josh."

"It's the truth."

"No, it's not. The truth is, you're not the Josh I remembered." She looked over at Will. Her face was stone, but he could see through it to the emotions roiling around inside her at the moment. "What about Nate?"

"They took him to the blue tent." He looked over at Josh. "Kid."

Josh looked up, his face shell-shocked.

Gaby was moving around the tent, looking for supplies. She picked up a backpack from the ground—Josh's—and stuffed in anything she could find. Busy work. She didn't want to look at Josh. Didn't want to see the heartbreak on his face.

"How many collaborators are in the camp?" Will asked Josh.

"Too many for you to kill them all," Josh said.

Will grinned back at him. "Are you sure about that?"

"Assuming you could. Then what?" he said, his voice challenging. "Look around you, Will. No one here wants to leave. The gates are open. They're not leaving because they don't want to. Look outside if you don't believe me."

"I've seen enough. I've also seen the pregnant women in the blue tent. You're breeding blood farms, Josh."

"No. You're looking at this all wrong."

"You're turning the human race into chattel. Open your eyes."

"No!" he shouted.

Will lifted a finger to his lips. "Don't do that again."

"Or what? You're going to shoot me?" Josh looked as if he might laugh. "They saved me from the lake, Will. Not you."

"I couldn't come back for you. Not with the others and the supplies at risk."

"You could have, but you didn't. You made a choice. Just like I did."

"Is that what you tell yourself?"

Gaby walked back over to them, avoiding Josh's searching eyes. "I'm not leaving without Nate."

Will nodded. "Yeah, I figured."

"So what's the plan?"

Josh was staring at Gaby. "You lied about him," he said accusingly. "He's not just some guy."

Will thought Gaby would keep ignoring him, that she'd pretend Josh had never spoken. But she surprised him by turning around and looking Josh in the eyes. "I didn't lie to you. I did just meet him this morning. He didn't have to come here, but he did. I don't care what you think this is, Josh, but he's my friend, and I don't leave my friends behind."

"What about me, Gaby?" That might have been a question, but Will thought it sounded more like another accusation.

"What about you, Josh?"

"You're going to leave me again? After three months? After everything I've done—"

"For me?" Gaby finished. "I never wanted this. I *don't* want this. Stop fooling yourself into thinking this is all for me."

"But it *is*," Josh said, almost pleading now. "Why can't you see that? Everything I've done, everything I've accomplished, it's all for you. This is how I'm going to keep you safe, Gaby. *This*."

"Look at me, Josh." Gaby stepped toward him, and though they were the same height, somehow she seemed to tower over him anyway. "I don't need your protection. I never did, and I never will. So you can stop lying to yourself about why you've done the things you've done. It's *bullshit*, Josh."

Josh's entire body seemed to flinch under her words, and he looked away.

Will holstered his gun. "All right, kids. Enough with the *Days of our Lives*. We're going to get Nate. Everyone. Together."

"Then what?" Gaby said.

"We'll cross that bridge when we get to it."

WILL WALKED THROUGH the camp toward the big blue tent for the second time. This time Gaby was beside him while Josh led the way up front. The kid walked awkwardly, as if he had to force his unwilling legs to move. He hadn't tried to run yet, which surprised

Will. He wondered if Josh was afraid of getting shot trying to escape, or if he still thought he could salvage this somehow.

Gaby. He's still clinging to hope that he can convince her. That's why he hasn't run.

Josh's gun holster was empty, but no one seemed to notice. The few men in hazmat suits they saw along the way either nodded to Josh, who wasn't wearing his gas mask, or didn't acknowledge him in any way. They did the same to Will and Gaby. Somehow, all of this made sense to these people.

They've had it too good for too long. They don't know how to do it any other way.

Will felt a little bad for Josh. He believed the kid when he said everything he did was to protect Gaby. He had seen them together in the days before Josh "died." Everything the kid did, he did it with the singular goal of keeping Gaby safe. The problem for Josh was that the Gaby he remembered was an eighteen-year-old high school senior. That Gaby was long gone. The fact that this Gaby survived the Mercy Hospital attack, while most of Mike's people died, was proof of that.

"The towns," Will said. "Where are they, Josh?"

"They're everywhere," Josh said.

"You didn't build them from scratch?"

"There was no need, not with so many small towns just lying around."

"So you're just repurposing them."

"Yeah."

"Your idea, or Kate's?"

"Both," Josh said. There was none of the pride Will had heard earlier when Josh was trying to convince Gaby. "It seemed easier, and most people don't care. Swap out the carpets, fix the windows and sometimes the doors, and it's almost like new again."

"Except for the blood, and the stench of death."

Josh didn't reply.

"You're moving the next group tomorrow," Will said. "What time?"

"I haven't decided."

The kid really is in charge.

Will looked around him at the camp, at the woods beyond. "Are they around?"

"Who?" Josh said.

"You know who."

"A few."

"How many is a few?" Gaby asked.

"A few hundred. Maybe a few thousand. It's not like I've sat down to count."

"In the forest," Will said.

"Yeah."

"I didn't see any while I was running through earlier."

"Neither did I," Gaby said.

"You wouldn't. They—" He stopped.

"What?" Will said. "They what, Josh?"

"They're very good about hiding from the sun," Josh said. "But you already know that."

"WHAT NOW?" GABY said, when they were inside the blue tent.

"This is where it gets dicey," Will said. "If anything happens, grab Nate and run. Even if you can't get to him, you need to run, Gaby."

"Not without Nate."

"Gaby…"

"Not without Nate," she said stubbornly.

He sighed. "All right. Not without Nate."

Will wondered if Josh had heard their little back-and-forth. Maybe not. The tent was loud with conversation and noise, the sounds of people eating, drinking, and even snoring. It was entirely possible Josh hadn't heard, but it was also very possible he had heard every single word, including Gaby's very clear pronouncement she wasn't going anywhere without Nate.

Ah, teenage love in the apocalypse. So unpredictable.

"Where would they take Nate, Josh?" Will asked.

"He's being watched by armed guards, so it'll be one of the private tents," Josh said.

"Lead the way."

Josh led them across the large room toward the dozen or so smaller tents lined in a row near the back. One of the tents belonged to Zoe, the doctor, and Will was relieved to see it wasn't her tent that Josh was making a beeline for. The one they were approaching had an armed man in a hazmat suit standing outside of it. The label on his left breast read "Henry."

The man saw them coming and nodded at Josh.

"How is he?" Josh asked.

Henry shrugged. "He's alive. Doctor's in there with him now."

Josh slipped inside the tent, and Will and Gaby followed. Will glimpsed Henry looking after Gaby, ignoring him completely. It was a good thing Gaby was between the two of them. Will was still waiting for his Givens cover to get blown, but apparently the guy hadn't been all that remarkable or made much of an impression on anyone, judging by how little reaction the name Givens got from those he had met so far.

There was a second man in a hazmat suit standing near the back of the tent, his gas mask clipped to his hip. His label read "Williams." He looked bored and was staring down at an old copy of *Playboy*.

Nate was shirtless and lying on a cot in front of a woman in a white doctor's coat. Fresh gauze was wrapped almost entirely over the left side of his body, all the way down to his elbow, as if someone were getting ready to turn him into a mummy. He looked cleaned up, but that wasn't hard to do; the last time Will had seen him, Nate had been covered in blood and dirt.

Nate opened his eyes when he heard them coming in. He might not have recognized Will with the gas mask on, but he didn't have that problem with Gaby.

The doctor was putting her supplies into a small bag as she stood up. Will knew who she was before she even turned around.

"How is he?" Josh asked.

"He'll live," Zoe said. Then she looked over at Will, standing behind Josh, and smiled a bit. "Hey."

Will nodded back at her. "Doc."

"You got my list?" Zoe asked Josh.

"What list?" Josh said.

She looked irritated. "I gave Givens the list of everyone going on the transport tomorrow. I also told him about the problem with the trucks getting too hot during the trip."

Josh glanced briefly at Will, then back to Zoe and nodded. "Oh, that. He told me."

"So?" Zoe said.

"So what?"

"The transport arrangements. You'll change it for tomorrow?"

"Yeah, I'll do that."

"Good." She looked back over at Will. "Seriously, Givens, you must really like that gas mask. I haven't seen you without it all day."

"Yeah," Will said.

Dammit, Will thought when he saw Williams looking up from the *Playboy* at the mention of Givens's name. The man's eyes zeroed in on Will's face.

"Givens?" Williams said. "Bullshit. You're not—"

Will drew his Glock and shot Williams in the chest. A thin bullet hole appeared in the suit as Williams collapsed, all the blood captured inside the fabric as if it were a vacuum.

Gaby quickly scrambled forward and snatched up Williams's rifle, while Will spun around just as Henry, the other hazmat-suited guard, pushed his way into the tent.

"What the hell's going on?" Henry said.

Will shot him in the head.

Zoe stumbled backward, shocked, eyes darting from Josh to Will to Henry's body on the grass floor. She bumped into Gaby, who pulled out Williams's handgun—a 9mm Beretta—and handed it to Nate.

Nate sat up on the small cot with a grunt and reached for a shirt that looked about a size too big hanging from a hook nearby. He pulled it on with his one good hand, until Gaby hurried over and helped him into the sleeves. Nate grimaced with pain the whole time, but tried not to show it. It was a losing battle, though, and he looked worse than some of the walking wounded Will had seen from his time in Afghanistan.

Josh whirled on Will, his face red with anger. "Why did you do that? You shouldn't have done that!"

There was already a commotion outside the tent. He heard heavy footsteps, and men's voices shouting for people to get out of their way.

Will pulled off the gas mask and looked past Josh's and Zoe's horrified faces at Nate, as Gaby struggled to do the bottom two buttons on his shirt. "Can you walk?"

Nate nodded grimly. "I can walk."

Will looked back at Josh and Zoe. "The two of you are coming with us."

"What?" Zoe said. "Just go!"

"Sorry, doc, but we need hostages." He focused on Josh. "And I get the feeling Kate made it very clear to everyone that you're her golden boy. Am I right?"

Josh said nothing.

"Gaby, Nate," Will said.

He didn't have to tell them the rest. Nate, still leaning against Gaby for support, positioned himself behind Zoe, while Gaby pulled Josh in front of her, standing the two hostages between them and the tent entrance, as the sound of running feet got louder as they drew nearer.

Will slipped out his cross-knife and moved toward the back of the tent. He shoved the knife into the fabric and sliced it across, then down, before pulling the flap aside to reveal the blue color of the bigger tent directly behind it.

"What's going on in there?" a voice shouted from the front of the tent. "Josh? Doctor Zoe? You both still in there?"

"Answer him," Gaby said. She was calm, but there was an edge to her voice.

"Doctor Zoe and I are being held hostage!" Josh shouted back.

"By who?" the voice asked.

"Doesn't matter," Gaby said.

"Doesn't matter!" Josh shouted.

"Williams? Henry?" the voice asked.

"Dead!"

While they were exchanging questions and answers, Will had slashed his way across the back of the tent, then continued through the blue fabric behind it. He sliced from top to bottom, then side to side, before peeling it back to reveal open air and the frightened faces of civilians staring back at him. They immediately began running away, except for a couple of boys eating apples who stopped to gawk, until older people dragged them away, too.

"Stay back or we'll kill them!" Gaby shouted behind him.

He went through the makeshift "door" first. "Gaby, Nate…"

Josh and Zoe followed him out, with Gaby and Nate closely behind them. Nate was essentially working with one good arm, his left hanging uselessly at his side.

"You going to die on me, Nate?" Will asked.

Nate gave him a forced grin, then wiped at a thick bead of sweat along his temple. "I'm good. They gave me some great pills back there, and the doc was nice enough to sew me back up."

Will nodded. He didn't believe a single word of it, but if he could walk… "Gaby, take Josh up front. Nate stays in the middle. Hold on to my rifle and lead me and the good doctor."

Gaby grabbed Josh by the arm and led him forward. Will could see the hurt expression on the kid's face as he silently obeyed. Gaby seemed to be moving on automatic pilot, like some kind of unfeeling automaton. He knew better, of course. She had simply shifted into what he called War Mode. He and Danny did it all the time during combat. It was easier to compartmentalize the superfluous and concentrate on the matter at hand—survival. Gaby was far from ruthless and emotionless at the moment, but she was putting on a good front.

That's my soldier.

Will was backpedaling with Zoe in front of him, which made walking difficult. He made sure to keep a firm grasp on her arm so she didn't stumble, and when she did, he was there to keep her upright—at least, for the most part.

Will didn't think the "don't come in or we'll kill them" threat was going to last very long, and it didn't. They hadn't gone more than twenty meters through the camp before he saw the first hazmat suit poking his head out from the slashed tent flaps in front of him.

Zoe gasped at the sight of the man emerging out of the tent in pursuit, perhaps expecting everything to suddenly devolve into gunfire with her caught in the middle. He didn't blame her. She was probably close to being right.

"Relax," Will said.

"Relax?" she said, almost shouting the word out. "Go to hell, Givens!"

Yeah, Givens, to go hell.

When more hazmat suits started emerging out of the tent flaps, Will fired a shot into the ground in front of the first man. He quickly retreated, tangling up with the man trying to come through behind him. It was almost comical. They disappeared back into the tent, but he didn't think that was going to last for very long, either.

"Where are we going?" Gaby shouted from behind him.

He couldn't see Gaby or the direction she was heading. He only knew when to go straight, to turn left or right when Nate tugged on his M4A1, as if he were a seeing eye dog leading his blind master. It was a crude form of stacking, but there were no other ways for him to keep an eye behind them while still moving the entire time.

"One of the vehicles outside the fence," Will said.

"Where are the keys?" Gaby asked. The question wasn't directed at him.

"In the cars," Josh said.

"You leave the keys in the cars?"

"No one's going to steal them. I told you, they *want* to stay here. Why can't you understand that?"

"Less chatter, more walking," Will said.

They began moving faster through the camp, and Will struggled to keep Zoe upright in front of him. He wasn't sure if she was moving slowly on purpose, or if she was just terrified and her legs were locking up under her.

People were scrambling out of their path, and by now the hazmat suits had emerged out of the blue tent, with more appearing along their flanks. He didn't have a clue what they were doing; he only knew that they weren't shooting, which confirmed his belief that Kate had made it perfectly clear Josh was her avatar in the daylight.

An eighteen-year-old kid, Kate? You could have done better.

He fired a shot into the air and the hazmat suits darted for cover.

Temporarily, anyway.

Soon they were back out and following them again.

Will pulled Zoe tighter against him, heard her grunt a bit.

"Gaby, how we doing?" Will shouted.

"Almost there!" she shouted back.

More men in hazmat suits were converging on them now. He counted a total of ten, then eleven—and those were just the ones he could see trailing them and moving in on his left and right. He glimpsed a man taking careful aim with a bolt-action rifle.

Will shifted Zoe over so she was directly between him and the would-be shooter. "Sorry, doc."

"What?" she said, even more alarmed than she already was.

The man with the rifle pulled his eye away from the scope and lowered his weapon slightly, though not completely.

"Gaby, give me a sitrep!" Will shouted.

"Gate!" she shouted back.

Nate tugged on the M4A1 and Will moved right and found himself backpedaling through one of the unlocked gates. He risked a quick glance over his shoulder at a row of vehicles—the five-ton transports, Jeeps, and too many trucks to count. The ground under the vehicles was wet, and mud clung to the undercarriages, especially those of the five-tons.

He felt Nate let go of the rifle. Will waited at the gate, his gun pressed into the side of Zoe's neck where it had been for the last few minutes during their trek through the camp. The hazmat suits had gathered in front of them now, spreading out along the other side of the fence. They weren't engaging in anything resembling tactical maneuvers that he could see, but they looked fidgety and anxious, which was never a good sign with people armed with assault rifles.

Now or never…

"Will!" Gaby shouted behind him. "You coming or what?"

Will slipped his head behind Zoe's, then looked back at the others. Nate was behind the wheel of a white Ford F-150 and Gaby was pushing Josh into the backseats.

"Come on, doc," Will said, dragging her toward the open front passenger side door.

The men in hazmat suits looked conflicted, unsure whether to follow, shoot, or let them go. He could see them exchanging looks, talking to each other. A lot of head shaking, a couple of the men trying to take control, but most of them looking unsure.

Thank God for amateurs.

"Jesus, you're trying to get me killed," Zoe said, gasping against him.

"Let's hope that doesn't happen," he said.

Will finally reached the truck. He glanced in at Nate, settling in behind the steering wheel. "You good?"

"Good enough," Nate said.

"In you go, doc."

Will shoved her into the open back door with Gaby and Josh, slammed the door closed, then dived into the front seat.

Almost instantly, he heard rifle fire and the front windshield spiderwebbed as Nate slammed his foot down on the gas. The F-150 skidded, fighting for purchase against the muddy ground.

It finally got enough traction to back up, Nate spinning the wheel as if he were some Hollywood stunt driver. Will had absolutely no idea how the kid managed it with just one good arm.

Then they were moving forward, slashing along the hurricane fencing to their left, men in hazmat suits running and firing after them. He heard the *ping ping ping!* of bullets going into the sides of the vehicle. Then Nate slammed down on the brake and spun the steering wheel again, and they were suddenly back on the dirt road with trees everywhere.

Will turned around and looked into the backseat, at a horrified Zoe sitting behind him in the middle. Josh sat against the window to Zoe's left, while Gaby caught her breath to the doctor's right. Gaby had her Glock in her lap, aimed at Zoe and Josh.

"We good?" Will asked.

Gaby nodded. "No bullet holes."

Will looked over at Josh, but the kid's face was turned against the window. "Josh—"

Before Will could finish, Josh jerked on the door handle, flinging open the door and disappearing outside in a rush of wind. Gaby screamed his name and Nate slammed on the brakes. The F-150 skidded to a reckless, sliding stop.

"Holy shit," Nate said. "Did he just jump out of a moving car?"

Will threw his door open and climbed out. Josh was picking himself up from the road thirty meters back. He looked to be in one piece, but was cradling his left arm. Josh stared back at him, almost daring Will to come get him.

Kid's got balls.

"Should we go back?" Nate asked, leaning over the front seats.

Will shook his head and climbed back into the truck. "Let's go."

Nate put the truck back in gear and stepped on the gas. As they shot up the road, Will looked at his side mirror and saw two trucks, men in hazmat suits mounted on the backs, appear behind Josh. They slowed down when they saw him, and he calmly, almost leisurely, walked over to one of the vehicles.

Then Nate made a turn and Will couldn't see them anymore. Will thought about telling the kid to slow down, but he seemed to be handling both the truck and his own pain well enough.

He looked back at Gaby instead, saw the unasked question in

her eyes. "He's alive," Will said. "Hurt, but alive."

"Are they chasing us?" she asked.

"I don't think so."

"Why aren't they?" Nate said.

"Maybe he doesn't think there's a point."

"Who? The kid?"

"Yeah," Will said. "The kid."

"Nate shouldn't be driving," Gaby said.

"I'm fine," Nate said.

"The hell you are. You could barely walk an hour ago."

"That was an hour ago. The doc gave me some really good pills back there. Right, doc?"

Zoe didn't answer. She stared forward in silence, looking dazed.

"Anyway, I'll let you know when I can't drive anymore," Nate continued. "But I'm good for now."

Will turned his attention to Zoe. "You okay, doc? Any bullet holes?"

She seemed to remember where she was and glared back at him, just before lunging forward and slapping him across the face with surprising speed. Gaby grabbed her and pulled her back, but Zoe never took her eyes away from him. If she could, he imagined she would drill lasers through his eyeballs.

"Go to hell, Givens," Zoe said.

"My name's not Givens," Will said.

"You can still go to hell, whatever your name is."

Will sat back in his seat, trying to shake off the stinging in his cheek. She was a hell of a lot stronger than she looked.

"That was fun," Nate said, grinningly crookedly at him. "Let's not do it again anytime soon, huh?"

CHAPTER 27

GABY

ABOUT TEN MINUTES after they exited Sandwhite Wildlife State Park, Will pulled off the hazmat suit and got behind the wheel of the Ford F-150. In the backseat, Zoe cleaned up Nate's open shoulder wound—which had begun bleeding again—and applied a fresh bandage, tossing the blood-soaked one out the window.

Gaby had been reluctant to let Zoe even touch Nate, but she finally relented when the older woman gave her a firm look and said, "I know you don't trust me, but I'm a doctor, and I'm not going to let your friend bleed to death if I can help it."

Zoe kept her promise, cleaning Nate's wound, then dressing it back up with the supplies from Will's pack. When she was done, they propped Nate up between them so he could lean his head against Gaby's shoulder. She slipped an arm around his waist just to make sure he didn't fall down.

When they finally reached the town of Harvest, Gaby half expected to see Harris, Kellerson's sniper, lying in wait for them again. She listened for gunshots that never came.

Will pulled off the main highway and drove west along the small streets for about thirty minutes, heading deeper and deeper into the main center of town where they could become lost among the buildings. He finally stopped, then guided the truck toward a two-door auto body garage called Fredo's. They drove past a sign featuring a cartoon character holding a wrench, and the promise of "Mechanic on Duty." Fredo's was squeezed in between a combination Phillips 66 gas station and Burger King, and an empty building with a "For Rent" sign in the window.

Will parked the F-150 and climbed out with his rifle. He entered the office next to the garage, then came out of a side door and went around the back. Gaby waited with Zoe, still holding the Glock she had taken from Josh, just in case.

"He called you Gaby?" Zoe said.

"Yeah, that's my name."

"I figured that."

"So why'd you ask?"

"I'm just trying to be friendly."

"You can stop now."

The older woman sighed. "When are you going to let me go?"

"You'll have to talk to Will about that. I don't even know why he brought you along. If it was up to me, I'd just shoot you."

Zoe went quiet.

Will returned, pulled up one of the garage doors and went inside.

"Would you really do that?" Zoe asked after a while.

"Do what?" She knew what Zoe was referring to, but the mischievous side of Gaby felt like hearing the other woman say it anyway.

"Would you really shoot me in cold blood?"

"Who says it would be in cold blood?"

"I don't have a weapon. I'm harmless."

"I don't see that."

"No, I don't have a weapon," she insisted.

"Not that. The second part."

"That I'm harmless?"

"Yeah."

"You may be younger than me, but you're clearly more adept with those weapons than I am. Besides, I don't think I could take you in a fight."

Gaby almost laughed. "I wish you'd try. I'd crush your throat. That is, if I don't break your nose and shove the loose bones into your brain first."

She heard Zoe swallow audibly on the other side of Nate. Gaby smiled to herself.

"What you were doing back there," Gaby said, "with the pregnant girls. That makes you dangerous."

"I don't understand."

"You're working for them. The ghouls. The bloodsuckers. Whatever you want to call them. That makes you dangerous. Add in your medical training, and that *really* makes you dangerous. I would shoot you just to keep you out of their hands, so you can't do any more harm."

Zoe didn't answer.

Will climbed back into the truck. He noticed the silence, and there must have been something about Zoe's face that gave away their conversation.

"What's going on, ladies?" he asked.

"Nothing," Zoe said.

"Just girl talk," Gaby said.

"Uh huh," Will said, not believing a single word of it.

He reversed the truck, then turned a full 180 degrees in the driveway before backing up into one of the two empty garage ports.

Gaby climbed out of the truck and walked outside to pull security with the AR-15 she had snatched up during their escape. The weapon felt wrong in her hands, and she longed to have her old M4 back. The barrel on the AR-15 was too long, and she was even slightly annoyed by the ugly tan color. But at least whoever owned it before her had converted it to full-auto, so there was that.

Sunlight was fading in the horizon, and she could barely make out the gray stones of the highway from this distance. Will had chosen a good spot to lay low for the night.

Zoe climbed out, and when Gaby looked back, she saw the other woman doing everything possible to avoid her gaze.

"We'll stay here for the night," Will said.

"Then what?" Zoe asked, arms wrapped tightly around her chest. "What happens to me?"

"I need you to keep an eye on Nate, make sure he survives the night."

"And then?"

"We'll revisit that question tomorrow."

She sighed, frustrated. "Do you have any painkillers? He's going to need them."

Will pulled out his pack, took out a bottle, and handed it to her.

"Generic Vicodin," Zoe said, reading the label. "It'll do."

"Gaby," Will said.

She walked into the garage and they pulled one steel door down, then the other. There were no ways to lock the doors except for a latch that could be easily flicked open. The room was suddenly bathed in darkness, until Gaby heard a soft crackling sound and Will's face lit up, illuminated by a soft green glow stick. He put it on the dashboard and climbed back in behind the steering wheel.

She squeezed into the back with Nate, lifting his head and resting it in her lap. She stroked his hair, matted with sweat, and looked down at his calm, almost contented face. His lips even looked as if they were curling up into a smile, as though he knew she was doting on him.

Zoe climbed into the front passenger seat, her face illuminated by the glow stick. Will pulled out some strips of beef jerky from his pack and passed them around. Zoe took the offering gratefully, pulling open the wrapper and chewing ravenously.

"Tell me about the towns," Will said.

Zoe didn't answer right away. The older woman was sitting directly in front of her, so Gaby couldn't see her face. She did see the seat moving uncomfortably from time to time, depending on what Will was asking.

"What about them?" Zoe finally said.

"How many are there around the state?"

"I only know of three."

"You've been to all of them?"

"Just two."

"Including the one they're scheduled to transport to tomorrow?"

"Not that one, no."

"How big are these towns?"

"Big."

"Give me dimensions."

She sighed. "I don't know. I didn't exactly get out and measure them."

"Ballpark."

"They're good-sized towns, I guess. More than one street."

"How many people were there?"

"There were 500 in one town, and about a thousand in the other."

"How many were supposed to go to this third town?"

"From my camp alone, around 700."

"How many camps will be relocating their people over to this third town?"

"Josh told me two other camps from around the area."

"Jesus, how many camps are there?" Gaby asked.

"There are five that I know of," Zoe said.

"As big as the one we just left?" Will asked.

"No. This last one was the biggest by far. The others are about half the size, some smaller."

"And they all have pregnant women in them?"

"Yes. They…encourage it."

"I bet the guys don't mind," Gaby smirked.

"No, I guess not," Zoe said.

"So you go around the camps, making sure everyone's getting laid?" Will asked.

Gaby smiled at the question.

"I'm a doctor," Zoe said defensively. "Someone has to look out for them."

"How many doctors do they have working the camps?"

"I haven't been to all of them, like I said. But of the five that I've visited, there are about twenty of us spread around. Actual doctors and nurses. Most of the ones you saw in scrubs back at the camp were volunteers."

"Twenty doctors and nurses for five camps. That's a lot of work."

"Yeah, I guess."

"And you don't see anything wrong with it?"

Zoe didn't answer right away.

"Doc?" Will pressed.

"What do you want me to say?" She sounded angry, which surprised Gaby. There was real emotion there, and her voice rose slightly. "I did the best I could, but there's only so much you can do. And I was tired of the running, the hiding…watching people dying that I couldn't save."

The seat in front of Gaby creaked as Zoe leaned back against it heavily.

"I thought I was dead at first," Zoe continued. "When it all began, there were twenty-nine of us. We were like you, running and hiding, barely surviving. Then one night they caught us, and I went to sleep. I don't know what happened. It was some kind of induced coma, I know that now."

Phase Two. The blood farms...

"Were you alert?" Will asked. "During the coma?"

"Sometimes." She paused. "It's hard to tell. Sometimes I remember images. Flickers of memory, but they're hazy, and it's never for very long. A creature bending over me, over one of my arms...my legs..." She shook her head. "It's all a blur. I can't make out details, just the feeling of helplessness. Unable to move, unable to make a sound, unable to... It's better to pretend it's all just a bad dream."

She stopped talking for a moment. Will didn't push it, and Gaby wasn't sure if she really wanted to know more, either. The idea of a blood farm was grotesque enough, but getting details about what happened inside one of them, from someone who was a victim of it, felt almost perverted.

"Then one day I woke up," Zoe said. "It's months later, and suddenly I have this dream. This creature, with glowing blue eyes, giving me a choice. But it wasn't much of a choice. Go back to sleep, or wake up and help people. It wasn't much of a choice, like I said."

Zoe pulled back the long sleeves of her white doctor's coat that she still had on and showed Will her arm. Gaby leaned over a bit and saw fading teeth marks against pale skin. She had no doubt there were similar markings along Zoe's right arm too, and maybe other places as well. Will had told her about what happened at those blood farms, and Blaine and Maddie had confirmed it. The ghouls fed on you, night after night after night...

She shivered slightly in her seat.

"I guess I'm weak," Zoe said. "I rationalized it, of course. History will look at me and frown. But what's that saying? History is written by the winners. Tell me, Will, do you really think you can win this war?"

Will didn't answer. He sat silently in his seat, staring out the bullet-riddled windshield at the pulled-down steel garage door.

"I didn't think so," Zoe said, and leaned back against her seat for the night.

SHE MUST HAVE fallen asleep, because when Gaby opened her eyes again, it was pitch dark inside the garage. The glow stick was still giving off light, so it couldn't have been more than a few hours since she had dozed off.

She saw the back of Will's head in the driver's seat, along with the barrel of his M4A1 peeking out over the space between the two front seats. Nate was sleeping soundly in her lap with that stupid grin still on his face. There was the sound of snoring in front of her, the front passenger seat slightly reclined back.

Gaby picked up the AR-15 from the floor and leaned it between her leg and the door. Will had split his ammo with her—three magazines for the rifle and three more for the Glock. Only Will would carry that many spare magazines with him. One of his favorite sayings was that the only thing soldiers liked more than bullets was even more bullets. She felt better with the rifle next to her, and even better knowing they were loaded with the right kind of bullets. She stuffed the regular ammo she had snatched from the camp into her pack, just in case.

When she looked up, Will was holding something in front of her. She smiled and took it. "Thanks. Where'd you get it?"

"I grabbed a spare back at the Archers. Just in case."

Gaby pulled off her shirt. It was still sticky with Nate's blood, but more than that, it was the smell. She tossed it out the window and slipped on the new T-shirt, ripping the tag off the sleeve. It was a bit loose, but it fit well enough after she tucked it into her pants.

"How's Nate?" Will asked.

"Out like a light."

"His breathing?"

"Pretty normal."

"Good."

"What do you think? About Zoe."

He didn't answer right away. "She believes she's doing what she has to. Taking care of the others."

"Josh thought the same thing." She remembered how earnest he looked while explaining his actions to her.

What happened to you in those three months, Josh?

"He really believed it," she said. "Every single word of it. I don't know if he's changed that much, or if I have." She paused. "Is it me, Will?"

"You're still you, Gaby."

"Am I?"

"If there's one thing I've learned, it's that training doesn't change you. Training only brings out what's already inside. You can't turn shit into diamonds, but you can wipe away shit from one."

Gaby smiled. "That's a nice visual, Will, thanks."

He chuckled. "This moment of Zen, courtesy of Danny."

"He came up with that?"

"Yeah, a while back."

"What do you think they're doing right now on the island?"

"Danny's probably making bad jokes, Carly's probably rolling her eyes at him, and Lara is probably soaking in the tub. Naked. Looking beautiful…"

She smiled. "TMI."

"Not nearly enough."

"You wanna know something funny?"

"What's that?"

"You and Lara are probably the most functional couple I've met."

He turned around in his seat and grinned back at her. "Really."

"Yeah. Sad, right?"

He shrugged. "Better than the alternative, I guess. Although she must be pretty pissed at me right about now."

"You left Benny and the others before I could come back with the radio on purpose, didn't you? So you wouldn't have to tell her you weren't coming back home."

He didn't answer her right away. After a while, he said, "Yeah."

"That's really shitty of you, Will. She's probably worried out of her mind right now."

"I didn't know what to tell her."

"She would have understood."

"Maybe. But I was probably going to die out here, Gaby, and I didn't want the last words she heard from me to be an excuse why I'm not coming back to her."

"You chickened out."

"I guess I did."

"You're an asshole, Will."

"I know," he said quietly.

WILL WAS JUST as surprised as she was that they had made it through the night unscathed. They climbed out of the truck in the morning and threw open the garage doors, drinking in the warmth of the sun like drunks with their booze.

Gaby went back to check on Nate while Will wandered off. Both Nate and Zoe were still asleep in their seats. She had only gotten a few hours in last night, and Will had gotten even less than that, since every time she opened her eyes during the night he was still staring alertly at the garage doors.

Will didn't return until twenty minutes later.

"Found one?" she asked.

He nodded. "How does a sports car sound?"

"As long as I can step on the gas and it goes, I'm good."

They climbed back into the truck, and Will drove them over to the Phillips 66/Burger King next door. There were two vehicles lined up along the gas pumps—a red Ford Mustang GT and a slick-looking black GMC truck.

Zoe woke up when they were halfway there. "Where are we going now?"

"Next door," Will said.

"Oh," she said, sounding disappointed.

Will maneuvered the Ford until it was parked parallel with the Mustang, except the noses of the vehicles were pointed in opposite directions. The sports car would have looked shiny and new if not for the thick layer of eleven-month-old dust. Gaby got out of the truck with a rag and wiped down the thick grime that covered the front windshield. It gave way grudgingly, revealing the clean front seats underneath. No blood, and the key fob was sticking out of the ignition.

"How much would a car like this have cost me?" Gaby asked.

"$22,000 for the base model, easy," Will said. "Twenty-five with some luxuries."

"There goes the college fund."

"Lucky for you, I'm going to take the F-150 in a straight-up trade."

"Now that's a deal," a voice said behind her.

She looked over at Nate, peering out of the open truck door. "Lay back down," she said.

"I'm fine."

"Stop being an ass and lay back down."

He smirked, then laid back down with his feet sticking out of the open door. "I'm really fine."

Zoe was stretching lazily next to the truck. Gaby was surprised she hadn't taken off running at the first opportunity. She would have, in the same situation.

"Give him a final look-over, doc," Will said.

Zoe climbed back into the Ford. "How are you feeling?" she asked Nate.

"Like someone poured concrete on my head and then tried to bury me," Nate said.

"That's the Vicodin talking."

Zoe swapped out Nate's bloody bandages and put on fresh ones, while Gaby opened the Mustang's unlocked driver side door. Dust erupted from the black leather seat as soon as she sat down. It would have been nice if she could roll down the windows, but that required power.

Will, meanwhile, had pulled out a siphoning tube from his pack and was sniffing the Mustang's open gas tank. He had lined up the two vehicles and stuck one end of the tube into the Ford's tank, then sucked on it until liquid started flowing slowly through the tube. He quickly stabbed the other end into the Mustang's, transferring gas from one car to the other for about five minutes before cutting it off.

"Is that enough?" she asked.

"The Ford doesn't have that much to give. You'll need to search for more gas along the way, or find something else less shiny to drive."

Will climbed back into the Ford and maneuvered it until it was parked nose-to-nose with the Mustang. He popped the truck's hood, and Gaby fumbled around with the Mustang until she found a lever underneath the steering column. Pulling it, she heard the sports car's hood pop open. Will climbed back out and Gaby watched him hook the jumper cables between the two batteries.

When he finally gave her the thumbs up, Gaby turned the key in the Mustang's ignition. The car struggled for about five or six seconds before it finally turned over and roared to life, so loudly that Gaby instinctively pulled her foot off the gas to quiet the beast. She climbed out of the Mustang and left it running.

Zoe stood outside the truck, cleaning her hands on a rag that was already covered in dried blood.

"How is he?" Gaby asked.

"Better than yesterday," Zoe said. "You're taking him to the island?"

"That's the plan."

"How far is it from here?"

"Beaufont Lake," Will said.

"I know where that is," Zoe nodded. "I used to go fishing there with my dad when I was a kid. It's nice. So you guys are on the island? Song Island, right?"

"Right," Gaby nodded.

"So what about me?" She looked at Gaby, then at Will. "What happens to me now?"

"You're coming with me," Will said.

She frowned. "Why won't you just let me go?"

"I will, but not yet."

"When? I already told you everything I know."

"I still need to know more."

"But *why?*" she asked, sounding very much like a child.

"*'If you know the enemy and know yourself, you need not fear the result of a hundred battles,'*" Will said.

Zoe sighed. "What the hell does that mean?"

◄━━ ━━►

"ARE YOU REALLY going to leave Will?" Nate asked.

He was reclining in the front passenger seat of the Mustang, stretching out his legs as far as they would go. She could hardly tell he had been shot twice yesterday unless she peeked underneath his shirt, where his entire left side was wrapped tightly in gauze. It helped that he wasn't wearing his old, blood-covered shirt and had a bottle of generic Vicodin in his pocket.

"That's the way he wants it," she said.

She watched Will through the windshield, waiting for the gas inside the GMC to finish transferring over to the F-150. She could see the outline of Zoe's head in the front passenger seat, probably still fuming.

"That's what he wanted last time," Nate said, "but you followed him out here anyway."

"He also made a good point."

"What's that?"

"Take you to Song Island before you bleed to death."

"I won't bleed to death, Gaby. Zoe made sure of that. If you want to go where Will goes, I'm good with it."

"Why?" she asked.

"Why?"

"Why are you so nice to me? Besides the fact you're desperate to get into my pants, I mean."

He chuckled. "What, that's not enough?"

"No," she said, still serious. "Why the devotion to someone you've only known for one day?"

"A day and a half."

"Don't deflect the question."

"That wasn't my intention."

"Answer the question," she pressed.

"Because you're...you."

"What does that even mean?"

"Besides the physical appearance—which is pretty damn spectacular, big nasty looking gash on your forehead and an outrageous amount of scars and bruises notwithstanding—"

She had to smile at that.

"—the rest of you is pretty awesome, too."

"Like what?" she said.

"You're really making this difficult."

"What about me specifically makes you willing to risk your life over and over again? It can't be just the potential for sex."

He sighed. "The first time I saw you, I thought you might be it."

"What's that?"

"You know. *It.* The one. The girl I've been waiting for."

She was speechless.

Nate laughed. "Oh, shit, now you're going to make fun of me, aren't you?"

She shook her head. "No."

"No?"

She shrugged. "I asked, and you answered."

"So…"

"So, what?"

"So…that's it?" He gave her a strange look. "I confessed that the only reason I've been following you around like a lost puppy is because I have this totally abstract notion of you being 'the one,' and all you can do is shrug?"

"I don't know what to say."

"Well, say something."

"Thanks?"

"That's it?"

"I told you, I don't know what to say."

"Hunh," he said.

"What does that mean?"

"It means I would really like to kiss you right now, but I'm afraid you might punch me."

"I probably would."

"See?"

"If it makes you feel any better, the old me would be sucking face with you right about now."

"Damn, really?"

"Absolutely."

"Dammit."

She smiled, then opened the door. "I'll be right back."

She climbed out of the Mustang and walked over to Will. He looked up from the gas tank as she approached.

"You're still here," he said.

"We decided we're coming with you."

"Gaby…"

"Nate's fine."

"And you believe him?"

"Yes." Gaby leaned through the open F-150 window and looked across the front seat at Zoe. "How's Nate? The truth."

Zoe looked confused by the question. "He's fine. Why?"

"Is he in any danger of bleeding to death anytime soon?"

"Unless he plans to get involved in a gladiator fight, then no."

Gaby looked back at Will. "He'll be fine. We'll keep back, stay in support. Besides, if I go back without you, Lara is going to kill me."

"No, Gaby," he said.

"Why the hell not?"

He motioned for her to follow him. She did, and he led her almost to the very end of the parking lot. She glanced back at Zoe, realizing it was because he didn't want the other woman to hear. Zoe had apparently come to the same conclusion, because she stared curiously after them.

"What is it?" she asked in a softer voice.

"I'm going to do some recon," Will said. "That's all. The truth is, I'm better on my own."

"What about the doctor? You're taking her with you."

"She's a necessity."

"For what?"

"In case it gets FUBAR."

She knew what that meant. FUBAR. *Fucked Up Beyond All Reason.* Military jargon for when everything you planned went completely awry. Will was doing what he always did. Hoping for the best, but preparing for the worst.

"She's my bargaining chip," Will continued. "But I can't keep an eye on her and at the same time worry that Nate is going to bust a stitch and bleed to death. Even if it's unlikely, the possibility exists. Besides, I need you to go back to the island and tell Lara I'm fine."

"And you're just doing recon," she said doubtfully.

"That's it," he nodded.

"No hero stuff?"

"Scout's honor."

"You were never in the Scouts."

"Let's pretend I was."

She stared at him, trying to read his face. He looked back at her, as cool and calm as he always was. Unflappable. Unreadable.

Like I could ever read him.

Gaby looked back at Zoe. "Can you trust her?"

"No," Will said without hesitation.

"But you're willing to risk it anyway."

"I need to know."

"Need to know *what*, Will?"

"What the hell they've been doing out here. Not just in the

camps, with the pregnant women, but in these towns they're taking over. I need to know if we can fight it, or if we even should."

"If we even should? What does that mean?"

"Things have changed, Gaby. The world's changed while we hid on the island. Why do you think they haven't attacked us in three months?"

"Josh seemed to think it was because of him."

"Josh is delusional," Will said. "They haven't been attacking us because we don't *matter* to them. What's a handful of humans trapped on an island compared to what they've been doing in these camps? We're insignificant. That's why they haven't bothered."

"Josh said the camps were just the start."

"That's what worries me. What's on the other side of the camps?"

"The towns."

"Yeah. The towns. I need to know for sure."

She couldn't blame him. The same questions had been bugging her ever since she learned what was going on in the camp. And that wasn't even the end of the line. There were the towns…

"All right," she said. Glancing over at the Mustang, she saw Nate curiously watching her back. "I'll take Nate on ahead to the island. What should I tell Lara when I make contact?"

"Tell her I'll be back by tomorrow. Later this evening, if everything works out."

"Right," she said, smirking back at him. "Because things have always worked out great for us in the past."

CHAPTER 28

WILL

HE DIDN'T MOVE from the Phillips 66/Burger King until nine in the morning, about an hour after Gaby and Nate had left in the Mustang. When his watch clicked over to nine, he turned on the F-150 and pointed it out of the strip mall and back toward I-49 in the distance.

Zoe sat quietly in the front passenger seat through most of the trip. She didn't speak until they were almost at the highway.

"You're going to follow them to the town, aren't you?" she finally asked.

"What makes you say that?"

"All those questions last night."

"I guess there's a reason they gave you a medical diploma."

She snorted. "Are you always this much of an asshole?"

"Pretty much, yeah."

He turned left, merging back onto I-49 and slipping into the mostly barren northbound lane. They were the only thing moving for miles, which both comforted and concerned him. The fact that Josh hadn't bothered to pursue them remained in the back of his mind. He had hardly slept at all last night, and had spent most of it listening for the sounds of car engines that never showed up.

What are you doing out there, Josh?

"So who's Lara?" Zoe asked.

He thought about not answering.

"I'm just going to keep asking," she said.

He sighed. "She lives on the island."

"Is she your wife?"

"No."

"Girlfriend?"

"I guess."

"You guess? So you don't know?"

"I haven't really thought about it."

"Oh no? I bet she has. A lot. That's what we do, you know. We think about these type of things."

"Good to know."

"Wow, you must have majored in asshole in college."

"Greek history."

"Greek history?"

"Yeah."

"You majored in Greek history in college? That was unfortunate."

"Yeah."

"You don't talk much, huh?"

"No."

"So Lara likes the strong, silent type, is that it?"

"You'd have to ask her."

"Is that your way of telling me you won't kill me after this?"

"I'm not going to kill you, Zoe."

"No?" She stared at him for a moment, as if trying to gauge his trustworthiness. "I can take that to the bank?"

"Why do you think I'm going to kill you?"

"How the hell should I know. I never met you until yesterday, and back then you were named Givens. I don't know anything about you. Why you're doing what you're doing, or how you could so cold-bloodedly shoot those two men back in the tent."

"I had no choice."

"You could have wounded them."

"Too risky."

"You're good at it," she said. It wasn't a question. "The killing part."

He didn't answer.

"I guess everyone has something they're good at," she said, turning her head into the breeze outside her open window. "So why Greek history?"

"What do you have against the Greeks?"

"Nothing. Some of my best friends are Greeks."

"Is that right?"

"No."

"Hunh."

"You're a real conversationalist, Will."

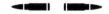

HE WENT BACK to Sandwhite Wildlife State Park, but this time he didn't take the off-ramp. Instead, he stopped a half kilometer from the exit and climbed out, then scanned the flat, gray concrete highway for signs.

Zoe looked at him strangely when he settled back into the Ford twenty seconds later. "What are you doing back here, Will? Do you have a death wish?"

"Not the last time I checked."

He put the F-150 in drive and continued up the highway.

"So what are we doing back here?" she asked.

"You'll see."

"Great. Another surprise. You're full of them, aren't you?"

"You have a very acerbic sense of humor for a doctor."

"Do I?"

"Yes."

"I'm just trying to piss you off."

"Hmm."

"Not working?"

He shrugged and kept driving.

He didn't stop again until he had almost passed Sandwhite completely, and only when he saw another on-ramp. He put the truck in park, climbed out, and saw what he had been looking for.

Large tire tracks caked in mud, curling from the on-ramp and onto I-49 heading northbound. They weren't quite faded yet, so they weren't more than a few hours old. The tracks overlapped, but not so much that he couldn't tell there was more than one vehicle driving in a convoy. He guessed Josh was using either all or most of the military five-tons he had seen back at the camp.

Will climbed back into the Ford.

"Tire tracks," Zoe said. "From the big transport trucks. You're using the mud falling off them to track them. You're smarter than you look."

"I'm sure there's a compliment in there somewhere."

"They're not going to last, you know. The tracks."

"They'll last long enough. I don't see Josh moving that many people for that long of a distance. Like you said, it can get pretty hot in the back of those transports."

"How did you know they would be heading north and not south toward us?"

"South takes them back into Lafayette. There aren't any towns big enough to settle everyone at the camp between here and the city. There was always only one direction for them to go—north."

"You really are smarter than you look," she said.

Will grunted and drove on.

⬅▬▮ ▮▬➤

IT WASN'T HARD to track the trucks. The trails were visible from the high perch of the F-150, and he drove for thirty minutes or so, doing forty-five miles per hour because of the lack of traffic. After a while, the tracks turned right onto an off-ramp, then merged onto State Highway 106.

"Have you been here before?" he asked Zoe.

She shook her head. "No. But like I said, they have camps and towns everywhere. I'm sure there are more that I don't even know about."

He drove along the two-lane state highway for another ten minutes, passing mostly overgrown farmland, with the occasional stables or abandoned silent tractors, reminders that at one point people used to live and work here. Wild grass had begun to reclaim the land, and as soon as the buildings were covered up, there wouldn't be any reminders at all that man once tilled them.

He passed a small bayou and kept going for another ten minutes. Houses began cropping up on both sides of the road. A pair of two-story farmhouses, one white and one slightly brown—or maybe it was faded or dirty white—stood next to each other.

Soon, the tracks told him to turn left along a new stretch of state highway.

More farmland, until he saw smoke rising in the distance. Will slowed down and, purely out of habit, pulled over to the side of the two-lane road.

There were three columns of smoke drifting lazily into the air farther up the road—two kilometers, give or take. Close enough for the sound of a car engine to be heard, especially with so few noises, except for the chirping of birds and clicking of crickets around them. He thought about Josh and how smart the kid was. An ambush or two wouldn't be out of the question.

"The town," Zoe said. "Looks like you found it."

"Looks like it."

"So what now?"

Will looked around at his surroundings.

More overgrown farmland, a long ditch, and the bayou curving slightly to his left before evening out to run parallel with the road again. He remembered passing a couple of farms back down the road.

"When was the last time you went for a walk, doc?"

LIKE MOST BARNS in rural America, the one he chose was painted red, with a slightly burnt orange shade. It was wide and long, and he had no trouble driving the Ford F-150 inside once he opened the large twin front doors.

There was enough darkness inside to worry about ghouls hiding in the shadows, forcing him to spend a few minutes poking around the old bales of unused hay on the first floor. He started breathing through his mouth against the metallic mold smell, stepping around spores along the back walls and floors that were visible in the bright pools of sunlight spilling in through holes that pockmarked the building. He finished by climbing up the rickety steps to the second floor and scanning in a complete 360.

Satisfied, he returned to the Ford and slipped on his pack, then shouldered the M4A1.

Zoe followed him out of the truck. "Are you going to kill me, Will?"

"You already asked me that."

"I wanted to make sure you hadn't changed your mind."

"No," he said. "I promise, I'm not going to harm you, Zoe."

He pocketed the key fob and left the barn. After Zoe followed him out, he swung the big wooden doors closed, then made sure the latch caught.

"I don't know what you expect to find here," Zoe said. "It's a town. With people. What else is there to see?"

"We'll see."

"Oh, clever."

He started off, Zoe following behind him. He expected her to bolt at any moment, take her chances anywhere but with him, but she didn't. Instead, she followed him quietly, the only noise coming from her footsteps.

Will glanced at his watch: 10:45 A.M.

He pointed them toward the smoke, keeping to the field of tall grass along the roads for cover.

"I should have worn hiking shoes," Zoe said behind him.

"Stop complaining."

"Says the guy with boots. I only have tennis shoes."

"Tennis shoes are all-purpose."

"Not when you're walking across farmland. What kind of shoes does Lara wear?"

He didn't answer.

"You don't happen to have a pair of boots in that bag, do you?" she asked.

"I had a pair of shoes I picked up for Lara, but I had to throw them away."

"Boots?"

"No."

"Too bad. I could use a pair of boots. Even those clunky army boots. Tell me about Lara."

He ignored her.

"Come on, you know you want to. Is she pretty? Blonde? Brunette? Probably pretty. I also bet you have a thing for blondes, don't you?"

He pretended he couldn't hear her.

"Who doesn't like blondes? Everyone likes blondes. You wanna ask me if I'm a natural blonde?"

He didn't.

"I am. In case you were wondering. Lara's a blonde, right? I knew it. You don't know it, but you have a type. You wanna know what it is?"

He kept walking, looking forward.

"You know you wanna," she said. "Admit it, and I'll tell you. Will? Can you hear me up there? God, you suck."

<hr>

"IS IT EVERYTHING you expected?" Zoe asked.

It looked like something out of an old Western, sections of the place separated into grids, all connected by one long main street. Brick and mortar buildings lined the sidewalks, their signs repurposed with simple names like Bakery, Supplies, Clinic, and one for Administration. There were more he couldn't see from his vantage point. Smoke drifted out from chimneys.

Apartments were interspersed among the businesses, and people were moving leisurely on the other side of open windows and fluttering curtains. A woman was hanging laundry, while a redheaded kid leaned over the windowsill watching the streets below. A pair of preteens in shorts raced along the sidewalk, dodging adults.

What end of the world?

There was a fountain in the town square, where a big white tent had been set up. Transport trucks were parked nearby, and a line of people stood in a semi-organized circle that snaked around the tent. Armed figures in hazmat suits moved among them, but unlike back at the camp, these men looked alert.

They're expecting trouble.

He was lying flat on top of a small hill about 200 meters from the edge of town, peering through binoculars. Zoe sat behind him, rubbing her feet.

There were no gunmen on the rooftops that he could see, which made the place look more accommodating than it really was. Or maybe it really *was* that welcoming? He remembered what Jenkins, the man he had met yesterday in the camp and who had tried to squeeze him for information about the towns, had said. The man was anxious, even eager, to finally get settled.

"I think I made the right decision. Still, it would be nice to finally get to one of these towns I keep hearing about. Get on with living."

A low rumble preceded the appearance of two military five-ton transport trucks, entering the other side of town. They moved through the street, coming to a loud, crunching stop behind the other parked vehicles next to the white tent.

People hopped out of the back of the first truck. Men and women stretching, shaking hands and hugging. An air of happiness, of a long journey finally come to a fruitful end, showed on their faces. A pair of women with clipboards appeared, greeting the newcomers, while teenagers pushed carts and handed out bottled water and food. Pregnant women were helped down the back of the second truck, and they automatically became the center of attention.

"What's happening in the white tent?" Will asked.

"The one with everyone lining up outside?" Zoe asked.

"Yes."

"Processing. It's where they sign in to the town and get assigned housing. Later, they're given work details."

"Work details?"

"It's a town, Will. People have to run it. They're given work based on their qualifications. For instance, I would get assigned to the clinic."

"So what poor slob gets garbage duty?"

"I guess whoever doesn't have a skill they could use somewhere else. Isn't that what you do on the island? Delegate jobs?"

She had a point, but he decided to keep that to himself. He said instead, "And anyone can come and go as they please?"

"That's the idea."

"But you don't know for sure."

"I've never seen anyone leave. Why would they want to? Everything they need is there. Food. Water. Shelter. And they don't have to be scared at night."

"Bottled water?"

"The towns I've been to all had spring wells. I'm guessing this one does too, or they wouldn't have settled here."

"And the creatures, they don't come into town at nights?"

"I've never seen them."

"How do they know to stay away?"

"Probably the same way they know not to harm the guys in

hazmat suits."

Kate tells them. Or one of the other blue-eyed ghouls.

The line outside the tent moved slowly, but no one seemed to mind. He couldn't hear their chatter from where he lay, but their body movements told him everything. This was where they wanted to be, and the overwhelmingly positive energy emanating from them was hard to miss.

Will watched them in silence for a moment.

"It's a good deal," he said finally, grudgingly. "As long as the townspeople keep feeding them blood."

"Donating," Zoe said.

"Po-tay-to, po-tah-to."

"They're not like you, Will. They're not soldiers. They're just trying to survive the end of the world the best they can."

"Why did they choose the small towns? Why not the bigger cities with all the supplies still on the shelves? Just for the well water?"

"I never asked."

"You don't have any theories?"

"You'll think I'm crazy."

"Indulge me."

"The others and I were talking—the other medical staff—and we think it's because they want us to start over. A fresh start. The cities are filled with reminders of the old world. Our achievements, our art, our evolution as human beings. Out here, surrounded by farmland, woods… It's like going back to our roots. No power, no electricity… It's easier to believe the last two centuries never happened."

"Back to the olden days, is that it?"

"Something like that," Zoe said. "I know you don't approve of this, Will. But those people down there, they want to be there. What right do you have to tell them they can't?"

"It's unnatural."

"According to you. Who gave you the power to decide for them what they should or shouldn't do with their lives? Look around you, Will. The world as we know it is gone. It's not your place to tell anyone what to do with however many days, weeks, or months they have left."

Goddammit, she makes a good point.

Will crawled back to her and slipped the binoculars into his pack. He pulled out a bottle of water, took a sip and offered her the rest. She drank hungrily from it and didn't stop until she had almost drained it.

"Maybe you're right," he said.

She gave him a surprised look. "Really?"

"Don't be so surprised."

"Sorry," she smiled.

"I don't have the right to tell anyone down there what to do with their lives."

He saw her face softening, maybe even looking a little bit pleased. "So what happens now?"

Good question. What happens now?

He didn't answer her right away. Will looked up at the cloudless sky. It was bright and warm, with barely anything resembling a breeze. It would be different on the island. There was always a nice wind blowing across Beaufont Lake. Cool lake water and soft, mushy sand under his feet. And Lara. He missed Lara most of all.

"Will?" Zoe said. "What happens now?"

"I go back to the island and you can head into town. The people down there are from the camp I took you from, so they'll know you didn't go with me willingly. You shouldn't have too much trouble fitting right back in."

"Thanks."

"You really think I was going to shoot you?"

She smirked. "You did shove a gun against my temple the first time we met."

He chuckled. "Point taken—" he started to say, but stopped when he heard the *crunch crunch* of heavy boots against dry, brittle grass behind him, coming from the other side of the hill.

Will unslung his rifle as Zoe froze, alarmed by his sudden movements. He crawled back to the top of the hill and looked down.

Three men in hazmat suits were moving steadily up the other side, the sun reflecting off their bright white suits. Two of them were wearing their gas masks, while the third had his clipped to his hip. They were near the very bottom of the hill and seemed to be struggling with their footing.

He saw them about a second before they spotted his head peering over the crest of the hill, and instantly one of them opened fire with an AK-47. When that happened, the other two began shooting, too.

Will ducked his head as the dirt and grass around him exploded, chunks flickering into the air. He slid his way back down to Zoe.

Her eyes were wide and glued to him. "What's happening?"

"I'll see you around, doc." He leaped to his feet and raced down the hillside, then threw a quick look over his shoulder at Zoe. "Stay down so you don't get shot!"

Will hopped the last three meters down to the bottom of the hill and continued running at full speed. It didn't take very long for gunfire to fill the air again, bullets speckling the ground to the left and right of him.

But they were lousy shots, and as amazing as it seemed, each subsequent new round seemed to land further and further away from him. He didn't bother to return fire, and instead concentrated on adding more distance between him and the hill. He pretended as if he weren't running away from gunfire, but running back toward Lara.

Yeah, that's the ticket.

After thirty seconds of nonstop sprinting, he had extended his lead enough that the shooting stopped. That allowed him to slow down to a nice, unhurried pace.

Like running in the park…while being shot at.

He thought about Lara and the island again. Sarah's cooking, Danny's corny jokes, and watching the girls, Elise and Vera and Sarah's daughter Jenny, being girls. But most of all, his mind's eye was filled with images of Lara.

It didn't take long before he felt shooting pain from his thigh, the everlasting gift from the helicopter crash. It had been so long since he noticed he was even injured down there that the sudden jolts took him momentarily by surprise. He pushed it into the back of his mind, then away entirely.

It worked…for a few seconds.

Lara could take care of that. Back on the island.

Back to Lara…

Out of the corner of his eye, he caught the glint of blue metal and heard the loud, familiar roar of man-made machinery before he even glanced to his right side and saw it.

It was a big blue truck, emerging from around the wide base of the hill.

It was moving fast—and was pointed right at him like a heat-seeking missile. There were two men in the back of the truck, wearing hazmat suits and holding on for dear life as the truck slid, crunched, and spun against the loose ground under its massive tires.

The truck sped right at him, gobbling up the distance between them in the blink of an eye.

FUBAR. Definitely FUBAR.

Will spun around, lifted the M4A1, flicked the fire selector to full-auto, and pulled the trigger.

CHAPTER 29

GABY

THEY TOOK I-49 southbound back into Lafayette, doing thirty-five miles per hour because Gaby didn't quite trust her driving skills. It wasn't like she had a lot of practice on the highways, especially in something as souped up as the Mustang GT. Thankfully, there weren't a whole lot of obstacles for her to maneuver around, though she knew all that would change once they neared the city.

"I'll drive once we get closer," Nate said.

She glanced briefly over at him. He did look a lot better. Then again, it wasn't hard to improve on yesterday, when he was covered in his own blood and half dead. And she had seen him driving with one hand back at the camp, with people shooting at them. Even Will had looked impressed.

She nodded. "Okay."

"Really?" he smiled. "I was expecting a fight."

"Goes to show you don't really know me."

"Point taken."

She found herself looking forward to reaching Beaufont Lake by midafternoon, and the image of riding a boat back to Song Island, over the familiar calm of the lake's surface, made her smile into the wind outside the open window.

Nate noticed. "What was that? Was that a smile? Holy shit, now that's hot."

"Don't be an asshole."

"My bad."

"'My bad'? I haven't heard that in a while. The last person who said that—" She didn't finish, because the last person who had said that was Josh.

Back in Beaumont.

Back when he was still…Josh.

What happened to you, Josh?

"What's wrong?" Nate asked. "Did I say something wrong?"

"No." She shook her head. "I was just thinking about a friend."

"I'm sure Will's fine."

"Not Will…"

"Oh." It took him a moment, then he nodded knowingly. "That kid back in the camp? What was his name, Josh?"

"Yeah."

"You guys were more than friends. That's the sense I got, anyway."

"We were."

"A lot more?"

She nodded.

"I'm sorry," Nate said.

"Don't be sorry. It had nothing to do with you."

"What happened to him? How does a kid that young become one of those guys? It seemed like he was leading them, too. They wouldn't shoot us because we were using him as a shield, right?"

"I think so, yes."

"Was he always like that?"

"No. That Josh back there…" She struggled for the right words. "It wasn't the Josh I knew. We survived together. Josh and me, and another guy named Matt. For eight months. We hid and ran and survived together in one dark, dank basement after another. We hadn't met Will yet at the time. We were just three stupid kids. Honestly, I don't know how we managed to survive for so long."

"What happened to Matt?"

"We lost him."

"Wow, I'm a total idiot. Sorry."

She gave him a pursed smile. "You didn't know."

"I should have, though. I've been out here for a long time too, and what else would have happened to Matt if not…for what happened to him."

"It's okay."

They didn't say anything for a while, and she was grateful for the silence.

Of course, it didn't last.

"So, this island," Nate said. "It's got rooms, hot showers, and a never-ending supply of fish?"

"Uh huh."

"Awesome. Because I love all three of those things. Especially the hot shower part. I don't know if you've noticed, but I haven't showered in, oh, about two months."

She wrinkled her nose. "That explains the smell."

TRAFFIC ALONG THE I-49 started clogging up about four miles out of Lafayette, and eventually Gaby didn't trust her driving enough to keep going. She slowed down, then stopped altogether and put the GT into park.

She looked over at Nate as he was unbuckling his belt. "Are you sure you can drive?"

"Gaby, it's two things—stepping on the gas and turning the steering wheel. I only need one arm for that."

She nodded, and they climbed out of the GT and switched places.

Gaby laid her AR-15 across her lap for easy access, while Nate adjusted the seat to accommodate his longer frame. He put the car back into drive, looking very comfortable driving with one hand, and soon she forgot to keep an eye on him.

Nate drove up the highway for a while, before the congestion forced him onto the shoulder. The GT scraped by a couple of stalled vehicles, the loud grinding of paint against paint like a banshee's shrill cry.

"Try not to lose any more paint," Gaby said. "It's my first sports car."

"I'll do my best."

Soon, Nate had slowed down to ten miles per hour—then five, until they were essentially crawling along the highway. Gaby wondered if they would make better time if they got out and started walking. It had been so much easier yesterday in the Beetle, but of course there was a reason for that. The road out of Lafayette had been cleared by the Humvees and their steel plows, whereas the road back in was still stuffed with vehicles abandoned eleven months ago.

"There's less traffic over on the northbound lane," Gaby said. "Maybe we should switch over before we get any further into the city, use the path those Humvees cleared out for us."

"Good idea."

They were still far enough outside the city limits that the highway's lanes weren't partitioned with concrete dividers yet, so there was nothing to keep Nate from crossing over onto the northbound lane. After that, he was able to push the GT back up to fifteen miles per hour, then twenty.

"And they say girls are bad with directions," Nate said.

"I think you've got the genders mixed up there, buckaroo."

He chuckled. "'Buckaroo'?"

"Something I picked up from this guy named Danny. You'll meet him on the island."

"I don't have to fight him for your affections, do I?"

"Why? You don't think you can win a fight for my affections?"

"Right now I'm a bit gimpy. I do have two bullet holes in me, you know. Give me a break."

"Still, a real man would work through those disabilities."

"Now you're just trying to hurt my feelings."

"Is it working?"

"Just a tad," he said, pinching his thumb and forefinger together.

◄━━┃ ┃━━►

LAFAYETTE WAS A lot thicker with traffic than she remembered. By the time they reached the Marabond Throughway, they had already been forced off the highway and onto the feeder roads.

And Gaby was glad for it. She had greeted the idea of retreading the same stretch of I-10 where Jen's helicopter had fallen out of the sky only a few days ago with dread. She and Nate had managed to avoid the site entirely the last time only because he had insisted on using the feeder roads before hopping onto the I-49.

There was a chance Jen, Amy, and the kid with the button nose were still up there. Will and Danny theorized that the ghouls took dead bodies for whatever reason, but no one really knew for sure. Gaby hadn't then, and still didn't now, feel like finding out either way.

So they took the feeder roads again, and while it was slow going because of the GT's width, she didn't complain. It was difficult to get through most of the heavy pileups, but the Mustang was strong enough to bully its way through most obstacles in their path. By the time they were driving parallel to the I-10 heading westward, Nate was spending more time on the sidewalks than in the streets.

"Car's not going to last for long," he said. "The grill looks like a pretzel, and we might have to slide out the window *Dukes of Hazzard* style pretty soon."

"Maybe we should start looking for a replacement."

"Shout if you see something. Maybe another Beetle. Or even better, a motorcycle or ATV."

She kept an eye out, but every car was either a sedan that wasn't much of an improvement over the GT, or a truck. Lafayette, like Texas, had a healthy inventory of trucks.

"How's the gas look?" she asked.

"Dangerously low. And it might take a day just to get out of here. Too bad you don't still have the helicopter."

"Yeah…"

Nate sighed. "Shit, I'm sorry, Gaby. I know you lost friends in that crash. I need to think before I talk." He paused, then added, "I have a big mouth. Everyone says so. I'm sorry. Shit, I'm so sorry."

She didn't know why she did it, but Gaby leaned over and gave him a peck on the cheek. Then she quickly sat back down and stared out the front windshield as if nothing had happened.

"I should shoot my big mouth off more often," Nate said.

◄▬▮ ▮▬►

"IS IT NEAR here?" she asked.

"Across the highway," Nate said.

"We should swing over."

"Why?"

"I need to grab another radio to contact the island. They must be sick with worry by now."

She was talking about the pawnshop, the same place they had found the ham radios two days ago. They were coming to the intersection now, and Nate took a left and went under the I-10. Another block later and they were at the familiar strip mall with Leroy's and its bent burglar bars.

Nate parked in front of the pawnshop, and Gaby climbed out with her rifle and looked around. There was always something about the stillness of a city that made her paranoid, as if she could feel the ghosts of the former occupants watching her from every window, every door. It was unnerving, and she shivered slightly.

The muddy, foreboding look from the clouds didn't help to calm her nerves. It was barely one in the afternoon, but it already looked like four or five, as if darkness were trying to creep up on her.

"See if you can find us another car," she said.

"Not a whole lot of choices," Nate said, scanning the area.

The parking lot didn't have much to offer, though at this point any vehicle they could get running was preferable to the Mustang. She didn't realize what bad shape the vehicle was in until she had to literally kick the jammed door open. A good chunk of the door was sliced, as if some wild, mechanical animal had gone to town on it with steel claws; the grill was hanging miraculously by a few random wires.

She went into Leroy's, using the same section of broken windows she had crawled through two days earlier. There were still patches of darkness in the back of the store where the sun couldn't reach, which made her sling the rifle and draw her Glock. She preferred the handgun in close quarters.

Gaby stood still for a long moment, sniffing the air, listening to every sound. There was just the soft wind outside the store and the quiet patter of her heartbeat. She scanned the darkness, waiting, waiting...

Come out, come out, wherever you are.

When nothing came out, she breathed a little easier, went around the counter, and grabbed one of the radios, then pulled a pack of batteries from a nearby rack. She crawled out of the pawnshop and stood back up under the moody skies.

It had gotten so dark so quickly that for a moment Gaby was taken aback.

It's going to rain...

She put the radio on the badly damaged hood of the Mustang and plugged in the new batteries, then powered up the radio and spun the dial until she found the designated emergency frequency. She knew it by heart. Everyone did, even the kids. Will had made sure of that, in case they ever found themselves out here and needed to contact the island.

Hope for the best, expect the worse, right, Will?

She just hoped someone was monitoring it on the island at the moment.

Gaby picked up the microphone and pressed the transmit lever. "Song Island, come in, this is Gaby. Can anyone hear me over there? Over."

She released the lever and watched Nate peer inside a white Ford Fusion across the lot. She guessed he was looking for a key. After a while, he gave up and moved to the next car, a gray two-door Kia hatchback.

"This can't possibly be Gaby," a voice said through the radio, "because the Gaby I knew was a virgin when she left us a few days ago, but I'm hearing stories of sex in hospitals and other shenanigans."

She smiled at the sound of his voice. "I miss you too, Danny."

"Oh, shit, it is Gaby!" Danny said. "How the hell are you, kid?"

"Alive and kicking."

"Good to hear it. What about the other guy? Willard or something."

"He was fine the last time I saw him. We split up this morning."

"Lara'll be glad to hear that. Personally, I don't know what she sees in him. But back to you. Where you calling from, kid?"

"I'm still in Lafayette, looking for a new ride." A dark patch of shadow fell over her and Gaby glanced up at the darkening skies. "I'm not sure I'm going to make it back today, Danny. It's looking like it might rain."

"I can see the clouds from here. Must look even worse up close."

"I've definitely seen brighter days."

"How are you for shelter?"

She looked around her at the strip mall. A Family Dollar store, a Wallbys Pharmacy on the other side, and a small mom-and-pop ice cream shop next to a Subway. The pawnshop behind her was probably the most secure building in the entire area, thanks to the burglar bars.

"Manageable," she said.

"Took you a while to answer that," Danny said.

"Just getting my bearings."

"Are you alone?"

"I'm with someone. We've been traveling with Will since yesterday."

"How is he or she with a gun?"

"Not bad. We'll be fine if we have to stay the night. How is everyone over there? Are you guys managing without me?"

"So far, so good. Hey, Lara's here."

"Gaby," Lara said, her voice sounding breathless over the line. Gaby imagined her racing to the Tower as soon as Danny radioed her. "Are you okay? Where's Will?"

"I'm fine. And Will was fine when I saw him this morning."

"What happened? Did you guys split up again?"

"He sent me back while he went to do some reconning."

"What's he reconning?"

Gaby told her about the camp and the pregnant women. About the towns, where people were being relocated, and everything Zoe had told them last night.

Then Gaby added, almost as an afterthought, "Josh was there. He's still alive."

"Josh is *still alive*?" Lara said, the shock registering even over the radio. "How is that possible?"

Gaby told her. Josh falling into the lake. Getting fished out by the collaborators. When she got around to what Josh had become, how he had been working with the ghouls, her voice threatened to break and she had to choke back the emotions.

She found, to her surprise, that she was more angry than sad.

Dammit, Josh. What the hell are you doing?

She was angry at him for thinking he needed to protect her and for putting it all on her. And she was angry for the loss of Jen and Amy and the button-nosed kid. The last few days only served to remind her all over again of how much she had lost, how much she still stood to lose.

Nothing lasts forever anymore. Not even my fond memories of dead loved ones.

"Oh, Gaby," Lara said. "I'm sorry. Are you sure you can't make it back today?"

She looked up at the sky again, at the gray clouds moving in. "It's looking pretty bad, Lara. I'm not sure we should risk it."

"What about shelter for the night?"

"There's a pawnshop that could work."

"Where is it exactly, in case we need to find you later?"

"It's in a strip mall at the intersection of Weston Street and Pillar Street, a couple of blocks from the I-10 freeway."

"And it looks safe?"

"It might be our best option right now. That, or go look for a house with a basement."

"It's your call, Gaby, you're the one over there. We'll still be here tomorrow, and the day after that."

She watched Nate all the way across the parking lot, peering in at a white Dodge.

"How are Benny and the others?" she asked. "Are they fitting in?"

"Fish and cold drinks, hot showers and clean rooms," Lara said. "What's not to like? By the way, Benny's been asking a lot about you. Is there something I should know?"

"It was a one-time thing."

"Does he know that?"

"He's a guy," she said.

Lara laughed. "Take it easy on him. He seems like a nice kid."

"He is." Nate was walking back toward her now, twirling a key ring on one finger and looking very proud of himself. "Lara, I have to go for now. I'll call back in about an hour with an update, let you know if we decide to push on down south or if we're packing it in for the day."

"It's good to hear your voice again, Gaby. You had us really worried."

"I'm sorry we didn't call earlier. Things were...hectic the last couple of days."

"I know about Mercy Hospital. I'm just glad you're both alive."

"Will wanted me to tell you that he expects to be back by tonight, maybe tomorrow at the latest."

"And he said he was just doing some reconning?"

"He promised me no hero stuff."

"And he's fine...?"

"He had all of his teeth, yeah."

Lara laughed again. Gaby could tell it was nervous laughter. She couldn't imagine what Lara had been through the last few days, and she felt guilty for having gone so long without radioing back home.

"That's good to hear," Lara said. "I've always been fond of his teeth."

"I'll see you soon, Lara. If not today, then the day after. Who knows, Will might actually beat me back to the island."

"Hope springs eternal. All right, go do what you have to do, then call me back in an hour."

"One hour."

She put the mic down as Nate leaned against the hood across from her.

"Song Island?" he asked.

She nodded. "What did you find?"

He held up the key, then pointed to a small, blue four-door Toyota Yaris in front of the Wallbys. "Small enough for ya?"

"Does it run?"

"Let's find out," Nate said.

THE YARIS WAS still in relatively good condition. It was a small, painfully compact car, though somehow it had managed to build in four doors anyway. The leg room wasn't anything to crow about, but since they would be in the front seats anyway, that wasn't really a consideration.

Gaby went through the glove compartment while Nate used a hose they had found in Leroy's to siphon gas from the GT into the Yaris, leaving just enough in the Mustang to jumpstart the Yaris's dead car battery. When the Yaris was running again, they smiled at each other.

"Song Island?" he said.

She nodded. "Why not? Song Island or bust—" She hadn't finished when a drop of water hit her on the head. Gaby sighed. "Or not."

It had gotten much darker while they weren't paying attention, and as soon as she looked up, more drops of rain splattered the car's dirty roof.

"Well, at least the car'll be clean by the time we get to Song Island," Nate said.

"Captain Optimist," Gaby smirked.

"Captain what?"

"Nothing. Get in."

They climbed back into the Toyota just as the rain really began coming down, pelting and washing away the dust and grime from the front windshield.

"Let's drive it around to charge up the battery," Nate said. "We can decide what to do in the meantime."

She drove in circles along the parking lot while the rain poured down around them, the unrelenting tapping against the roof sounding like gunfire. Twenty minutes later, with the rain still making puddles over the parking lot, Gaby drove back to Leroy's and put the Yaris into park.

She looked over at Nate. "Tomorrow?"

"Probably the smart thing to do."

"Should we look for another place?"

"We might not find one with burglar bars."

"Yeah, but those burglar bars aren't exactly in place."

"I could bend them back into place."

She gave him a doubtful look.

"What?" he said. "I absolutely could, even with just one good arm."

"What about the house you guys were staying in?"

"It's up to you. I'm good either way. Pawnshop or dank basement?"

She thought about it. "I used to live out of dank basements. Never was a big fan of it. Besides, they didn't bother with the pawnshop before, even with the bent bars. There shouldn't be any reason for them to pay attention to it now. Right?"

"Are you trying to convince yourself or me?"

"Both?"

He shrugged. "There was a door at the back. Looked like an office. It would probably be a lot more comfortable than a basement."

She thought about it for a moment, then nodded. "All right. Let's hope it has a couch at least."

Gaby grabbed her rifle and pack and hurried out, rushing through the wall of rain. Nate followed her into the pawnshop, the two of them crawling through inch-high puddles. Water had flooded in through the broken glass opening and reached all the way to the back in thick, cold rivulets.

They were shivering from the wetness and the cold chilly air by the time they made their way into an office in the back, where they found a big desk with bags of old chips that had gone rancid months ago inside one of the drawers. A small fridge in the corner held warm bottled water along with some spoiled food.

Gaby left the office door open to ventilate the room of the thick smell of abandonment. There was just enough sunlight from outside to light their movements. The room had two doors—the one into the pawnshop and another one in the back. There were, thankfully, no windows to worry about, and the place hadn't been touched in eleven months, which put her mind further at ease.

She opened the back door by sliding the deadlock and leaning out, saw a large forest clearing behind the strip mall. A bulldozer sat in the middle, surrounded by muddy water. Two trash dumpsters stood sentry at the end of the lot, rainwater bouncing off their lids.

"Anything good back there?" Nate asked from behind her.

"Just a couple of dumpsters."

She closed the door and locked it, then walked over to an old leather couch next to the desk and fell down with a loud, satisfied *whump!*

Nate sat down next to her and handed her one of the warm bottles from the fridge. "This is the life, huh? How could you possibly ask for anything more than this?" He sniffed the air. "What in God's name is that smell, anyway?"

"Abandonment," Gaby said.

"Oh. I was afraid it was me."

She drank from her bottle, then opened her pack and took out some beef jerky Will had given her earlier. She handed one to Nate.

"I must have eaten a hundred of these things," Nate said. "They're starting to taste really gamey."

"Better than nothing, so stop complaining."

"Why are you always so bossy?"

She smiled and ate her beef jerky without any hurry, listening to the *tap-tap-tap* of the rain against the roof.

"How's your arm?" she asked.

"A little sore."

"You have any pills left?"

He fished out the bottle of generic Vicodin from his pants pocket and shook it, listened to the *clink-clink* of pills inside. "Should get me to the island in one piece. Lara's a doctor, right?"

"Third-year medical student."

"Close enough."

He opened the bottle and swallowed a couple of pills, then sat back with a sigh. She sat quietly next to him, enjoying the *tap-tap-tap* of the rain above them and the stillness of the building.

"What do you think Will's doing now?" Nate said after a while. "You think it's raining where he's at?"

"I don't know. It looks like a pretty big storm. Danny could see it from the island."

"Good," Nate said. "This city could use a little cleansing flood."

CHAPTER 30

WILL

WILL HAD ALMOST died—really, *really* almost died—only once in his life. That was thirty years ago when he had been born. The doctors told his parents he was a complicated pregnancy and that there was a very good chance he would die during childbirth, along with his mother. His parents, perhaps with more than a little of the famous stubbornness people often accused him of, refused to accept the diagnosis. Especially Will's mother, Charlene (Charlie to her friends). Will was born one week early, fighting and screaming and gasping for air. He lived, and so did his mother.

So death wasn't anything new to Will, even if he didn't exactly remember any of the details of the last time it had come for him.

This time, though, he remembered every second of it in excruciating detail.

The bullet chopped into his side, just above the waist. It was a through-and-through, which was the good news. The bad news was the ground exploding and clumps of dirt and grass cascading all around him like waterfalls.

Will continued squeezing the trigger on the M4A1. The magazine burned through half of its load in a matter of seconds, and the carbine felt lighter in his hands with every passing heartbeat as a result.

It was a Ford Bronco, maybe ten years old by the looks of its paint job and well-worn front grill, and Will aimed for the front windshield. He stitched it from forty meters away and kept firing as it kept coming. The truck's entire front windshield crumpled under the volley, and the driver jerked on the steering wheel as bullets slammed into him.

The truck made a sharp (too sharp) turn and spun, sending the two men in hazmat suits in the back flying across the air as if they had been shot out of a cannon. It helped that the two idiots were too busy shooting at him to hold on to the vehicle. One of the men landed on the ground a split second before the truck came tumbling over and crushed him into the dirt as if he were an ant. The truck continued rolling until it finally smashed into a meter-deep ditch that cut across the farmland, depositing window fragments and pieces of sheared metal into the surrounding grass.

Will quickly searched out and found the other man who had been tossed from the truck. He lay twenty-five meters away and looked unconscious.

He didn't have a lot of time to take in the wreckage before the air was filled with new gunfire and the land erupted with dirt and grass again.

The three men who had been chasing him from the hill were coming, but they were still a good fifty meters away. They were also running and shooting at the same time, which from experience Will knew wasn't exactly the best way to hit a target—even one that was standing still the way he was.

He calmly ejected the spent magazine and slipped in a new one, then flicked the fire selector to semi-auto. He willed his breathing to slow down, pushing aside the adrenaline keeping him upright despite the flow of blood pouring out of him.

Lara could deal with that later.

He took a deep breath and shot the closest man in the chest. The man looked as if someone had tied a rope around his neck and had suddenly yanked on it. One second he was on his feet, running full-speed, and the next he was lying in the thick grass, unmoving.

Will swiveled, and as he took aim on another target, a bullet came dangerously close to scalping him. He flinched and shot the second man, aiming for the chest, but got him in the hip instead. The man stumbled and went into a crouch. Will blinked sweat out of his eyes, then shot the man again, this time getting him in the chest. The man toppled forward and into the tall blades of grass.

The third man had reached the overturned Bronco and he dived behind it for cover.

Will turned and resumed jogging back toward the barn, ignoring the scorching pain from his right side. He put a hand down there, hoping to slow the bleeding at least just a little bit. He shouldn't have bothered, because his hand was soaked with gushing blood almost immediately. What didn't cover up his hand poured out behind him. He was probably leaving a wet, bloody trail that even a blind man could follow.

The third guy found his courage and leaned out far enough to take a shot at him. A bullet buzzed past his head, but Will ignored it and kept jogging. The guy shot again, but the bullet landed well off target this time.

Someone needs target practice, he thought, chuckling to himself. Or did he?

Will slowed down until he was just walking now. Briskly. Maybe. It felt like a brisk walking pace, but he could have been just imagining that part. Just like he was probably making up the sudden reemergence of pain from that piece of glass he had pulled out of his leg two days ago.

Phantom pain. That's all it is.

Yeah, that's the ticket.

He couldn't hear any more shooting behind him. Maybe the guy had given up? Or maybe he was waiting to get closer so he could put a bullet in the back of Will's head. Either/or. Will just didn't feel like running anymore. This brisk walking pace was good enough. Probably.

The burnt orange barn with the stashed Ford F-150 was visible in the distance, still about half a kilometer away. It looked like a tiny red dot under the clear, bright sky.

The sun was very high up today, raining heat mercilessly down on him. God, it was hot all of a sudden. Will blinked once, twice, and for a moment almost lost his bearing against sunspots forming and bursting repeatedly in his line of sight.

He reached into his pack and pulled out the first bottle his fin gers groped. He didn't bother reading the label. He twisted off the cap with some effort, swaying a bit, and shook two pills into his mouth.

He paused for a second, then gulped down two more.

Better safe than sorry, right?

He snapped the cap back on the bottle and shoved it into one of the empty pockets on his cargo pants. He had a feeling he'd need it again pretty soon anyway. Easier access and all that.

His vision started to blur, and he thought he could hear the sound of water dripping against the grass. Like rain on a rooftop. He wasn't even moving that fast anymore, and he still kept expecting the third guy to finally catch up and shoot him in the back of the head from point blank range.

Any moment now, buddy. Any moment now...

How far had he walked, anyway? Ten meters? Twenty? Fifty? It felt like half a day.

Surely, he was almost at the barn?

Then why was the goddamn red dot still a tiny red dot in the distance?

Every other second he expected to hear gunshots. Or the familiar drone of a pursuing vehicle. Did they only have one truck in the entire town? Probably not. He remembered seeing those five-tons. What other vehicles were in the town? Maybe not that many. He remembered the empty streets, people walking around. Like that couple with those two kids...

Back to the Stone Age. The only thing missing are horses and carriages. Yee haw.

The red dot in the distance started jumping from left to right, then right to left. Or was that him? When did he stop moving in a straight line?

It wasn't long before he heard voices. At first he thought he was muttering to himself. That was a bad sign. Talking to yourself was not good, especially after you'd been shot.

But then he noticed the sound was coming from behind him.

Finally caught up, huh, buddy? Good for you. Good for you...

But the voice sounded familiar and female, and he distinctively remembered the third guy being male. A big guy. Kind of fat. Definitely not female.

Lara?

What the hell was Lara doing all the way out here? She was supposed to be on Song Island, safe and sound. He did a lot to get her there, because he cared for her. Hell, he loved her. Had he told her that before he left the island? God, he hoped he had. It would suck if she didn't know how he felt.

She probably hated his guts by now. He didn't blame her. He should have called her days ago. He should have waited for Gaby to come back with the radio and called her. She would have understood.

Lara...

The voice was insistent and calling his name. And it was getting closer.

Lara, for God's sake, what are you doing out here? It's not safe.

He couldn't put his thoughts into words, because when he opened his mouth, only haggard breathing came out.

And it was painful. And difficult.

And really, *really* painful.

So he stopped trying.

But the voice persisted, and soon Will felt something against his left arm. He tried to lift his rifle to fight back, but it was too hard, and he surrendered. Something warm and soft pushed against him, and Will looked over, but he couldn't see much of anything through the sheets of sweat covering his eyes.

Or was that blood?

God, he hoped he wasn't bleeding from the head. That would really suck.

"Jesus, you're dying," the familiar female voice *(Not Lara)* said.

Will grunted. He wasn't certain if he had successfully formed words with his sounds, but he must have, because the familiar female voice chuckled next to him.

"You're such a dick," it said.

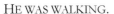

HE WAS WALKING.

Then he was inside a building.

Then he was inside a vehicle.

Then he was moving again, but this time it was more like floating.

No, riding.

Riding in a vehicle.

Clouds passed by above his head, outside an open car window. Bright, white clouds. When he was a kid, his mother *(Charlie to her friends)* used to tell him that if he stared long enough, the clouds would magically transform into whatever he was thinking at the time. When he got older, he realized it was just his imagination at work. But he still loved his mom anyway. She was a beautiful woman, kind and generous, and he never heard her say a bad word about anyone.

"You're still alive?" a voice said.

There was a lyrical quality to the voice that he appreciated, as if it were reaching down from the clouds floating above him.

"God, how are you still alive?" the voice asked. "You must have lost at least two pints of blood out there. What are you, 200 pounds? You lose any more and you're never going to wake up. Can you hear me? No, of course not. Just keep staring at those clouds."

He wished the voice would shut up, because it was ruining what was, up to that point, a perfectly good staring-at-clouds moment. It had been so long since he'd allowed himself to indulge in such pointlessness that getting interrupted made him feel cheated. These eleven months had been one battle after another, and he was tired of fighting. So goddamn tired.

"Oh, shit," the voice said. "You're bleeding again!"

Oh, so that's what that dripping sound was. I thought someone had left a faucet running.

He closed his eyes and the clouds disappeared. He might have also rolled off the seat and landed on the floor, hitting his head against the door, but that could have just been his imagination.

Yeah, that's the ticket.

THE SECOND TIME Will opened his eyes, it was to the rhythmic *plop-plop-plop* of rainwater. He was lying on the front passenger seat of the Ford F-150, reclined back as far as it would go. He was shirtless, and there was fresh gauze wrapped around his midsection. The throbbing pain felt like a sledgehammer pounding his brain in tune to the *plop-plop-plop* of the rain outside.

He groped along the side of the seat, found the lever, and pulled it. The seat lifted him up into a semi-sitting position. He stared out the bullet-riddled windshield and into a muggy, dark-gray world, sheets of rain falling over a familiar opening.

He was back in Fredo's auto body shop in the city of Harvest, in one of its garage ports. For a moment, he was alarmed that it was nightfall. With some effort, he was able to lift his hand until he could see his watch: 5:11 P.M.

Why is it so dark?

"I can't believe you're still alive," a voice said.

Will looked over at Zoe, sitting in the driver's seat, watching him with curious eyes. Her white doctor's coat, covered in dried blood, was thrown over the headrest, and he thought she looked odd in just a T-shirt and pants.

"You're supposed to be dead," she said.

"Am I?" His voice was labored and quiet. Was he whispering?

"You lost at least two liters of blood back there. Probably closer to three. But all it did was knock you out for half a day. What are you, the Terminator?"

He managed a grin. The truth was, he hurt. Every inch of him, and all he wanted to do was lie back down and go to sleep for a long, long time. But he didn't, because it was too dark outside and his instincts kept him awake because of it, even if his watch told him it was only because of the rain.

"Do you always carry thread and needle around with you?" she asked.

"It seemed like the thing to do."

"I tried to suture your wounds, but you were bleeding too much. I'll have to do it later when you're stronger. By the way, what happened to your leg?"

"I was in a helicopter crash."

"What about your left arm?"

"Someone shot me."

"Christ."

"Yeah." He sat up a little bit more. "How long has it been raining?"

"About thirty minutes."

"We're back at Fredo's?"

"I didn't know where else to go." She looked conflicted. "And you were bleeding so badly, I wasn't sure if you would survive anyway. But you did. Just barely."

Will felt sticky, as if he were sitting in gum. He looked down at his seat, and even in the semidarkness saw that it was covered in blood. His blood. It stuck to his clothes, and his shirt, dark black with blood, was crumpled on the floor at his feet. It had been white when he put it on this morning.

"Do you have another shirt?" she asked.

"I did, but I gave it to Gaby last night."

"That explains the bloody shirt I found outside."

He nodded and laid his head back down. "You saved my life."

"Yeah."

"Why?"

"I'm a doctor. What the hell was I going to do, let you die out there?"

"There was a third guy…"

"He gave up and ran back to town after you took off."

"He didn't try to stop you?"

"I think he was confused. And scared."

"Good for me, then."

"Yeah, really good for you. There weren't that many guys in hazmat suits back in town. Most of them were probably en route, bringing over more people from the other camps. If there had been just one more vehicle back there, we wouldn't be having this conversation."

"Must be my lucky day."

"Yeah, lucky you."

She picked up a water bottle and handed it to him. He drank greedily, devouring the whole thing in a couple of gulps.

"It's rain water," she said. "I'll refill it later." She took the bottle back and continued to watch him. "I can't figure you out, Will."

"What's got you so confounded, doc? I'm not that deep."

"The fact that you keep fighting, when everyone—or most everyone—has given up. I know you have the island, but instead of going back to it, what do you do? You run over to the camp. Then the town. Why?"

"Know thy enemy."

"It's more than that. You want to save people, don't you?"

"You're the first one to ever accuse me of that, doc."

"I doubt that. Maybe you and I are more alike than I thought. We both can't stand the idea of people who need help not getting it."

Is that it? Maybe…

He said instead, "Decent working theory, I guess."

"What you have to realize is that those people back there don't want your help. They're perfectly satisfied with where they are. To you that may sound unfathomable, but they're not like you, Will. They're not soldiers." She looked out the windshield, into the pouring rain. "Not everyone can fight forever. Not everyone wants to."

He watched the rain with her. Slowly, he began to enjoy the melodic *plop-plop-plop* against the garage roof, the almost calming effect of water cascading to the concrete driveway in front of them.

After a while, he said, "Thanks again, doc."

"How's the pain?"

"Like someone's poking me in the eyeballs with a spear."

She reached into the back for his pack, unzipped it, rummaged around, and then took out a bottle and read the label. "You don't have much left. Looks like you might have given all the good stuff to Nate."

"Not everything." He pulled out the pill bottle from his cargo pants pocket and tossed it to her.

She read the label before giving him a concerned look. "How many of these have you taken?"

"Four, I think."

"Oxycodone. How are you even still awake after four of these?"

"Persistence."

She smirked. "Well, no more of this." She shoved it into the pack and opened the pill bottle she had brought out earlier. "Hydrocodone. It'll stave off the pain for a while and won't knock you out completely. I assume that's something you want?"

"Good call."

She handed him two pills, then opened her door and climbed out. "I'll go refill the bottle."

Will popped the pills into his mouth and swallowed, then spent the time watching her sticking the open water bottle out into the rain while doing her best to keep from getting wet. She came back later, shaking the rainwater out of her hair, and handed him the bottle. He drank half of it, even though he wasn't really thirsty.

"You carried me back to the barn by yourself?" he asked.

"Well, shouldered you, anyway. I don't think I could have actually *carried* you. Frankly, I was shocked you were still on your feet after you closed your eyes. I'd never seen anything like that before. It was like your body just knew it had to keep moving, even if the rest of you shut down."

"I told you I was special."

"That, or you're really, really stubborn."

"That too."

They exchanged a brief smile.

"Why are you still here?" he asked. "I put a gun to your head and threatened to kill you yesterday."

She sighed. "Isn't it obvious? I'm an idiot."

He chuckled. "No, that's not it. What's the real reason?"

She looked out the front windshield at the falling rain. "Maybe I can help you."

"To do what?"

"Fight the creatures. Or ghouls, as you call them."

"I thought you said their deal was acceptable, that it was even preferable to how you were living before."

"You don't understand," she said, looking back at him. "I don't want to change anybody's mind. The people at the camps. In the towns. They've decided, and I'm fine with that. But that doesn't mean we can't try to improve their lot anyway."

"I don't understand."

"You don't have to be *against* the people in the towns to keep fighting the ghouls, Will. From what I've seen, you have no interest in harming those people. Am I right?"

"Of course not. Why would I want to hurt them?"

"Exactly. It's just you versus the ghouls and the people in haz-mat suits. What you call collaborators. And you're only violent with them because you have no choice. Is that also right?"

He nodded. "I don't want to hurt anyone unless I have to. I've seen the blood farms, the before-picture of when people like you were in those induced comas. I know what you've been through, doc, and maybe I wouldn't have agreed to the deal myself, but I can understand why you and the others did."

"So there's no conflict," she said, nodding. He wasn't sure if she was trying to convince him or herself. "We fight the creatures, but not the people."

"That sounds like a solid plan," he said, and closed his eyes.

"Are you okay?" Zoe asked.

"I think I'm bleeding again. Can you do something about that?"

He heard her moving around. "Shit, Will, I was going to wait until you're stronger to suture your wound, but I might have to do it sooner. Can you—"

"Do it," he said.

"It's going to hurt."

"Just do it," he grunted.

His last thoughts were of Gaby, and he wondered what she was doing back at the island right this moment. Probably walking on the beach with Nate. Or Benny. He wished her luck in choosing. God knew they all had to grab happiness wherever they could these days.

At least one of us made it back to the island...

CHAPTER 31

GABY

GABY OPENED HER eyes to silence and darkness. She climbed off the couch, her sudden movements waking Nate in the process. He had been asleep next to her, dozing from the medication, and she was surprised he was even alert enough to feel her moving.

"What's going on?" he said, his voice groggy.

"I think I heard something," she whispered back.

His voiced dropped to match hers. "What?"

"I don't know. Stay here."

She groped around in the darkness for her pack, unzipped it, and pulled out a glow stick. She pocketed it and grabbed the AR-15 leaning against the wall nearby and moved across the room toward the door. Her ears were up, listening to every sound, every heartbeat, every labored breath between her and Nate.

She crouched in front of the door, reached up, and twisted the deadbolt. With one hand, she slowly pulled open the door a fraction—just enough to see out—while making as little noise as possible. The night was so quiet that any little sound might as well be an announcement that they were inside the pawnshop.

"What do you see?" Nate whispered behind her.

She wasn't sure what she saw, so she said nothing. The inside of the pawnshop was still wet, puddles of water pooling over the tiled floor, most of it concentrated near the front where Nate had broken the glass and bent the bars back to access the building.

It was pitch black outside, and the damn moon had chosen this night to go into hiding; she couldn't make out anything, not even the parking lot beyond. She could just barely discern the counter in front and to her left, and the shelves to her right.

Other than that, it was like staring into the abyss.

Nate crouched next to her, his breath warm against the back of her neck. Thank God he was quiet. Benny would have been lumbering around like a giant in the dark.

"What do you see?" he whispered again.

"Nothing," she whispered back.

He stared for a moment, then shook his head. "I can't see anything. Less than anything."

"Yeah…"

"I—" He stopped in mid-sentence.

"What is it?" she whispered.

He pointed toward the windows and slightly to the left.

Her heart skipped at the sight of a ghoul moving quietly from left to right, sliding across the front of the pawnshop with that unnatural, almost ballet-like grace they had about them. There was only one and it was small, its appearance more fragile than she was used to seeing. It peered inside the pawnshop, searching with beady eyes, upturned nostrils sniffing the air.

Can it smell us?

Gaby tightened her grip around the cold brass of the doorknob, preparing herself mentally to slam the door shut at a moment's notice. Not yet, though, not yet. It hadn't seen them, and moving too quickly now would be giving away their position.

We should have looked for a basement. Stupid. So stupid.

She watched the small, malformed ghoul moving across the front glass wall of the pawnshop. It was looking at something else now, something outside the store.

Keep going. Just keep going, you little shit.

Then it stopped at the broken section of the window.

No…

It lowered itself to the ground, toward the opening.

No!

"It's going to come through," Nate whispered.

She heard the sound of Nate sliding the Beretta out of his waistband.

"Nate," she whispered.

"Yeah?"

"Take my Glock and the two spare magazines on my right hip."

"Why?"

"They have silver ammo."

"Right, silver bullets."

He put his Beretta away and drew her Glock from its holster, then opened one of her pouches and pulled out the two spare magazines.

"Is this all we have?" he asked.

"More magazines in my pack, but they're loaded with regular ammo."

She remained still, watching through the small opening as the ghoul slowly slid under the window.

Dammit.

The good news was, there was still just the one. She could deal with that. Too bad she had never gotten around to arming herself with a silver knife, the way Will carried that cross-knife of his everywhere. She was going to have to make a lot of noise just to kill this one ghoul, which would risk bringing more—

She hadn't even finished the thought when two—no, four—*ten* more ghouls had appeared out of the darkness and were swarming toward the pawnshop from the other side of the window.

Oh, God.

Then ten became twenty, and suddenly there were too many to count. She didn't know where they had come from—nowhere and everywhere. Like moths to the flame, squirming, pushing, and fighting to enter the pawnshop at the same time. So many that they began clogging up the entrance like hundreds of black worms wriggling in the ground, their individual silhouettes impossible to make out against the blackness. She got queasy as glass shards sticking along the broken windows sliced into their flesh, drawing thick clumps of blood that dripped, dissolving in the puddle on the floor.

And still they pushed, wordlessly, soundlessly, anxiously—*desperately*—to get inside.

The first creature she saw—the painfully small one—was the first to make it through, pushed on ahead by the amorphous blob behind it. It slid against a puddle, almost out of control, but quickly gathered its wits about it and looked across the darken room and *hissed* at her.

As the ghoul rose to its feet, Gaby pushed the door open wider and shot the creature in the chest.

Even before the creature fell, two—three—*five*—were already leaping over its collapsing form and bounding across the room, moving with such incredible speed that Gaby found herself staring, fascinated and awed by their ferocity.

"Gaby!" Nate shouted behind her.

Gaby stood up, switched the AR-15 to full-auto and squeezed the trigger.

Bullets speared flesh and chipped bone and kept going, the creatures' soft, non-existent muscle doing nothing to stop the velocity of the silver rounds. The windows spiderwebbed, the *pak-pak-pak* sound of impact like the raindrops from earlier. What sounded like a bullet ricocheted off one of the metal bars and pierced a ghoul, even as more of them fell and flopped to the floor as if they were slipping and sliding.

For a brief instant, she almost wanted to laugh at the comical sight.

She dropped seven of them in the first burst, but they hadn't all crumpled to the floor yet before another wave began squeezing their way through, cutting and slashing and eviscerating themselves against the broken glass.

"Gaby!" Nate shouted again. "Close the door!"

Gaby couldn't really hear him, because she was too busy emptying the rest of the magazine into the jagged hole where the wet floor met the opening, where the ghouls were fighting—each other and the shards of glass—to get through. The sound of silver slapping into flesh, continuing, hitting more flesh, deflecting off bone, and digging into the parking lot beyond was like a melody—a death song filling the quiet, silent night.

It was almost beautiful.

Then the window disappeared, and there was just a wall of moving prune flesh—gaunt, bony faces and dark, unforgiving black eyes looking back at her.

"Nate!" she shouted. "The desk!"

Gaby stepped backward and slammed the door shut. She twisted the deadbolt into place, ejected the spent magazine and ran over to her pack, pulling out a fresh one and shoving it back into the rifle.

One down. One to go.

She pulled out the glow stick and cracked it, then tossed it on the floor in the middle of the room. The office lit up, just as the sound of falling glass rattled from the other side of the door, and she knew they were breaking through, no longer willing to wait in line. She could already hear the cacophony of bare feet slapping against tiled floor, splashing water that had settled across the store.

Gaby slung her rifle and reached for the other side of the desk. Nate, on his own, had managed to push the big, heavy oak furniture a good five feet. Gaby grabbed the other end and, grunting with the effort, lifted it up. Nate did the same on his end, using both hands, though his right was doing most of the lifting. She didn't want to imagine the kind of pain he was feeling at the moment. She couldn't afford to care. Not now, not with the creatures bearing down on them.

They moved to the door one desperate inch at a time, the desk between them. She could feel sweat pouring down her temple, cheeks, and dripping off her chin. Nate's face was a twisted mask of pain, and he grunted with every successful inch.

They were almost at the door when the first ghoul smashed into it on the other side. The entire frame trembled under the impact.

She moved faster, and Nate, sensing her urgency, fought to keep up.

"How we doing this?" he grunted.

Thoom-thoom-thoom!

"Angle it, on its side, tabletop against the door!" she shouted back.

Thoom-thoom-thoom!

The attack on the door had increased in intensity and speed with every passing second. The doorknob quivered and the wood quaked and the frame splintered with each impact.

Thoom-thoom-thoom!

Thoom-thoom-thoom!

At last they were at the door, and Gaby dropped her end and rushed over to Nate's side. They exchanged a brief nod, and with a heavy, simultaneous painful grunt, upended the desk until the bulky object was standing on its side.

"Push!" Gaby shouted, and put her shoulder against the underside of the desk as Nate did the same next to her.

She didn't stop pushing until the desk's tabletop slid perfectly flat against the door. It almost instantly trembled as soon as the two pieces of wood touched.

Thoom-thoom-thoom! Thoom-thoom-thoom!

Gaby backpedaled, taking each step, each breath, almost in tune with the relentless, unceasing pounding. Nate mirrored her actions, though she barely noticed him until his labored, ragged breathing seeped into her flaring senses.

"Do you think it'll hold?" Nate asked between gasps.

Thoom-thoom-thoom!

"No," she said quickly.

"Damn." He pulled out the Glock from his waistband, his right pocket bulging with the two spare magazines. The Beretta was stuffed behind his back. "How did they know we were in here?"

"I don't know," she said.

"We should have gone looking for a basement."

"Yeah."

A loud crash rang out, and she knew the door had just come free from its frame on the other side of the desk. Splinters flickered into the room, along with torn fragments of the wall that shot at her like projectiles. She twisted her body instinctively and swatted the air, batting away a few loosened chunks.

"We're fucked," Nate said.

"Not yet." She glanced behind her at the back door.

Nate followed her gaze. "Isn't it more dangerous out there?"

"There are two dumpsters in the back…"

Thoom-thoom-thoom!

"So we're going dumpster diving after this?" He grinned, his face comical in the green fluorescent glow. "Awesome. Although, I always pictured my first date with you being a little cleaner."

"This isn't the time—"

Another massive *Thoom!* and the desk slid back a few inches, squealing loudly as its edges dug into the tiles. Peeking out above the shorter desk, she could see the top portion of the door, opening slightly, though how the door managed to stay on its hinges was baffling since there didn't seem to be much of a frame left.

They took another involuntary step back, then another one. She lifted her rifle, and Nate raised the Glock.

The first creature poked its head out of the right side of the desk, trying to squeeze its way through. Its slim, emaciated body moved like a skeleton draped with black flesh instead of something that was actually alive.

She shot it in the head and the creature flopped to the floor.

Nate stared at the dead *(again)* creature, almost as if he couldn't believe it. "Silver bullets. Holy shit."

"Aim for the biggest part of their body," she said. "It doesn't matter where you hit it, as long as you hit it with silver."

Thoom-thoom-thoom!

Two more creatures emerged out of the left side of the door. Gaby shot the one that was almost through, while Nate put the other one out of its misery. The creatures' bodies smacked against the floor, where they lay still—before they were jerked unceremoniously back through the door to make room for the next wave.

Another loud crash, and the desk moved backward another two inches.

Gaby slung her rifle and rushed forward, throwing her shoulder into the desk. Then Nate was there doing the same thing and they moved the desk an inch at a time back against the door.

A ghoul struggled to squeeze through the slight opening next to her, so close Gaby could smell the rancid odor seeping from its pores. She shot the creature's arm at point-blank range, rendering flesh and snapping bone as if it were powder. The arm flew off at the elbow joint and streaked across the room.

The relentless hammering continued on the other side of the door, over and over again, pounding into every inch, top to bottom, side to side, an endless sea of blows, never ending, never pausing for even a second to let her breathe.

Thoom-thoom-thoom! Thoom-thoom-thoom!
THOOM-THOOM-THOOM!

"Push!" she grunted.

"What do you think I'm doing?" Nate grunted back.

Nate gave her a look, his face almost ethereal in the green fluorescent of the glow stick. And he did push, legs struggling desperately under him, sheets of sweat breaking out across his face. She prayed to God his stitches didn't snap free at that very moment.

They managed to push the desk another inch back against the door, when a loud, massive hit shook both of them to their core. She didn't know they were even capable of that kind of power, and her mind was still reeling, trying to justify it, even as she and Nate both took a stunned step back.

By the time they gathered themselves and threw their bodies back against the desk one more time, the door had reopened another two inches and one of the ghouls had managed to squeeze through the small sliver.

It leaped inside, moving so fast she only saw a blur before she heard the *click-clacking* of bones against the tiled floor. Its skin, stretched tight over deformed bones, made for an odd, grayish tint that looked as if it were moving slower than it really was. But her eyes were lying to her because she knew it was fast, darting from the door to the side wall.

Gaby stepped away from the door, tracking the creature with her rifle. It raced to the back of the room, toward the couch, and bounded over it. It ran with purpose, moving around the back instead of attacking head-on, each second bringing it closer to her.

"Dead, not stupid," Will always said.

She fired—and *missed!*

The damn thing was actually zig-zagging across the room in order to make her aim more difficult.

So she feigned a shot, made as if to shoot by jerking the gun toward it—and got it to zig instead of zag (*"Don't shoot at where the target is, shoot at where it's going,"* was a mantra Danny had drilled into her head). She squeezed off a second shot and clipped it in the neck. Just barely. It was enough, and the ghoul stumbled and went down as if it had run into a wall.

Thoom-thoom-thoom!

THOOM-THOOM-THOOM!

Gaby spun around just as the desk and door and chunks of the wall exploded behind her. She felt rather than saw Nate stumbling back, disoriented, trying to shake off the blow, then losing his balance and crashing to the floor with a loud expelling of breath and pain.

The desk had collapsed to the floor, returning to the position originally intended for it—on its legs. The door, or what was left of it, hung from a single hinge, the frame forced free from the wall, leaving behind little more than a jagged rectangle.

She looked past all of that at the nebulous blackness moving and shifting and surging through the opening. She didn't even have time to count how many were in the pawnshop beyond the door, or how many were clamoring over the backs of the ones in front of them, trying to be the first into the room, the first to take what they wanted from her, from Nate.

The first to taste their *blood.*

She flicked the fire selector on the AR-15 to full-auto and fired, the magazine emptying at an incredulous rate, the weapon recoiling against her over and over and over again. She swung it from left to right, then right to left.

They stumbled and fell and climbed over each other. Every bullet she fired pierced soft flesh and glanced off bones to kill one, two, sometimes three more behind them. She was getting good value for her money, every bullet taking down multiple ghouls, but it wasn't enough.

It wasn't nearly enough.

For every one that staggered to the floor and didn't move again, two more—*five* more—took its place.

There were too many. There were simply too many.

And they kept coming.

And coming…

"Gaby!" Nate shouted behind her. (When had he gotten behind her?)

Gaby heard his voice only because she had stopped firing; the magazine was empty. She backed up, hitting the release switch to pull out and slam in her final magazine before looking back.

Nate was at the door, one hand on the deadbolt, the other on the lever. She could see blood soaking through the fabric of his shirt over his left shoulder, the red color spreading along his left arm. He looked deathly ill, but was somehow still standing.

"We have to go!" he shouted.

She nodded, turning around just as two ghouls came within inches of scratching her face. She didn't have time to aim and fired from the hip instinctively, slicing them in a short burst. They fell, the bullets that killed them continuing on, knocking three more ghouls off the desk seconds after they had scrambled on top of it.

Clumps of flesh, smelling like garbage and decaying meat, along with viscous liquids made of things she'd rather not think about, splattered her shirt and neck and cheeks, and she could have sworn some got in her hair, too.

"Do it!" she shouted. "Do it now!"

She kept backing up, firing into the thick, shapeless mass of quivering flesh flooding through the door over and around the fallen desk. It didn't matter where she fired. One section of the room was the same as the other. It looked as if the bullets were punching into an ocean. An endless sea, as deep as the universe, moving forward to take her into its final embrace.

She felt the large gush of cool wind behind her, and knew Nate had thrown open the back door. She waited to hear his voice, calling to her to come already, that there wasn't any time left to make their escape.

The dumpsters. If they could get to the dumpsters…

But there were no sounds from behind her, no Nate screaming, urging her backward. She wondered if he was dead, if opening the back door had only allowed more creatures waiting outside to come in.

She had to turn, had to look back, but she couldn't. There were too many in front of her, that if she took her eyes off them for even a second, it would all be over. They would make up the distance and that would be it. That would be the end.

"Nate!" she shouted.

There was no response.

She kept firing, counting the number of bullets. Too many, too fast, too—

Empty.

She looked over her shoulder—

Nate was on the floor, his body in a heap.

And something else—a second figure—was rushing toward her. Dark, tall, and *wearing a white hazmat suit.*

As her mind tried to process what she was seeing, the stock of a rifle smashed into the side of her neck. Gaby gagged, more from the shock than pain, and dropped her rifle, falling to her knees. Groping at her neck, she struggled to breathe.

She looked toward Nate, at the open back door, as a second hazmat-suited figure darted inside, leaping over Nate's prone body. The man's gas mask made for a fiendish sight in the green of the glow stick, as if he were an alien invader coming to take her. It moved toward her with surprising speed, and before she could stand up and fight, it grabbed her and held *(embraced?)* her.

Then darkness, as the world was swallowed by black-skinned creatures blotting out everything around her. Glimpses of blurring flesh and bottomless pits moved toward her, then *past* her.

The arm around her was so tight it threatened to choke the life out of her. She wanted to fight, but barely had any strength to keep her eyes open. And the pain from her neck was impossible to ignore. She gagged, trying to remember how to breathe again. But it was difficult. It was so difficult…

Her vision started to fail her and everything became heavy. Slowly, slowly, she realized trying to breathe was too challenging, and the last thing she remembered was the sound of screaming…and she knew it wasn't coming from her.

CHAPTER 32

WILL

HE DREAMT OF Lara. Of white sandy beaches. A perfect breeze and the soft glow of blonde hair in the sun. Soft skin under his fingers, and kissable lips.

Lara...

"You know how to make a girl jealous," a voice said.

He opened his eyes slowly, painfully. The spiderwebbed front windshield of the Ford F-150 was the first thing that came into view. Behind that, sunlight filtered in through holes along the steel garage door and from crevices around it.

"What time is it?" His voice sounded more like a guttural groan. How long had he been asleep?

"Morning," Zoe said.

"What time?"

"You have a watch. Look at it."

"I can't feel my arms."

Zoe leaned over, lifted his right hand, and showed him the face of his watch: 9:15 A.M.

"There," she said. "Happy?"

"I slept through the night?"

She smiled down at him. "Yes and no."

A bottle of water magically appeared in her hand. She tipped the opening against his lips and he opened his mouth and drank. Rain water. It still tasted better than no water, and his throat was parched.

"You slept through the last two nights," she said.

"Two nights?"

"You almost died, Will. Again." She frowned at him. "Honestly, I don't know how you're still alive right now. You're basically seventy percent flesh and blood and thirty percent sutures. You almost bled out the last time you were conscious."

"Good thing I'm stubborn."

"No kidding."

He struggled to sit up. She put her hand on his chest and pushed him back down. She must have been stronger than she looked, because he couldn't move at all against her palm. That, or he was half dead and had little strength to resist.

"Slowly," Zoe said. "Okay? Slowly."

He laid back down and calmed his breathing. Better.

"The good news is, your sutures are holding and you're not bleeding anymore," she said.

"The bad news?"

"I tried washing your shirt in the rain, but I'm not very good at laundry."

She held up his shirt. There were still blood stains on it, and it smelled like rain. He smiled and took it, put it on the dashboard for later. She offered him the bottle again, and he drank some more.

"Lara," she said.

"What about her?"

"You kept saying her name in your sleep."

"I guess I was dreaming about her."

"I figured," she smiled. "Hungry? I've been filling you up with nothing but water for the last two and a half days."

"There's food in my pack…"

"There *was* food in your pack. I ate it." She picked up a plastic Phillips 66 bag from her floor. "But the gas station next door had some food on the shelves. Lots of stale chips, Pringles, and plenty of beef jerky and other nonperishables."

She took out a can of Dole fruit and pulled the tab free. He smelled syrup-drenched artificial flavoring and immediately thought of Gaby.

At least one of us made it back home…

"You need to be careful about going outside the garage by yourself," he said.

She gave him a wry look. "Give me a break. I've been doing it for the last two days while you were sleeping on your ass in here. I know you're the big bad Army Ranger, but I do have some survival instincts of my own, you know. Besides—" she picked up something from the dashboard—his cross-knife "—I had this. You religious or something?"

"No."

"So what's with the cross?"

"You see a cross, I see a knife."

"So, cross-knife?"

"Something like that."

She handed it back to him, and Will slipped it into its sheath along his left hip.

"Did you have to use it?" he asked.

"No."

"Anyone looking for us while I was out?"

"I don't know if they were looking for us specifically, but while I was outside I saw a lot of movement along the highway the last few days. And a couple of vehicles came close enough a couple of times that I could hear them from inside the garage." She pulled open a stick of Jack Link's beef jerky and took a bite. Teriyaki-flavored beef drifted from her seat to his. "This thing isn't half bad. I can see why you like it."

He sporked a chunk of pineapple into his mouth, tried to chew it a little bit before swallowing.

"Can I ask you a question?" she said after a while.

"I'm not sure I could stop you if I wanted to, so go ahead."

"Would you have really shot me back there at the camp, if the others had opened fire on us?"

"No."

"Oh."

"Because if they opened fire, chances are one of them would have shot you by accident first."

She glared at him. "God, you're such a dick."

He wanted to laugh, but the most he could manage was a soft chuckle.

She went back to eating the jerky while he fished out the final piece of pineapple, then tilted the can over his lips and drank down the sugary liquid.

When Will lowered the can, he saw that the garage had gotten noticeably darker. He checked his watch just to make sure his internal clock wasn't out of whack. No, it was still just 12:11 P.M.

"It's getting darker," he said. He glanced up at the roof. "Rain."

The first drop hit Fredo's rooftop on cue, quickly followed by sheets of rain pouring down across the holes and crevices along the closed garage doors.

"Good thing I went shopping earlier today," Zoe said.

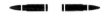

THE RAIN MADE him feel better, and allowed him to relax and concentrate on not dying. The daylight kept the ghouls away, and rain kept the collaborators hunkered down. He wasn't sure if they still had pursuers, but he always liked to keep his options open.

He got some of his strength back, enough that he could climb out of the truck on his own and walk around in the tight confines of the garage while barefoot. (He didn't recall when Zoe had taken off his boots.) Every muscle ached and joints popped with every move, but he kept shuffling anyway until he got the hang of it again.

Zoe watched him carefully, and he wasn't entirely sure if it was admiration he saw in her eyes or pity. Probably a combination of both. Eventually, he got enough strength back to pull his shirt on.

By three in the afternoon, the rain was still pounding on Fredo's, and water had seeped into the garage under the closed doors. He slipped his socks and boots back on and continued his movements. He felt better with every step, every hour on his feet. His strength wasn't there yet, and it would be a while before he was his old self. The good news was that he barely felt the sutured wound along his thigh, and the one in his side was manageable as long as he didn't think about it too much.

He ate his share of the beef jerky and canned food Zoe had scavenged from the Phillips 66 next door. Whenever they ran out of water—which was often—they refilled it outside in the rain, taking turns. Zoe regulated his medication, not that there was enough variety to choose from. The pain was unavoidable, but he soldiered through it and thought of something else.

The island. Lara. Danny's bad jokes. Sarah's cooking.

He was at least heartened that Gaby and Nate had probably

made it back to the island by now. He had no way of knowing for sure, but Gaby was resourceful, and even injured, Nate had proven himself to be a good companion for her.

Teenage love in the apocalypse lives after all.

———◂▬▬▮ ▮▬▬▸———

WHEN HE OPENED his eyes again later that night, it was pitch dark inside the truck, and he couldn't hear the sound of rain anymore, only the soft and steady *drip-drip-drip* of leftover water falling off the sides of the building.

Nightfall.

He could see the whites of Zoe's eyes. Her knees were pulled up to her chest, hands over her legs. She was staring at him as he stirred awake.

"They're outside," she whispered. Her lips trembled, making it sound as if she were stuttering.

He looked down at his watch, the hands glowing bright green in the darkness: 10:39 P.M.

Will twisted slightly in his seat, grimacing with the pain *(Ignore it)*, and reached into the back for his M4A1 rifle. There, the cold but comfortable feel of well-worn metal. He pulled it forward by the barrel and into his lap. He ran his hands over the carbine, checking to make sure everything was where it should be.

Zoe was looking at the closed garage door in front of them now. Moonlight filtered in through the tiny crevices at the bottom and along the sides, as if the door were glowing in the dark. Figures— thin, gaunt shapes—darted across the other side, never staying at one spot for very long, and the sound of splashing puddles that had accumulated in the parking lot after the day's rain.

How many? More than two. Possibly five. Likely more than that.

His gun belt was on the floor. He reached down and tugged the Glock gently out of its holster and checked to make sure he had a full magazine inside. He slipped it back into the holster, the slide of the Glock's plastic polymer against leather like fingernails on a chalkboard. He carefully wrapped the gun belt around his waist and pulled it tight, ignoring the brief flash of pain. He was glad he had swallowed extra painkillers when Zoe wasn't looking.

His pack rested between the two front seats; he picked it up and calmly, silently searched for the spare magazines inside. He had two spares for the M4A1 and two for the Glocks. All silver ammo. He had given the rest to Gaby.

"What are we going to do?" Zoe whispered, her voice impossibly strained.

He shook his head. *"Nothing."*

Her eyes trembled and widened, over and over again.

"We'll be fine," he whispered.

There was a loud *bang!* as one of the ghouls crashed into the steel garage door. The whole building seemed to shake for an instant, before another one of the creatures smashed into the same door just as it was settling.

Zoe almost screamed, but somehow managed to stop herself in time.

"Did you latch the garage doors?" he asked.

Will had dispensed with the whispering now. The ghouls clearly knew they were inside, and he could see the number of figures increasing through the slits. There were so many that they completely overwhelmed the slivers of moonlight that were once visible.

Twenty. Maybe thirty...

Zoe managed to nod back at him, her voice trembling when she answered. "I couldn't find the keys to lock them in place."

"It's okay, neither could I."

He had looked everywhere the first time they had spent the night at Fredo's, but the keys were nowhere to be found. The garage doors were simply latched, but not locked. It was one of the reasons why Will didn't like staying in a place more than once. Betting on the ghouls missing you two times in a row was asking for trouble. Betting on three days in a row was begging for it.

Dead, not stupid.

"We're going to die, aren't we?" Zoe said suddenly.

"No."

She was trying to read his face. Will smiled back at her. He had mastered hiding his emotions years ago. Fear, happiness—things that could be tempered with the right combination of resolve and denial.

He was very aware that there was a way out of this. The hazmat suit. It was still crumpled on the floor behind his seat, where he had tossed it days ago after they escaped the camp. He could put it on and probably survive tonight. *Probably*. He wasn't entirely confident that was even true. Were the ghouls ordered not to attack *any* hazmat suits? Or just people wearing the uniforms at certain locations?

Too many questions, too many possibilities.

Not that it mattered. There was Zoe to think about. She had saved his life, even when she didn't have to. He couldn't pay that back now by grabbing the suit and leaving her to fend for herself. Besides, there was still a way out of this.

"We'll be fine," he said. "I just need you to stick with me, okay?"

"I don't want to die, Will."

"You won't."

Zoe jumped at the sound of footsteps moving across the roof above them. The truck's windows were open, as they had been for the last three days. He could hear the steady, unmistakable patter of soft, bare feet treading over wet, loose gravel.

Definitely more than one. Probably a dozen…

"Oh, God," Zoe whispered. "What are they doing up there?"

They're probing, looking for a weak spot.

He said instead, "I need to get behind the steering wheel, Zoe, and you need to get in the back."

"Why?"

"Just in case."

He could tell she wanted to ask, *"Just in case of what?"*, but she didn't. Maybe she already knew, or maybe she didn't want to know.

He grabbed her hand when he saw her reaching for the door handle. "No, just climb into the back."

She untangled her long limbs, then slowly (and so, so cautiously) climbed into the backseat. Will slipped over and settled in behind the steering wheel. He laid the M4A1 across the front passenger seat, the stock facing him for an easy grab. He made sure he knew where the power switches for the windows were—right next to his left arm, along the driver's side door. That was important, since both front windows were open. He wondered how long it would take them to close. Five seconds? Maybe.

Zoe had left the Ford's key in the ignition. He could hear her letting out short, labored breaths behind him, like machine guns. He didn't blame her. The sound of ghouls moving above them was disconcerting. He had been through it countless times, and it still got to him.

"Will?" she whispered, her voice barely audible.

"Yeah?"

"Was I wrong? For doing what I did? At the camps, with all those pregnant women?"

The question surprised him, especially since she had defended herself so well. But there were very real doubts in her voice now. Doubt, and very real regret.

"No," he said. "You did what you had to do. No one can blame you."

"Do you?"

"No. I don't blame you, Zoe."

"Thank you."

He nodded, and slowly tuned out the noises from above. That was a distraction. He could almost sense them trying to lull him, like sirens grabbing at his attention.

Instead, he focused on the garage door directly in front of him. That was where the danger would come from. It would take too much effort to crash through the roof, but the doors, held down by a simple latch that could be opened from both sides, was the real problem. All it would take was for one ghoul to realize that...

Then he saw the door moving slightly—ever so slightly—and Will put his hand over the key. Behind him, he heard a soft *click*, and grinned at the image of Zoe putting on her seatbelt.

Buckle up, here they come.

Before he had even finished his thought, they threw the garage door open—first one, then the other—with such a sudden explosion of sound and fury that he actually jumped. His senses, already overloaded, went into overdrive when he glimpsed darkness beyond and the ghouls packed into the parking lot.

Then every inch of him erupted into action.

He flicked the key in the ignition and heard the F-150 roar to life about the same time the first ghoul leaped through the door, which was still in the process of sliding open, and landed on the hood, scrambling on all fours up to the damaged window. Will ignored its gaunt face and slobbering mouth—caverns of twisted and brown and yellow teeth—and slammed his fingers down on the power window switches. His right hand was already moving, falling down on the gear shift and pulling it into drive.

The ghoul was perched directly in front of him, glaring through the windshield with intense dark eyes, as if it could will itself through the bullet holes. Will slammed down on the gas pedal just as two— three—*four* more of the creatures flung themselves through the air and landed on the hood with loud *thumps*.

More *plopped* against the windshield and careened off as the F-150 powered forward and burst out of the garage, all four tires spinning desperately under its massive bulk.

The headlights had popped on automatically as soon as he turned the key, and Will saw a sea of ghouls crowding around the parking lot. They seemed to fly at him, landing and bouncing off the hood and windshield and sides of the vehicle like baseballs, each impact denting and cratering but doing nothing to halt the momentum of the almost 5,000-pound vehicle.

He heard the loud crunch of bodies and bones and skulls under the truck's large twenty-nine inch tires, most of it lost in the roar of a powerful engine designed to tow over 11,000 pounds. Against that kind of brute force, creatures that were essentially bags of skin and bones didn't stand a chance.

By now both windows were fully closed, though that didn't stop the ghouls from endlessly smashing into them with their fists—and skulls—anyway. It was a hail Mary of sharp, bony bodies, jackhammering fists, and flailing legs coming from everywhere even as the truck battered its way down Fredo's driveway and into the streets, splashing puddles as it went. The truck's magnificently bright headlights flashed across scowling faces and shrunken bodies.

There had to be hundreds. *Thousands.* The streets were lined with them. Wall upon wall of shriveled figures, so many that eventually even the truck began to slow down under the onslaught, the number of crushed ghouls clogging up the tires and undercarriage.

"There's too many!" Zoe shouted from the backseat.

Gee, thanks for the fine observation, Zoe.

He jerked the steering wheel and took the F-150 off the streets and into the grass. Instantly, he felt the difference in how the vehicle handled, minus the bodies trying to cling to it from every inch of the roof, hood, and sides. He was pretty sure a number of the creatures had leaped into the truck bed and were now clinging on for dear life, but he didn't have time to look in the rearview mirror to make sure.

Now that he had abandoned the strip mall, he was moving through uncharted territory. Literally. The ground before and around and under him was constantly shifting, from smooth asphalt to concrete to grass and back again. Every bump and hop and sudden dip threatened to send them careening to their deaths. The truck was rising and falling more than it was moving on solid ground. It took all of his concentration not to broadside parked vehicles or take a tree head-on.

And through it all, the cascading sounds of bodies bouncing off the hood and grill and back bumper. The squeal of flesh trying to grapple onto the smooth sides of the truck to no avail. The constant glimpses of marble eyes, like small rain drops of tar, pouring at him from left and right and front and back, and at one point, he swore they were falling out of the sky, too.

We're going to die. Soon, the truck will run out of gas, and we're going to die.

Then, like a tunnel opening up in an ocean of nothingness, he saw it in the distance. It was long and lean and looked tiny, but that was only because it was still too far away to see in any detail. It was bright, blinding whiteness in a dark universe. He remembered seeing it days ago when he first drove through Harvest. It was a kilometer away, maybe more.

Doable.

He stepped on the gas and the truck poured it on, crunching ghouls and turning skulls and bones to dust and pulverizing skin into paper. Would that even kill them? He wasn't so sure. He had seen ghouls moving with half their heads literally caved in, seen severed hands still acting like they had minds. Compared to those things, getting caught under a truck's tires was probably child's play.

Behind him, Zoe was screaming. He wasn't entirely sure why she had suddenly let loose. Was it the fear? The sight of the ghouls flinging themselves at them with wild abandon? He couldn't really blame her; if he were seeing it all for the first time, he might have lost it, too.

He tuned her out instead and concentrated on the objective in front of him. Literally. It was getting closer, becoming more and more real as the truck tore across the open land. He was leaving the ghouls behind, but he had no illusions that this small victory was going to last. He could outrun them, but only for a little while.

There were too many; they were simply everywhere, coming out of every inch of darkness around him. And they weren't going to give up. Not as long as he was out here in the wide open with them.

He slammed his foot down on the accelerator and willed the truck to go faster. In the back, Zoe was screaming her head off.

Plan Z, Danny.

You would have loved this one, buddy...

CHAPTER 33

LARA

WILL WAS DEAD. Gaby, too.

There were no other explanations as to why neither one of them had contacted Song Island since she'd last heard from Gaby. If he was still alive and capable, Will would have attempted to contact her by now.

Unless he's dead…

Whatever optimism she had managed to cling to vanished when Gaby missed her check-in yesterday. Even Benny, who had been hobbling around the island beaming with anticipation of Gaby's return, had begun to realize something had gone very, very wrong.

Danny, too, took the silence badly. "That fucking rain. I should have told her to push on through."

She wanted to tell him not to blame himself, but it was a moot point. Like Will, Danny took responsibility for Gaby. The two of them had molded her into a soldier in their image, and in so many ways, became brother figures to her.

It's not your fault, Danny, it's my fault. I should never have let them go.

If I hadn't insisted on the medical supplies, if I didn't have so much faith in Will, if I had argued harder against taking Gaby…

…if…if…

It took Stan, one of the people who had arrived with Benny, to get her mind back to the work of the island. For a while, anyway.

She stood outside the main generator building at the Power Station, listening to Stan, wishing she were somewhere else, but grateful to be there at the same time.

This is Will's job, she thought, listening to Stan as he explained how Song Island's generator worked. Stan was an electrician and had spent the last few days looking at the island's energy set-up, jotting down notes, diagrams, and spending more time at the Power Station than he did at the hotel.

"It's an amazing piece of machinery," Stan was saying. "The energy grid for the entire island is designed for maximum efficiency. Even with half of the system unaccounted for, I don't see why we couldn't crank up the AC in the summers and heating in the winters."

Stan went on, but Lara had already stopped listening.

This is your job, Will. You should be here right now. You should be in charge. Not me. I'm not ready for this. I was never ready for this.

After a while, Stan seemed to realize that she wasn't listening. He stopped talking and put a reassuring hand on her shoulder.

"They'll show up," Stan said. "They looked pretty capable. Give them more time, and they'll show up."

She nodded and tried to smile back at him, but she knew it came out badly. "Can you handle this place by yourself?"

"I don't see why not. As long as the power grid doesn't suffer some kind of catastrophic damage, this thing could conceivably keep running for years with just some basic maintenance."

"Do you need anything? Supplies?"

"Plenty," Stan said.

"Make a list, and we'll try to fill it when we do supply runs later in the week."

"I'll get on it."

She left him, and was glad when she made it back to the pathway and her teeth stopped chattering.

For a place that was so vital to the health of Song Island, the Power Station was her least favorite building. Not only because of the intense vibrations emanating from the generator, but because having to walk anywhere close to the small, walled off shack next door made her squeamish, even now, months after Danny and Will had collapsed the tunnel entrance along the shore. She always imagined she could *feel* them in there, back again after Will had cleared them out a few days ago…

Will, goddamn you.

She was on her way back to the hotel when her radio squawked.

It was Danny: "Lara, got a minute?"

She unclipped the radio. "What is it, Danny?"

"Roy has something to show you."

She took a breath. She didn't want to talk to Danny right now, much less Roy. She had barely managed to summon enough energy to talk to Stan, and the only reason she had even done that was to get away from the hotel, from the others. She needed the time alone that the long walk supplied, and she wasn't quite ready to give it up yet.

She keyed the radio. "Danny, can it wait?"

"Lara," Danny said, and there was something in his voice—an insistence—that she hadn't heard before. "You'll want to see this."

"I'll be there soon."

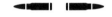

"WHAT IS IT?" Lara asked.

"It's a laptop," Roy said.

"I can see that, Roy. But why am I looking at it?"

They were on the third floor of the Tower, with nightfall spreading across the lake outside the windows. She spent the entire time trying to ignore the darkness, and the image of Will and Gaby out there, trying to survive another night.

If they're even still alive...

Roy was sitting at the table in front of a laptop. There were two ham radios on the tabletop now, one on each side of the computer. The radio she was familiar with, that was still dialed into their designated emergency frequency and waiting to hear from Will and Gaby, was in one piece, while the one Benny had brought back with him looked gutted. Its cover was open, and there were multicolored wires connecting it to the laptop, which was also open at the back. Clearly, Roy had been doing more than just tinkering with the devices.

Danny leaned next to one of the windows, eating fried fish on a ceramic plate. "I told Roy Rogers here to go crazy with the spare radio, and he goes and does that."

"What is 'that'?" she asked.

"He wants to spread the word about the ghouls. Their weaknesses, their bad skin condition, and that ghastly smell that's like getting tossed into a year-old dumpster."

"Danny filled me in about the computer program that brought us here," Roy said. He indicated what looked like a series of random numbers running inside an open window on the laptop's screen. "I couldn't duplicate exactly what the people who sent the FEMA broadcast had, but I think I got the gist of it. I've connected the two devices so we can now control the ham radio's operations through the laptop. And, I've added some improvements."

"What kind of improvements?" she asked.

"Instead of broadcasting on one frequency, it'll broadcast across all of them, across all the bands, one after another. This way, we'll be able to send the same recorded message over and over, twenty-four hours a day, seven days a week, but not be limited to just one frequency."

"And it's all automated?"

"As long as the laptop's running and the Tower's still standing, yeah."

"Jinx," Danny said.

"Oops, sorry," Roy said. "You know what I mean."

"What do you think?" she asked Danny.

Danny shrugged. "It's not a bad idea and we don't really have anything to lose. The broadcast doesn't take that much power, and we still have the other radio for everything else. We know a lot about these buggers, maybe more than most people out there. Seems like the nice thing to do, don't you think?"

She nodded, then looked back at Roy. "What do you need to set everything up?"

"Everything's already set up," Roy said. "I just need a message to send out there." He picked up the radio's microphone and held it out to her. "Fire away."

She stared at him, then at Danny. "Me?"

"You're the boss," Danny said.

"Danny…"

"Carly's not going to do it. She hates the sound of her own voice. And Sarah's not going to do it, not after…well, you know."

"What about Bonnie? She used to be a model."

"We asked her," Roy said. "She says models are seen, not

heard."

"We talked, and we all agreed you should do it," Danny said.

"You 'talked'?" she said. "When did that happen?"

"It's a secret. We do that, you know, talk behind your back. Quite often, actually."

"Why does it have to be a woman, anyway?"

"Tokyo Rose, Axis Sally, Hanoi Hannah…"

"Really, Danny?"

"Point is, it's gotta be a woman. Makes people feel all warm and fuzzy."

She sighed. "What should I say?"

"It should be short. The facts, but nothing about us or our location. I like Roy Rogers here and all, but we don't need people showing up every day. It'll get crowded real fast."

She nodded. "I guess I'll sleep on it."

AFTER ROY LEFT to go eat, Lara stayed behind in the Tower with Danny. They stood next to each other, ignoring—but intimately aware of—the darkness covering the island and the lake outside the windows.

Neither one said anything for a while. She imagined he was thinking the same things she had been turning over in her head for the last few days.

About Will, about Gaby…

"I need to know," she said after a while.

He nodded. "It's a good thing I know where to start looking."

"The pawnshop."

"She gave us the address. Too bad we don't have GPS, but we'll make do. I hear they invented maps and such that work just as well."

"It'll be dangerous, Danny."

"Why wouldn't it be?"

"Will would hate me for asking you to do this. He always says either him or you should be here on the island at all times."

"Willie boy has been known to make sense every now and then."

"And you'll have to leave Carly…"

"I'll talk to her tonight and leave at sunup."

"She'll hate me."

"Probably."

Lara sighed. Then, "Who can you take with you? Blaine's still hurt, even though he pretends he's not."

"Maddie, maybe. Or Roy."

"Roy?"

"He's a lousy shot, but all I need is a warm body to distract the other guys."

She smiled. "You don't mean that."

"Don't I?"

"No."

"Maybe not."

They stood in silence again.

"If they're out there, I'll bring them home," Danny said after a while.

"I know you will," she said.

"OKAY?" SHE ASKED.

"Um, not yet," Benny said. "Give me a sec."

She waited patiently as Benny moved his finger around the laptop's touchpad, directing the pointer onscreen. He clicked a couple of times, but the program she had seen running when Roy was working the same laptop last night didn't show up.

Morning sunlight flooded in through the windows along the Tower's third floor. She had barely slept last night, her mind filled with thoughts of Will and Gaby, and now Danny's leaving. Her eyes had looked red in the bathroom mirror, as if she had been crying all night, though she didn't remember doing it. Maybe she had just blocked it out.

"Benny?" she said.

"I almost got it."

"Maybe I should come back later..."

"Roy showed me how this thing works. I don't know why it's not working now—" Finally, the familiar-looking program appeared on the screen. "There."

She gave him a half-hearted "good job" smile.

Benny picked up the ham radio mic and handed it to her. "You can start whenever you want, and I'll clean up the audio later. Do however many takes as you need."

She nodded. She was always planning on one take. It was a simple message and relatively short. She had already run it by Carly and Danny, and they had given her the thumbs up. Even so, she wished Will were here. He would know if she had gotten it right.

Will, please be alive. I don't know what I'd do without you.

Lara took a breath, then pressed the transmit lever.

"TO ANY SURVIVORS out there, if you're hearing this, you are not alone. There are things you need to know about our enemy—these creatures of the night, these ghouls. They are *not* invincible, and they have weaknesses other than sunlight. One: you can kill them with silver. Stab them, shoot them, or cut them with any silver weapon, and they will die. Two: they will not cross bodies of water. An island, a boat—get to anything that can separate you from land. Three: some ultraviolet light has proven effective, but flashlights and lightbulbs with UV don't seem to have any effect. We don't know why, so use this information with caution. If you're hearing this message, you are not alone. Stay strong, stay smart, and adapt. We owe it to those we've lost to keep fighting, to never give up. Good luck."

CHAPTER 34

WILL

THE CITY OF Harvest, Louisiana, like most small towns around the United States, maintained a backup water supply in a water tower. The one Will and Zoe were on now was fifty meters high, with the word "Harvest" stenciled down the side in big, blocky black letters to make them stand out against the bright white paint. It was the stark whiteness of the structure against the darkness that Will had spotted from a distance.

Getting up the water tower was simple enough. All it took was climbing. A lot of climbing. Fast climbing. Fifty meters up. He was pretty sure he was going to die about halfway, but somehow, some way, his stitches held, and miraculously he wasn't bleeding by the time he got to the top.

The ghouls were on their heels by the time Will flung himself onto the tower's cone-shaped roof. He had his pack over one shoulder, the M4A1 over the other, and he unslung the rifle and fired down, killing the closest ghoul—already halfway up the ladder—and slicing through three more behind it. They fell like dominos, tumbling backward, knocking loose more ghouls. It looked almost amusing, like a Three Stooges gag.

Will counted every bullet he fired, painfully aware of how many he had left in his arsenal. The current magazine was already minus the three rounds he had used back at the collaborator town, leaving him with twenty-seven.

One…

He couldn't see the white Ford F-150 parked at the base of the tower anymore. It was simply gone, engulfed by the teeming mass of creatures racing toward the structure that rose out of the center of Harvest like a beacon.

Come one, come all! Free human blood! Come get them—if you can!

He must have laughed out loud, because he caught sight of Zoe out of the corner of his eye looking over at him, half terrified and half perplexed.

She was clinging to the tower's roof, her shoes scraping for better contact against the smooth metal surface. Not an easy feat, given the day's rain, which had made climbing and keeping a grip on the ladder's rungs difficult. The leftover wetness also made accidentally slipping down the slanted rooftop a very real possibility. The tower itself didn't have any protective railing at the top, which meant if you dropped off the side, you *dropped.*

Smartly, Zoe was using the metallic telecom antennas jutting up from around the sides of the tower as foot stops to keep from sliding off. The structure looked like a huge aboveground grain silo, with a massive girth that extended from top to bottom instead of the flat base and pencil-thin middle section of most water towers he was used to seeing.

Will had perched himself directly over the ladder extending up from the ground below. It was the only way up, which was more than he could have possibly hoped for. One way to access the rooftop meant only one spot to cover. When he realized that, he suddenly got excited. Up until that point, this had been a suicide run. But now, there was a chance. A slim one, but it was a chance nonetheless.

Yeah, that's the ticket.

And they were coming, all right—not that he had any doubts they wouldn't be. If he had learned anything about the ghouls, it was that 1) they weren't stupid; and 2) they were persistent. Goddamn persistent.

So he kept firing down, but only when the closest ghoul was within five meters of reaching the top. That ensured point-blank accuracy, and allowed for more creatures to be lined up directly below his target so the shot would keep traveling down, gravity giving the silver bullet an extra burst of speed for maximum collateral damage.

And he kept count of every bullet he fired.

Fifteen...

He mumbled a curse each time a bullet ricocheted off a bone and was deflected in a direction other than straight down. It was rare, but it happened.

Twenty-two...

Will pumped the twenty-fourth and twenty-fifth round into the flesh of two separate ghouls, then fired the final two shots in rapid succession while the ghouls were still more than five meters from him, in order to give himself time to reload.

One magazine down, two to go.

The stitches along his side were holding, and he didn't see blood seeping through his shirt when he glanced down. Thank God Zoe knew what she was doing when she put him back together. He looked over at her now, staring down at the squirming black horde gathered below them, so many that even the grass seemed to have been swallowed up. Her face was frozen in horror, her mouth slightly open, as if she wanted to scream but couldn't get the sounds out.

He turned back to the ladder and fired the first bullet from the second magazine and watched three—no, four—ghouls tumble from the ladder.

One...

Another shot sent another three down, before the bullet bounced off track.

Two...

The water tower was cold against his backside, and he was high up enough that he could feel the chill night air. His pants were already soaked through.

Five...

He took a moment to snap a glance down at his watch, glowing underneath the darkness. 12:33 A.M.

Not bad. He only had to hold them off until...when? 6:30 A.M.? 7:00 A.M.? Close enough. It wasn't the worst situation he had ever faced, though he imagined it would be easier if Danny were here.

Or Lara.

Or someone besides a terrified doctor.

Seven...

Zoe hadn't moved from her spot on the angled roof, her feet

spread out in front of her, each shoe pushing against a jutting cell tower. He almost smiled; she looked like a pregnant woman giving birth.

She looked over at him, her entire body trembling, making her stutter the words: "We're going to die, aren't we?"

"Of course not," he said. "Don't fall, and we'll be fine."

"Don't fall," she repeated. She looked back down at the creatures below. "Don't fall…"

Eight…

"Don't look," he said. "Lay down on the roof and don't look and don't move."

She was clearly unconvinced, but she lay down against the cold slanted metal surface anyway.

Nine…

After the first fifty or so ghouls, the rest began moving at a crawl. He was so used to seeing them attacking at frenzied speeds that watching them climbing up the ladder, being careful with every step, every rung they reached for, was a revelation. For every ghoul that managed to climb, another lost its footing or grip and went tumbling down into the pit of writhing flesh below.

Eleven…

"How many bullets do you have left?" Zoe asked, her voice still shaking.

"Enough."

"Are you sure?"

"Yes," he lied.

Thirteen…

⬛▬▬ ▬▬▶

HE WAS ON his last magazine when he started thinking about alternatives.

One…

He had the Glock. That was fifteen more silver bullets. He also had two more magazines in his pouch. That was good for thirty more rounds, for a grand total of forty-five. Which, judging by the speed the ghouls were climbing, would probably get him through another three hours. One hour per fifteen bullets.

Captain Optimism. Danny would be so proud.

Six...

He had his cross-knife. The problem with the knife was that he needed to wait for them to get all the way up before he could strike. Potentially hazardous work. One grab around his wrist, or if the knife lodged in too deep, and he would lose it—and himself right along with it, because stabbing, even downward, required leaning over the edge.

Doable, but risky.

Then there was the whole numbers game. He could only take down one at a time, which meant for every ghoul he dispatched, another would be right behind it, giving him very little time to recover. He couldn't count on Zoe to take up any slack. He didn't think it was possible to even pry her from her current spot.

Eleven...

His watch read: 3:19 A.M.

Zoe looked half asleep, lying with her back against the angled roof. Every few minutes she would lift her head slightly to make sure she hadn't slipped while she had her eyes closed. If she was afraid of heights, she hadn't said a word as he urged her up the ladder. Of course, she was probably fueled at the time by enough adrenaline for a half dozen people.

Sixteen...

A slight wind had picked up, and Will turned his face into it. He could see most of Harvest from his perch. Or at least, as much as he could pick up with the naked eye. The moon was not being very cooperative, and he had lost the bright headlights of the Ford F-150 within the world of murky blackness, shifting flesh and glinting black eyes swarming the base of the water tower.

A sudden burst of motion drew his attention, and he looked over to find Zoe fighting with her footing, having somehow ended up slightly crouched, knees bent, with one hand bracing against the cool metal under her. After some frantic struggling, she managed to push herself back into position.

"You okay?" he asked.

"I must have fallen asleep," she said breathlessly.

He turned his attention to the ladder and the nearest ghoul clinging to it, ten meters down. He waited for it to make up the distance, then shot it in the face a few seconds later. The bullet pierced the creature's chest and caught two more under it, sending all three plunging down. They knocked loose two more from the ladder as they fell.

Seventeen...

"How many bullets do you have left?" she asked.

"Plenty," he said.

"But *how many?*"

"More than enough." Before she could press him again, he added, "Get closer, Zoe, so I'll be able to catch you if you doze off again."

She scooted over slowly, taking her time. She flinched when he leaned over the ladder and fired his eighteenth bullet without warning. He sat back and held out his hand. She took it and let him pull her closer until she was sitting only a few inches away. She immediately sought out the safety of the nearby cell antennas with her shoes.

Will leaned over, watching the closest ghoul climbing from thirty meters away. The creature reached up and took another rung and pulled itself up slowly...

He slung his rifle and dug into his pack. He pulled out the gas siphoning tube, unrolled it, then looped one end around his belt and cinched it tight. He leaned toward Zoe and reached for her waist, hooking his fingers into her belt.

"What are you doing?" she asked, alarmed.

"I'm going to tie you to me, so I'll know if you slip again. Early warning system."

"But what if you fall?"

"Then you're coming down with me."

Her face turned pale.

"I can go days without sleeping if I have to," Will said. "Can you?"

"Do I have a choice?"

"Yes. You can fall."

"So, no, then."

He grinned back at her, then looped the other end of the tube around her belt. He pulled at it to draw her closer, before tying it into place. He left a meter length between them so they could still move without forcing the other along. He wasn't entirely sure if the hose would hold if one of them actually did fall off the tower, but he kept that doubt to himself.

He leaned over the ladder, shot another ghoul in the chest, and watched it tumble into the darkness below, this time taking five more along with it.

Twenty…

◀▬▬ ▬▬▶

HE STRETCHED THE final rifle magazine a few minutes past 4:00 A.M.—4:14 A.M., to be exact.

When she saw him slinging the M4A1 and drawing his Glock, Zoe said, "You're almost out of bullets, aren't you?"

"I have three magazines for the Glock."

"Will that be enough?"

"Forty-five bullets in all."

"How many bullets did you have for the rifles?"

"Thirty."

"How many magazines?"

"Three. But one magazine only had twenty-seven rounds."

"Eighty-seven bullets got us from eleven o'clock to three in the morning," she said. "Four hours. Forty-five bullets will only get us two more hours. We'll still be ninety minutes short of sunup, Will."

Great, she can count, too.

"I'll make it last," he said.

"No, you won't."

He was struck by the matter-of-fact tone in her voice. The fear seemed to have been replaced by what sounded like resignation.

"What happens when the bullets run out?" she asked.

"I still have my knife."

"Your knife…"

"We'll be fine."

Say it a third time and maybe she'll actually believe you.

"You're full of shit, Will," Zoe said.

Or not.

He leaned over the ladder and shot a ghoul from five meters away. The bullet pierced its chest, hit a second ghoul directly below it. They tumbled free, knocking only one other ghoul with them this time.

Sonofabitch.

The rest continued to climb steadily, either unimpressed by or oblivious to the deaths of the others. He couldn't even see the dead ghouls below, and figured they were crushed under the live ones fighting their way to the ladder to be the next one up.

Two...

FIFTEEN...

Will didn't wait to watch the ghoul flip off the ladder. He immediately ejected the magazine, catching it with his other hand and jamming it back into the pouch *(just in case)*, then instinctively grabbed the next—and last—magazine.

He slipped it in, worked the slide, and leaned over the side of the water tower.

The closest ghoul was only ten meters away. Will watched it climb for a moment, one arm over the other, impossibly patient and determined, and unfathomably fearless. He wondered if they even still had the same concept of life and death anymore. Once you've already "died," did it matter if you died again? Even if it was permanent this time?

"How many?" Zoe asked.

"What?"

"How many bullets do you have left?"

"This is it. Fifteen more bullets in the magazine." He heard her chuckle, and looked over. "What's so funny?"

"You didn't bother to lie that time."

He wasn't sure if she looked horrified or amused. Maybe somewhere in between.

"I would have, but it's obvious you know how to count," he said.

He heard flesh slapping metal and leaned over and shot the ghoul in the head. It tumbled, taking two down with it.

One...

Zoe's entire body had become a living spring next to him, the siphoning tube connecting their bodies quivering each time she shifted or moved, which was every few seconds. It had also gotten much colder up here, and Zoe's entire body was shaking. He had gone numb and couldn't feel the vibrations coming from her, of course, but he could see the tube trembling out of the corner of his eye.

Will glanced down at his watch: 6:09 A.M.

Almost there…

"Will," Zoe said.

"Yeah?"

"What happens when you run out of bullets?"

"We'll improvise."

"The knife?"

"Yeah."

"We're going to die," she said, her voice so low he almost didn't hear.

He shot another ghoul, watched it do a swan dive off the ladder, somehow managing not to take a single creature with it.

The next ghoul took its place.

Two…

He fired again, and this time was rewarded with the sight of the creature collapsing straight down, taking one—then two—ghouls with it.

Three…

He noticed they were moving faster up the ladder now, and it wasn't going well. For every ghoul that managed to scramble up two rungs without falling, two either lost their footing or grip and tumbled down. That didn't seem to deter the rest, and they continued clamoring, moving faster and faster up toward him.

Why?

Maybe they sensed he was running out of bullets. Or maybe they—

The sunrise. They know it's coming.

His watch confirmed it: 6:31 A.M.

Come out, come out, wherever you are, Mister Sun.

He fired, knocking three off the ladder.

Four…

"Zoe," he said.

"Yes?"

"You need to get ready."

"Get ready for what?" she said, her voice quivering noticeably again.

6:55 A.M.

They were coming up too fast, surging up the ladder, returning to the same frenzied pace when all of this began. It was all he could do to slash and stab with the cross-knife and suck in a fresh breath of cold air before another one tried to grab at his wrist or ankle to pull him down.

Thank God turning into ghouls hadn't granted them any special strength; he was able to shake them off, at times kicking them loose from whatever they were hanging on to and sending them fluttering back down to the mass of bodies below.

Not that it stopped them. Or slowed them down for even a second.

Zoe was moving next to him, navigating the small, precious space at the edge of the water tower. She grabbed on to the cell antennas as if they were a lifeline, shuffling left then right, trying to keep up with his movements. She had to keep moving, because each time one of the ghouls reached the top, Will had to step back before he could slash or stab. Then once the ghoul fell, he moved forward again, back toward the ladder to greet the next one up.

He marveled at their persistence, their ability to shun all sense of self-preservation. They didn't stop. Not for a second. The tide kept coming, churning, one after another, and for every black-skinned thing he dispatched, another took its place.

And they kept coming, and climbing, and coming…

…and climbing…

7:01 A.M.…

When was sunrise? 7:10 A.M.? 7:20 A.M.?

Whatever the time, they could sense it. The ghouls were desperate to get up to the rooftop, as if they knew they only had a few minutes left. Will couldn't see light in the skies or on the horizon. He didn't know how much time was left. How much longer he had to hold on. So he stabbed and slashed, moving back, then forward again, then back…

And they kept coming.

Again and again, again and again…

7:09 A.M.…

He was covered in slabs of thick black blood and torn flesh. The smell was overwhelming, assaulting his nostrils, making his eyes flare uncontrollably, his skin tingling with the acidic stench of death and decay. He wiped at copious globs of fluid that dripped from his hair down to his forehead and into his right eye. He spat out something that tasted like flesh, but it could have been dirt, or garbage, or some kind of filth he had no name for.

Zoe did her best to keep out of his way, struggling to hold on to the antennas, the two of them literally tied together by a hose that wasn't designed for the task. Still, it was better than nothing, and it allowed him to keep track of her without having to look back, because he didn't have time for that. He prayed she didn't slip and fall, because if she did, he would go over the side right along with her. Unless, of course, the tube snapped. That was possible, too.

Amazingly, he had begun to get feelings back in his body. The more he moved, the more sensations returned to his hands, to his legs, and to his joints. It took all his strength to keep scrambling, stabbing and slashing, kicking and punching. They were weak things, like striking bags of flour. They relied on numbers, which was useless when there was only one path up the water tower.

He had to stay clear of their mouths and the crooked yellow and brown teeth, like caverns of smaller bones trying to gnaw at him. Those were dangerous. Blood itself didn't do anything to you, but if they bit you, the direct transfer of fluids was what caused the infection.

Teeth of Death. I should write a book.

7:15 A.M...

Goddammit, where's that damn sun?

Slowly, he became aware that the speed with which each new ghoul appeared had begun to flag. They were coming up at longer intervals now, and he was able to breathe a little bit before he had to engage another one.

He killed a ghoul, then kicked it in the chest and watched it flip over the side, and waited for the next one.

The cross-knife in his right hand was covered in blood and skin, viscous things that looked like a concentrated form of foul-smelling sweat dripping over his fist. He was only dimly aware of his ragged breathing, and his legs screamed at him for rest. His lungs burned, but it was nothing compared to the fire burning away in his side.

Was he bleeding again?

He looked down. No. No blood. Well, not the red kind, anyway.

A little rest right about now would be nice.

No. Not yet.

Not yet…

He waited for the next one to emerge up the ladder, but it didn't come.

He kept waiting…

"Will, what's happening?" Zoe said behind him.

He shook his head and stood perfectly still.

Will hadn't looked over the tower in a while. He hadn't had the opportunity.

But now he did, and he saw there wasn't a single ghoul on the ladder. They were all on the ground, and as he watched, they began to dissolve, like a pool of black ink flowing away from the base of the tower, until the grass below became visible again. And there, the Ford F-150, unveiled as if by magic *(Ta-da!)*.

"They're leaving," Zoe said, her voice breathless, as if afraid just saying those two simple words out loud might jinx it somehow.

He checked his watch: 7:18 A.M.

"Oh my God, are they leaving?" she asked, her voice shaking, filled with hope.

"I think so, yeah."

"Oh my God, Will. Oh my God."

She rushed forward and grabbed him—and almost knocked him backward and off the side of the tower. He managed to right himself at the last moment and held on to a telecom antenna to keep from falling.

"You did it," she said, gasping for breath, somewhere between crying and screaming with joy. "You did it, Will. I can't believe you did it."

Something caught his attention.

A flicker of something distinctive below, in the corner of his eye. Something *blue*.

He looked down and saw, among the writhing black canvas, something that stood out. It was about forty meters from the base of the water tower, and it didn't move as the ghouls flowed around it, like Moses parting the Red Sea. It was looking back up at him, and Will saw intense, bright blue eyes radiating out of the darkness.

Will didn't know how he knew, he just knew who it was.

Kate.

Not the Kate he remembered, but the Kate that Lara had seen that night outside the Green Room in Harold Campbell's facility. He had dreamt of her, but she came to him in those dreams as the old Kate, the woman he remembered and for one night, loved.

This new Kate, this *ghoul* Kate, was another creature entirely, and despite the distance, he could see its deep blue eyes pulsating. They weren't like the blue of Lara's—these were more intense, like staring into the sun. He couldn't look away. They drew him in, fascinating him.

Then Kate smiled.

No, not Kate. *A ghoul.* He had to stop thinking of her *(it)* as Kate. This was the enemy now. This creature.

It turned and walked away with a preternatural grace that was almost majestic. He watched it go, the other ghouls squirming around it, swallowing it up—or was it the other way around?

They merged into the darkness, becoming one…then nothing.

Just like that, they were gone.

A few minutes later, the first slivers of sunlight poked through the clouds. He smiled at the sight and pushed away all thoughts of Kate, remembering all the sunrises with Lara on the beach back at Song Island instead.

7:25 A.M. Sunrise.

Good to know, good to know…

CHAPTER 35

GABY

SUNLIGHT DREW HER out of a deep slumber, whether she wanted it to or not. Her head seemed stuck in some kind of cocoon where just thinking was difficult, and it felt as if she had been sleeping for the last few centuries. Every part of her body ached, and there was a lightness to her chest that wasn't normal, as if she were still asleep and dreaming all of this.

Nate.

She sat up on a bed that was almost as big as the one in her hotel room on Song Island, but fluffier, like sleeping on clouds. She swung her legs off the bed and took in the room. A closet to her right, windows in front, and a door to her left. Barren white walls, and old-fashioned wooden floors.

Gaby blinked away the sun, loose hair falling over her face. She swiped at them and stood up. She regretted it almost immediately, and had to reach over to the wall to keep from falling. Her legs were jelly and her stomach growled from hunger. Her throat was sore and felt constricted, and she flinched when she touched it.

She forced herself to pad across the room, determined to reach the window, drawn to the bright warm light. Voices from outside made her move faster. Strength returned to her legs with every step, and by the time she reached the window, she felt like herself again.

Almost.

Dainty peach-colored curtains lifted gently against a slight breeze flowing through the open window. At the prospect of meeting other people, she became aware that she wasn't just shoeless, but wearing only white cotton panties and a bra. She didn't remember either articles of clothing when she had lost consciousness last night.

Was it last night? It felt longer.

She brushed aside the curtains and was confronted with burglar bars over the window. She peered down at the city street below her. No, not a city, more like a small town in the countryside. She should know. She had lived in a small town for most of her life.

People moved along the sidewalks. Adults and children in civilian clothes. A pair of men rode by on horses in the street, the *clop-clop-clop* of horseshoes against concrete making for a strange sound and an even odder sight.

Where the hell am I?

She made sure to keep herself hidden, very aware of her half-nakedness. A woman was holding a boy's hand as they stood on the sidewalk watching the men on horseback pass them by. The boy waved at the horsemen. They waved back. The woman smiled, even beamed.

This isn't right.

She looked behind her at the door and walked quickly over to it. She grabbed the doorknob and to her surprise, it turned—except the door didn't move. There was a deadbolt or some kind of lock on the other side. She pulled at it harder, but the door wouldn't budge. She leaned toward it, listening for sounds. There was nothing.

She banged her fist once on the door, shouted, "Hello? Can anyone hear me?"

She waited, ear pressed against the smooth wood, but there was no reply.

Where the hell was she?

Gaby slammed her fist into the door again, and shouted louder, "Is anyone out there? Can anyone hear me?"

Finally, she heard footsteps approaching. Heavy footsteps.

Combat boots.

Gaby scanned the room, looking for a weapon. She felt naked without her guns.

There was nothing in the room that could be mistaken for a weapon. Whoever had put her in here had made sure of that. There were just the big pillows on the bed and the duvet she had thrown aside when she woke up. A small end table next to the bed, spalted maple, with tall, thin legs, and an armoire next to the window.

"Adapt or perish."

Gaby moved quickly across the room and picked up the end table by two of its legs. It was surprisingly light and barely weighed more than a pound despite its length. She hurried back to the door, moving on tiptoes to keep the noise down. She lifted the nightstand up to her shoulders, positioning herself near the hinges of the door so that whoever opened it wouldn't be able to see her right away.

She sucked in a breath and waited.

The footsteps finally reached the door, and moments later, she heard the deadbolt retracting. Then the door opened slowly, cautiously, and she gripped the legs of the end table even tighter. A man's head peered in, looking toward the bed, and she saw the barrel of an AK-47 over the man's shoulder.

She smashed the table down on top of the man's head, breaking all four legs on impact. The man slumped to the floor and Gaby grabbed the door and threw it open and—

Stared at a man holding a Glock in her face.

He was short, and for a moment she thought he was a kid. As the adrenaline faded, the kid morphed into a man who stood five feet away from the door. It suddenly occurred to her that he had probably used the first man as bait.

He motioned for her to step back, and she did. He grinned, showing perfect teeth—except for a big gap in the front, which looked like a dark tunnel surrounded by white pearls.

"I told this dummy you were probably going to try something," the man said. "Girls, I told him, you just can't trust them. Always conniving, am I right?" The short man stepped over the other man stirring on the floor. "Can I call you Gaby?"

"Sure," Gaby said, "as long as you tell me where I am."

"You can call me Mason."

"That's not what I asked."

He grinned. He was either very satisfied with himself, or maybe that was just his natural look. Either way, she battled the urge to leap forward and punch him in the face.

"Where the hell am I?" she asked.

She had retreated all the way back to the bed. She saw the way Mason looked at her—leered at her, really—but she had learned to detach herself from that kind of overt pig behavior a long time ago.

Now, she allowed him to get a good look while she used the time to go over her options.

Not that she had very many at the moment, but if training with Will and Danny had taught her anything, it was that there were always options, a way out. You just had to look for it. The problem was, some were trickier to recognize than others.

She used the time to gather intelligence, looking past Mason without letting him know she was doing it. There was a long hallway behind him, doors, and the beginning of a staircase at the far end.

"L15," Mason said.

"What?"

"This place. L15."

"L15?" she repeated. "What kind of name is that?"

Mason holstered his gun. He had wisely kept a large enough distance between them that Gaby estimated she would need at least a full two seconds to reach him. That was plenty of time for him to see her coming.

The asshole's smarter than he looks.

"They haven't gotten around to giving the place a proper name yet," Mason said. "Right now it's just L15."

Behind Mason, the first man was slowly pulling himself up from the floor. He got to his knees and rubbed at his head, and when he saw blood on his palms, he gave Gaby a nasty glare.

Mason glanced back and chuckled. "You might want to get that looked at, Mac. You don't look so hot."

Mac picked himself up from the floor with some effort, made sure he still had his AK-47, then stumbled back through the open door, dripping blood as he went.

"How did I get here?" Gaby asked.

"You don't know?" Mason said.

"I don't remember."

"It'll all come back to you eventually."

"Where's Nate?"

"Who?"

"The man I was with."

"What do I look like, your personal assistant? How the fuck should I know."

Mason turned and stepped over the pieces of the end table scattered on the floor. For a second—just a second—she considered rushing him, but he was too far away, and her chances were slim.

"They'll bring you some food soon," Mason said, stepping into the hallway. "If you're smart, you won't try this again. I'm a patient man, but some of these guys, like Mac? Not so much." He looked back at her, one hand on the doorknob, eyes roaming her body without an ounce of discretion. "There are clothes in the closet. It's been a while since these boys have seen a hot piece of ass like you, so you might want to cover up, show less skin, if you know what I mean."

He closed the door and she heard the deadbolt sliding back into place, then footsteps fading into the background.

Gaby remembered flashes of images from last night—*was* it last night? Maybe longer, from the way her stomach was growling. Her tongue felt as if it were moving across an arid desert.

Nate…

The loud, rumbling sound of an approaching vehicle *(vehicles?)* invaded her thoughts. She hurried across the room and back to the window, and saw a group of green military transport trucks moving down the street. She remembered them from the camp in Sandwhite Wildlife State Park, though these were probably not the same ones. Or were they?

People in the streets had stopped to watch as five of the trucks entered town, moving at very slow speeds. Not that they had to. There were no other vehicles anywhere that she could see, unless you counted the half dozen people on horseback.

As the trucks drove under her window, Gaby glimpsed the faces of men, women, and children looking out from the back flaps. Bright, smiling faces. *Eager* faces. The trucks came to squelching stops, and people began climbing out of the backs. Pregnant women, dozens of them, were helped down from their own transports. More people came out of buildings, gathering in the streets and converging on the newcomers, offering food, water, handshakes, and hugs.

They think this is salvation. This place. This…L15.

She felt a hollowness in her stomach that had nothing to do with the lack of food. Her mind spun, trying to understand, processing everything she was seeing, everything she had learned the last few days.

Sandwhite. Josh. And now, L15.

She remembered what Will had said, back when they first discovered the camp in Sandwhite: *"I think we're looking at the next phase of whatever final solution the ghouls are moving toward."*

Was this it? The final solution? Humans living in towns run by ghouls?

She shivered even as she listened to the bright, contagious laughter coming from the street below her, the very real, very unmistakable sounds of people delirious with happiness.

This is how mankind ends. Not with resistance, but with laughter...

CHAPTER 36

WILL

"SO MANY CARS," Zoe said. "You'd think there would be at least one that would work. My feet are killing me."

They had been walking for the last hour, ever since they climbed down from the Harvest water tower and discovered the Ford F-150 destroyed. The truck's engine was gutted and the battery missing. Will expected the truck to be useless after the damage it endured last night, but the fact that they took the battery was unexpected. He wondered if it had anything to do with Kate being here last night. The ghouls tended to act unpredictable when the blue-eyed ones were around.

His pack had felt disturbingly light as he climbed down the water tower, reminding him that he was carrying around empty magazines for the carbine and Glock. They walked away from the water tower, over the cemetery of bones bleached white by the sun around the base of the structure. The lingering smell of vaporized flesh was suffocating and Zoe threw up twice before she finally made it to the other side. Zoe took twenty minutes to clean his bandages and check his stitches, breathing through her mouth the entire time.

After an hour of walking, the highway didn't look any closer. Will hadn't been able to see where he was going last night as he fled the ghoul horde; he had only known where he was heading—the bright, white-painted water tower.

"Where are we going anyway?" Zoe asked after a while.

"The highway."

"And after that?"

"Lafayette."

"That's far away."

"Yup."

"Can we really walk all the way to Lafayette in one day?"

"Sure we can."

She gave him a doubtful look.

"It's only thirty-eight kilometers," Will said. "Give or take."

"Kilometers?" she smirked. "What are you, European all of a sudden? What's that in miles?"

He sighed. "Twenty-three miles ish."

"Better."

"See? Not too far."

"How long in terms of walking?"

"Three miles an hour at regular walking speed. That's—"

"Over seven hours, Will. Without stopping for food or water."

"We can always pick up our speed."

She gave him another doubtful look.

"Or I can put you on my back and carry you," he said.

She managed a smile. "Now you're talking."

"I was kidding."

"Oh," she said.

THEY STOPPED AT a Shell gas station and raided the shelves for food, warm bottles of water, and anything else they could eat or drink. Will stuffed the pack with supplies, then grabbed a pair of cheap T-shirts off a rack and swapped one of them with his blood-soaked one. He poured water over his head and shook off as much leftover ghoul smell as possible, then slipped on a yellow and purple cap. He grabbed an extra one for Zoe and waited for her outside on the curb.

Zoe came out looking refreshed. She was apparently better at cleaning herself than he was. Zoe had also swapped shirts, and her long drying blonde locks fell across her face and shoulders.

"Did you even wash?" she asked, wrinkling her nose at him.

"I did the best I could."

"Your best sucks. I could have given you a hand."

"Maybe next time." He handed her the spare baseball cap. "For the sun."

"Thanks."

She slipped it between her legs, then grabbed her hair in a big bundle and somehow got it into a bun, tying it in place with a rubber band. Lara could do that too, and for the life of him he could never quite figure out how they managed something so complicated so effortlessly.

"Hungry?" he asked.

"Famished," she said, and took a spicy Jack Link's beef jerky that he had pulled out of his pack. "So, Lafayette?"

"Lafayette. Then Song Island after that."

"And hot showers."

"And hot showers," he nodded.

AFTER ABOUT AN hour of searching every store that stood between them and the highway, he finally located a small hunting outlet called Renny's in a strip mall. He swapped his blood-stained pants, well-worn combat boots, and socks for new ones off the rack. He also found plenty of ammo under the counters. Will grabbed as many 9mm and 5.56x45mm rounds as he could find and reloaded his weapons, then shoved as much as he could carry into the pack.

He left Renny's feeling better about his chances of getting back to the island than he had all day, and went looking for Zoe.

She had spent most of her time going through the cars in the parking lot. When he caught up to her, she gave him an approving look. "You still smell like something died, but it's an improvement. Hell, from a distance I might even mistake you for handsome, Will."

"I'm sure there was a compliment in there somewhere. Any luck?"

"I didn't find a working car, but I did find something that might be even better."

She led him across the parking lot to a Jeep Wrangler squeezed in between a red Taurus and a black minivan. It wasn't the Jeep she wanted to show him, but two mountain bikes clinging to its back.

One was bright yellow, the other white, and both were held in place by looping steel chains with separate padlocks.

Zoe looked back at him, then at the knife in its sheath. "Can that thing cut through steel?"

"No."

"Damn. Any ideas how to get the bikes free, then?"

"Did you search for the keys?"

"You think they're around here?"

"Usually people keep their keys in one big bundle. Like on a key ring."

"Good point." She hurried over to the Jeep's front door, opened it, and leaned in, then came back out a few seconds later with a large key ring. "It was in the ignition. I turned it, but the car didn't start, so I just assumed it was worthless."

She tossed it to him. Will flipped through the dozen or so keys, found two identical small ones, and tried them on the locks, opening both.

"Awesome," Zoe said with a big smile. "All those years of riding the stationary bike at the hospital gym will finally come in handy."

THANKS TO THE bikes, they were able to reach the highway much faster, and before long they were heading south on the I-49 highway back toward Lafayette. There was little traffic this far out from the city, so they were able to bicycle anywhere on the road for long stretches.

Will estimated they did eleven kilometers in the first hour, about only half as much as he was hoping for. Despite her supposed long history of bicycling, it had been exactly eleven months since Zoe had actually climbed onto a bike, so she had to rebuild some of her lost stamina. That slowed them down, though he didn't mention it. They stopped twice to drink and eat to keep up their strength.

He was happier with their progress in the second hour when they managed fifteen kilometers. Soon, they were moving along the shoulder as traffic began to thicken and more cars started to appear ahead of them.

Will glanced at his watch as they pushed further into Lafayette.

They had crawled down from the water tower at 7:35 in the morning, and it took them another two hours before they found the bikes. They were pushing one in the afternoon by the time they finally spotted Lafayette in the distance, along with the sea of vehicles shimmering across the highway in front of them.

Zoe pulled up alongside him. "You think we can bicycle all the way down to Beaufont Lake before nightfall?"

"Not a chance," Will said without hesitation.

"Damn. I was so hoping for one those hot showers you promised, clean some more of this...whatever this is off me."

By 2:30 P.M., Will could see the pretzel-like Marabond Throughway, where I-49 reconnected with Interstate 10. The sight of the large blocks of concrete, like the heads of a hydra, made him briefly think about Jen's helicopter. He wasn't looking forward to seeing pieces of it still scattered along the length of the highway when they finally reached that part of the city.

There was a brief rush of wind as Zoe raced past him.

"Zoe, slow down," he said after her.

She threw a mischievous grin back at him. "I told you I was good at this. Ten years of biking at the gym, remember?"

"Pull back, I don't want you getting too far ahead."

"Oh come on, the big tough Ranger can't keep up?"

"Zoe, pull back."

She ignored him and pushed forward when the gunshot shattered the air, like lightning striking the ground an inch from his ear.

In front of him, Zoe was falling sideways off her bike. Her head landed so hard on the concrete that he was afraid she might have split it open. The bike spilled under her legs, front reflectors cracking against the highway.

Will was already jumping off his own bike, pushing it away from him, even before the gunshot finished its echo across the skyline. He reached for his rifle with one hand and grabbed Zoe with the other, dragging her noncompliant body all the way behind the back bumper of a beat-up Ford Bronco.

Gunshots rained down on them instantly, shattering windshields and tearing into the highway around them like missiles.

He didn't stop moving until he had her completely behind the truck and propped up against the bumper, just as the rear windshield collapsed under the onslaught. He unslung the pack and held it over his and Zoe's head as glass fell down on them.

Zoe stared back at him, lips quivering, eyes wide with terror. He couldn't tell if she was panicking, dying, or both. She flinched each time she heard a bullet *ping!* off a vehicle.

He grabbed her and looked behind her, saw a hole in her shirt and blood flowing out the back. The bullet had gone through her, which was a good sign, even if the sheer amount of blood pouring out onto the highway suggested otherwise. A through and through was a good thing. He was proof of that.

"I have to stop the bleeding," Will said.

She nodded back, then gasped audibly when a bullet chipped the concrete a few feet from her. Will opened his pack and pulled out a spare T-shirt and a roll of duct tape.

"This is going to hurt," he said.

"Do it," she said, barely getting the words out through clenched teeth.

He mouthed a countdown from three to one, and when he got to *one,* she removed her hands and he shoved the T-shirt against her side. She let out a loud squeal of pain, thrashing involuntarily against him. Will stretched the shirt around her body along one side, covering up both bullet holes. She did her part, pressing both bloodied hands back down over the shirt, while he ran the duct tape around her once, twice, taping the shirt to her body.

The gunfire from up the highway hadn't stopped, though it had lessened. He guessed their ambushers were trying to gauge if they had hit anything. A final bullet *zipped* above their heads, passing through where the back windshield used to be, and vanished into the hood of a blue Hyundai.

Zoe was trying to control her ragged breathing, sweat pouring down her face. He couldn't tell if she or the pain was winning.

"You're doing good," he said.

He reached into the pack again, pulled out a bottle of pills, and deposited it into her shaking palm.

"Don't take too many, you might get addicted," he said, smiling at her.

She somehow managed to grin back. "You're such an asshole."

She popped open the bottle and upended it against her lips, swallowing without chewing.

Will slipped toward the edge of the back bumper and pulled the nylon pouch with the baton and mirror out of the pack. He snapped the baton out to its full sixteen inches and connected the mirror to the end before easing the rod out from behind the Bronco and using it to scan the highway.

At first he saw only parked vehicles—a glut of them, crammed from one end of the I-49's southbound lane to the other—but then he began to pick up movement.

There was definitely more than one, peering out from behind cars, fifty—maybe sixty—meters ahead. Which convinced him whoever had fired that first shot had jumped the gun. He would have kept going, oblivious to what awaited him up the highway if the man hadn't shot early. That was one of the first things you learned in a war zone—patience and calm in the face of an approaching enemy. That, and you never spoil a perfectly good ambush by firing too early.

He spotted four men, each one wearing a hazmat suit, though none were wearing their gas mask. He was almost sure there were more than four of them from just the sheer volume of gunfire. At least five, with a possibility of six, maybe even seven if he was really, really unlucky.

He watched one of the men moving across the length of an old '80s station wagon with wood paneling. The car was parked across the lanes, probably after spinning out of control. The man was shuffling away from the front passenger-side window where he had been crouched earlier. He moved laterally toward the hood, where he rested a hunting rifle and fired off a shot.

The mirror attached to the baton exploded, showering Will with glass fragments. He dropped the baton with a curse, then reached down and pulled out a thin shard of glass sticking out of his right arm. He flicked it away, ignoring the little trickle of blood.

The problem was the guy who had just fired that last shot. He remembered the man from the camp. The one with the bolt-action hunting rifle, equipped with the big scope. The guy just shot a mirror that was only three inches in diameter from fifty meters. Big rifle-scope or not, that was pretty damn impressive.

"Nice mirror!" a voice shouted. It was male, deep, and it sounded familiar. "Where'd you get that? Archers? Nice place to shop. We were gonna hit it later ourselves, stock up and whatnot."

Will didn't answer. Instead, he listened to the man's booming voice rattle down the length of the highway, before it eventually died in the breeze.

"He sends his regards!" the man shouted. "Your old buddy! Josh!"

Josh?

"He wanted to be here himself," the man continued, "but he had other business. He told me you'd be coming back in this direction sooner or later. Of course, we thought you'd be coming by car, not bicycles. That really threw us for a loop, let me tell you!"

He had heard that voice before, over the radio.

"Kellerson?" Will shouted.

"Bingo!" the man shouted back.

Sonofabitch.

He looked back at Zoe. Her face was pale, but she wasn't trembling nearly quite as much as before. She stared back at him with sunken eyes and seemed to be breathing fine, though that might have just been a combination of adrenaline and pills.

"We'll be fine," Will said. "Trust me, okay?"

"Okay," she nodded back.

He couldn't tell if she actually believed the lie or if she was humoring him. It was impossible to read anything in her face at the moment. He wondered if he had looked that spaced out after getting shot a few days ago.

"Hey, you still alive back there?" Kellerson shouted. "It goes without saying, we can do this all day. Got supplies and more ammo than we know what to do with them. And night ain't your friend, but then you probably already know that, don't you?"

Will scooted back toward Zoe and felt her pulse. Weak, but it was still there.

"You're doing good," he smiled at her. "I'll be back, okay?"

She didn't respond. He wasn't sure if she couldn't, or if she didn't want to. He could almost feel her drifting away, leaving her body.

"Hey, Will!" Kellerson shouted. "Josh told us you were a badass ex-Army Ranger. I gotta say, I'm unimpressed, man!"

Even before Kellerson finished the word "man," Will was darting across the highway. There were only two meters between the Bronco and a large Suburban minivan in the next lane. It was a quick dash, with only the two mountain bikes in his way. Will had to leap over them, raising his profile higher than he wanted.

He heard a gunshot and a bullet *zipped* past his head, almost taking his ear off.

And he saw something else in the half-second he was in the air—a man in a hazmat suit on the other side of the concrete barrier that separated the south and northbound lanes. The man had apparently been making his trek down the highway for a while and was only ten meters from Will's position when Will spotted him.

The man froze, looking like a kid caught doing something he wasn't supposed to. Will landed behind the minivan and snapped off a quick shot in the man's direction. He managed to hit the man in the right shoulder and watched him spin and drop, disappearing behind the concrete barrier.

Will ducked his head just as the minivan's windshields exploded, and glass poured down on top of and around him. Bullets that didn't pelt the Suburban's sides—the *ping ping ping!* going into metal like chimes—dug lengthy grooves across the highway floor.

He leaned out from behind the Suburban and glanced at where he had last seen the man in the northbound lane. He saw a thick head of blond hair bobbing along the barrier, fleeing back up the highway. Will considered taking a shot to finish the man off, but that would have involved leaning almost completely out from behind the minivan, and he had a feeling the guy with the hunting rifle was waiting patiently back there at the station wagon for a shot. Throughout the torrent of gunfire, Will had heard the familiar rattles of M4 carbines, but not a single shot from a bolt-action rifle. The man was just waiting for him to make a mistake.

Then the gunfire stopped, and there was just the heavy silence of a dead city again.

That, too, didn't last.

"Hey, Will!" Kellerson shouted. "You still alive back there?"

Will didn't answer.

"Come on!" Kellerson continued. "Cat got your tongue? You know you're not going anywhere. This is it, buddy! This is the end of the line! Make it easier on yourself and the blonde! Throw out your weapons and I'll end it quick. Scout's honor!"

Will glanced toward the highway barrier again, expecting another figure to rush up alongside it, having used Kellerson's taunting as cover. The man was talking so much Will thought it had to be a trick, some kind of clever diversion.

But no, there was no one on the other side this time.

He's just a loudmouth, after all.

"Will?" Kellerson shouted. "This is getting boring, man. I'm giving you till the count of five, then we're coming. I got no time for this Alamo bullshit! You ready, buddy? *Five!*"

Will looked back across the lane at Zoe. Her eyes were closed, and she looked on the verge of sliding off the Bronco's back bumper at any second. After three solid seconds of staring, he couldn't tell if she was still breathing.

He thought about how she had come back to rescue him when she didn't have to…

"*Four!*"

He flicked the fire selector on the M4A1 to full-auto. If they tried to bull rush him, he could probably take three, maybe four if he was *really* lucky.

Captain fucking Optimism.

Not that he had much of a choice. He and Zoe were dead if he stayed still.

"*Three!*"

They had stopped firing, and he guessed they were getting ready to do exactly what Kellerson had promised—move on him. Of course, they weren't going to make it easy to pick them off. They would probably do it slowly, moving between vehicles, keeping behind cover the entire time. Eventually, they would reach him. That was the problem.

Eventually they would be right on top of him.

"*Two!*"

Will was going to stand up, take the fight to them, when he heard a series of gunshots—and this time the bullets weren't coming *at* him or hitting the Suburban or scalping the highway around his vicinity. Instead, the gunfire sounded like they were coming from a handgun—a Glock—and they were hitting cars up the highway— *behind* the ambushers.

The hell—?

Will stood up behind the Suburban and peeked through the broken windows. The hazmat suits were returning fire on *someone else* further up the highway. The figure was wearing black and had ducked behind the highway barrier on the northbound lane after drawing their attention, and bullets were chopping into the thick concrete block in front of him, spraying the air with a fine white powder.

For a moment, he thought it was the blond who had tried to flank him earlier, but no, it couldn't have been the same person. That guy was wearing a hazmat suit, while this one was dressed all in black. It looked like some kind of assault vest, too.

Then there was a single, very deliberate shot, and Will saw the man with the hunting rifle flinching as something hit him in the chest. He collapsed to the highway, disappearing behind the '80s station wagon he had been using as cover.

A second player.

There was a second shot, and another man stood up, grabbing at his neck as blood gushed out between his fingers. A third shot knocked the man down for good.

Kellerson's men were returning fire in the direction of the second gunman now. The man was leaning out from behind a white van with "Arnold's Plumbing" stenciled across the side, along with a cartoon picture of a toilet with a smiley face. The shooter, also wearing dark black *(assault vest?)*, had slipped behind the van to dodge the return volley. Bullets stitched the side of the van and shattered windows.

Will quickly came out from behind the Suburban and moved steadily up the highway, using the distraction to his advantage. The phrase *"The enemy of my enemy is my friend"* rushed across his mind.

He flicked the fire selector on the M4A1 back to semi-auto as he spotted the closest man in a hazmat suit to him, standing behind a Dodge Ram. The man was reloading his M4, desperately trying to jam the magazine in but having a difficult time lining it up. Will shot the man twice in the back and watched him disappear behind the truck.

Another man in a hazmat suit stood up from behind a brown Buick, directly in front of Will. The man was lifting his rifle and spinning around, but Will beat him to it and shot him once in the chest. The man staggered backward but didn't go down. Will saw the familiar rectangular lump of a Kevlar vest over the man's chest and shot him again, this time in the face.

Two figures flashed across his peripheral vision, moving out from cars in front of him. The white-clad men raced across the lane toward the concrete barrier. One of them threw himself over it so fast he tripped and fell down on the other side. Someone shot the second man in the back before he could make the jump, and he stumbled and comically hit his forehead on the concrete divider, sliding down it face-first.

Will hurried out from behind the Buick and glanced over at the plumbing van, seeing a familiar face grinning back at him over the distance.

Sonofabitch.

Will returned the man's grin, then jogged over to the barrier and leaped over it, landing on the other side. He moved up quickly toward the hazmat suit that had stumbled and fallen. There were fresh blood splatters along this side of the highway, most likely from the blond he had shot earlier.

He found a man in a hazmat suit lying on his back near the divider, still alive and holding on to his right arm, which was twisted at an odd, unnatural angle. One of the man's knees was scraped and bloodied, and his M4 rifle lay forgotten at his feet. The man looked over as Will jogged toward him, and for a moment—just a moment—Will was sure he would reach for his weapon.

But he didn't. Instead, the man lay still until Will was finally standing over him.

Will looked past the man and up the highway, and spotted another hazmat suit-clad figure lying on its stomach about ten meters farther up the northbound lane. The blond he had shot earlier. The poor bastard had apparently run into someone else who had finished him off.

Will turned his attention back to the man at his feet. He was in his forties, and in another time, another place, Will would have pegged him as a husband with two kids, a house in the suburbs, and a wife that constantly browbeat him about drinking or smoking too much. The guy looked completely average and plain.

"Kellerson?" Will said.

The man grinned up at him. "Shit, you cheated. You had reinforcements."

"In my defense, I didn't know they were coming."

"That right?" Kellerson said.

"Yeah."

"Okay, then, I guess that changes everything." Kellerson sighed.

"So what happens now?"

Will pulled a silver-chromed .45 Smith & Wesson revolver out of Kellerson's holster. "Nice gun."

"Thanks. I stole it."

"I figured."

"Then again, is it really stealing if it's just lying there?"

"Probably not."

Will heard footsteps and looked over at a blond in his mid-twenties coming toward him from the other side of the barrier. He was wearing a stripped-down black assault vest and throat mic rig, and was holding a Glock in his hand. He looked almost shell-shocked.

"You good?" Will asked.

The guy stared back at him, as if unsure how to respond. Finally, he nodded and said, "I think I'm okay."

"Okay's always good."

"You must be Will," he said.

"I must be. Got a name?"

"Roy."

Will nodded at the dead blond. "You?"

"Yeah, he sort of just ran into me," Roy said, almost embarrassed. "I got really lucky."

"You're one of the newbies that showed up on the island. You came with Bonnie and the others."

"Yeah."

"Nice work, Roy."

"Thanks. I was just doing what Danny told me."

Danny appeared, eating beef jerky out of an Oberto bag, his rifle slung over his shoulder. He looked as if he were on a casual stroll. "Well, well, well, look who I gone and stumbled across. You look like shit, buddy."

"Good to see you, too," Will said. "How's Lara?"

"She's miffed. But good. Bossing the whole island around while you were gone."

"That's my girl."

"I keep telling her to move on, that she's way too good for you. You never call, you never write, you never visit. You're no damn good, I say. She could do so much better."

"You're a real pal, Danny."

"My advice? Put on a cup before you step back onto Song Island."

"Noted."

Danny glanced down the highway. "I saw someone else with you back there. Wouldn't happen to be Gaby, would it?"

"Gaby?" Will looked back at him. "Isn't she back at the island? She left me days ago."

"She didn't show up. That's why I'm out here. Lara sent me to come looking for you two idiots."

Will frowned. "I don't know where she is."

"From what I can tell, she had major ghoul trouble at a pawnshop off the highway where she was staying. It looked like a hell of a fight. That's where we were coming from when we heard your little spontaneous block party up here."

Gaby.

Dammit. He was hoping at least one of them had made it back home.

"You found blood at the pawnshop?" Will asked.

"A lot, yeah," Danny said.

"Shit."

"You talking about the blonde?" Kellerson said. "Josh's girl."

Will looked down at him. "What do you know about it?"

"Lots."

"Bullshit."

"Blonde. Five-seven. Gorgeous. Hard to forget a piece of ass like that."

Will and Danny exchanged a look, before Will focused his stare back on Kellerson. "Is she alive?"

"Last time I saw her," Kellerson said.

"When was this?"

"A day ago."

"The blood back there was old," Danny said. "At least two days. If he saw her a day ago, that means she's still alive."

"What else do you know?" Will asked.

Kellerson grinned back at him. "Why should I tell you? You're just going to kill me anyway. Howzabout we make a deal first. I tell you what I know, and we forget this little unfortunate incident ever happened. What do you say?"

"Danny," Will said, "there's someone down the highway. Her

name's Zoe. I don't know if she's still alive or not. Behind the Bronco."

"Come on, kid," Danny said to Roy. "Let's go lend a hand."

"What's he gonna do?" Roy asked.

"Don't worry about it. Willie boy's a real smooth talker when he wants to be. How'd you think he got Lara in the first place?"

Roy gave Will and Kellerson a hesitant look before turning and following Danny down the highway.

"You wanna hear a joke?" Danny asked.

"Sure, I guess," Roy said.

"A priest, a rabbit, and a horse walk into a bar…" Danny began, his voice fading down the highway.

Kellerson was staring up at Will, though he seemed to have lost some of his earlier confidence. "We have a deal?"

Will pulled out his cross-knife. The sunlight glinted off the silver double-edged blade.

"You're bluffing," Kellerson said, his eyes shifting from the knife to Will and back again. "You're not going to kill me. You'll never find the girl if you do."

"I don't have to kill you," Will said. "I just have to make you wish you were dead. But you are going to tell me everything you know. If you make me ask a question twice, I'll take a finger. When I'm out of fingers, I'll start taking toes…"

EPILOGUE

IT WASN'T FAIR. He had given up. He had given in. He had even donated blood, for God's sake. How many times did they ask him to give blood, day after day, and how many times did he say no?

Never. Not once. Not fucking once.

And here he was anyway, running for his life.

It wasn't fair. God, why was it so damn *unfair?*

He was a good guy. He tried to do the right things. He even took care of those women and that idiot out of Oklahoma. But then they finally reached the island and that bitch Lara, and everything fell apart.

It was so unfair. Why was the world so goddamn unfair?

West could hear them, even though he couldn't see them. Not that it was easy to see anything in the pitch darkness. There was barely any moonlight. Even the moon was hiding behind the clouds, giving him almost nothing to navigate by. It was all he could do not to trip or run right into a tree. Even so, he had stopped counting the number of times a branch slashed at his body, slicing at his cheeks and drawing blood. At least the new scars took his mind off his old wounds.

It's not fair. It's not fair!

Another branch nearly took his head off, but he ducked just in time, felt the leaves brushing against his already wet hair. Even out here in the chilly night, he was sweating from every pore.

How long had he been running? A few minutes? A few hours? It was hard to tell. Time was an elusive bastard.

His body ached from head to toe. The old wounds were coming back with a fury.

But he kept running, because there was no other choice. He couldn't go back. They wouldn't let him go back. It wouldn't be so bad if he wasn't out here alone. He was never good at being alone, that's why he and Brody got along so well. It was good to have someone watching your back, someone you could trust. But Brody went and got his head blown off by that Mexican on the island—

Snap!

West told himself not to look back, to keep running. Don't stop. Don't look back and don't stop. There was nothing back there but death.

Don't look back!

But he couldn't help himself and he looked back.

It glared at him from a tree branch, perched like some kind of gargoyle from hell, prune-black skin almost invisible against the unrelenting darkness of the woods. But he could see its eyes—bright blue, gleaming like a pair of precious jewels.

He had always heard the whispers, people who claimed to have seen them in person. *Blue-eyed bloodsuckers.* West had scoffed at the idea. Now, looking back, he wondered if he had just dismissed the stories because he chose not to believe, because believing opened up possibilities he didn't want to accept.

It stood up on the branch, stretching, until it was upright. It looked so human that for a moment he found himself staring, even as he ran and—

He stumbled and fell and rolled, tucking in his shoulders at the last moment *(You idiot!)*, until his forward momentum drove him into the trunk of a large tree. Pain exploded across his body and he ended up on his stomach, writhing in the dirt on the wet ground.

No! No!

Finally, after what seemed like hours, he managed to turn over on his back, but he couldn't find the strength to get up. Instead, he reached up to his head, where most of the pain was coming from. He felt something sticky against his palm.

Blood. Of course he was bleeding. His skull had probably split open.

Tap-tap.

West looked up and saw the blue-eyed creature crouched on a branch above him *(How did it get up there so fast?)*, looking down at him with something approaching...amusement? Was the damn thing having fun at his expense?

It's so unfair.

Its blue eyes really did seem to glow up close, but that could just have been the contrast of blue against black. Or maybe his mind was making all of this up, a result of the concussion and subsequent pain. That was possible, too.

Crunch-crunch.

West looked forward as another blue-eyed creature walked toward him—slowly, effortlessly, in that strange motion that was at once so human and supernatural.

There were *two* of them?

Crunch-crunch.

No, not two. He wished there were just two, because a third one was coming out of the night to his right, blue eyes blazing.

Then he looked to his left, at a fourth one.

Four of them. My God. There are four of them.

The one above him jumped down, startling him. West kicked at the dirt with his shoes and scooted back until he bumped against the tree. Oh God. Now he was trapped. He had no place to go.

It's so unfair...

They stood around him in a half circle, watching him. There was something about one of the blue-eyed creatures that looked different. It took him a few seconds of staring before he finally realized what it was. The other three were male, but this one, the one standing closest to him, was female. He was sure of it. There were even small bumps on its chest where breasts used to be. And the hips were wider, though he couldn't imagine what it would need wide hips for anymore.

The female blue-eyed bloodsucker smiled at him. "Run," it said, its voice almost a hiss, breaking through the natural sounds of the woods.

Fear sliced through West's core like thousands of knives. He didn't understand. Run? Did it want him to run?

Then it did something else he had never seen the creatures do—the female *smiled* at him.

"Run," it said again.

He scrambled up with some difficulty, his sneakers slipping under him. The blood was still coming down the side of his head, and it was hard to keep his balance as a result. That was it, wasn't it? It was the bleeding, not the crushing terror that made every step precarious, every movement extraordinarily clumsy.

Somehow, he managed to climb back to his feet. He turned, skirted the tree, and continued fleeing through the woods. He tasted blood in his mouth, more dripping down his chin. He must have gashed himself even more than he thought.

He wiped at a thick patch of it and flicked it away.

Snap-snap!

West told himself not to look back. He knew what was back there. He shouldn't look back. He should keep running for all he was worth.

How did it all go so wrong? He wasn't a bad guy. What did he ever do to deserve this?

He looked up at the sky, but he couldn't see much of anything over the thick tree canopy swaying against a slight breeze. How long before the sun came out? How long before he could stop running?

Too long. Too damn long.

Crunch-crunch!

He screamed at himself not to look back. He knew what was back there. How many were back there. Four. There were four of them.

Four!

And they were playing with him. This was a game, one he had no choice but to take part in, because the alternative was to sit down and die. He couldn't do that. West wasn't a quitter. If he had been, he would never have survived the end of the world.

Screw that. West was a fighter. It was too bad Brody wasn't here with him. He could have used his buddy's help. The two of them could take on anything…

…except an island led by a little blonde girl.

No!

He saw the tree branch on the ground, twenty yards away. It was as long as his arm and twice as big. He used to play baseball when he was a kid. He was good as it, too. Then again, sports always came naturally to him.

You wanna play? Let's play!

West went low at the last second and snatched up the branch just as he was about to pass it. At the same time, he dug the heels of his sneakers into the soft, wet ground, slowing down his momentum until he came to a complete stop.

He spun around, clutching the tree branch with both hands, raising it back, imagining that he was choking up on a Louisville slugger.

He turned, ready, shouting, "Come get me, you bastards! Come get me!" so loud that his throat stretched and ached.

West became aware of a madman laughing hysterically somewhere in the woods.

Made in the USA
Middletown, DE
26 June 2015